William Chalmers Burns was only twenty-four, and only recently ordained, when he preached in Dundee for the saintly Robert Murray McCheyne. We know him best for that great flood of revival at St. Peters Church in those early years. However, Dr. Michael McMullen warmly presents the whole of this godly man's revival preaching and missionary zeal, with portions of his compelling journal, and letters and sermons never before published. *God's Polished Arrow* is about the sacrifices and massive affect of an eminently holy man.

Jim Elliff,
President, Christian Communicators Worldwide

The sacrifice and challenge of obedience to God's calling today can be better understood upon reflection on the lives of saints and pioneers of a former era who laid the foundation for what God is doing today. William Chalmers Burns was one of those unheralded servants and missionaries of whom many would be unaware. This itinerant preacher was used mightily of God in his native Scotland but turned his back on the acclaim gained from revival movements in local churches to respond to the passion of his life, sharing the gospel in China. A contemporary of J. Hudson Taylor, Burns sacrificed material comforts, suffered illness and harassment, and labored unto death in order bring the good news of Jesus Christ to the interior of China in the mid-nineteenth century. This unique biography by Dr. Michael McMullen, including Burns' letters, sermons and journal entries, will be an inspiration and blessing to all who read it and a model for those responding to God's call in the twenty-first century.

Jerry Rankin,
President, International Mission Board,
Southern Baptist Convention

Sometimes while reading stirring biography I wonder why I read anything else. The life of W.C. Burns falls into this category. Like David Livingstone, John Paton, and his colleague in China —Hudson Taylor, Burns was a flint-faced pioneer. Few men have seen more of the Lord's evident blessing on their preaching than Burns. Fewer still have seen such dramatic results both in their own homeland and among previously unreached peoples. I am delighted to see Michael McMullen providing the church with a fresh reminder of what God has done—and can do—through men like W.C. Burns.

Don Whitney
Associate Professor of Spiritual Formation,
Midwestern Baptist Theological Seminary

Christian Focus Publications publishes biblically-accurate books for adults and children. The books in the adult range are published in three imprints.

Christian Heritage contains classic writings from the past.

Christian Focus contains popular works including biographies, commentaries, doctrine, and Christian living.

Mentor focuses on books written at a level suitable for Bible College and seminary students, pastors, and others; the imprint includes commentaries, doctrinal studies, examination of current issues, and church history.

For a free catalogue of all our titles, please write to
Christian Focus Publications,
Geanies House, Fearn,
Ross-shire, IV20 1TW, Great Britain

For details of our titles visit us on our web site
http://www.christianfocus.com

God's Polished Arrow
William Chalmers Burns

by
Michael McMullen

Christian Focus

I would like to acknowledge my debt of gratitude to Midwestern Baptist Theological Seminary and for all the love and support of the Faculty, administrators and students whilst I have been there. I would also acknowledge all the love and support we as a family have received, from the members and friends at WhiteChurch Baptist Church, Kansas City, Kansas.

© Michael McMullen
ISBN 1 85792 395 2

Published in 2000 by
Christian Focus Publications
Geanies House, Fearn, Ross-shire,
IV20 1TW, Great Britain

Cover design by Owen Daily

Contents

Biography of W.C. Burns

I dedicate this book to our two children, Evangeline and Zachary. I have come to realize that children can be very much like books, they take a great deal of hard work, but the results can be wonderful. And Evie and Zach are just that, two wonderful children. One hopes too, that the books one produces will have very good effects, and that is our prayer too for you two.

Biography
of
W. C. Burns

Biography Introduction

This book is entitled *God's Polished Arrow* because that is what Burns desired that he himself would be. He longed, he wrote, that God might find him as a polished arrow, and that He might use him as an arrow flying straight, swift and true towards its target. This volume is divided into four main sections. The first section is an account of the life and labours of William Chalmers Burns, a record which draws upon his extensive Journal entries and other manuscript material, much of which was previously unpublished.

In the course of research for a previous volume *The Passionate Preacher*, also published by Christian Focus Publications, in which I discovered and transcribed many previously unpublished sermons by Robert Murray M'Cheyne, I was fortunate enough to also discover previously unpublished manuscripts from the hand of William Chalmers Burns. These manuscripts form part of the wonderful and priceless holdings of the Special Collections department of New College Library, University of Edinburgh.

The aim of this present volume is to bring to remembrance one of the truly great giants of the Christian Church, and to challenge her once again to see in William Burns an example to obey God's call no matter what the cost. The holiness and the glory of God meant everything to William Burns, and his one real fear was that any glory might go to him and not to his Lord. His consuming passion was to make known the wonderful grace of God in Christ and he would literally give his life to that end. Therefore, as you read this volume, treat what you read as not just another book to pick up and put down, but as a direct challenge to see whether you too can say with Burns, 'Here I am, send me.'.

Burns became almost overwhelmed with the thought of those in foreign countries who were perishing without the good news of Christ. He often felt the burden of their cries of help as if they were calling to him. He was in Glasgow one day and his mother walked straight up to him but he remained oblivious. When he did finally see her, she said it was as if he had come from a great dream. When he spoke she says it was with deep emotion: 'O mother! I did not see you: for when walking along Argyle street just now, I was so overcome with the sight of the countless crowds of immortal beings eagerly hasting hither and thither, but all posting onwards towards the eternal world, that I could bear it no longer, and turned in here to seek relief in quiet thought.'

Even though Burns sensed a real call to the foreign mission field, no doors opened for several years and he spent those years preaching, often against real opposition, including in Ireland and Canada. Most of his years, however, were spent in his native Scotland, but with remarkable divine blessing. Many were converted and built up in the faith. It seemed that wherever Burns went Revivals went with him.

Burns was chosen by Robert Murray McCheyne to be his stand-in at Dundee, whilst he went to the Holy Land on a Mission to the Jews. Whilst Burns was at St Peter's real Revival broke out and meetings were held every day for months on end. Burns records that it was like a pent-up flood breaking forth; tears were streaming from the eyes of many, and some fell on the ground, groaning and weeping, and crying for mercy. It was a similar scene in the town of Kilsyth when Burns helped in the Communion time there and the services would last for five hours or more, because people were so convicted and God's presence was so strong. Thousands were coming to the meetings and many stayed until three in the morning.

As for China, Burns was commissioned as the first missionary to China of the English Presbyterian Church. He never accepted the call lightly or quickly. He sought the counsel of his friends, family and, of course, the Lord. A friend reminded him of the speech that he gave to Edinburgh University's Students' Missionary Association in which he said that when young men gave themselves to the Lord for the work of the ministry, they were not to prescribe to Him where their field of labour should be, but should be willing to go anywhere, 'even to China'.

Burns sailed alone for China in 1847, he would die there in 1868. The journey took five months and he suffered from almost daily bouts of nausea. In China he lived very meagerly, even in the eyes of his humble Chinese neighbours. There was a disturbance in his neighbourhood after a petty robbery had occurred and an excited crowd was running past Burns' lodgings in heated pursuit of the suspect. When someone wondered whether they should look in there, the crowd responded, 'Oh! you need not look there, it is only a poor foreigner.'

He was robbed and stripped of his clothes and few possessions on more than one occasion. He learnt Chinese and would travel from village to village explaining to all who would listen the way of salvation. In just one week, for example, he preached in more than 30 villages. He believed the need for workers to join the missionaries already in China was so great that he gave back £250 to the Mission agency, a whole year's salary, to encourage them to respond practically too.

He translated *Pilgrim's Progress* into Chinese. It was a continuous translation and that made it different from that which already had been printed. He also edited a collection of hymns for Chinese worship which soon became a real favourite. He befriended Hudson Taylor and they travelled and preached together for almost a year. 'Such a friendship is beyond price,' wrote Hudson Taylor, 'William Burns is better to me than a college course with all its advantages, because right here in China is lived out before me all that I long to be as a missionary.'

Burns was particularly concerned to press ever inwards into China's mainland. He founded churches and sometimes schools. In 1867 he caught a cold which turned into a fever, and from that he never recovered. When people visited him he spoke of both life and death: when he spoke of life, he said what he would do if he had the energy; when he spoke of death, he prayed that others might be found to continue the work that God had begun through him.

Very soon after his death, Rev Charles wrote to his mother: 'China and its labours, far from the ear and eye of man, was his sphere. He had literally buried himself in that vast land; a noble living burial! No doubt, also, his system was spent. He had done his work (not a short one, be it remembered) in such a manner that even his robust constitution was undermined. His brother Islay Burns wrote: 'His whole life was literally a life of prayer, and his whole ministry a series of battles fought at the mercy-seat.' A fellow-missionary in China, Rev James Johnston, said these words at a meeting of the China Mission: 'The faith and patience of this devoted servant of God is an example to the Church, and to every labourer in the Lord's vineyard.... he left the impress of his character and piety wherever he went. Missionaries felt it, and converts felt it, and have been heard to say, that they got their idea of what the Saviour was on earth, from the holy calm, and warm love, and earnest zeal of Mr Burns' walk with God.'

Chapter 1

Early Life, Conversion and Call to Ministry
(1815-1839)

God has given great gifts to his Church, and amongst them he has raised up and given many godly men and women. One such is the subject of this book, William Chalmers Burns. William was born on 1 April 1815, in the manse of Dun, the fifth child and third son of William Hamilton Burns, the minister there. In 1821, his father was appointed to the charge of Kilsyth and the family moved from Dun to there. Kilsyth was a village of 3000, a combination of weavers, colliers and shopkeepers. The move went well and family life in the manse was cheerful, warm and secure, which is not surprising when one hears the contemporary descriptions of William's father and mother. Islay Burns, William's brother, describes their father at this time as one who was

> gentle, reverend, gracious, full of kind thoughts, devout affections, and fresh genial sympathies – serious without moroseness, cheerful and even sometimes gay without lightness, zealous, diligent, conscientious without a touch of impetuous haste, and carrying about with him withal an atmosphere of calm repose and staid measured dignity ... the very model of a type of the Christian pastorate which is fast passing away.

But of their mother, Islay writes that she was his direct counterpart in many ways. She was 'of a nimble buoyant active frame, alike of body and mind: she was all light and life and motion, and was as it were the glad sunshine and bright angel of a house which had otherwise been too still and sombre.'

The records show that William did well at school, but above all he loved sport and outdoor exercise. 'My brother's bent especially was at this time,' comments Islay, 'decidedly in the "muscular" direction. He gave far greater promise of becoming a mighty hunter than a deep student bearing the pale hue of thought. Strong of limb and of sanguine temperament, his heart was in the open fields and woods, and in all manner of manly and athletic exercises.' William would go out early and spend long days with his fishing-rod on the Carron water on the other side of the hills. He wandered for hours along the hedges and through the fields with an old carbine, borrowed from the village blacksmith, 'in search of sparrows and crows.'

His interest then, obviously lay outside study as such at that time, but he did have two favourite books, which were *The Pilgrim's Progress* and *The Life of Sir William Wallace*, who like Burns himself, is currently enjoying a degree of rediscovery and reassessment regarding their respective significances in their own fields. The former book he read and re-read, during a time in which an accident confined him to the house. The latter volume he purchased with a half-crown given him when a very little boy by Dr Hamilton, a close family friend.

He may have loved the outdoors, but as said, he did well at school. The parish school at the time was under the care of Rev. Alexander Salmon, who later went to Sydney: 'a teacher of rare intelligence and skill', records Islay, who it seems was one of the first Scottish teachers to, 'substitute an intellectual interest for the old iron sway of the ferula'. William became a good reader, good at mathematics and accounting, and learned too the rudiments at least of Latin. When he thought about his future, William had no inkling as to a future following his father. His thoughts turned to the land and the possibility of earning a living from working it. 'His declared resolution was to be a country farmer, like the fathers of most of his school companions and friends.'

If nothing more were said of his character as a boy and young man, then this would be a very superficial portrait. Now and again there are glimpses of a deeper side to him, a side which would become much more prominent in later life. Islay records one touching example of this. William owned a dovecot. It was his 'special property', but it became, what the family termed as, 'redundant'. William was instructed by 'higher powers' that some of his favourites should fall a 'sacrifice to the public good'. William decided to take the place of the executioner himself, a task he did reluctantly, but one which he considered would be discharged more mercifully by him than another.

So when the day dawned, there was William, gun in hand at the corner of a wall, a little distance from his targets. He 'took aim resolutely but tremblingly at one of the devoted flock perched on the ridge of the house, between him and the sky. The shot missed its mark, but unhappily only partially. The poor bird was sorely wounded in the foot, but not killed; and gathering up the broken and bleeding limb beneath its wing, he stood on the other, silent and motionless, a spectacle of agony. Instantly his heart smote him for the deed he had done.' Burns no longer saw himself as the executioner, but as the cruel murderer, and he stood there, rooted to the spot for hours, gazing up at his wounded victim, with his eyes streaming.

Not long after this, a maternal uncle visited the family and saw in the twelve-year-old something special, something different, and he persuaded William and Elizabeth that, when he returned to Aberdeen, they should let him take with him their son. The plan was for William junior to spend the winter with this respected lawyer and begin a short time of study at the Aberdeen Grammar School, which was then at the height of its fame. After some consideration they agreed and William became a student at that prestigious school. It was an opportunity he did not waste and which obviously helped to shape him for his future call. His brother believed, probably quite rightly, that his time at the school awakened and trained 'that remarkable faculty for the study of language which stood him in such good stead in the missionary labours of later years'.

After spending just one year at the school, he then proceeded to enter the Marischal College of Aberdeen University. Again, William was well placed in his studies. He stood fifth on the list of bursars or open scholars in the College, from among more than one hundred competitors. But after only two sessions, William had decided to leave the University in 1831 to seek the law as his career. How did he come to his choice? William himself was quite frank and open about this: money and status. He later said that his mind was filled with the temporal benefits that those who practised the law constantly reaped.

However, his father had always hoped deep down and prayed that his son would become a minister too, and it must have been hard for him to give his blessing to the choice of his son, but he did. But God was moving and working. It was no coincidence, therefore, that before he left for Edinburgh, several supernatural things occurred, which declared that God was bringing about his purposes. One of these included the fact that one day William overheard his father praying and it seems that the words of that prayer were used by God, as his father prayed, to become the foundation of the change that God would bring about in the very son he was praying for and about. William overheard his father praying very quietly, 'there can be no doubt where his heart is, and where he is going.' Islay adds that, 'it was not long before the great decisive change took place, and may possibly have been the first living seed of grace that sunk into his heart.'

Another incident which took place while William was still in Aberdeen, and which led the family as a whole to regard the year 1831 as a year of special grace from God to them, concerned the eldest of William's sisters. She had been living in Edinburgh a life away from God and away from the family. But God apprehended her too, and she returned to the Kilsyth manse, 'desiring, whatever others did, that she might serve the Lord.' This only added to the discomfort that William was feeling at the increased spiritual fervour within the manse, which had only recently been heightened when it became a regular feature to read aloud, between lunch and the evening meal, some religious books. This was too much for William and each time he would, without saying a word, slip out of the house. 'He was to our view,' all the saved of the family thought, 'the least likely subject of grace in the family.' How encouraging should all believers find this! What an encouragement to pray without ceasing! What confidence this should give us, to come and keep coming to the throne of grace!

This meant, then, that as he moved to Edinburgh to begin his proposed law career, God was already working mightily in the heart and life of William Burns. The plan was that he would join his uncle Alexander in his Edinburgh office and become an articled clerk. Everything seemed to be heading that way, except that no one had really expected God to intervene in the way that he did. But the love and prayers of his father were obviously not wasted, and this should be an encouragement to all who have had children who have left the family for the world. God used a variety of means to reach William's heart, and in some lives those whom God strives with may respond fairly quickly, whereas others may seem to have hearts that are so hard, they will never return to Christ. His father must have despaired at times that William might become so enticed with the things of the world that he would never see his need of a Saviour. But he did not give up.

'The means by which my change of heart was brought about were these, I think: Mr Bruce's preaching, which engaged me much, and the fear of sudden death from the approach of cholera were preparatory. A letter from my sisters at home, in which they spoke in a single sentence of going as pilgrims to Zion, and leaving me behind, proved a word in season and touched my natural feelings very deeply.'

Having begun to stir William's mind to things other than mere riches and luxury, God then used a book William's father had given him as he left for Edinburgh. There is much to learn from how this loving father acted. He did not seek to force his son into the kingdom: love never forces. He did not seek to stop his son choosing his own life. He obviously advised his son, but he respected the choices that his son made. He continued to pray for William and knew that his prayers would be heard and answered, however long that took. But he knew, too, that God by his Spirit could use any spiritual material he could put into the hands of his son to speak to his soul, when he, his natural father, could not physically be there.

The key month for Burns was December 1831. Two things are of note. Firstly, the correspondence which took place in that month. He received a joint letter from the family in Kilsyth. The letter itself is no longer extant and the contents themselves were not even remembered by the writers, even only a little while after the letter was sent, but God used whatever they said. We know this for Burns often referred to it later, as one of the chief means of awakening him. In his reply of 5 December 1831, Burns astonished the family, when he wrote:

> I am extremely obliged to you for your excellent letter, also to papa, and I look forward to our correspondence as a thing that shall afford me great pleasure when I am fairly settled away from that dear home where I have enjoyed so many happy days, and where in all likelihood I shall never be resident again. I wish you would recommend to me, or send me some good religious reading.

At that request, the family sent him Thomas Boston's *Human Nature in its Fourfold State*.

The second thing that occurred that month, December 1831, took place at his then lodgings, 41 York Place, Edinburgh. It was a Sunday, and probably having very little to do, he picked up the book which his father had given him before he left Kilsyth. It was Pike's *Early Piety*, and Burns himself records what God did through the words of that book: 'little did [Pike] know what use God was to make of it, little did the author of that solemn treatise know one òf the purposes for which he wrote it! In one moment, while gazing on a solemn passage in it, my inmost soul was in one instant pierced as with a dart. God had apprehended me.'

But this was not Burns' conversion, only his awakening, for he records of that day that 'an arrow from the quiver of the King of Zion was shot by his Almighty sovereign hand through my heart, though it was hard enough to resist all inferior means of salvation.' But only one month later, Burns was able to write that he had become 'a child of grace', and that he now knew that 'the Spirit of God [had] shone with full light upon the glory of Jesus as a Saviour for such as I was'.

His father's prayers had been answered mightily as had those of his sisters too. But they could not have imagined to what degree God would answer. As the Lord himself tells us, he is able to answer in ways far above what we might ever even think, and that is what he did. For no sooner did William feel himself 'saved by a sovereign and infinitely gracious God', in that 'same instant almost I felt that I must leave my present occupation, and devote myself to Jesus in the ministry of that glorious gospel by which I had been saved'.

What we also discover is that just as God was working in William Burns' heart, so he was working too in the circumstances of his life. William had gone, as we have seen, to be apprenticed to his uncle in Edinburgh. For this to be sealed, all Burns' academic certificates from Aberdeen had to be received in Edinburgh. Some had arrived, but not all. There was one outstanding certificate of attendance and this delayed his being bound for the period of his apprenticeship. Having received the forgiveness of sins and a clear call to serve his Master, and being free to train for that task, William planned to return to Aberdeen, the clear prospect in his mind being to be prepared for the ministry.

But before all this had reached such an advanced stage of planning, Burns left Edinburgh for Kilsyth to tell the family of what the Lord had done in his life. The family remember that one evening, suddenly and most unexpectedly, William walked into the manse. His face betrayed something had happened, but it was not a face of joy, it was a grave look, and all his mother could ask, was, 'Oh! Willie, where have you come from?' To which he answered still gravely, 'From Edinburgh.' 'How did you come?' was the next question, to which he replied matter of factly, 'I walked.' This provoked a silence in itself, as all knew the distance to be thirty-six miles. All knew something serious had occurred: all probably suspected something bad. Burns now stood on the hearth-rug, with his back to the large fire, and we can never fully imagine the family's joy, when his next words were, 'What would you think, mamma, if I should be a minister after all?' The house was now one commotion, as Burns sought to recount how the Lord had arrested him and that he had had no rest in spirit until he had set off for Kilsyth to tell them and obtain their consent to give himself to the ministry of Christ. His brother could not contain his joy, and he ran along the long passage to their father's study and there threw himself down on his knees and wept before the Lord.

There is not much that still remains for us to read from that period in Burns' life, only one or two letters. In one, written to his sisters soon after his conversion, 20 February 1832, even while he was still in Edinburgh, we can see something of how quickly he began maturing in his faith:

> I feel it often a great encouragement to me to persevere in that life upon which I have entered, that I do not make for heaven alone; but though there be few that find 'the strait gate' and the 'narrow way', yet that my nearest and dearest friends upon earth are my fellow-pilgrims to the 'heavenly Canaan'. Let us encourage and exhort one another in following and trusting in the Lamb who was slain, and who now intercedes for all who trust in him, at the right hand of the Father. I have been apt, as is I believe the case with many young Christians, to make my safety depend upon my feelings, and consequently to feel miserable when not engaged in religious exercises, and to despise in some degree the ordinary business of life; but I have for some time past been coming to juster and more stable views.... Let not the question be with us, 'How near must we be to him in order to insure our safety?' But how much communion can we possibly attain to while here on earth?

With the family's blessing, William Burns moved back to Aberdeen. But doing this so soon after leaving there meant that he came upon several who had known him before his commitment to Christ. They recognized an immediate and great difference. With his eyes being opened, his work too benefited and in his first session of study at Aberdeen he was placed first in the Senior Mathematics class. But he achieved even more in his final session, when he was placed equal-first with one other for the Mathematics scholarship of the University, a prize which was then and for a long time after 'the highest attainable distinction in the University'.

After his graduation in 1834, he proceeded to Glasgow, the nearest divinity hall to his family in Kilsyth, for his divinity studies. His time there was not particularly noteworthy. The spiritual nature of things there were at a low ebb, though he was able to make friends with several students who were like-minded in their determination to serve Christ with all they had. He did win a medal for Greek, but what stands out more was the time he spent as a founder-member of the University's Students' Missionary Society. They learned and discussed together the stories of some of the giants of missionary faith and heroism. They looked at shining examples from the past, the Martyns and the Brainerds; they looked too, at some of their contemporary men, the Marshmans and the Duffs. They were so filled with the truth of what God could do, that 'our hearts burned within us, and we longed to go forth and mix ourselves with life, in the great battle that was going on in the church and in the world around'.

It was in such an atmosphere that his heart and mind were opened to the real possibility of him taking the good news of Jesus Christ abroad. But it was while he listened to the words of Dr James Kalley, who was then about to sail for China, that Burns purposed to consecrate entirely and absolutely his whole being and life to the service of Christ, and especially to missionary service. It subsequently transpired that Kalley was actually prevented from sailing for China through ill health. But what God did was use Kalley's words to move another, as it were, almost to take his place.

Whilst he continued at Glasgow, Burns had no blinding flashes of inspiration, no visions of where his Lord would have him go. He was being obedient to his call and was certain that the One who had called him would prepare and use him in whatever ways he thought fit. He knew, too, that compared to the God who had lifted him up and compared to the task that lay before him, he was nothing, and he would often record reflections in words such as these:

> I am approaching ... an era of my history, if we except the time of conversion, the most important that can occur to a human being in this world. Soon must I offer myself, miserable as I am, to the Church of God as a candidate for the work of an evangelist; and still more, that Church must decide, so great is the honour I have in prospect, whether in this land or among the perishing heathen it shall be my lot to preach to sinners the unsearchable riches of Christ crucified.

William Chalmers Burns was licensed to preach the gospel by the Presbytery of Glasgow on 27 March 1839. Things had gone well; God had kept his servant, and now the door of service for William was wide open. The usual course for a probationer would have been to become an assistant in a parish until his probationary time and studies were complete. But Burns was aware that all was not usual. He would become almost overwhelmed with the thought of those in foreign countries, perishing without the good news of

Jesus Christ. He felt the burden of their cries of help as if they were calling to him. He could see their need and God was filling his heart with a concern to respond.

One revealing illustration of the effect that this was having on his life was recounted by his mother. She tells of how she was on business in Glasgow centre one day, and she was walking through the Argyle Street Arcade. Suddenly, there was William her son walking directly, but obliviously, towards her. Though she went straight up to him, he was still not conscious she was there. And when she spoke to him, she says that he started so much that it was as if he had come from a great dream. When he did speak, she says it was with deep emotion: 'O mother! I did not see you: for when walking along Argyle Street just now, I was so overcome with the sight of the countless crowds of immortal beings eagerly hasting hither and thither, but all posting onwards towards the eternal world, that I could bear it no longer, and turned in here to seek relief in quiet thought.'

Burns felt so deeply his personal responsibility to spread the gospel, especially amongst those who had never heard, that after much prayer and reflection, he wrote to his father 'to request that, if he thought good, he should communicate with Dr Gordon, the convenor of our India Committee, and let him know that, should the Church deem me qualified, I would be ready to go as a missionary to Hindustan.'

This his father did. The reply of the Committee was so encouraging to William that from that moment on, Burns records that he looked upon himself 'as publicly devoted to the missionary field. In my own soul, and in all my public duties connected with missionary meetings, I felt from that time forward a greatly enlarged measure of the presence and blessing of God, tending to confirm me more deeply in my cherished hope and purpose.'

Burns had officially finished his course and could have left in the summer of 1838, but, he says: 'partly because I found myself profitably engaged in study, and still more, I believe, because I waited in expectation of a call to the missionary field, I remained at College during the following winter, and in the spring of 1839 a proposal was made by the Colonial Committee that I should go out for a season to fill a charge at St John's, New Brunswick, and proceed direct from America to India when the India Committee should require me.'

Burns had no reason to think that the Committee would think otherwise concerning this proposal, but in the event, they did refuse, stating that they wished their agents to be free to go when wanted, and so there, Burns adds, 'the matter ended'. The open door that had seemed the clear route for him to take had closed as firmly as it had suddenly seemed to open. Burns looked to God and prayed that he might not become discouraged, but that he might pray and expect all the more.

Burns did not have to wait too long. God had opened his heart to the cries of the foreign masses, but he would be sent in God's timing and not his own. So for the next nine years, God used Burns to win many souls in his own country.

The next stage of the working of God in Burns' life came by way of letter. Burns might not have been travelling abroad, but another young preacher of the gospel was, and he needed another man of God to look after his flock. Robert Murray McCheyne was never strong, and when his health became a greater cause for concern, he was advised to travel abroad. He was invited to be a member of the Church of Scotland's Mission of Inquiry to the Jews. But he was most reluctant: he worried that his beloved people might suffer if their under-shepherd was away. Whom could he trust? Who would be a blessing to them and not a curse? After much prayer, McCheyne believed William Chalmers Burns to be just that man.

Burns was willing to go wherever his Lord might send and use him, but his last thoughts were of being sent to the people of Dundee. But because both men were obedient, Dundee and Kilsyth saw the hand of God move mightily in awakening and revival. 'This was at the very time when Mr McCheyne, about to set out for Palestine, wrote, asking me to take his place at Dundee. I found myself unexpectedly free to do this, and being speedily licensed I entered on my duties in that memorable field.' It was now April 1839.

But in case one gets the impression that being a servant of God makes for an easy road, and that the doors open and close without trial or the need for God's constant guidance, only two months after beginning his ministry at St Peter's, Dundee, Burns received troubling letters. The first came from the India Committee. 'It was,' says Burns, 'the call that I had looked for'. They were asking him outright to travel as missionary to Poona in Bombay; but he was already committed. Why did this have to happen now? But Burns was not prone to worry, and he prayed to God for guidance. Very soon after, he received a second letter. This one, he wrote, 'only increased the difficulty'. It was a call from the Jewish Committee, with an open door to go to Aden and Arabia.

At the very time he was seeking God's will for his life and ministry, the July Communion at Kilsyth would be taking place. So Burns went there, not knowing that the answers he looked for would become as clear as day. Burns records that he was used of God 'in a way so remarkable for the awaking of sinners', that when he returned to Dundee, and found himself at the centre of a great spiritual awakening there too, how could he think God would will him anywhere else! He immediately wrote to both Committees that, while his views regarding missionary work remained unchanged, yet he now knew that he must for the time remain where he was 'and fulfil the work which God was laying upon me with a mighty hand'.

Chapter 2

The Year of 1839

Awakenings in Dundee and Kilsyth

Robert Murray McCheyne is still remembered and revered as one of the most godly, gifted and fruitful ministers that God has ever given to the church in Scotland. His reputation was little different at the time when he was the minister of St Peter's in Dundee. An overflowing congregation, yet rich in spiritual life and growth, was the fruit of his holy life and ministry, and yet McCheyne did not live beyond his twenty-ninth year.

McCheyne had only been at St Peter's for two years when he began to display some medical symptoms that alarmed his friends. It was soon clear that his bodily health was suffering to an increasing degree from the work demands that he was placing upon it. He soon began to suffer from severe heart palpitations after any great exertion, though it quickly became much worse, even affecting him as he studied. It was soon his constant experience. His doctors advised that he must immediately cease from all public duties, fearing that damage to his lungs might be caused if this did not happen. This resulted in McCheyne leaving Dundee for his father's home in Edinburgh at the close of 1838. He left in full hope that the rest and the change might mean that he would be back amongst his flock in a week or two.

On 5 January 1839, he wrote to a friend that his desire was that 'this affliction will be blessed to me.... Ah! there is nothing like a calm look into the eternal world to teach us the emptiness of human praise, the sinfulness of self-seeking and vainglory, to teach us the preciousness of Christ, who is called "The Tried Stone".' In another letter, he wrote in an almost prophetic way that:

> I sometimes think that a great blessing may come to my people in my absence. Often God does not bless us when we are in the midst of our labours, lest we shall say, 'my hand and my eloquence have done it'. He removes us into silence, and then pours 'down a blessing so that there is no room to receive it'; so that all that see it cry out, 'It is the Lord!' This was the way in the South Sea Islands. May it really be so with my dear people!

That same year, McCheyne's pulpit supply, William Chalmers Burns, would be God's agent to bring that very divine blessing that McCheyne had prayed might come to his flock.

During McCheyne's stay in Edinburgh, Dr Robert S. Candlish came to see him and as they talked about the Mission to Israel which had then recently been agreed upon, an idea suddenly suggested itself to Candlish. He asked McCheyne what he would think of 'being useful to the Jewish cause, during his cessation from labour, by going abroad to make personal inquiries into the state of Israel'. McCheyne recorded that at the proposal, his heart was filled 'with joy and wonder'. His doctors gladly consented to the plan as a way of giving much needed rest and recuperation to his exhausted body.[1] Not surprisingly the news of his proposed absence alarmed his flock at St Peter's and many wrote letters begging him to reconsider. To one of these well-meaning parishioners he replied:

> I rejoice exceedingly in the interest you take in me, not so much for my own sake as that I hope it is a sign you know and love the Lord Jesus. Unless God had himself shut up the door of return to my people, and opened this new door to me, I never could have consented to go. I am not at all unwilling to spend and be spent in God's service, though I have often found that the more abundantly I love you, the less I am loved. But God has very plainly shown me that I may perform a deeply important work for his ancient people, and at the same time be in the best way of seeking a return to health.

McCheyne sought God for one who would be a faithful shepherd whilst he was away, one who would feed the flock and gather in

---

1. An account of their travels to Palestine was written by Andrew Bonar. *Mission of Discovery* is published by Christian Focus.

those who might stray during his absence. The Lord granted his desire and William Chalmers Burns was sent of God to Dundee. In a letter to Burns dated 12 March 1839, in words reminiscent of his desire for God's blessing to fall upon his people and in words which clearly reveal the heart of an all-loving under-shepherd who seeks only God's glory, McCheyne wrote:

You are given in answer to prayer; and these gifts are, I believe, always without exception blessed. I hope you may be a thousand times more blessed among them than ever I was. Perhaps there are many souls that would never have been saved under my ministry, who may be touched under yours; and God has taken this method of bringing you into my place.

What needs to be said at this point, which has been overlooked by previous biographers, is that according to letters to and from McCheyne, Burns was clearly the man of McCheyne's choice and was a surprise and rebuke for others. The choice of Burns was probably a surprise, because to fill McCheyne's pulpit would take someone quite out of the ordinary, someone tried and tested, and upon whom it was clear God's blessing rested. Yet William Burns had no proven track-record of church growth, in fact he had little track-record at all, for at the time that he was approached to take McCheyne's place, he was still in a state of being unlicensed to preach by the Church of Scotland. St Peter's Kirk-Session, too, in an unpublished letter to McCheyne dated 11 March 1839, were hesitant, for though they agreed to the selection of William Burns, they clearly indicated their doubts that anyone would be able to replace McCheyne, either in the work of the parish, or in their affections.

The choice of Burns was also seen as a rebuke to some, for on 1 March for example, we find the following words in an unpublished letter that Alexander Somerville wrote to McCheyne: 'Your silent rebuke by your letter to Burns this morning, let me see what you were thinking of.' He then went on, 'I delivered your message to Burns who liked the idea very much of taking your place for a season.... He will return an answer to you later himself.' However, Burns soon met personally with McCheyne to discuss and pray over the proposal and again Burns said he would need a little more time.

His agreement to stand in McCheyne's place came in another unpublished letter, dated 11 March:

> My dear sir. I have been endeavouring since I saw you to discover, by deliberation and the advice of friends, accompanied by special prayer for the light and guidance of the Holy Spirit, the will of God in regard to the important proposal made to me by you. And now as far as I can discern any path, it appears to be this, that I am bound to leave myself at your disposal, and, in case you shall still see cause for asking me to enter on your sphere of duty during your absence, to cast myself on that grace promised in the covenant which is sufficient to fit the weakest instruments for accomplishing that which yields a reverence of glory to God. I confess I am afraid to speak in such terms as these; for though it be true that God can fit even one for such a mighty work as this which is proposed, yet I have too much reason to fear that the work of the Spirit is making little progress, or even going back, in my own soul.

In fact, Burns says that he hoped that McCheyne had been 'directed to some other in whose hands you would prefer to leave the weighty charge of your people's souls. If however you still desire that I should attempt this work, I dare not refuse from any inability which the Lord who calleth me to his service is able and willing to remove.'

On 22 March 1839, McCheyne wrote his last letter to Burns before he left for the Holy Land. He began this letter with the words, 'My dear friend'; 'for I trust,' says McCheyne, 'I may now reckon you among the number in the truest sense.' This was a friendship which grew and blossomed from that time onwards. McCheyne informed Burns that the Committee in charge of the Mission had resolved that McCheyne should leave that Wednesday. This meant that any advice he wanted to pass on, he would have to do by letter and so he did. In this godly counsel it is easy to see McCheyne's concerns both for the one standing in for him and for his people whom he loved so dearly. Consequently, McCheyne advised Burns to:

Take heed to thyself. Your own soul is your first and greatest care. You know a sound body alone can work with power; much more a healthy soul. Keep a clear conscience through the blood of the Lamb. Keep up close communion with God. Study likeness to him in all things. Read the Bible for your own growth first, then for your people. Expound much; it is through the truth that souls are to be sanctified, not through essays upon the truth. Be easy of access, apt to teach, and the Lord teach you and bless you in all you do and say. You will not find many companions. Be the more with God. My dear people are anxiously waiting for you. The prayerful are praying for you. Be of good courage; there remaineth much of the land to be possessed.

On the 27th of that same month, William Burns was licensed to preach the gospel by the Presbytery of Glasgow. The next two Sundays he spent with his father at Kilsyth, and then with fear, trepidation and real expectation, he left for his duties in what he later referred to as 'that memorable field' of Dundee. As has been noted, St Peter's was a thriving congregation of about eleven hundred people. The flock had high expectations and many travelled from great distances to sit under the blessed ministry of McCheyne. The real test would be how Burns would be accepted by those who had become used to the richest of fare. Burns was obviously well aware of the challenge that faced him, but he was well aware too, that the God McCheyne served was the same Lord that he himself served and by whom he had been called.

In fact, it was Burns' own clear sense of insufficiency that actually played a major part in persuading him to accept the call to Dundee, for Burns was utterly convinced that without God he could do nothing; nothing, that is, that would bear fruit, nothing that would last. It did not make any difference, he would say, whether that was a short children's talk or the request to take McCheyne's place. Repeated journal entries testify to the fact that Burns believed that without the strength and help of the Holy Spirit, he could accomplish nothing at all. It is also clear from his *Journals*, that this became the guiding principle of his whole life and ministry.

Robert Murray McCheyne was twenty-five years old when he left for the Holy Land; William Chalmers Burns was only twenty-four when he travelled from Kilsyth to Dundee to stand in his place. Members of St Peter's have recorded how their hearts trembled for Burns when, on that second Sabbath in April 1839, he ascended the pulpit of their beloved pastor, for he appeared to be a 'mere stripling'. When we remember the closeness of their ages, one must wonder whether it was the volume of work that McCheyne had had to cope with that had made its mark on him in such a striking way, making him appear well beyond his years.

But it seems it was at the first sound of Burns' voice, as he led the people of St Peter's in divine worship, that they began to love and accept him, recognizing almost immediately in him and through him, the voice of the Master of their beloved pastor. They perceived that the young man who now stood in front of them was clearly God's man for the hour. Evidence of God's hand amongst them was also soon apparent, with a clear increase of spiritual hunger amongst the people, and one of the church officers made his own remarkable record of that time:

> Scarcely had Mr Burns entered on his work in St Peter's here, when his power as a preacher began to be felt. Gifted with a solid and vigorous understanding, possessed of a voice of vast compass and power, unsurpassed even by that of Mr Spurgeon – and withal fired with an ardour so intense and an energy so exhaustless that nothing could damp or resist it, Mr Burns wielded an influence over the masses whom he addressed which was almost without parallel since the days of Wesley and Whitefield. Crowds flocked to St Peter's from all the country round; and the strength of the preacher seemed to grow with the incessant demands made upon it. Wherever Mr Burns preached a deep impression was produced on his audience, and it was felt to be impossible to remain unconcerned under the impassioned earnestness of his appeals. With him there was no effort at oratorical display, but there was true eloquence; and instances are on record of persons, strong in their self-confidence and enmity to the truth, who fell before its power.

In a letter which Burns wrote to his sister only a matter of days after arriving at St Peter's, he gives us a very illuminating insight concerning his first impressions of Dundee and the work to be done there:

I would gladly fill my sheet in narrating what I have been able to ascertain of my situation and circumstances here, were it not that I must husband every moment of my time for my engagements in visiting the sick and dying, examining intending communicants, and preparation for the Sabbath that is approaching. I am not left without many circumstances to encourage me in my arduous labours; not a few hearts seem in a good measure prepared to hear the gospel as the Word of God, and some I have met with whose experience in the spiritual life affords the strongest stimulus to my own growth in grace, and whose ideas of Christian ministrations will, I fear, make me to appear among them as an ignorant babbler. They appear, however, as a very kind and not uncharitable class of people, as far as I can discover; they will, I hope, pray for as well as censure me.

Burns knew well the dangers associated with such a successful ministry, especially at such a young age, and repeatedly made journal entries to that effect. These records were written in such a way that he might remind himself where the source of his strength and help really lay and to whom all the glory must go. On 25 April for example, he writes, 'Discovered through grace, an awful hungering after applause from man, and came home fearing that God may utterly forsake me in consequence of my self-seeking in his service.' Then on 6 June he records how one he called A.M. came with real joy to tell him that God had clearly spoken to her and helped her, as he had done under McCheyne's ministry. 'I told her not to cast sparks from hell into my inflammable heart, to give thanks to God, and to beware of commending man.'

Burns also makes it clear that he was aware that before there could be any real work of God amongst the people he was ministering to, there would have to be much seeking of God's face for that end, as he had become aware had been the case in previous awakenings. So on 25 April we find him praying, 'O for a spirit of humble wrestling prayer for the outpouring of the Holy Spirit, that sinners may be awakened, and saints greatly edified and advanced!'; and on 29 April, 'O that Christ were exalted and man forgotten among this people! Come from the four winds, O breath, and breathe on these slain that they may live.'

But if Burns was aware of those two things, that pride was an ever-present temptation and that in the economy of God serious and sustained prayer and pleading came before the showers of divine blessing, he became well aware too, as he admits, that his own preaching was incomplete. For he writes that 'during the first four months of my ministry, which were spent at Dundee, I enjoyed much of the Lord's presence in my own soul ... but though I endeavoured to speak the truth fully, and to press it earnestly on the souls of the people, there was still a defect in my preaching at that time which I have since learned to correct.'

That deficiency, as he refers to it, was his tendency to hold back whilst preaching. 'I never came, as it were, to throw down the gauntlet to the enemy by the unreserved declaration and urgent application of the divine testimony regarding the state of fallen man and the necessity of an unreserved surrender to the Lord Jesus in all his offices in order that he may be saved.'

Once he had diagnosed the problem, however, his ministry went from strength to strength, and soon after he was told of some in the congregation 'who were shedding silent tears under the Word of the Lord'. The flood-gates were lifting and the hand of God would soon move for many to see, both in Dundee and back at his father's parish of Kilsyth.

God's blessing began to fall in Kilsyth, because in July of 1839, William Burns returned there to help at the Communion season, at the very time that God was preparing to use Burns as his agent to prepare the people for the store-houses of heaven to be opened and to be poured upon the people.

Burns arrived at Kilsyth in late July and was to spend a little more than a week-end there, but that is all the time it took for God to begin such a mighty work that it is remembered still, over 160 years later. Burns preached on the Friday evening from Psalm 130:1, 2, a subject that had obviously been pressing on Burns' heart, for he had recently spoken on the same subject in Dundee after studying John Owen's treatise on this Psalm. His message was delivered, he says, 'in a manner in some degree fitted to alarm unconverted sinners and sleeping saints'.

On the following day he preached at Banton, a little village adjoining Kilsyth at which an extension church had been erected through Burns' father's labours, and there he preached from Psalm

103:3 'with considerable assistance, as far as I can recollect'. His uncle, Dr Burns of Paisley, sensed God's hand upon his nephew, and asked William to take his place at Kilsyth on the Sunday evening. Burns also assisted in the Communion Table Services and then on the evening preached from Matthew 11:28. His memory was stirred and his heart was moved, as he thought back over all the many lost and wasted years that he had spent amongst those same people, many of whom were still like he had been, in darkness and without Christ. He was moved to such a degree, that he announced he would speak to them once more before returning to Dundee. He would speak that coming Tuesday morning in the open-air at the market place.

When Burns looked back to that Tuesday morning, he referred to it as one 'of the Lord's wondrous works'. The weather necessitated a change of venue, something which Burns later recognized as 'a wise providential arrangement'. Burns was a popular preacher, and it was known that he would soon be away, but it was obvious that many more had gathered to hear Burns in the outdoors than would normally have gone within church doors. So Burns and others shepherded all in their path through the streets and on to the church. 'When I entered the pulpit, I saw before me an immense multitude from the town and neighbourhood filling the seats, stairs, passages, and porches, all in their ordinary clothes, and including many of the most abandoned of our population.' In fact, the church was overflowing, with nearly fourteen hundred people being present.

Burns took as his text Psalm 110:3, and spoke on the subject of 'the day of God's power'. He recounted to his hearers some of the wonderful awakenings that Scotland had already experienced, including the time when the young John Livingstone preached in Shotts in 1630 and it pleased God to save hundreds of souls in a short time. Burns told the people that Livingstone had actually been on the point of finishing his message, when a few drops of rain began to fall and the people took this as their cue to begin putting on coverings. Livingstone then asked them if they had any shelter from the drops of divine wrath and, from this heaven-sent illustration, he exhorted them for another hour to flee from the wrath to come and to run to Christ.

During the whole of the time that Burns was preaching, all listened 'with the most riveted and solemn attention, and with many silent tears and inward groanings of the spirit'. But just as Burns was speaking of Livingstone's challenge:

> I felt my own soul moved in a manner so remarkable that I was led, like Mr Livingstone, to plead with the unconverted before me instantly to close with God's offers of mercy, and continued to do so until the power of the Lord's Spirit became so mighty upon their souls as to carry all before it, like the rushing mighty wind of Pentecost. Suddenly as God's Spirit moved in their midst, many 'broke forth simultaneously in weeping and wailing, tears and groans, intermingled with shouts of joy and praise from some of the people of God. Some were screaming out in agony; others, and among these strong men, fell to the ground as if they had been dead; and such was the general commotion, that after repeating for some time the most free and urgent invitations of the Lord to sinners, I was obliged to give out a psalm, which was soon joined by a considerable number, our voices being mingled with the mourning groans of many prisoners sighing for deliverance.'

His uncle and his father both also spoke at the gathering, and after it was announced that there would be a further meeting that evening at 6.00 p.m., the meeting was closed a good five hours after it had begun. This was no flash in the pan either. For some time all business in the town was suspended. Meetings for prayer and preaching of the gospel were held every successive night, both in the church and in the open-air. There were often thousands who gathered for these times of preaching. Crowds of inquirers flocked at every invitation to the vestry or manse to seek spiritual counsel from Burns or his assistants. Trains from Glasgow and other nearby towns brought thousands of curious and interested people, who swelled the numbers already touched. Prayer meetings for all ages sprang up everywhere in the village and the surrounding areas, and ministers from all parts of the country came to the aid of the overworked Burns.

The *Glasgow Argus*, which condemned the 'extraordinary scenes' of hundreds of people calling out for mercy and fainting from the intensity of their feelings, was later forced to admit that 'the excitement is indeed altogether remarkable, and is deeply attracting the attention of the religious public'. The *Presbyterian Review* of October 1839, on the other hand, responded quite differently: 'A whole community setting their faces to seek God! The world thrown aside, earthly interests forgotten, that eternity might be remembered. What a scene!'

It is often said that a work of God should be judged by the results that are tangible and not just spiritual. Is there any evidence of general change in Kilsyth and the surrounding areas? There most certainly is. A statement was read at the time by the minister of the parish to the presbytery of the bounds. It is most illuminating:

> The waiting on of young and older people at the close of each meeting, and the anxious asking of so many, 'What to do'; the lively singing of the praises of God, which every visitor remarks; the complete absence of swearing and of foolish talking in our streets; the order and solemnity at all hours prevailing; the voice of praise and prayer almost in every house; the cessation of the tumults of the people; the consignment to the flames of volumes of infidelity and impurity; the coming together for Divine worship of such a multitude of our population day after day; the large catalogue of new intending communicants giving in their names, and conversing in the most interesting manner on the most important subjects; not a few of the old careless sinners and frozen formalists awakened and made alive to God; the conversion of several poor colliers, who have come to me and given the most satisfactory account of their change of mind and heart, are truly wonderful proofs of a most surprising and delightful revival. The public-houses, the coal-pits, the harvest reaping fields, the weaving loomsteads, the recesses of our glens, and the sequestered haughs all around, all may be called to witness that there is a mighty change in this place for the better.

Burns could only stay in Kilsyth a little longer because of the pressing responsibilities in Dundee, and he returned there on 8 August. But if he imagined that things would be nearly the same as when he had left them, he was to be much mistaken. After arriving back in Dundee, he found himself in the midst of scenes little different to what God was doing in Kilsyth. How his heart rejoiced to at last see the flood-gates lifting in Dundee too. He had seen little evidences earlier that some were being touched under his ministry, such as signs of deeper attention than normal and real anxiety in some that had before shown no concern at all, but these were mere mist-drops compared to that which God was soon to pour down. Burns returned on the Tuesday, and by the Thursday Dundee was to be touched as Kilsyth had been only a little time earlier. What is also worthy of note is that Andrew Bonar tells us in his *Memoir of McCheyne* that it was on that very day, 8 August, that McCheyne was stretched on his bed, praying with all his remaining strength for his flock back in Dundee. But McCheyne and Bonar knew nothing of the remarkable works of God in Scotland until they were in sight of home.

The Thursday prayer-meeting at St Peter's was held as usual, and afterwards Burns explained why he had been delayed in returning to Dundee, as he recounted to them the marvellous things that the Lord was doing in Kilsyth. He invited those to remain who felt, as Bonar records, 'the need of an outpouring of the Spirit to convert them'. One hundred or so stayed back, and after Burns had spoken to them 'suddenly the power of God seemed to descend, and all were bathed in tears'. There was another meeting on the Friday evening with similar results, except that on that evening Burns decided to make the vestry available 'to those who might feel anxious to converse'. As soon as he opened the door however, a vast, eager crowd rushed in. 'It was like a pent-up flood breaking forth; tears were streaming from the eyes of many, and some fell on the ground, groaning, and weeping, and crying for mercy.'

From that night, Friday 11 August onwards, meetings were held every day for many weeks, and it seemed that the whole city was touched. Burns himself tells us that the church was so crowded every night, many had to be turned away and that after every service there were throngs of people remaining behind for prayer and counsel. Prayer-meetings sprang up all across the area, composed of old and young alike; several were even run and attended only by children. On 28 August, for example, Burns records that 'in the forenoon the church was densely crowded, and in the afternoon every corner was filled, so that I could not, without much difficulty, force my way to the pulpit; hundreds were forced to be excluded.'

At the heart of these awakenings lay the sovereignty of God: that God will touch people as and when he will. But there are also responsibilities laid upon those who desire to see God move in wonderful ways. Prayer is obviously one, but faith that God will move is another. Not the belief that he can, but the faith to lay hold of God and to plead for his grace to be sent in waves on the people.

This was where William Chalmers Burns stood. Like William Carey, he expected great things from God and attempted great things for God, but always in the knowledge that without God he could do nothing. Burns knew, too, that the people must in some way share that expectation and so what we find Burns doing is the very same thing that his predecessor Mr Robe did in previous revivals. By way of preparing the ground he read accounts of what God was doing or had done. In other words, he sought to increase and nurture the faith and expectancy of God's people and to challenge the hearts and minds of unbelievers. Robe had been a regular correspondent with Jonathan Edwards, and when Edwards sent accounts of the awakenings in New England, Robe would eagerly read them to his own people. For his part, Burns read accounts of the revivals under Robe himself. This obviously produced certain reactions amongst the hearers. They became filled with a sense of expectation that if God had done such remarkable things in the past, then he could easily repeat such wonders. They became filled too with a sense of the urgency and need of constant and believing prayer. So we find Burns recording numerous examples, for instance on 2 September:

> In the evening Mr Macalister preached an excellent sermon, after which I read Robe's narrative, and engaged in prayer more than once for the outpouring of the Spirit, which I think we received more signally perhaps than on any former night, if we except the very first meetings. There were many crying bitterly; one fell down, when near the end I stopped and sat down in silent prayer for five minutes, that all might be brought to the point of embracing Jesus.

The fruit continued to be evident. Not only was the church filled to overflowing every night with hundreds waiting behind for further instruction, but every other available hour Burns had was taken up with praying and counselling with individual seekers. Up to forty people would often be found at his door, and as they waited to be seen by Burns, they would gather to pray together in smaller groups in an outer room. Even when all seemed to be finished, eager groups would stay around the preacher as he retired to his vestry, hoping to hear some last words of parting counsel, blessing and prayer. Sometimes Burns found it almost impossible to return home; crowds would simply follow him wherever he went. On 19 September, for example, Burns writes:

> When we left the session-house we met a great multitude still waiting to hear the word, and some of them in tears. Many of these came along with us to the west end of the town, and when we came to Roseangle, Mr W. at my suggestion engaged with them in a parting prayer on the highway side, under the starlight faintly shining through the dark windy clouds.

Burns knew that when he was close to God, when he was and had been dependent upon him, was when he felt God's strengthening most. If his prayer-life waned at all, even if it was due to the ongoing duties the awakening created, he was very quickly aware of the lack of closeness of God's Spirit. Prayer then became all-important to Burns and he would do all he could to spend time alone with God even in the midst of his busy days.

Burns sometimes recorded these meditations, so for example we have him writing the following in mid-September:

> Come, Lord Jesus, come quickly! O scatter the clouds and mists of unbelief which exhale afresh from the stagnant marshes in my natural heart, the habitation of dragons, and pour afresh upon my ransomed soul a full flood of thy divine light and love and joy, in the effulgence of which all sin dies, and all the graces of the Spirit bloom and breathe their fragrance! Nor do I pray for myself alone, but for all my dear friends, and for my father, mother, brothers and sisters, and for all the people here; and for all the ministers of every name whom Jesus hath called to preach his gospel, and for all who shall tomorrow hear or read the glad tidings of great joy which shall yet be to all people! Lord, hasten the latter-day glory! Come quickly, and reign without

bounds and without end! And now wash me in thy blood, whose price I cannot tell, but need to cleanse me, so great a transgressor am I. Glory be to thee, O Lamb of God, and to thee, O Father, and to thee, O Holy Ghost, eternal and undivided! Amen!

In that same month of September 1839, Burns began a new volume of his journal, which he entitled, 'A Record of the Lord's Marvellous Doings for me and many other Sinners at Dundee, 1839.' It consists for the first seventy-four pages of notices of individual cases of awakening and earnest inquiry. Most are brief and fragmentary entries. What one learns from this journal, however, is that McCheyne obviously had access to it afterwards, for he has made a number of his own notes next to Burns' own entries, adding information concerning the individuals Burns refers to. Against the name of one he wrote, 'Holds on her way rejoicing, October 1840.' Against another, 'I trust goes on well and steadily, October 1840.' By another entry McCheyne noted, 'Admitted her to the communion; she seems a true disciple of Christ, October 1840.'

But after beginning that volume, Burns was soon to be found back in Kilsyth. He returned there on 21 September to help with a second Communion Service, organized because so many had recently been converted in the awakening which was still taking place. He preached on the same afternoon that he arrived, with, as he writes, 'much assistance'. On the following day, Communion Sunday, in the tent there were about ten thousand people gathered for worship. Mr Rose preached first and then Burns followed with a message on Isaiah 54:5, which lasted for two hours. Burns again preached that evening at 7.00 p.m. in the tent, whilst Rose preached in the church. Burns' outdoor meeting lasted for about three hours, 'the moon being full and the sky unclouded', and Burns noted that 'there was visible among the people a far greater awakening than during any part of the day'.

But when Burns returned home, he noticed that his father and Mr Rose had not yet returned, and it struck him too that those who were willing could continue to meet in the church and stay there 'all night in prayer to God for the outpouring of the Spirit.' When he and others returned to the church, there were already many in prayer and after the bell was rung the church was soon filled. Many were awakened during that meeting, and though they left the church at 3.00 a.m., Alexander Somerville and Burns had to remain in the session-house 'with the distressed, instructing and praying till between five and six o'clock, when we went home to rest'.

But these days of God's Spirit did not allow much time for rest, and Burns was again preaching later that day in the tent to a congregation of two thousand. Burns knew that there were many ministers and preachers in the tent that day and he was anxious, not having had time for special preparation. But Burns again proved the faithfulness of his Lord, for having cast himself on God, 'he did not prove a wilderness to me, a land of darkness, but aided me beyond all my expectations'. At the church evening service, Charles J. Brown preached, and Burns felt constrained to ask those 'who knew that they were still unconverted, to remain, coming down into the front seats below to be addressed and prayed for. By thus assigning them particular seats rather alarmed and staggered Mr Brown, and, as I afterwards found, my father also and many other of the ministers present.'

Many in fact came forward, so many that all the seats were taken. After further singing and prayer, Burns exhorted both those in the seats and those in the church generally to accept Christ and to close with him. 'There seemed to be a general and sweet melting of heart among the audience, and many of the unconverted were weeping bitterly aloud, though I spoke throughout with perfect calmness and solemnity.' They were not able to leave the church until about 1.30 a.m., but this was not the end of the work, for many went straight from the church to the session-house, 'where my father had been with not a few in distress during the greater part of the meeting, and then he and Mr Rose continued for several hours longer, witnessing, as they told us when they came home, the most wonderful displays of the Holy Spirit's work.'

But we are not just dependent on William Burns' own record of the events in Kilsyth. We are fortunate that Burns' father also wrote down his own recollections of that period, together with his own personal thoughts. It is of added benefit in the sense that here we have the judgments of the pastor, admittedly the father of the evangelist from whom much of the work stems, but he will still have to take back the reins and pick up the pieces when William finally leaves for the last time:

> Having been preceded, accompanied and followed by a very unusual copiousness of prayer, the showers in answer were very copious and refreshing. We are daily hearing of good done to strangers who came Zaccheus-like to see what it was, who have been pierced in heart and have gone away new men. Our own people of Christian spirit have been greatly enlivened and strengthened, and some very hopeful cases of apparently real beginnings of new life have been brought to our knowledge. I feel grateful to the God of grace and God of order in our churches, that there has been such a concurrence of what is true, venerable, pure, just, lovely and of good report, and that little indeed has escaped from any of us which can justly cause regret.... The solemn appearance of the communion tables, and the delightful manner in which they were exhorted; the presence of not a few unusually young disciples at the tables; the seriousness of aspect in all, and the softening and melting look of others, made upon every rightly disposed witness a very delightful impression.... For ninety years, doubtless, there has not been in this parish such a season of prayer and holy communings and conferences, nor at any period such a number of precious sermons delivered. The spiritual awakenings and genuine conversions at this time are not few, and it is hoped will come forth to victory; but the annals of eternity will only divulge the whole.

Burns again left these wonderful scenes to return to St Peter's, and to the remarkable happenings that were also occurring there. But it is typical of Burns, that even in the midst of all that was taking place and being demanded of him, he still somehow found the time, opportunity and strength to occasionally make evangelistic journeys to other places. One such visit was to Paisley, which took place on his way from Kilsyth to Dundee. He preached there in the High Church to a densely crowded mass of people, and 'saw not a few in tears'. The next day found him preaching in the morning at Kirkintilloch, and in the evening at Denny. But something further happened before Burns even reached Paisley. He was sitting in the boat to Glasgow when a man whom he knew, John Marshall, suggested to him that he 'should have worship here'. Burns' ready reply was that 'if it is agreeable to all it will be agreeable to me'. Those near to Burns all agreed and then the Captain appeared saying, 'Will you allow me to open the steerage door as the passengers there would like to hear?' They all gladly agreed to this and in a few moments Burns found himself, to his own admitted astonishment, standing at the partition door and praying and singing with all on board.

After Paisley, Burns then journeyed onwards to Dundee. As at Kilsyth, several ministers came to assist Burns at the Dundee October Communion season, as fishermen in the midst of a great harvest of the sea. Burns' good friends the Bonars came to help, and the number of people was so great that three congregations had to be formed. The church held the largest number with Burns addressing them, and two smaller groups met in adjoining school rooms and each was addressed by one of the Bonars.

Later that October, Burns visited the Edinburgh Orphan Hospital, which was run by one of his friends, a Mr McDougall, and which had been greatly supported by George Whitefield in the previous century. Burns went into the little pulpit of the chapel and, with the orphans gathered before him, read from Psalm 103, 'Such pity as a father hath....' He felt quite overpowered with sympathy for the children there in their orphan state, mingled with 'grateful wonder at the love of God in dealing so kindly with them. In prayer also I had considerable enlargement, and ... I felt unusually melted myself, and yearned over them, I think, in the bowels of Jesus Christ. Some of the boys and girls were crying, and when I bade them farewell, they unwillingly and with many tears withdrew.' Burns' prayer for them was typical, 'O Lord, think upon each of these dear children, convert them all to thyself through Jesus, and raise up from among the boys a great band of holy and devoted ministers and missionaries of Jesus!' Only eternity will reveal the fruit of such a prayer from such a man.

Burns received a letter from McCheyne confirming that he would return to Dundee on 23 November. On the following Sunday, which would be the last Sunday before McCheyne would be back, Burns announced that McCheyne was due to return that coming week. But as he spoke he was quite overcome and could speak only a little more. The people left the hall very slowly and many waited in the passage and in the gallery until Burns was ready to leave. As Burns moved through the passage there was much weeping from the people and he stopped there to pray with them for quite a time. It was similar outside the church, and as Burns looked over the people he silently prayed that amongst them there might be 'not a few jewels to shine for ever in the crown of Emmanuel the Redeemer!'

McCheyne was preaching in Hamburg when he read of the outpouring of God's mercy in Dundee, but there was little detail and so he wrote to his parents, 'we are quite ignorant of the facts, and you may believe we are anxious to hear.' McCheyne prayed all the more earnestly both for his own ministry and for his flock, and he sent to Burns, by way of a fellow-worker, the following encouragement:

> Do not forget to carry on the work in hearts brought to a Saviour. I feel this was one of my faults in the ministry. Nourish babes; comfort downcast believers; counsel those perplexed; perfect that which is lacking in their faith. Prepare them for sore trials. I fear most Christians are quite unready for days of darkness.

As McCheyne and Bonar headed for Scotland, McCheyne received a letter from R. S. Candlish dated 8 November. This unpublished letter reveals both Candlish's regard for McCheyne, as well as his reaction to Burns' work in the revival in Dundee:

> We hear much that is cheering and encouraging of what is going on in Dundee. At the same time there are circumstances which lead me to suggest that it will be necessary for you, coming in at this particular stage of the work, to proceed with due caution and deliberation, and even in some particulars with a certain reserve and suspense of judgment, for a time. I say this to you frankly and confidentially ... being very sure that you will not misunderstand me. I do not say it in the spirit of ... suspicion, but out of a real desire to see what I regard as a decided work of God, turned to the best account. For this end I think your return home at this juncture ... may be most providential .... I cannot conceal from you that there are ... some points of considerable delicacy, and I feel persuaded that both in regard to the

wholesome progress of the work at Dundee, and the general cause of the revival of religion, and the judgment to be formed respecting it, much may depend upon you.

In Bonar's *Memoir*, we should not be surprised to discover therefore, that after such a letter, as soon as McCheyne set foot on British soil, he sought out as much detail as he could concerning what had and what was occurring in Dundee. But any fears that might have arisen seem to have been allayed, for Bonar adds that 'he had no envy at another instrument having been so honoured in the place where he himself had laboured with many tears and temptations ... he rejoiced that the work of the Lord was done, by whatever hand. Full of praise and wonder, he set his foot once more on the shore of Dundee.' The hour of the renewing of Burns' and McCheyne's personal friendship came at 6.30 p.m. on 23 November. Burns met McCheyne at his house and had 'a sweet season of prayer with him before the hour of the evening meeting'. When the time came for the service both went together to the church. Every seat was filled, as were all the passages: even the very stairs up to the pulpit were crowded, 'on the one side with the aged, on the other with eagerly-listening children.'

Both men entered the pulpit together, but it was McCheyne who opened the time of worship with songs and prayer. McCheyne later commented that the singing was very different from what it had been; 'so tender and affecting', he said, 'as if the people felt that they were praising a present God.' McCheyne also later wrote to the Bonars that 'Everything here I have found in a state better than I expected. The night I arrived I preached to such a congregation as I never saw before. I do not think another person could have got into the church, and there was every sign of the deepest and tenderest emotion.'

After the singing and prayer and some words from McCheyne, Burns then spoke from 2 Samuel 23:1-5 and the service ended at 10.00 p.m. They returned to McCheyne's house together and spoke at great length about many things connected with God's will and God's work, including both men's future plans and prospects. Burns judged McCheyne to still be in 'weak health, and not very sanguine about ever resuming the full duties of a parish minister. O Lord, spare thy servant, if it be for the glory of thy name, and restore his full strength that he may yet be the means of winning many souls for Jesus. Amen.'

That Burns was held in high regard by the members of St Peter's is to be seen not just in their emotions, but also in their gift to him of more than a hundred volumes of theological books 'a token' of their affection and unqualified approbation of his ministry, reported the *Dundee Courier* of 31 December 1839. But what did McCheyne think of Burns the preacher and of the revival which, Bonar says, was still falling, 'drop by drop...from the clouds', even after McCheyne's return? In the same letter quoted above, from McCheyne to the Bonars in December, McCheyne does comment on both Burns and the scenes which met his eyes:

> There is a great deal of substance in what he preaches, and his manner is very powerful, so much so that he sometimes made me tremble. In private he is deeply prayerful, and seems to feel his danger of falling into pride.
>
> He then adds this is a pleasant place compared with what it was once.... I have hardly met with anything to grieve me. Surely the Lord has dealt bountifully with me.... I have not met with one case of extravagance or false fire, although doubtless there may be many.

With the return of McCheyne, Burns' relationship with the congregation of St Peter's did change, but it did not end. Because of McCheyne's delicate health, Burns remained at Dundee for a period to assist his friend in the parish. It meant too, though, that Burns was able to travel on a much wider scale, and was often away to various parts of the country, preaching the gospel with wonderful results. By December, however, Burns was obviously thinking as to his future, for on the 6th he wrote in his journal that he was 'in great difficulty in knowing my own duty, whether to remain steadily in Dundee or to visit it only among the many places which seem at present ripe for the harvest'. In the meantime he continued his evangelistic visits, guided simply by the calls which came to him, and going in the power and strength of the Holy Spirit.

Chapter 3

Itinerant Evangelism Through Scotland
(1840–43)

'Ripe for the harvest' is how William Burns regarded the many places that the return of McCheyne now enabled him to travel to preach to all the more. It is very clear from Burns' journal that he fully expected the right preaching of the gospel to bring forth fruit. As we have noted, it had not always been this way with him, but now that he brought his hearers to a point of decision about Christ, he was fully persuaded that the Spirit would open the hearts and minds and wills of many of those who heard the Word. He was likewise persuaded that this may often result in physical manifestations, and it was this truth that would later lead to problems in Aberdeen. In fact, 'he had,' said his brother, 'very exalted views of what might be expected even in these latter days from the outpouring of the Spirit, in answer to the earnest prayers of a reviving Church.... That memorable scene [Pentecost] he regarded not as an isolated event, but as a pattern of what the Church might hope in any age to see, it might be even still more gloriously.'

We learn, too, that Burns did not regard the most startling outward manifestations of the Spirit's working seen at Pentecost as exceptional, but evidences that the Spirit was working and signs that should be looked for in every age. Shortly before William went to St Peter's, he and Islay were walking from Glasgow to Kilsyth, and a discussion began on this very subject. Islay asked him whether in spite of the fact that it was the same Spirit working, the reserve and self-restraint of modern man might mean that people would respond much less dramatically than was recorded as taking place at Pentecost. William could not agree. For him, the mighty rushing wind of the Spirit coming in power would, in any age, be such that not only the Church would hear, but 'even the world itself should not be able wholly to close its ears'. Neither men could fully know then that the very place they were at that moment walking towards would provide the evidence that would testify to the remarkable truth of William's words. 'Probably he himself,' comments Islay, 'even while arguing the possibility of such a thing, little dreamed that it was in truth so near at hand.'

The close of 1839 saw William Burns travelling a good deal, as he preached in various villages, towns and cities. In November, he was to be found in Perth, which would later become the place he would settle at for a little while. Whilst on a short visit there, he was asked if he would stay to preach later that day, and when he agreed, some men were sent to give intimation of this. The result of even this short and partial notice was that the church was crowded and hundreds had to be sent away who were not able to get in. He then travelled on and arrived next in St Andrews. From that place we have recorded a wonderful testimony concerning Burns, from one 'whose name will long be fragrant in the city and neighbourhood of St Andrews':

> To many that season, I trust, was the birth-time of their souls, and to believers a time of great revival and refreshment. To me, it was a feast of fat things, and I trust of great blessing. Certainly I never heard the gospel message so clearly preached, so unfettered, so unbeclouded; and as faith cometh by hearing, so faith came to my soul, and, out of obscurity, I saw and felt the love of God in a way so melting and so overflowing as to make me weep. May I never lose the impression produced by that sermon from these words: 'He that believeth doth enter into rest.' What an exhibition of the fullness and freeness and completeness of salvation to the believing soul! 'Doubting Castle' was quite demolished; every chain struck off; closed lips opened to shout for joy and sing praise to our redeeming God.

In the early part of December 1839, we find Burns detailing a whole list of places that he went to and preached at. Some of these included Greenock, Dundee, Port-Glasgow, Paisley, Bo'ness, Dunfermline, Perth; and on Tuesday 10 December, he was back at Kilsyth. Whilst there, he met widow Miller:

> a remarkable old woman, who was converted on Monday evening, July 29th, while I was speaking. She appears to be making marvellous

progress in the knowledge and love of Emmanuel, and being naturally of a superior cast of mind, she makes the most beautiful and striking remarks. She said, for instance, 'Oh! You must rouse them, you must rouse them tonight, just as a mason drives his chisel with his mell upon the stones; and are we not all stones – rough stones, till God hew and polish us? You roused them before, just as if you were to put a cold hand on a man's warm face.'

But it would be Perth where the Lord next led him to stay a while, and there to see his hand pour out upon that place showers similar to that which Kilsyth and Dundee had both previously witnessed. He arrived there on Christmas Day 1839, and he would labour there for several months to come.

Only four days after arriving, he was already preaching at meetings which he described as being 'very similar to some of the Lord's most gracious visits at Kilsyth and Dundee. Praise and glory to his matchless name!' On the following day, Monday December 30, hundreds gathered to hear him preach in the afternoon. That was followed in the evening by an immensely crowded gathering in the Gaelic Church. He says he was 'much aided', and that there was 'great solemnity', and 'some in tears'. 'After the blessing I spoke a little to some that lingered; much affected. I was pressed by them to go into the session-house. It was overflowing; all in tears nearly. Sang, read, spoke and prayed for an hour – they would not go. Mr Stewart concluded with prayer; the tears were standing in his eyes; indeed it was an affecting scene!'

Such scenes became commonplace for the time he remained in Perth. For example, on 31 December, 'the vestry was filled with weepers with whom we had to pray and sing a long time.' On 5 January, he preached to another 'densely crowded' church, where he was told 'thousands went away without getting in'. But it was not just in actual church buildings that we find Burns sharing the gospel in Perth. There are journal entries describing how he witnessed as he walked on the roads; as he travelled by steam-boat; as he stopped at wayside inns; when he visited markets; and even when he journeyed into 'the haunts of vice and crime'. All were to him, says Islay, 'the fit arena in which to fulfil his divine ambassadorship, and "compel men to come in" to the house of God.'

But even whilst he was so busy in Perth, Burns still was able to find time and energy to make evangelistic journeys to several other areas. In this way he visited at different times during this period the parishes of Auchtermuchty, Strathmiglo, Dunfermline, Muthil, Stanley, Auchtergarven, Caputh and Kinfauns. As March was closing, so was his time of ministry in Perth. He had received repeated and urgent invitations to visit Aberdeen, and he was now feeling unable to resist them any longer. He felt, too, that his time at Perth was ending, that he had remained there long enough to fulfil the functions of a distinctively evangelistic ministry. What was needed now, he believed, was more that of a pastoral nature, and he was assured that that would be most effectively performed by those who had been his constant helpers and supporters whilst he had worked in Perth. Amongst these, he especially named Revs. Milne and Gray.

It is to Mr Milne that we can now turn, as he gives us a summary of that which took place under the ministry of Burns:

> God's people were quickened; backsliders restored; the doubting and uncertain brought to decision and assurance; hidden ones who for years had walked solitary brought to light, and united to a family of brothers and sisters; a large number of the worldly, thoughtless, ignorant, self-righteous turned to the Lord; a peculiar people growing up, who are separate from the world, know and love one another; watch over, exhort, and aid one another, and seem to grow in humility and zeal.

On 7 April 1840, William Burns said goodbye to a large crowd of friends who had gathered to wish him God's blessing as he left them for Aberdeen. He had not long arrived in the city before he found out why he had received so many repeated requests for him to come and preach. He was constantly in demand to minister:

> Sermons to densely crowded audiences in three several churches on each Lord's Day; prayer meetings in the morning and afternoon, and a public address in the evening of each weekday, with generally an additional hour of counsel, instruction and prayer, for those whose intense anxiety still detained them after the long service was over, with words by the wayside and conferences with enquirers and young

disciples at all other available hours, constituted the daily history of
his work, so far as it can be written by man, for weeks together.

For several months Burns was occupied thus. On the evening
of 26 April for example, he was preaching in the open-air in Castle
Street, to an immense audience. He was conscious there of more
of God's presence, he says, than on any previous occasion in
Aberdeen, as he 'laboured to pull sinners out of the fire. The
impression was very deep; many weeping, some screaming, and
one or two quite overpowered.' At eight o'clock, he adjourned to
the North Church. After a service there, the people were dismissed,
but many were so deeply moved that he could not get away. Along
with Mr Murray, Burns then proceeded to speak to those who had
remained, about four hundred in number.

On 1 May, Burns temporarily left Aberdeen in order to answer
a number of other requests that he had received for him to go and
preach outwith Aberdeen. Even though he had been in Aberdeen
for less than a month, so much had taken place that he briefly
summed up what had already occurred:

I am now come to the end of my sojourn in Aberdeen, and must
notice a few general features in what met my eye and ear. We had
meetings every morning to the end, in Bon-accord Church, which
were very sweet and solemn, and increased in size towards the end. I
also continued to meet almost every afternoon, from one to three,
with anxious inquirers. Many that came to these meetings, as well as
many that called at the house, seemed in a most promising state, and
altogether, upon a review of all I saw of this kind in Aberdeen, there
seemed to be very hopeful symptoms of an extensive awakening.
And now, Lord Jesus, grant me and all thy people there, the Holy
Ghost as a Spirit of praise for all the tokens of thy glorious and gracious
presence there; and may those who were impressed by thy power not
be left to fall back into their former security beneath the abiding wrath
of God, but be brought to wash in thy blood, and put on the glorious
wedding-garment of thy righteousness, and adorn the doctrine of God
their Saviour by a life and conversation becoming the gospel; and to
thee be all the glory! Amen.

After leaving Aberdeen, Burns headed for Dundee. But he was physically and mentally exhausted, and suffered the symptoms of that for several weeks. Thus at Dundee, on 3 May, at the conclusion of the Sunday services, he writes, 'I was tired and had not much of the Lord's comfortable presence in my work, feeling that I needed rest for the body and a season of solemn retirement to meet with the Lord in personal communion.' Then at Stirling, on 6 May, 'I did not come here with an expectation of doing much, on two grounds. First, that my bodily strength was much reduced; and second, my mind needed recreation to restore its elasticity and power.'

Yet even in the midst of this, the Lord was using him as his instrument. On 13 May, for example, after preaching and as he was looking up the stairs as the people were coming down, his eye fixed on one young man in particular. Burns then pointed to him and said loudly, 'Will you come to Christ?' The man said nothing but left hurriedly. But the following day, the young man came to Burns in deep distress. He told him that he was a smith from Scone, who had attended Burns' meetings in Perth. He said he had often wanted to be awakened, and wondered how he was so little moved, when so many around him were. That was the state he remained in, until the previous night, when Burns' words were so remarkably directed to him. They had gone like a knife to his heart and brought him to the foot of the cross.

Burns however was becoming increasingly weak, but still he would not give up, endeavouring to fulfil engagements he had already made. But when he became too ill to carry on, he was forced to take time away from his busy schedule. He stayed with his friends, the M'Farlanes, at Collessie manse, and he never forgot their kindness. After less than two weeks, Burns was again preaching with renewed vigour. He travelled through the area of Fife and met with extraordinary encouragement from ministers and people alike. Even those ministers whom he considered would have been most against his way of doing things gave him support. In the parish of Anstruther, all the ministers brought their congregations together to hear him preach. In their midst, Burns says, 'some of the most hardened sinners of the town were seen turning pale as death and shedding tears' as he appealed to them. Two days later he wrote:

> I spent the day chiefly alone, seeking personal holiness, the fundamental requisite in order to a successful ministry. I was in Burleigh Castle for an hour on the first floor, which is arched and entire.... Before me I had to the right Queen Mary's Island in Lochleven, and to the left the Lomonds, where the Covenanters hid themselves from their persecutors, and I stood amid the ruins of the castle of one of their leaders. The scene was solemn and affecting, and I trust the everlasting Emmanuel was with me. O that I had a martyr's heart, if not a martyr's death and a martyr's crown!

Leaving that locality, Burns made a number of preaching-visits, some short, others involving staying a little while, to Strathmiglo, Milnathort, Cleish, Kinross, Dunfermline, Stirling, Gargunnock, Kippen, Kilsyth, Glasgow, Lochlomond, Glen Falloch, Lawers, Fortingall, Aberfeldy, Logierait, Moulin, Breadalbane, Tenandry, Kirkmichael and Inverarnan. Listing these places should give some indication of how constant was his activity and how much energy Burns needed. At Lawers, even though the day was not good, Burns spoke in the tent to a congregation which numbered more than fifteen hundred. In the evening, they met in the church which seated five hundred, and which was crowded; 'a good many were in tears, and one cried aloud as we were dismissing them.' On the following day, the church was again crowded; 'when the blessing was pronounced a great many remained in their seats, and some of them began to cry out vehemently that they were lost.'

On 23 August, Burns crossed the loch to preach at the missionary station of Ardeonaig. The tent was placed on the hillside behind the manse, very nearly on the spot where it had stood in the days of previous revivals. 'There was an immense assembly, collected from a circuit of from twelve to twenty miles, which could not amount to less than 3000.' Burns recorded that he 'felt a great uplifting of the heart in pride before God', and this made him conclude more abruptly than usual. But this made Burns cast himself all the more on the Lord. As he prayed that afternoon, 'I found the Lord very gracious, and had a sweet anticipation given me of the Lord's presence in the evening, when we were to meet in the church.' He preached from Psalm 102 and spoke particularly of Christ's love. When the time came for separating, 'some individuals began to cry aloud. I tried to quiet them, as I am always afraid that they are in danger of drawing the attention of many who are less affected away from considering the state of their own souls. However, they could not be composed.' Burns took them, along with many others in a similar state, to the manse, and after much prayer he 'sent them away, though not in the best state for going so great a distance'.

The following day there were similar scenes. But as Burns sought to prepare to speak on a Scriptural passage, he was so overcome with a sense of his pride once again that 'I could fix on no passage to speak from'. Even as he stood in the pulpit leading the worship, he had no idea of what he would bring to the people. He opened the psalm-book and his eye rested on Psalm 69:29. 'The suitableness of the words to my own spiritual state attracted me, and I began to make a few remarks in consequence upon them. I soon however got so much divine light and assistance in commenting upon them, that I spoke from them I suppose for an hour, much affected in my own soul, and to an audience in general similarly moved.' Burns and the other ministers had hardly entered the manse, when they were besieged by many men and women, who 'came in after us, in deep distress of soul, with whom we had to pray again'.

On 25 August he was preaching in Lawers once again and this time the congregation numbered at least seven hundred. Many had travelled great distances to come and hear. Burns was later informed that for a quarter of a mile from the church 'every covered retreat was occupied by awakened men and women, pouring out their hearts to God'. The minister of the area told Burns that that night was the most solemn season that he had seen. Burns ended that diary entry with the following short prayer, 'Praise, praise! O humble me, good Shepherd, and be thou exalted over all! Amen'

His final day of preaching in that area was on Friday, 28 August. A public meeting had been arranged at Kiltire, four miles west of Lawers. 'The house was crowded, and many were outside at the windows. There must have been two hundred and fifty in all.' The people were 'deeply solemnised and tenderly moved'. As he walked home he 'overtook a few of the people. They said nothing, but walked in thoughtful silence, and in some cases wept. In looking back upon this work from the beginning till now, it appears to me more clearly the fruit of the sovereign operations of God's Spirit than almost any other that I have seen. We have never needed to have any of those after-meetings which I have found so necessary and useful in other places; the people were so deeply moved under the ordinary services. I never saw so many of the old affected as in this case. The number of those affected are greater in proportion to the population than I have ever seen, and there has been far less appearance of mere animal excitement than in most of the cases that I have been acquainted with.'

On 8 September Burns was to be found in Moulin, preaching to about five hundred in the open air. 'The people were bent down beneath the Word like corn under the breeze, and many a stout sinner wept bitterly.' On the Sabbath, Burns had moved on to preach at Logierait. 'An immense congregation assembled at twelve o'clock in the churchyard, with whom I continued uninterruptedly until 5 p.m., singing, praying and preaching the Word of life. The people were very solemnly affected, indeed more visibly so than on any previous Sabbath that I have been in the Highlands; at one time many were crying aloud in agony, and tears were flowing plentifully throughout the audience.'

Burns left the Highlands on Wednesday, 16 September, to return to the scene of his former labours in Aberdeen. After arriving back in the Granite City, Burns began a series of meetings on week-days and on Sabbath days, and the great numbers of those attending never decreased for the months that he held them. So great were the numbers of those who were responding to the preaching, that Burns records that special times set aside specifically for counselling the anxious became not meetings but congregations. On 22 October Burns preached in the crowded Trinity Church. He began at seven o'clock. They parted at ten, but so many crowded around him outside that he had to return with them to the Church:

The place was filled in a few moments, and almost all fell on their knees and began to pray to the Lord. I continued to pray and sing and speak with these until after twelve o'clock, having frequently offered to let them go, but finding that they would not move, and feeling in my own soul that the Lord was indeed in the midst of us. This was the most glorious season, I think, that I have yet seen in Aberdeen. Many poor sinners lay weeping all the night on their knees in prayer, and some of the Lord's people present seemed to be filled with joy.

The following evening, Burns spoke to about three hundred and fifty mill-girls in a local school. He spoke of the lost state of sinners, and the enormity of many sins:

and the impression was so great that almost all were in tears, and many cried aloud. This impression seemed so deep and genuine, that it continued the whole evening afterwards, and though I dismissed them 3 or 4 times, hardly any would go away, the greater part crying aloud at the mention of dispersing. Accordingly we remained until after eleven, and even then the greater part remained behind me, and the beadle could not get some of them away for a long time after this. It was indeed to all appearance a night of the Lord's power.

That same week, Burns tells us that he agreed to meet with anxious inquirers at the session-house of North Church, but when more than two hundred and fifty turned up, he wisely decided that they should all go to the church itself. 'Some of them seemed in the deep waters, and a great many were weeping silently.' Burns was later informed that at the local mills, locals saw something they had never seen before; many of the mill workers coming to work carrying Bibles with them.

The following month, things were happening in the same way. Burns preached in the East Church: 'The church was choked as soon as opened. There could not be fewer than two thousand five hundred.' Night after night it was apparent to all that something remarkable was occurring in their midst. Multitudes would begin weeping as Burns revealed Christ's love to them. There was much religious excitement throughout the city, and for many it seemed almost out of control. Burns always sought to keep the emotion down, that people might respond to the Word and not as a result of their emotions being moved, but for many the movement of God's Spirit in their hearts was too much to contain. The newspapers became involved, and Burns' name and some not wholly positive accounts of some of his meetings appeared in the local press.

Two major questions were being asked. Firstly, were the meetings that this man was holding dangerous, were they causing people to become far too over-excited, or were the physical manifestations, in particular, expected consequences of what seemed to be taking place? The second question turned more on the issue of whether the excitement itself was in many cases an excitement of fear rather than of love, and for that reason also, the charge went, the more liable to prove temporary and prove of little lasting worth. It would not have been enough for Burns and his supporters simply to have argued that this was a work of the Spirit of God, for as it was said at the time, a divine work was all the more sure to be marred to some degree by man's touch; and surely, it was argued by some, that work would have been helped and not hindered, had the protracted and exciting meetings and services been fewer, and the hours of still and meditative seeking of God more.

In the eyes of the Church of Scotland in particular, whatever was happening was remarkable and they had many questions to ask, not only of Burns but of themselves too. The result was that the Presbytery of Aberdeen appointed a Committee of Inquiry, which would sit under the chairmanship of Rev. William Pirie (who later became Professor of Divinity in the University of Aberdeen). God's hand is to be seen clearly in how the Committee acted and reported. William Burns himself said that the proceedings were conducted with candour and fairness, and in such a manner as to bring to light the essential elements of the truth of the matter. It could have been very different. It seems that one of the major factors in the establishment of the Committee was the nature of that newspaper report already mentioned, which appeared in the *Herald*. If the report had simply been believed without question, then one can only guess what might have been the outcome.

Burns left Aberdeen on 5 December to take temporary charge of a new church in Dundee (this was before the Committee was even formed). He set out at 6.40 a.m. with the Dundee mail coach, but he would not be leaving unnoticed. 'A number of my young friends had found out the time of my departure, and stood by on the pavement in tears. The mockery of many around made our tongues silent: we looked at each other, with Jesus in our heart's eye I hope, and wept.'

Burns may have thought that he would not see Aberdeen again for quite a while, but that was not the case, for after only a short time away, he was called back to Aberdeen to appear before the Committee. The particular newspaper report was produced. It consisted partly of a supposedly verbatim account of the proceedings at the meeting held on 23 November in the Bon-Accord Church; together with this, was a leading article which made many bitter remarks about that which was alleged to have taken place. Burns was then asked several questions about that which the article claimed was true.

Q. Could you state those peculiarities of the Herald's report which makes it, as you have said in your letter to Mr Mitchell, a 'caricature' of what was spoken by you on the occasions referred to?

A. Among these peculiarities, I may mention the following as occurring to me at the moment:

1st, The manner in which the whole is printed, by the use of hyphens, and the parenthetical insertion of remarks by the reporter. The reason of my speaking with peculiar slowness on the occasion referred to, was to prevent, if possible, the charge of trying to excite the people being brought against me by the enemies of the work present.

2nd, The omission of sentences throughout which are necessary to exhibit the true connection of what was said, and the consequent bringing together, and in some cases mixing up, of things which, as spoken, stood apart.

3rd, The entire omission of what was said during the last hour of the address, the insertion of which is indispensable to give a just impression of the whole service.

4th, The omission of some introductory remarks, in which the speaker explained his reasons for addressing those who seemed to have come as spectators, rather than those 'anxious inquirers' for whom the meeting was intimated, a circumstance which led the speaker to leave the text on which he was to have spoken, and to enlarge in a remonstrance with those whom he supposed to have come from questionable motives.

Q. Assuming it to lie as a religious exposition delivered from the pulpit, by a licentiate of the Church of Scotland, would you hold the report in the Aberdeen Herald (supposing it to be correct) as becoming, decent, and in conformity with Scripture?

A. I have no hesitation in saying that the report in the Herald, if read under the idea of its being accurate, and without a knowledge of the particular circumstances in which these meetings took place, would seem open to the charge of being incoherent in the connection of its meaning, and not well fitted to edify the hearer. Indeed, I have myself met with judicious and godly friends who have been led to fear that the speaker had been impudent in the case referred to, while, on the other hand, I have not met with any serious person of sound judgment who was present at the meeting and thought that anything unscriptural or unbecoming in the circumstances had been said or done. Nor do I myself, in the recollection of what took place, know of anything which ought to be condemned by those who hold sound views of Bible truth.

Q. You admit that the words, 'This is the outpouring of the Spirit,' were used by you; how did you know that at the time?

A. This was my own deliberate conviction at the time and continues to be so. The grounds on which I was convinced of this were not merely those appearances of deep solemnity and a humbling sense of sin which were manifested by many of the people, but also my general knowledge of the state of many of them, from private conversation and the testimony of others. No one can see the propriety of introducing such a statement, unless he had been present and had witnessed the circumstances in which it was made.

Q. How did those appearances of deep solemnity and humbling sense of sin, to which you have referred, manifest themselves in the hearers at the time?

A. The appearances to which I have alluded are that deep solemnity which one can judge of when present, and all the usual outward marks of grief and humiliation. It is no doubt difficult to judge of such a matter from visible tokens, and specially so in regard to individual cases. But, as I have already said, the conviction which I expressed was not founded solely on the appearances visible at that time, but also on the grounds stated in answer to the previous question; nor would I think it safe to judge of such a matter by almost any appearances, if taken apart from the causes which produced them and the effects by which they are followed.

Q. When you used the words referred to, 'This is the outpouring of the Spirit,' how was it possible for you, in conformity with the explanation given in your last answer, to tell what the effects would be?

A. I am fully convinced that it is a matter of the utmost difficulty to judge, in regard to a particular individual, that the concern which that individual feels is the effect of special and saving grace, but, at the same time, I have no doubt that any one who is acquainted, from Scripture, and especially by experience, with the saving work of God's Spirit, can on good grounds conclude that the Spirit of God is working remarkably among a people, even before time has fully proved the effects of that work upon the lives of individuals.

Q. Did you know a great proportion of the parties before-hand?

A. I was accustomed to meet them almost day by day, to converse privately with those who were anxious, and, in this way, had an opportunity of obtaining a general knowledge of their religious state. I also heard, from various quarters, of the state of some of them when at work and when at home, and thus could more confidently judge that they were really impressed by divine truth.

Q. Did you witness any physical manifestations on that night?

A. If by physical manifestations be meant the indications of grief, alluded to in such texts as in Zechariah 12:10, 'They shall look on me whom they have pierced, and shall mourn for him, as one mourneth for his only son, and shall be in bitterness for his first-born': if this be meant, I did see such indications of feeling, and I would desire to see them on a far larger scale.

Q. It is meant, did you hear sobs, crying, screaming, or did you see any one faint or fall into convulsions?

A. I certainly did see, and expect to see in such cases, much weeping, some audibly praying to God for mercy, and occasionally also individuals crying aloud as if pierced to the heart. I don't remember that any one fell down or fell into convulsions on the night referred to, although I have occasionally seen such cases, both in Aberdeen and in other places, and among these, strong men in the prime of life.

Q. Do you think persons so excited can by possibility further benefit from pulpit ministrations?

A. I should think that the most direct means of composing persons under such spiritual concern, is the calm and tender ministrations of the gospel of Christ. Of course, if the bodily frame is so much affected as to prevent the intelligent hearing of the Word, no benefit can be derived from it. When people have fallen into a swoon, the latter is the case, and such persons had better be removed, but where there is much weeping, there may be at the same time the best preparation for listening to the exhibition of Christ.

Q. Am I to understand you, when you said, in a foregoing answer, that you did see persons weeping and audibly praying to God for mercy, and occasionally also individuals crying aloud, as if pierced to the heart, that you considered these as sure evidences that the Spirit of God was savingly working upon these persons?

A. I have already stated very fully the grounds of my conviction that the Spirit of God was at that time powerfully working among the people taken as a whole, but I have a firm and growing conviction that there often are, at such seasons, individuals who manifest a great degree of feeling, and yet afterwards show that they continue in their natural state.

Q. Do you not think public meetings protracted until ten, or eleven, or twelve o'clock at night, likely to give offence, to interrupt family worship, interfere with family arrangements, cause family disputes, and to be hurtful to the interests of religion?

A. I confess I am more and more convinced of the great importance, in general, of a sacred regard to the ordinance of God in regard to family and secret worship, and of the importance consequently of having public meetings, as far as possible, concluded at an early hour; at the same time, I have no doubt that there are cases in which it is for the glory of God that public worship should be more protracted. In places where the people cannot meet earlier than eight o'clock, I have generally found that we could not end before ten o'clock, and this is the hour at which, generally, the public meeting has been dismissed, although, in a few cases, it has seemed necessary to remain to a later hour with those who were anxious about their souls.

Besides these oral statements, the following are some of the written replies to some of the questions proposed by the presbytery:

Q. Have you had many opportunities of seeing persons in different places affected at religious meetings in the way in which the persons referred to were affected in Bon-accord Church?

A. I have had many such opportunities.

Q. What have you found to be the result generally, in as far as the religious state of those persons was concerned, as displayed in their after-conduct?

A. I have known cases in which persons so affected, even to a great degree, have turned out ill; though I believe they were at the time really affected with a sense of their guilt and danger. In the generality of cases, however, I have had good reasons to hope that such persons underwent a saving change. They were at least greatly changed to the eye of man.

Q. Have you carefully inquired as to such results?

A. I have been careful to inquire as to these results, and often feel a burden of concern on my soul about the case of such persons, using all the means in my power to ascertain and to insure their consistency, and their growth in the knowledge of God.

Q. Have you found that, when persons have not been strongly affected, to all appearance, in religious meetings, they had been awakened to any great concern about their spiritual state?

A. I have found many who have been brought to a deep spiritual, and abiding sense of sin, without manifesting their concern to those around any farther than by silent tears or deep seriousness of demeanour. Such cases, if really deep, are in general, I think, to be marked for stability.

Q. What sort of persons have you generally seen much affected at such meetings? Were they those who had been utterly careless about religious truth, and very ill acquainted with the facts of religion, or those who had been accustomed to pay some attention to religious ordinances, and had an acquaintance with these facts?

A. They have been of both the classes mentioned in this question. I do not know that persons of little knowledge are harder to bring to a sense of sin than others better informed; the Spirit of God worketh when and where he pleaseth. But I think that I have found those persons generally most stable after they were awakened, who had full religious knowledge and especially who lived in godly families. Yet I know remarkable instances of persons becoming eminent for godliness in the most disadvantageous circumstances, and who seemed rather to get good than evil from seeing the wickedness of their relations around them.

Burns also sent a letter to William Pirie, as Committee chairman, in which he expressed his appreciation of how the Committee had conducted itself:

Allow me, also, here to express the kindness shown to me, by the Committee and the Convenor, at my appearance before them. The truth will always bear examination. In this case I fear nothing, except a superficial or prejudiced consideration of the facts. A close and holy scrutiny will indeed expose the emptiness of the work of man; but the work of Jehovah, like his inspired Word, the more it is examined will appear the more clearly to be worthy of his own infinite perfections.

The examination was in no way superficial, for the Committee extended their inquiries from that which had been occurring in Aberdeen to some of the other places that Burns had preached at, and which had similarly reported an outpouring of the Holy Spirit in power. The Committee hoped too that because some time had passed since Burns had been there, the real nature of what had happened might be judged, together with any lasting results that could be seen.

The Committee received much evidence in answer to the queries that it sent out to the various scenes of Burns' previous labours. What follows is the general findings of the Committee and the subsequent resolutions of the Presbytery:

The Presbytery, having taken into their solemn consideration the evidence on revivals of religion received by their Committee on that subject, resolved,

1. That a revival of religion, consisting in the general quickening of believers, and the conversion of multitudes of unbelievers, by the Holy Spirit, cannot but be an object of most earnest desire to every follower of the Lord; that the genuineness of such a revival is chiefly to be tested by the nature and permanence of the effects by which it is followed; that it can only be expected to flow from the use of the appointed means, accompanied with the abundant outpouring of the Spirit of God; that it should be made the subject of fervent and persevering prayer; and that, when such a revival takes place, it should not be dreaded or spoken of with levity, but should be carefully and seriously marked, and acknowledged with devout thanksgiving.

2. That the evidence, derived from answers to certain queries sent by the Committee to ministers and others in different parts of the country, amply bears out the fact that an extensive and delightful work of revival has commenced, and is in hopeful progress in various districts of Scotland, the origin of which instrumentally, is to be traced to a more widely diffused spirit of prayer on the part of ministers and people, and to the simple, earnest and affectionate preaching of the gospel of the grace of God; that this work in the districts referred to, many of which are locally far distant from others, has been attended with few of those evils which have generally more or less characterised seasons of great religious excitement; and that, on the whole, an amount of good has been accomplished, which loudly calls for gratitude and praise to Him 'who turneth the hearts of men as the rivers of water.'

3. That in the case of Aberdeen, to which the evidence more especially refers, it clearly appears, so far as the test of time can be applied to the subject, that a very considerable number of persons, chiefly in early life, have been strongly, and it is hoped savingly, impressed with the importance of eternal things, and are in the course of further instruction; that many of all ages have been awakened to a more serious concern about Christ and salvation than they formerly felt, and have been quickened to activity in well-doing; and that the labours of Mr W. C. Burns, preacher of the gospel, are peculiarly discernible in connection with these results. At the same time, the Presbytery cannot but regret that such an exclusive reference should have been made to two particular meetings at which Mr Burns presided, where the services were protracted to a late hour, and where much outward excitement prevailed, circumstances obviously liable to much inconvenience as well as misconception, while it appears from the evidence that many other meetings were held for religious instruction, through the same instrumentality, which could be liable to no such misconception, and where much good was wrought. And, upon the whole, the Presbytery are convinced that, if it had entered more into the nature of the inquiry to ascertain simply the extent of the awakening that has

been effected in this city and neighbourhood, the evidence of a favourable kind would have been such as to lead to increased thanksgiving.

4. That the Presbytery having considered the whole evidence that has been laid before them on this unspeakably important subject, feel themselves called upon to recommend to all ministers, preachers and elders within their bounds, in their respective spheres, to labour more and more diligently and prayerfully, in the use of all scriptural means, to promote the cause of vital religion, which needs so much to be revived among us; and they would also exhort and entreat all the private members of the Church to study to grow in grace, to abound in all the fruits of righteousness, and to plead more earnestly with the great Head of the Church, that he would pour out his Spirit more plentifully upon us, and bless his appointed ordinances, that the wilderness may become a fruitful field, and the fruitful field be counted for a forest.

Such resolutions were only to the credit of the Church of Scotland, when there must have been several voices calling for Burns to be admonished or have strict conditions laid upon his preaching. They clearly acknowledged his part in the revivals (under God); they clearly recognized that revivals had and were taking place in various parts of Scotland, and that Burns had played his part in many of those too; and they clearly encouraged in their statement all other ministers, preachers and elders to labour all the harder in a Biblical manner, that God might send even greater revivals which, they openly admitted, the land so desperately stood in need of.

In many ways, then, Burns and the nature of his ministry had been vindicated, but other than the fact that God's Name was not impugned, the outcome of the Inquiry would not have mattered too greatly to him. Whatever men might say, Burns was convinced and assured that he was about God's business, and that if he sought God's blessing and lived as God demanded, then God would use even such an imperfect instrument as himself. After appearing before the Committee, Burns soon returned to his itinerant evangelistic work. He headed, almost immediately, south of the border, for the great city of Newcastle. But if he believed that Newcastle would respond in the same wonderful way that other places had, and as soon, then he was to be sadly disappointed. As his brother wrote, William 'found himself in the presence of a power which, alike in its extent and terrible energy, startled and shocked him, and threw him back as scarce ever before on the power that is infinite and divine.'

A few days after his arrival in Newcastle, Burns wrote, 'The people of God are rallying in their places, and we have them of every name on our side. Ah! but the Lord is with me as a mighty, terrible ONE. This is enough.' Burns had been aware of the enemy of souls before his time in Newcastle, but he was more aware of that evil presence there than in any other place. He wrote to another minister-friend in Scotland, 'I ask it as a favour and plead for it, that you will lay before your people the case of Newcastle, an iron-walled citadel of Satan. Almighty power, and that alone, can make a breach and plant the banner of salvation in the Lamb on its proud ramparts. They must cry, they must wrestle; for the devil is in the field, and the day will be hot.'

Burns' preaching was not enjoying the blessing of God that he had hitherto been experiencing. 'The Scotch Church is low here; the audiences were not large. During the week I preached every night but Tuesday and Saturday, but chiefly to the churchgoing few, including some Christians, with a view to stir them up to come nearer to God.... Went out at meal hour and began to invite sinners. Very apathetic. The sleep of death is on the city.'

This is not to say, however, that Burns made no impact. He heard announced that a pleasure trip would be taking place that coming Sabbath, but because it would be 'of a more than usually offensive kind', his brother remarked that Burns' spirit was stirred within him to such a degree that he began a very visible protest. He made notices which he signed himself, and posted in every street and open place in the city. If Burns was generally unknown before this, that was not the case any longer. His brother wrote that Burns' actions fell like a bomb-shell in the midst of the community.

Burns composed a tract, which did not speak in any veiled way about the sins of Newcastle, and which threatened the inhabitants with the coming judgments of God. This too caused its own reaction, and it was not long before the newspapers of the area became involved, 'denouncing his proceedings'. Burns was actually informed by his friends in Scotland that the national newspapers were making the cities of the country 'ring with your doings in Newcastle.... The people in Scotland are thinking that the opposition must be awful.'

Burns soon gave up preaching in the churches of Newcastle, which were still remaining quite empty, and instead he took the message of the gospel to the people in the streets. He preached on the Quay, at the Spittal Square, in the Corn and Cloth Markets, and near the Castle. There were sometimes few, sometimes great audiences. Burns spoke from time to time of 'solemn attention'; 'very great attention and eagerness'; 'a very large and deeply solemn audience'; 'a large audience who stood riveted to the end'; of a 'service of three hours' duration, in the castle-yard where Whitefield preached of old'; 'a considerable audience who continued immovable under darkness and rain'; 'the people so much impressed that the stars were out in the sky before we separated'; and 'some of the old sailors on the quay weeping, and pressing their money on those who gave away the tracts at the end'. But for all this apparent 'success', we learn that there were in fact very few who ever sought him out afterwards for counsel and instruction.

After working in this way for most of the day, quite often Burns would then go out at night into the dark streets, carrying a bundle of his 'plain sentences', to see if God might lead him to some to whom he may 'hold out the torch of life eternal to some poor wanderer whom he might never hope to meet at any other place or time'. His diary contains records of some strange meetings in this manner. 'I offered near the mouth of the Arcade a copy to a gentleman half-intoxicated. He swore fearfully and said, "Oh, what a cursed country this is! I might go through every town on the Continent, and not meet with such another rascal as you infesting me. Rome is infinitely better than this."' On another occasion he writes, 'After the meeting I spent a half-hour on the street with tracts, and met with awful proofs of the enormous wickedness of the people, also with many whose language amid their sins seemed almost to be, "Oh! that I were saved, oh! that you could do me any good."'

But as time passed, even the partial interest that he had created began gradually to wane. The congregations in the churches where he preached remained small; the audiences who came to hear him in the open air became less numerous and less interested. Even some of his friends, who had begun with a real hope that Burns would be the instrument for a rich and widespread blessing, began to lose heart. 'I had hope at one time,' said one of his most ardent supporters, 'but now I confess it is gone. Every ear seems closed.' But Burns himself too almost despaired. Receiving a letter from Mr Parker, in which he expresses his astonishment that the people could bear his words, he writes in his journal bitterly, 'Alas! the people can bear anything here as yet. The body seems so dead, that though you plunge the knife to the heart there is no pain.' Yet there, at that point of utter despair of self, God was declaring that he had brought him to that point, that he might the more simply and wholly triumph in Christ. For in less than the passing of one more day, Burns was to see the mighty move of God once more through his ministry.

It began on Thursday, 23 September. The cattle-show was being held that day, and Burns had thought of taking the opportunity of preaching there. But during the day, Burns felt very weak and it crossed his mind not to go. But as he read the Scriptures, 'the passage turned up, "If thou say, Behold, I knew it not," and I was compelled to go.' When he arrived, however, he found that the show was in a park, which meant that there would be no possibility of preaching. But he used what opportunity there was with so many people, by handing out tracts, speaking to whoever would listen, and giving notice that that evening he would be preaching in the cloth-market. 'After dinner I felt my strength of body renewed, and had hope of something being done of God in the evening.' The events of that evening will be best recounted in Burns' own words:

A little after six we went to the scene of action, and found a great crowd around the place, many of them trying to see in through the windows, and multitudes waiting for the music at interval. I thought of heaven lighted with the brightness of a thousand suns, and of poor lost souls longing to be in when it is too late, and forced to hear from afar the joyful praises of the redeemed, loud as the noise of many waters. We had no sooner begun than an immense crowd gathered round.

Some of the enemies were enraged and urged the police to interfere, crying, 'Down with him, down with him.' The policeman told me that the people were disturbed by us within, but this was so absurd that he did not insist on it; and as he could not find us guilty of a breach of the peace, he soon went away. But although the enemy could not oppose us by legal force, they did not cease to show their deadly hatred of what was said and done. Once a stone was thrown, again a quantity of manure, which bespattered my clothes. Afterwards, in the time of prayer, when we were prevailing against them without hand, they raised a burst of horrid laughter, and pushed the crowd at the side on me with the view of overthrowing the pulpit. At this time I had to pause in the prayer, and when I began to tell them that they could do nothing without the Lord's permission, and that all they did would promote his cause, they were quieted for a time; and I was led out to speak with greater power, perhaps, than ever before in Newcastle, putting the sword into the very heart and bowels of the town's iniquities. At this time, and ever after it until ten o'clock, when we parted, there was the greatest solemnity, and a deep impression; and though I was frequently interrupted with questions, they all tended to bring out in a marvellous way the truth of God, so that they who put them were silenced and the people rejoiced.

During the first hour and half we were obliged to contend, at intervals, with a tumult of people all around the music in the Corn-market, and the movements of a travelling show taking up its encampment close to us. Even amid those trials, although increased by the contradiction of sinners, I was enabled not to waver nor faint; afterward, however, the meeting in the market broke up, the show people were quiet, the streets were nearly empty, and we worshipped the Lord amid solemn silence for another hour and half. At this time the singing was truly sublime; and the whole scene, when contrasted with what it had lately been, was fitted to deepen the impression of the Word in the hand of the Spirit. I did not speak on any text, but used the various circumstances of the feast so near as to set off by way of comparison and contrast the feast of fat things on Mount Zion. I did not proceed regularly, but from time to time noticed such topics as these:

That feast is for the body, this is for the soul; that is one of which you easily take too much, in this you cannot exceed; that is soon over, this will last eternally; that would tire and nauseate if often repeated, this becomes sweeter every day; that is only open to those who can pay for a place, this is provided freely for the poor: it is made free not because it is of little value, but because it is so costly that no money can buy it, and in order that it may be a feast for all; that is made on bullocks and fatlings, but this, oh! wonder of wonders, is made on the body and blood of God's own Son; the greatest sinners are welcome to it now, and the greater they have been they will sit nearer the head of the table as honoured guests, in order that the more the grace and mercy of Jehovah may be displayed to view!

At ten o'clock, Burns prayed the parting blessing and would have separated himself from the crowd, but when he got to the lamp and took out his Bible to look at a verse 'the whole crowd gathered round and stood with breathless attention while I read,' and he then shared with them things about his own conversion. They only parted in the end because 'the policeman desired it'. Burns then recorded his views on the day: 'Though I spoke nearly four hours amid such difficulties in the open air I was not fatigued, and am well today. Oh! that I were only well in soul, and fit to renew the combat. Come, Lord Jesus! come quickly! Amen! Amen! Glory to Jehovah!' On the following day, he prayed, 'Oh! how glorious a sight to behold this town awakened from its deep sleep, and calling upon God with the whole heart! "The waste cities shall be filled with flocks of men!" Be it unto us according to thy word. Amen.'

But only two days later, on the Sabbath, Burns says that as he was going out in the evening to preach, he was as a man with no strength and that he never felt as low as he did that night: 'I am dead, and that is all. I could not fix upon a text; indeed, every door of hope seemed closed, and I knew that God, and he only, could grant deliverance.' When he arrived at the Spittal, there were already many assembled, and in a few short moments, there gathered many more. In fact, 'the crowd became much greater than on any former day, and continued so, and even increasing to the end.' He announced the passage he would speak on with 'hope that the Lord would again speak by my unclean lips'. He then prayed, 'and in doing so I felt – more, perhaps, than since I came to Newcastle – as if a direct communication were opened between my soul and the Divine Mind. My heart was truly drawn out and up to God for the advancement of Emmanuel's glory, even more than for the salvation of guilty worms, as a heart-satisfying end.'

Immediately after this, Burns said he was enabled in a way quite new to him there, to declare to the people the sins of the city and their dreadful consequences in eternity: 'I also found myself in an agony to compel sinners to come to Jesus now, and not even the next hour, which I felt was not man's but God's. Indeed, I felt so much that I could almost have torn the pulpit to pieces. Oh! it was a glorious, an awfully glorious scene.' He closed the open-air meeting at a quarter to nine, encouraging everyone to go directly home, seeing that they had remained in the outdoors for such a long time. Burns had only been in his house a few minutes, when two friends came to him from the church, and told him that it was nearly full with a congregation entirely different from that which had been in the open-air, and that they had been waiting since seven o'clock! Burns headed directly to speak to them too of the good news of Jesus Christ.

On 14 November, 1841, for a temporary spell, Burns took the place of his friend, A. Moody Stuart, at St Luke's Church, Edinburgh. Moody Stuart had taken medical advice, and for the sake of a serious throat infection had travelled to Madeira to spend the winter there. An interested party recorded much of that which Burns accomplished whilst he was there, and the writer added these words:

Those who had the rare privilege of meeting him in private, and seeing his close walk with God, were at no loss to understand the power which attended his public ministration. With him the winning of souls was a passion; calm, but intense, consuming.

Along with his preaching on Romans and James, he taught various classes; he conducted children's work; he attended the College Missionary Association; he took a special care for, and interest in, the students who were attracted to his ministry; he visited the military barracks to speak to the soldiers and hand out tracts; he frequently visited and preached at the Shelter, the Jail, the Asylum, the Orphan Hospital and many other institutions. 'From the very refuse of society he gathered jewels for Emmanuel's crown. Very touching to see him giving tracts and speaking tender words to the fallen. To him they were lost pieces of silver, and the thought that they might even yet have Christ for their brother, and heaven for their home, filled him with a tenderness which he had no name for.'

From January to March 1842, along with his labours in Edinburgh, Burns was to be found regularly preaching in Leith. He preached to densely crowded and what Burns termed 'hungry' audiences. Even though the weather during those months remained severe, the numbers attending his meetings continued to grow so much, that even on the Wednesday evenings the crowds were overflowing. So deep was the impression on them, says Burns, that the people could not go away, even after the parting blessing. So he held an after-service for prayer and counselling, and such was the distress of those who remained, that they were removed to the vestry for further help. Robert Murray McCheyne helped in one of these services and to all intents and purposes, it looked 'as if the ever-memorable scenes of Kilsyth, Dundee, and Perth were to be repeated in Leith'. So widespread was the movement of God, that individuals said that the people of Leith 'were all going mad'. Many were converted to Christ; so much so, that Burns wrote that 'the Lord gave me spring, summer, and harvest, that winter in Leith'.

On another occasion, Burns went to the Quay at Leith to preach to the sailors there. He took three friends with him to distribute tracts and invite the sailors to come and listen. A large crowd soon gathered, but after Burns read the text, it began to rain heavily. He paused, and prayed that God would restrain the clouds that the people might hear God's Word. The rain continued, however, and they adjourned to a large shed at the head of the quay. But the moment that Burns opened his mouth to begin preaching, the rain ceased. As his brother records, 'I shall never forget the look of wonder with which that crowd gazed on the clear sky.' Burns approach was very astute. He spoke as if he had spent his whole life at sea: as he spoke he included many sea-phrases and he was listened to with great attention; and, rising to a climax, he cried, 'Sailors! the breakers are ahead! The storm is rising! You are running upon a lee-shore! In a few moments the ship (the world) will strike and go down! The life boat is Christ! It is lying alongside – it is ready to move off! Come away, sailors, come away, or it will be too late!'

Whilst Burns was still at St Luke's, the first Sabbath train to run between Haymarket Station in Edinburgh and Glasgow was planned to take place, and this stirred Burns to begin a major protest against what he saw as a major and unnecessary desecration of the Lord's Day. For the next three months, Burns' usual Sabbath duties consisted of four services: two he held at the railway station and two at St Luke's. He considered this railway development to be so grave that he resolved to hold prayer meetings for this issue, every Monday, Wednesday and Friday at noon; to supplement this with open-air preaching; and to turn his female class into an evangelistic service in the church. His brother describes this as the culminating point of his work in Edinburgh. The church was overflowing, but the people were filled with awe and 'every head was bowed', and it was felt that 'the living God was in the place.'

In the midst of his busy time in Edinburgh, Burns still managed somehow to make four evangelistic tours away from the capital. In April 1842, he preached in Milnathort, Bridge of Earn, Perth, Burrelton, Collace, Abernyte and Dundee. In June, he was to be found back in Dundee, but also in Kilspindie, Anstruther, Logie, Cupar-Fife and Falkland. In August and September, he made two tours to the Highlands of Perthshire. The gospel consumed him and he felt the pressing reality of the words, 'woe to me if I do not preach the gospel'. His brother Islay said William had a mind of keen insight and power, but he was one who was a great puzzle to students. His work, his circumstances and his methods 'were so exceptional; but those who were so minded could learn from him the greatest lesson of all for the work of the ministry – the omnipotence of faith and prayer.'

Islay and William remained close all through the latter's ministry in Britain. They generally met together in private twice a week. William would send Islay little notes, the contents of which Islay never forgot. On one occasion, William had asked Islay to come to breakfast, but William was later unable to keep the appointment. He left a note expressing his regret, and added, 'We are often disappointed in our meetings with man, but never in our meetings with God at a throne of Grace, where we are ever welcome in the blood of Jesus.' In another note, written from Dublin, William wrote, 'May the Lord carry on his own great work within and around us, and may we be enabled to glorify him in life and in death!' But it was the very last words that Islay believed he heard from his brother, that sum up the whole thrust of William's compulsion to preach Christ so well: for as William stood at his father's door one night in 1854, under cold November skies, he said, 'We must run!'

We have already had cause to mention his preaching tours to Perthshire, but to get some idea of what Burns actually undertook and accomplished in the service of his beloved Master, we are fortunate indeed to have a detailed itinerary of the week 14–21 August 1842:

Burns' fellow labourer during that week, we are told, was 'a fine fast trotter', with the name, 'Church Extension'. On Sabbath August 14th, Burns preached at Blair-Athole (1) for five hours in the churchyard to an assembly of at least 4000 persons; and (2) in the evening in the church for three hours to an audience that would have remained till daybreak. On Monday evening he rode to Moulin, and preached (3) to a deeply affected audience. On Tuesday, he rode to Kinloch-Rannoch (20 miles), and preached (4) in a park from two to five o'clock, to an interesting congregation of shepherds, gamekeepers, foresters, graziers, and cattle-dealers. After a hurried dinner, he went across the west shoulder of Schiehallion, known as one of the most trackless and difficult passes that there was in the Highlands, to Fortingall (18 miles); rode six miles farther to Lawers, crossed Loch Tay to Ardeonaig, preached (5) there on Wednesday at twelve, and recrossing the lake preached (6) at Lawers the same evening. On

Thursday he rode down to Grandtully (17 miles), and (7) preached with great power in the churchyard to a dense crowd. On Friday he rode up to Fortingall (12 miles), there he preached (8) in the open air from two to nearly six p.m., a sermon which made a deep impression, many of the audience being in tears; and returned to Grandtully the same evening. On Saturday morning he started at six for Balnaguard, preached (9) there at seven o'clock to a large company. He caught the mail-cart at half-past eight, reached Edinburgh in the evening, and preached three times (10, 11, 12) in St Luke's on the following day!

We even have, fortuitously and wonderfully recorded for us, some of the details of the actual events of his preaching during that week. At Blair-Athole, for example, we learn that the congregation 'was a most imposing sight'. Most of those who came to listen were men, and most remained standing for the whole time. 'The thirst to hear was so intense and the blessing which had crowned his previous visits so widespread,' says his brother, that almost the whole population of many surrounding and adjoining areas flocked to hear 'the great preacher of repentance' as Islay calls him. His text was John 18:11, 'The cup which my Father....' and we are fortunate to have a verbatim record of some of what William Burns said as he sought to explain the emblem, 'the cup': 'Wine is the strength or essence of the grape. God's wrath is his whole being as directed against sin. He looks upon sin as infinitely base and vile, and therefore he is indignant: and the wine of his holy anger is poured out in all its strength into the cup of his indignation. The wine was not diluted when the cup was put into the hand of the Son of God. Look at the anguish sin has wrought. The tears of mankind have never ceased to flow since it entered the world. No sooner do they dry on one cheek than they begin to run down the other: no sooner does one widow lay aside her weeds, than another begins the wail: and yet one diluted drop of God's wrath has done it all. What anguish, then, must have been in the cup which the Father gave his Son to drink!'

Many were cut to the heart on that day, and Islay remembered seeing a white-haired old man in the gate weeping bitterly, and saying, 'Oh! it's his prayers: I canna stand his prayers!'

With the dawning of the year 1843, massive upheaval in the national Church of Scotland would soon occur. The great men of evangelical doctrine and faith, men such as McCheyne and Burns, were fully behind the events that would shake both the Church and the land. The Disruption was a secession that occurred in the Church of Scotland in the same year as McCheyne's passing, the year 1843. One would be greatly mistaken to think of the Disruption as similar to the many other secessions which troubled the Church in Scotland. This was a major division and one that had been a long time coming. For years before, there had been open conflict between those in the Church who stood for the spiritual independence of the Church, and those who were not overly concerned with the State's involvement in that same Church. After several skirmishes, the Disruption took place in May 1843, when four hundred and fifty ministers of the Church of Scotland, led by the renowned evangelical Thomas Chalmers, left the established church to set up what became the Free Church of Scotland. The issue for evangelicals was clear-cut: either Jesus Christ is Lord and Head of his Church or he is not.

On 16 May, 1843, Burns left Fife and hurried to Edinburgh, that he might witness and share in the dramatic events that were then unfolding. Two days later, he records that he was 'honoured to join in the solemn procession of ministers, from St Andrew's Church to the Free Assembly Hall, Canonmills, walking between my father on the one side and Uncle George of Tweedsmuir on the other. This was a scene of which I know not what to say! The opening of the Free Assembly was graciously solemn. Surely the Lord was there.'

But the Disruption had a peculiar effect on Burns' ministry. The emphasis in Scotland had shifted, from the message of repentance and the need to be born again, to that which Islay Burns called, 'a time not so much for the awakening of life, as for the exercising and turning to good account of the life already awakened – a birth-time rather for the collective church than for individual souls.' Burns knew that there was much work to be done in post-Disruption Scotland, but it was not the form of work to which God had called him. His call was not, says his brother 'to rear, or even materially to assist in rearing, the outward fabric of the house of God, but to help by God's grace in gathering the living stones of which it was to be reared.' This resulted in Burns being the more willing to listen to calls which were coming to him, with increasing frequency and urgency, both from close and distant fields.

Chapter 4

Dublin and Canada
(1844–46)

Of the many calls that William Burns received in the early 1840s, one particular call came from Dublin, and it was to there he travelled in April 1844. His avowed intention was to preach the gospel particularly to Roman Catholics. After arriving in Dublin, he quickly chose a piece of ground where he could address his audience without obstructing the street, and there, night after night, he would be found, stand on a chair, preaching to any and all who would stop and listen. Not surprisingly, the crowds would often be very hostile, and would interrupt him and seek to make him angry, but Burns was not easily detracted. Sometimes, however, the uproar was so loud and continued for so long that Burns did have to stop for a while. Regularly his clothes would be torn, the chair on which he stood would be broken, and he was threatened and abused. It was recorded though, that not once did he ever lose his temper, or lose the joy from his face, so much so in fact, that those who were the ringleaders of trouble admitted that he was 'a good man; we cannot make him angry.'

It must be added, however, that Burns did have a bodyguard composed of three young men, who were members of the church whose minister Burns was staying with. Fortunately, they were always at Burns' side, and several times stopped men who were rushing at Burns, seeking to topple him from his 'preaching-chair'. The crowds would often shout questions at him, not usually to receive any teaching, but to trick him or confuse him, in a manner similar to that which occurred to Jesus in the Gospels. Burns recorded some of the questions that were shouted at him, and the following are examples:

Questioner: 'What book is that which you hold in your hands?'

Burns: 'It is the Word of God.'

Questioner: 'How do you know? Can you prove that it is the Word of God?'

Burns: 'I shall prove that it is if you deny it; but if we both of us admit it to be from God, why need I stop to prove it?'

Questioner: 'What is your commission?'

Burns: 'I shall read it to you, my friends, "Let him that heareth say, Come." Eleven years have now passed since I heard the Lord speaking to my heart, and saying, "Come", and ever since I have been saying, "Come" to as many sinners as were willing to listen to me.'

Questioner: 'You may go, we don't want you here.'

Burns: 'My friends, it is to those who don't want me that I am always most anxious to go; for I find that they are the people who have most need of me.'

Questioner: 'Bravo! From what country do you come?'

Burns: 'From Scotland.'

Questioner: 'Have you no sinners there?'

Burns: 'Yes.'

Questioner: 'Have you not much drunkenness in Scotland?'

Burns: 'Yes, a good deal.'

Questioner: 'Why did you not stay at home to convert the drunkards before you came over to teach us?'

Burns: 'For this reason: In Scotland the drunkards know that they are sinners, and do not attempt to justify themselves in their sins. But here I see people who curse, and drink, and tell lies, who say, nevertheless, that theirs is the true religion. Now these people must be labouring under a great mistake, and I have come to set them right in this matter.'

Questioner: 'But our church is the true church, and we have our priests to teach us and to keep us right.'

Burns: 'My friends, your saying that you are members of the true church does not prove that you really belong to it. Let me read you a passage from the Word of God. John 8:39, 44: "They answered and said unto him, Abraham is our father. Jesus said unto them, If ye were Abraham's children, ye would do the works of Abraham. Ye are of your father the devil, and the lusts of your father ye will do.'''

On one occasion, Burns decided to vary the commencement of his open-air service by the singing of a psalm. His Irish host attempted to dissuade him from this, by telling him, that as his audience knew nothing of the metrical psalms, nor of psalmody, his attempt to sing would really only result in increased bitterness and opposition against him. But Burns wanted to see the result for himself, and announced to the assembled crowd that they would sing Psalm 62. After reading a portion of the psalm, Burns began to sing the fifth verse. The crowd were, for an instant, taken by surprise, and listened to the first line in some astonishment, but it soon passed and then they broke out into a laugh of derision. As one, the crowd then rushed at Burns, just as he had completed the first two words of the second line. The three bodyguards drew Burns aside until the crowd swept by, and after quite a time, they placed him once more upon his chair. Burns then, with his usual composure, resumed the tune at the part of the line which he had reached before he was interrupted!

One evening, when he was forced to stop short in his preaching because the crowd rushed at him once again, and broke his chair, Burns went down along the quay on the other side of the river, to speak instead to the coal-porters. His friends were very concerned when he told them his plan, for all they could see was the very real danger he would be exposing himself to. Burns simply replied that he 'had never known fear'.

Burns arrived at the place along the quay where the coal-porters were, but as soon as he began to speak, an angry mob quickly gathered, and loud and threatening shouts drowned all his efforts to be heard. It was not long before the police came to investigate, but they 'kindly but firmly' required him to stop. But Burns had come to speak to them, and again he tried to be heard above the now even larger crowd. But those who had only been shouting before, now grew very ferocious and were present in such numbers that the police insisted that he should be silent and cross the river in the ferry. 'If you attempt to go back along the quay,' they told him, in no uncertain terms, 'we will not be answerable for your life.' 'But I cannot pay for the ferry-boat.' 'It will cost you only a halfpenny.' 'But I have no halfpenny,' he replied. At that, one of the policemen gave Burns one of his own, 'Here is one for you.' At that, Burns stepped down into the boat, and never wasting an opportunity, held up the halfpenny and cried to the still-assembled crowd, 'See this, my friends, I have got a free passage. In like manner, you may have a free gospel, a free forgiveness of all your sins, a free passage to the kingdom of heaven. Without money, and without price.' As the ferry left the banks, Burns carried on speaking to those who were travelling with him.

On another evening, Burns took up his usual preaching position at the Custom-house. He laid his hat on the ground and began to read, 'It is appointed unto men once to die....' He soon had a large and quite mixed audience, 'but, as usual,' he says, 'the Romanists introduced their questions, and when the answers came too near them they began to make a rush with the view of putting me down. A police officer also came and advised me to remove. I said I believed that I was trespassing no law – that that was the ground where Father Matthew spoke – and that I would not remove unless he had authority to stop me. He seemed to be a Romanist, and was evidently set on putting me down, so that after throwing the responsibility on him, and telling the people where I would preach tomorrow, I came away with a disturbed conscience. Dear people! They seemed intent on hearing, and followed me far on my way home despite of all I could do.'

Burns seems to have had very few positive responses to his preaching. But on one Sabbath morning, he was speaking as usual at the Custom-house, and he read and spoke from the Gospel of John, of the need for man to be born again. At the close of his message, someone said to him, 'Well, sir, if what you have said be true, you had much need to come from Scotland to tell it to us, for we never heard of this doctrine before.' On Friday April 12th, Burns wrote in his diary that at half-past nine in the morning he went down again to the quay. He asked a captain if he would allow him to stand on his ship to preach, but he refused. Burns then saw what he took to be a group of Romanist emigrants who seemed to recognize Burns and they began to mock him. He asked them why they were so unwilling to hear the Word of God. They answered that they loved it, 'but not from me'. But as they spoke,

> they mingled many oaths, which I told them certainly showed that they were not on the right way. A crowd gathered, and I had the best hour among them that I have had in Dublin. I was greatly aided in gaining their confidence. They threatened to throw me into the river at first, but I told them I did not mind that – they treated my Master worse.... One said something vile: I said, 'You know that when you go to confession you must confess that as a sin.' Another, hearing of confession, and thinking that I was speaking against it, said, 'What do you know about confession?' I said, 'Not much, but I am saying no more than I know', and repeated what he had said. He was pleased. One said, 'You must be saved by prayer and fasting'; I affirmed it, but showed the infinitely higher place of the blood of Jesus.... I was so full of God's joy in all this that I could not but smile, or rather laugh, in speaking to them.

But such experiences were few and far between. On the whole, his Irish friends were disappointed with the apparent lack of results, compared to what had taken place in Scotland. His host, Dr Kilpatrick, wrote that 'his addresses to our Presbyterian people failed to produce much visible impression. His failure in this respect disappointed and grieved me very much.' The people generally were also disappointed that his preaching seemed somewhat more shallow than they were used to, 'having been largely informed of the wonderful success which God had vouchsafed to him in many districts of Scotland, they expected to hear from him a fuller exposition, and a more specific application of scriptural truth, than he was wont to give; and they were somewhat dissatisfied to observe that his discourses appeared to be wholly extemporaneous.' And yet, Dr Kilpatrick also added that there was no doubting that the salvation of souls 'occupied and absorbed his daily prayers, his social converse, his public addresses, the whole course of his thoughts, the whole business of his life. Why are there not more of us like him? The need of such men is as urgent as ever; and we know that the grace of God is not less rich, nor his promises in

Christ less sure, nor his gifts less varied or less rich.'

We are fortunate to have another record of Burns' labours. H. M. Williamson, who later became minister of the Free High Church in Aberdeen, was at the time a student in Trinity College. In his diary of that period, he writes:

> I only saw him once in Dublin. I was then a student in Trinity College, and I remember well passing along by the custom-house. I came upon a crowd, which as I drew near appeared greatly excited. I stopped to listen, and I found that William Burns (as I afterwards came to know) was addressing them. I think I see him still: with what a strange calmness he spoke! with what meekness he met all their taunts! He was hooted, pelted, insulted, but quite unmoved he held open his Bible, and answered every onset by saying, 'But hear me, hear what God says to us in his blessed Word.' I remember he was speaking from John 10 concerning the good Shepherd and the door of the sheepfold. At times the crowd were quieted down to listen, and one at least of the hearers walked away, forgetting for the time Greek iambics and mathematical deductions, but filled with the thought, 'That stranger has a peace and a life of which I know nothing.' Next time we met was at the Duchess of Gordon's, Huntly Lodge, on his return on a visit from China; and I have never forgotten that happy season, or his last words, as, entering the railway-carriage, he said, 'Now for China!'

Burns remained in Dublin until 10 May, when he made the return journey to Scotland. In human terms not a great deal had been achieved, certainly nothing like the blessings that had previously occurred in Scotland. For the next three months, he was to be found preaching again in various places throughout Scotland. But very soon, Burns would arrive in Canada to continue his call to preach the gospel to the very ends of the earth.

In fact, William Burns was the third of his family to be actively involved in the service of Christ in that land, for his uncle, Dr George Burns, of the Free Church at Corstorphine, Edinburgh, had in 1817 been called to be the first minister of the Church of Scotland in St John, New Brunswick. With only a short interval, he remained in that important charge for fourteen years.

Yet another uncle, Dr Robert Burns, formerly of Paisley, was for fifteen years secretary to the Glasgow Society for sending out Ministers and Teachers to the Colonies of British North America, and was himself for twenty five years pastor and then Theological Professor at Toronto. Robert Burns actually arrived in Montreal in 1844, one of the first deputies as it were of the new Free Church of Scotland. Moreover, when he arrived, the question immediately asked of him was whether he had brought his nephew with him. It was the case, sadly, that the revivals in Scotland were spoken of much more in Canada than ever they were in Scotland itself.

The result of this was that when Robert returned to Scotland, he brought with him earnest commissions from the people of Quebec, Montreal, Kingston and Toronto, together with many other places, for William Burns and others of similar spirit to come and labour amongst them in that land. In fact, so much had been heard in Canada of the way God had blessed the ministry of William Burns in Scotland, that even before Robert set foot back in Scotland in June 1844, the proposal for William Burns to visit Canada had been sent from Canada to the Colonial Committee of the Free Church and received by them. When Robert confirmed that call, and after he had given further information, William was assured that the call was of the Lord, and he made arrangements to travel. In a few short weeks, William embarked in the brig *Mary* for Montreal, a free passage to and from Canada having been guaranteed to him by the generous Christian owners of the ship. Burns sailed from Greenock to Montreal on 10 August 1844, and reached Montreal on Thursday, 26 September.

The following extracts from his journal show the feelings with which he approached this new field of labour, and the spirit in which he entered on it:

In every circumstance even to the least, I have seen infinite grace towards me on this occasion. The ship in which I am is an excellent one. As there is no cabin passenger but myself, I have the cabin as quiet as my own study could be, and a state-room in which to meet with God. The means provided for me by the Lord have so exactly met my wants, that I go forth truly 'without purse', having only two shillings remaining in the world; and yet I am infinitely rich, 'having nothing, and yet possessing all things'. I trust I shall be enabled not only to pray much, but also to study more deeply the divine Word, and prepare more regularly for the profitable discharge of my awful trust.... I have got some beginning made among the crew. Tonight we had fine weather, and met on deck for worship. It was sweet and solemn, the voice of prayer and praise blending with the winds in the midst of the mighty deep. Oh that I may be prepared for glorifying God fully in my body and spirit, which are his!

On another occasion he wrote:

Today we have been becalmed, and I feel the retirement sweet. I think I can say through grace that God's presence or absence alone distinguishes places to me. But ah! I am yet untried. I know but little of what is in me as yet, and still less of the depth of his redeeming love.... I have sometimes had glimpses both of the depth of sin and of redeeming love; still, I will need very special teaching if I am to be of use in the western world.

On 2 September he recorded the following entry:

This morning beautifully clear; a gentle north-east breeze, wafting us to our desired haven, brought us in sight of American land, after a delightful run of 23 days. Our seasons of divine worship have been increasingly pleasant of late, although I see no mark of a divine work of grace in any one around. Part of my daily work has been to teach the ship-boys to read. One of them is an interesting black from Africa. Oh that my heart were enlarged in pleading for the ingathering of all nations to Emmanuel!

On 10 September he reached Quebec, a journey of thirty-six days. It was the Sabbath, and so he remained on board, conducting worship for the crew. On the evening, he disembarked and went straight to the market place, where he took up his 'position alone, and yet not alone ... and began to repeat the fifty-fifth of Isaiah'. A crowd of sailors, both Canadians and British, soon gathered. At first, they 'seemed mute with astonishment, but soon showed me that the offence of the cross had not ceased by their mocking and threatened violence'.

He later entered into conversation with two young sailors, who he discovered remembered well hearing him preach in Newcastle. Many of the sailors and soldiers that Burns saw there were very drunk, and he noted that 'though it were only to reach these two classes of degraded men, it would be to me a reward for crossing the great ocean'. He closed that portion of his journal by noting that the only book he had with him besides 'the book of God, is Owen on the Glory of Christ, which I find very precious indeed. I have had some seasons of great nearness to the God and Father of our Lord Jesus Christ, and have found his Word full of power and refreshment.'

From Quebec he travelled to Montreal, and on arriving there he met with many people he already knew. He was invited to stay with the Orr family, 'a godly couple from Greenock, in a delightful situation at the head of the town. Truly goodness and mercy are heaped on me.' Burns also rekindled his acquaintance with the same regiment of soldiers amongst whom he had worked at the Aberdeen barracks in 1840. He remarks that he was particularly amazed that 'about thirty godly men among sergeants and privates... have hired a room near the barracks in which some of them teach a daily school for poor children gathered from the streets, as well as a Sabbath-school, and in which they meet for social prayer every Friday from six to half-past eight'. But Burns did not even need to go looking for them to meet them again, for he had hardly arrived when he was informed that they wished him to attend their prayer-meeting, and then to preach on the following Sabbath. He was overjoyed, but could not have expected the sight that met his eyes:

When we got to the place I found such a scene as I never before saw: a room crowded with soldiers, wives, and children, who were met not to hear a man speak, but to wait upon Jehovah, as their custom was. It put me in mind of the centurion of old. I enjoyed the meeting exceedingly, speaking upon Moses at the burning bush. One of the soldiers prayed, as well as Mr M'Intosh and myself. In the soldier's prayer I was struck by the petition that they might cherish such expectations of good through my instrumentality as were warranted by his Word, and were according to his mind. They seemed all to feel too that nothing but the presence of God himself would be of any avail. I found it very affecting to them and me to allude to the church of our fathers in the furnace, and to the people of Ross and Sutherland, from among whom the regiment was at first raised.

But such was the high esteem in which Burns was held, both of that and of many other regiments stationed there, regiments who were composed of men from several different denominations and none, that on several occasions when soldiers were ill, whether they were English, Irish or Scots, Episcopalians, Presbyterians, or Roman Catholics, they sent him earnest messages pleading for him to come and pray. From that time we are fortunate, once more, to have the words of Hector Macpherson, the then sergeant-major of the regiment's band:

> I shall never forget the first sermon he preached on the first Sabbath after his arrival. He gave out in the usual way the 32nd Psalm to be sung, and had read the first four lines, when he began to unfold the feelings and experience of a penitent believer, in a way, to me at least, never opened up before nor since, and which was to my affected spirit as good news from a far land. It was like oil and wine to my afflicted spirit. It was also greatly blessed to others of my fellow-soldiers. The man of God continued to address us in much freedom of heart and of power for three hours, concluding somewhat abruptly, but with words which indicated a spirit of winning affection to every one: 'I see your time is up, but I hope to have farther opportunities of addressing you', and solemnly pronounced the apostolic benediction.

Another description given by a non-commissioned officer at that time, helps us to see something of the effect of Burns' preaching, even on the hardened soldiers of that day:

> I have known the Rev. WCB to send this famous regiment [the 93rd], these heroes of Balaclava, home to their barracks, after hearing him preach, every man of them less or more affected; not a high word, or breath, or whisper heard among them; each man looking more serious than his comrade; awe-struck, 'like men that dreamed they were'; and when at home, dismissed from parade, they could not dismiss their fears. Out of thirty men, the subdivision of a company under my charge, living in the same room, only *five* were bold enough that Sunday evening to go out to their usual haunts; and these must go afraid, as if by stealth, their consciences so troubled them; the other

twenty-five, each with Bible in hand, bemoaning himself. Now, looking at the whole regiment from what took place in this *one* room of it, you may be able to judge of Mr Burns' powers as an ambassador of Christ with clear credentials.

Burns preached and ministered wherever and to whoever he could. But it was the highways, streets and squares of Montreal that were his favourite areas to labour amongst. For the first few days, there was little real opposition, but it seems that because the majority of those who listened were Roman Catholics, the priests soon became aware of his presence and message, and became alarmed, and this resulted in direct and violent opposition. On Tuesday, 24 September he was preaching in the open air, in *Place d'Armes*, in front of the Roman Catholic Cathedral. This caused some to immediately oppose him. Many had gathered there to hear him:

> I had a fine opportunity, and felt the power of the living God with us. Towards the end our enemies made a commotion. The mayor of the city, a Roman Catholic, came to stop me, but was restrained by God. As we retired about half-past nine we were mobbed, chiefly as usual through the excessive fears of friends seeking to guard me from violence. The mayor offered his protection, but I said to the people in his presence, 'No one will harm me – it is my own friends who are creating groundless harm. I would ask all to go quietly home, and if any one is my enemy he will give me his arm and we will go together.' They quietly moved away. I put my hand on my white neckcloth and moved on unknown to the multitude. If the kingdom of Satan is to be disturbed here, this is but the shadow of what will yet come, and then shall many be offended.

Burns would return to preach at the very same place on many more days. He describes how he would be 'awfully mocked and pelted', though he does go on to add that thankfully they used 'nothing deadly'. On another occasion he writes that 'a great number assembled, and, in contrast with the previous night, they seemed to have ears given them to hear'. At least that is how it was for a while that day, although the situation soon changed, for 'afterwards they began to throw gravel and to jostle me in the crowd'. When some of the people tried to rescue him from further danger, the crowd rushed him. Eye-witnesses described the scene as 'most terrible'. The people were 'furious', and so Burns wisely sought refuge in a local shop. It was discovered later, that the only damage done was that his coat had been badly torn, his hat had been trampled upon, and his pocket-Bible, his constant companion, had been wrenched from his hands and torn to pieces.

On yet another occasion when Burns was preaching, a stone was thrown very forcibly at him, striking him on the face. It cut his cheek quite deeply and several soldiers had to intervene. Smiling, he was heard to say, 'Never mind, it's only a few scars in the Master's service!' He was taken to a local doctor, Dr Macnider, who was known as a godly man, that he might stitch the wound. No sooner had the doctor finished, than Burns was back at his preaching-post, exclaiming in a loud voice, 'I bear in my body the marks of the Lord Jesus.'

At Williamstown, the minister and the kirk-session denied Burns preaching-access to the Church. How apt it was therefore, that the local innkeeper readily allowed Burns to preach in his premises. Many came to hear. At Lochiel, Burns stood in a wagon by the side of the road and preached, standing as he did under an umbrella held by another to protect him from the burning sun. Later that same day, a local farmer allowed Burns to preach to a large crowd in one of his barns.

As he travelled through Canada, the interesting thing is that he usually declined the offer of transport that people sometimes made, choosing instead to travel as far as he was able on foot, the intention being to take advantage of all opportunities to share the gospel with any and all he might meet. Even when he was forced to travel otherwise, such as on the steamers across the lakes, he would preach on them to whoever might listen.

Burns soon realized that to reach Canada proper, he would need to be able to speak and to preach in French as well as English. He therefore set about learning French, and he was so successful in this that he not only preached in this newly-acquired language very soon after, but he actually wrote a large part of his Canadian Journal in French.

What has to be said, unfortunately, is that the response of Canadians generally to Burns' message was, on the surface at least, one more of indifference or even opposition at times, rather than of conviction and repentance: 'Alas! the spiritual deadness of this country is very great,' he wrote, 'sometimes I have been a little encouraged, but in general, spiritual religion which alone saves the human soul, appears to be very rare. Nevertheless, I have met with some people who seem to love the Lord. Yesterday, I tried again to preach out of doors, but with little success. They stoned and pelted me with mud, but by the grace of God I escaped danger.'

Burns would often list the various places he preached at, and because he travelled so widely and took his commission to preach so seriously, portions of his journal often resemble a kind of gazeteer of Canadian villages, towns and cities. To get some impression of this, I include here for example these entries from his journal:

I have preached at St Eustach, Lachute, St Andrews, Hawkesbury, L'original, Vankle-hill; Lochiel, Indian Lands, Kenyon, Roxbury, Finch, Martintown, Williamstown, Lancaster, Cornwall; La Riviere, De Loup, Lake Stove, Huntingdon, St Michaels, Durmann, North Georgetown; Ottawa, Bristol, Perth, Lanark, Dalhousie, Beckwith, Smith's Falls, Carleton Place, Brockville, Prescott, Kingston; Gonoque, Glenburnie; Cobourg, Belleville; Demorestville, Picton, Napanee; Fredericksburg, Peterborough, Ottonabee, Port Hope, Clarke, Newcastle, Toronto, Niagara, Streetsville, Esquesing, Oakville, Wellington Square, Hamilton, London, St Thomas, Williams, Lobo, Southwold, Dunwich, Aldbro, Mora, Eckford, Chatham, Amherstburgh, and Detroit in the United States.

One such of these preaching-tours took him to the Highlanders of Glengarry. As far as his impact there is concerned, we are fortunate to have a written record from the Rev. Alexander Cameron, the minister who went to work amongst these very same people shortly after Burns had been there. Cameron's record is most enlightening:

I found the people in a very interesting state of mind, many of them cherishing a tenderness of conscience and a brokenness of spirit, and thirsting eagerly for the Word of life. Some of all ages were in this condition, but especially young men and young women. The crowds that congregated on the Sabbaths at Lochiel, the most central station at which I preached, were sometimes very great. In the district of Glengarry, where there are now seven or eight ministers, there was then only one, Mr Daniel Clark of Indian Lands, and myself; consequently the people came from all quarters, travelling five, ten, or even twenty miles and upwards. Many of them started on the Saturday so as to be forward in time for the morning service. The poor Roman Catholics observing all this, thought the heads of their Protestant neighbours were turned. In one sense it was easy to preach to these thirsty souls, for the word of God was precious in those days. It was the same wherever I went; no matter where the sermon was intimated to be preached in any school-room or district, the place would be crowded, even although such meetings were continued in different places nearly the whole week, as sometimes happened in winter; and often a few of the more ardent spirits would attend all these meetings, travelling from place to place for this purpose. The face of things began gradually but steadily to change. Old customs and inveterate habits were one by one abandoned. Balls and merry-makings and New Year's festivals, so frequent in that country, were fast disappearing. Some of the leaders in such things with their own hands cast their fiddles and bagpipes into the fire; and instead of the sounds of revelry the voice of praise and spiritual melody began to be heard in their dwellings. Zion was meanwhile putting on her beautiful garments. Communion seasons were now more like those in old Ferintosh than the former scanty gatherings in the 'backwoods'. This state of things I ascribe chiefly under God to the labours of Mr Burns. Doubtless many other able and excellent men, especially some from the Free Church at home, laboured faithfully, and I believe successfully, in Glengarry; but the visit of Mr Burns in my estimation was the crowning visit, and the impression produced by his preaching and his godly demeanour was deep, pervasive and abiding. The great day alone shall fully declare it.

What a great truth this is! How many faithful servants of God have laboured for their Master, and yet seen only little fruit *in their own time*! But truly, that Great day shall declare for all to see, what was done in His Name and for His Glory!

From the hand of another minister there in Canada, we even

have preserved for us a wonderful description of that which motivated Burns:

> He appeared to have continually in view an impression that he should do something for God, for his own soul, for the souls of others, and for eternity. His conversation was that of a man of extensive information, who knew how to apply it effectually to the best of purposes. His disposition was amiable, his feelings were tender, combined with a clear judgment, great firmness, caution and patience, qualities essential to dealing properly with unreasonable persons and with difficult questions. He did not consider that he had a warrant to proceed in any sacred duty without a consciousness of having the divine presence. I have sometimes seen him on this point in very great perplexity, earnestly wishing and praying for a special message direct from Heaven, and doubtful which was duty, to proceed or to keep silence: like Moses who prayed, If Thy presence go not with us, carry us not up hence!

Whilst in Glengarry, Burns stayed at the house of one of the church's officebearers. But when he was making ready to leave, a great snowstorm blew up and Burns was forced to stay for a full week:

> We found him remarkably agreeable and sociable as a guest, entertaining us with incidents relative to his labours in Ireland, and those parts of Scotland where revivals have taken place. The recital of incidents connected with such themes always caused his countenance to beam with a heavenly joy. Much of his time also was spent in retirement and over his Bible, which he often carried to the table at meal times, referring to it whenever a pause in the conversation gave him an opportunity.

As the days passed, so an agreement that Burns had made to preach in the Indian Lands came closer. Burns' host agreed to try and get him there for that, notwithstanding the storm. He got ready a powerful team of horses and a strong sleigh and they set out, hoping to find a way through the deep snow. But the roads proved to be virtually impassable and for much of the time the horses simply floundered about in the snow. In some places in fact, the drifts were so deep that the horses were almost lost from their sight. At other times, the horses were so totally unable to make any headway at all, that Burns' friend had to manually clear what path he could for the horses to make some progress. However, when his kindly host happened to make a remark on the state of the conditions and said, 'This is awful!' he was instantly checked by Burns who said, 'Oh! my dear sir, there is nothing awful but the wrath of God.'

William Burns spent about two very full years in Canada before returning to Scotland on 15 September 1846. As for his physical health and condition, we learn from contemporary accounts that though he was still in vigorous health, yet he was showing very clear traces of exhaustion: 'The clear tones of a voice of more than ordinary compass and power were gone; his mind and spirit were worn and jaded; and he had already begun to acquire a certain *aged* look which he never afterwards wholly lost.'

Burns' call to be a missionary on the foreign field which he received early in his ministry, was a call which though delayed and then tried as it were in Canada, never left him. So when at long last, in July 1847, he finally set sail to fulfil that call, he recorded his thoughts about the ways and timing of God in his life. He began by stating that up until the Disruption of 1843, 'I appeared to have a special work to do in my own country, and having no call to the missionary field I thought no further of it than this, that I did not feel it would be lawful for me to settle at home, but only to comply with present calls of duty to preach the Word.'

For the next two years though, he found his 'heart very much drawn off from the home field – the days of God's great power with me seeming to be in a great measure past, and ecclesiastical questions having taken so deep a hold on the public mind, that it was not in a state as before to be dealt with simply about the question of conversion.' It was in these circumstances that Burns followed the interim call he received in 1844 to go to Dublin, as he says, 'to try the field there, but finding no great opening I returned to Scotland.'

There then followed from August, 1844 his two years of ministry in Canada:

In Canada I found sufficient evidence that it was indeed the call of God which I obeyed in going to it; but after labouring there for nearly two years, and having gone over the ground which seemed providentially laid out for me, I felt that unless I were to remain there for life, the time was come for my departure.... I accordingly sailed from Quebec for Scotland on August 20, 1846, having a deep impression that I should find no special work to do in Scotland that would detain me there longer than a few months, but feeling quite uncertain what would be my ultimate destination.

Whilst he was in Canada though, Burns received two unconnected and yet related letters, which confirmed in his mind that God's call to mission still rested on him. One of the letters was from an acquaintance of his who was in India, and this played its part in directing his attention once again to that particular land. The other letter was a call from the Free Church of Scotland's Continental Committee urging him to make use of his newly acquired proficiency in French, by agreeing to travel as their worker in Europe.

On his arrival back in Glasgow, he received a follow-up request to consider the Free Church's call, but Burns records that 'against this there were objections'. He was actually in something of a quandary. He just could not envisage that in a brief visit to Europe he really could have great success, and yet he was reluctant to commit himself for a prolonged period, believing that could easily interfere with God's call on him, which he was assured was to go and take the gospel to far more distant lands. 'At any rate,' he wrote, 'I felt that I could decide on nothing until I had paid a few visits to those home fields with which I had formerly been connected.' With these thoughts in mind, Burns spent the rest of 1846 responding to some of the requests for help that were sent to him, though as Burns himself said, 'I might have protracted the period indefinitely, being encompassed with invitations on every hand.'

This itinerating went on well until the December of that year, when Burns became troubled at the idea of carrying on as he was, with no clear guidance for the future. He therefore arranged a meeting with Dr Candlish. After sharing and praying together,

Candlish said he fully believed that it was Burns' clear duty 'to go as originally destined to the heathen', provided there were found 'no special cause' to detain him. He added that he would also 'confer with others on the subject'. Having consulted with others, what Candlish discovered was that there were actually no openings in India. But God was working, and the call that he had laid on Burns would be fulfilled at just the right time, and that time was, in God's economy, fast approaching.

In fact, while Burns' case was actually being discussed, a letter came to the Convenor of the Foreign Missionary Committee, Dr James Buchanan, from James Hamilton of Regent Square Church, London, who was also the Convenor of the English Presbyterian Church's Missionary Committee. Hamilton was asking whether Buchanan could recommend any suitable Scottish minister or preacher, who might be considered as their first missionary to China. The letter was written in quite urgent terms, for the Missionary Committee had planned such a mission for two years, but had been unable to find the person of God's choice to go. Dr Buchanan took this as 'a providential coincidence', but without letting Burns know, replied to the letter, mentioning several possible names, including that of William Chalmers Burns. It took only until the beginning of February for Burns himself to receive a letter from James Hamilton. Hamilton told Burns that the Committee knew of his call to foreign missions and that they had such an opening. Their question to Burns was simple: would he consider this opportunity as possibly being God's plan and purpose for him. Hamilton concluded by stating that the circumstances were such that they needed a quick reply.

What must Burns' first thoughts have been when he read this letter? How many different emotions must have pulsed though his body and mind, as he considered this momentous request? If the Committee believed that Burns was the type of man who would immediately respond, they would be sadly mistaken. 'I could only reply,' he recorded, 'that the matter was too varied in its bearings and of too momentous a character to be at once decided on; but that it would be the subject of prayer and consideration, as well as of conference with the servants of God around me.'

As soon as Burns' reply was received, the Missionary Committee instructed Hamilton to send Burns 'an express and earnest call to become their Church's first missionary to China'. Burns received this call, but still found himself unable, as he says in his own words, 'to arrive at a final decision'. It was not that Burns was not convinced of the importance or need of that particular field of labour,

> but when I considered on the one hand the manner in which God had hitherto called me to labour, and the many calls at home and abroad which I still had to preach the Word as heretofore; and on the other considered the uncertainty of my being suited to the peculiarities of the Chinese field, I felt embarrassed, and though I wrote a letter of acceptance, I could not send it off, but rather suspended the case by letting them know my difficulties, and my need of delay, with a view of getting further light. I also urged them in the interval to look out for others, and mentioned two ministers to whom they might apply.

Over the course of the next two weeks, that call to China gradually assumed more and more importance in his thinking and praying, 'and though some of God's servants seemed to doubt whether it was a field suitable to my habits, etc., yet the prevailing opinion seemed to be that I ought to go.' But before any firm commitment on his part was made, Burns headed for Kilsyth and the counsel of his family. However, what has also come to light is that soon after receiving Hamilton's letter Burns also received one from his friend and supporter, Mrs Barbour. She reminded him of his address to the Edinburgh University's Students' Missionary Association in which he said that when young men gave themselves to the Lord for the work of the ministry, they were not to prescribe to him where their field of labour should be, but should be willing to go anywhere, 'even to China'. Burns smiled when he read this and said to his brother that he did not remember having said *even to China*! Burns immediately then left the room and looked for the notes of that particular talk. When he found the place, his finger ran across the line, and as it moved it ran under the precise words, *even to China*!

He was soon able, therefore, to write to the Committee that he was still seriously considering their call, and would be obliged if they could send further information regarding the precise nature of the work they expected him to be involved in. He also asked if they could estimate the length of time it might take to acquire an adequate working knowledge of the Chinese language. Hamilton replied that he believed the difficulties in learning Chinese were often overestimated, but that in any case, Hugh Matheson, one of their Committee, was expected back from China in only a few weeks. He would be able to answer Burns' questions in a very precise way, and the plan was that Matheson would contact Burns on his return, with very up-to-date information.

However, before Burns even heard any more from the Committee, he was compelled to write himself:

> The impression of my duty now became so strong that I felt I could no longer hesitate about signifying my willingness to go, and on Monday I wrote to that effect. I saw that I would dishonour my profession of the gospel, and thus wound the honour of Jesus, if I seemed to linger any longer; and though I had not heard again from London, I felt that on general ground, and taking even the most discouraging view of the case, it was my duty to go forward.

What Burns did not know was that on that very day the Committee was meeting and hearing from Hugh Matheson a very discouraging account of the situation in China. It was such a negative report in fact that the Committee resolved to recommend to a meeting of the full Synod, which was due to meet at Sunderland the following week, to actually abort the plan of launching the mission to China. Even when they received Burns' letter of commitment, their view did not seem to alter any. We now know, from various additional documents, what some of those negatives in Matheson's report were: they included the number of missionaries already in the field; the difficulty of sufficiently mastering the language; and statements made about how closed China was anyway to foreigners.

When Burns was made aware of the Committee's new feeling, he was at a loss how to act or even really what to think, except he writes, that he saw that now matters were coming to a crisis and that the issue would be either to shut up my path toward China or set me free from their call altogether. I did not feel any sympathy with their proposal to draw back, and fearing lest they might do so, and thus dishonour the command and promise of the exalted Jesus, I was the more pressed in spirit to go forward, that such a consequence might be avoided.

He decided that there was little else he could do, but to go himself to Sunderland and speak to the Synod personally. So he set out and arrived in Sunderland on the Wednesday of the week they were meeting, ready to plead his case for the mission to proceed. What he was unaware of, however, was that the Synod had actually already met the day previously as well, and that in spite of the Mission Committee's very negative recommendation, the Synod's mind was fully set on pressing forward with their mission to China. All that Burns knew was that he was now fully resolved to tell the Synod when he appeared before them that China had become *his* field, and that whether the Presbyterian Church abandoned it or not, it would, under God, be the place God would take him. How surprised and amazed and full of praise to God he was then to discover the results of the Synod's proceedings the previous day!

So it was that Burns was called before the Synod to speak about his life and call. It is recorded that those who were present that day were much affected, as was Burns himself, so much so in fact, that he had to frequently stop speaking so as to compose himself, and somewhat prematurely he had to stop altogether. It took little further time for it to be resolved that Burns be ordained at 10 o'clock the following day, as the English Presbyterian Church's first missionary to China.

There is also wonderfully preserved for us, from this very period, the written record of an anonymous eye-witness, but one who was himself quite deeply involved in the actual process of the calling of Burns:

By far the most solemn and striking matter at the meeting of Synod has been the setting apart of William C. Burns as a missionary to China. Who could have believed that such would have taken place only two days before? Such an ordination has scarcely ever – if ever

– taken place. It is perfectly marvellous. The thing was done suddenly (2 Chronicles 29:36), yet I cannot think hastily, for God hath evidently been preparing his servant for it these months past. The more I reflect upon all the circumstances since the time of our first speaking to him on the 21st December, when we told him of the strait in which the Church was for want of missionaries to China, up to the decision of the Synod on the 21st April to ordain him the very next day, the more I am amazed at the wondrous things which have come to pass, and cannot doubt that God has been in them of a truth.

Even the charge itself that was given to Burns at the ordination service is quite remarkable and what follows is actually only a relatively brief extract:

This is a very solemn occasion to us, and it is also a very solemn occasion to you, dear brother. You yesterday told us how the Lord had directed your heart to offer yourself for this work, and to respond to the call of the Church to go forth unto the Gentiles. You told us that you did not require to return to your home, but were ready to set out with your little scrip on the morrow. And now, I would address to you the words of the Lord to Saul, 'Rise, brother, stand upon thy feet', Acts 26: 16-18. You have seen what few of us have; you have seen in the past the Spirit of God going forth in his wondrous power, giving testimony to the word of his grace, and the spirits of men bowing before him as mighty trees shaken by the wind. You have seen whole multitudes awed by his presence, and constrained to acknowledge that the Lord was revealing himself of a truth. Have you not seen these things? Can you not testify to them? The Lord hath now called thee for this purpose, that you may go forth a minister and witness of those things which thou hast seen. While yet a stripling he chose you for a great work by which he designed to prepare a people for a great event, and to bring many forth to testify for the Lord Jesus Christ as the great and only Head of the Church. But he also sends you forth to testify of those things in the which he will appear unto thee – in which he will YET appear unto thee, 'delivering thee from the people and from the Gentiles, unto whom now he sends thee.' Yes, brother, he has been preparing you for another work, and he will go before you to open up the way and guide you in all your steps.

Verse 18 was commented on by Dr Paterson, and he continued:

I charge thee therefore before God, and the Lord Jesus Christ, who shall judge the quick and the dead at his appearing and his kingdom; preach the word; be instant in season, out of season; reprove, rebuke, exhort, with all long-suffering and doctrine. For the time will come when they will not endure sound doctrine; but after their own lusts shall 'they heap to themselves teachers having itching ears; and they shall turn away their ears from the truth, and shall be turned unto fables' (2 Timothy 4:1-4). Yes, soon, very, very soon the time will come when they will not endure sound doctrine; for they have naturally itching ears, and turn away from the truth. 'But watch thou, in all things, endure affliction, do the work of an evangelist, make full proof of thy ministry.'

If nature be shrinking within you, if you feel yourself very weak in the contemplation of this great work to which you have been set apart, let me direct you to another passage (Matthew 28:18-20), 'ALL power is given unto me in heaven and in earth. Go ye THEREFORE.' Yes, he has all power and all authority, and must reign till he hath put all enemies under his feet. 'The earth is the Lord's, and the fullness thereof.' He is King of nations as well as King of his Church; he has power to protect and uphold, and he will deliver you from the nations unto whom now he sends you. Ah! look to him – to him alone. You may see the stars shining around you, you may think of many a bright light who has gone before into the dark places of the earth; but let me counsel you to turn from these, and look to Jesus. He is now on the throne, he will shield you, he will watch over you, he will send down an abundant unction on your soul, he will supply all your need. Go forth then in his strength. Remember that God hath given the heathen to his Son for an inheritance; remember that Jesus hath promised to be with you alway even unto the end of the world. Go forth even as a little child, led by him who walketh in the midst of the seven golden candlesticks, and who holdeth the stars in his right hand. May thy dwelling henceforth be in the secret place of the Most High, and thy lodging under the shadow of the Almighty!

After the service, Burns travelled to Newcastle and there preached in Great Market Chapel. Later, a considerable number were waiting to bid him God's blessing, and at his lodging all spoke of how marvellously the difficulties had been removed. Burns was astonished at the way God had so ordered circumstances. He noted how so little there was of man in the whole matter, how so little preparation in the world's sight, and yet how harmonious was the church.

The following morning at 5 o'clock, Burns left to catch the early morning train to London, on what would be the first leg of his long journey to China. One may be surprised to discover that there was no intention by Burns to return for a last short visit to Scotland. In fact many probably thought it was only right and proper that he should, but when he was publicly asked at the Synod when he could be ready to go, he replied unhesitatingly, 'tomorrow'. His brother, Islay, actually wrote that, 'This resolute tone and attitude of spirit was eminently characteristic of him. As a man that warreth, he entangled not himself with the affairs of this life, and moved about ever as a free and unencumbered soldier, ready at a moment's warning to march at the Master's command to any quarter of the world.'

What we also learn from Burns' brother is that at the time William heard that some timid persons had become daunted by the difficulties they were told of in regard to the China mission, he immediately packed his little carpetbag and set off for Sunderland. The morning of his leaving however, he spent in his father's study in prayer. When he emerged he said nothing, but shook Islay's hand and then looked solemnly around, as if, Islay really believed, he was taking a farewell look at the house. Islay was greatly overcome and watched William's receding figure with the very real sense that he would not return. When Islay went to the drawing-room to pray, he found the Gaelic Testament and Psalm-book neatly put into one of the shelves, as if his brother had finished with them. Islay remembered then saying, 'William will return no more.'

Chapter 5

China
(1847–1868)

William Burns was to sail to China on the *Mary Bannatyne*, which would sail from Portsmouth. But it was still at sea and so Burns used the opportunity to take several preaching engagements until it came time to head for Portsmouth. On Tuesday, 8 June he received word that a favourable wind had carried the ship, somewhat ahead of schedule into Portsmouth and that he needed to leave. Islay travelled from Scotland to be with his brother before William left Britain. On the *Bannatyne*, they prayed and read the Scriptures together. William's last words to his brother were, 'Remember our father and mother.' As Islay pushed off in a little boat from the ship's side, William called after him and pointed to his Bible, which he held up high for Islay to see, as if to say, believed Islay, that there was the only thing worth living for in all the world, and the one everlasting bond of union for those who are parted on earth:

> A fresh breeze sprung up; the light cutter flew before the wind, and in a few moments we had left the vessel far behind us; but long as I watched its lessening form in the deepening darkness I seemed to see him standing in the same attitude still. I felt that I had parted not from a brother only, but from one far above me, a true and eminent saint of God. Just as we were nearing the shore they had drawn up their anchor and spread their sails to the winds.

In his cabin later, Burns was to be found writing a letter home, and we learn from that letter that he too had similarly felt the strain and heaviness of parting from his brother:

> I felt it a great privilege to have Islay with me at the last. May this separation for the gospel be to each of us a blessing. Ah! what grace

is manifested in *such* a separation! Why am I not, as many, going forth in search of mammon; or put to sea, as some are, because they are unprofitable even in man's account on land? Who maketh thee to differ? O! to live under the full influence of Christ's constraining love! To us to live will thus be Christ, and to us to die will be gain.

During the first week at sea, even though Burns was very seasick, he did not give up on his language studies and even made good progress. However, as more days passed, he began to suffer from severe bouts of nausea almost daily and this did begin to interfere with his work. On Tuesday, 3 August he led an evening worship service for anyone who might care to attend. One of those present was a seventeen-year-old apprentice, by the name of Thomas M'Leod from Rothesay. At that meeting, Burns spoke particularly of the danger of sudden death, an ever-present danger to which they were all now more than ever exposed. M'Leod seemed attentive, Burns recalls, and when the question from the Shorter Catechism was asked, 'What is prayer?', M'Leod readily gave an answer. However, only two days later, at half-past four in the morning, Thomas M'Leod fell overboard and was drowned. Burns was honestly surprised how little lasting effect this seemingly had on those on the ship.

For five more months the ship sailed towards its destination and then at midnight on Saturday, 13 November, the *Bannatyne* anchored in Hong Kong Bay. Burns was met by several Christians and was given lodgings at the home of Mr and Mrs Power. He continued his language studies, but wrote that his 'progress in Chinese is slow compared with my desires'.

One of the first tasks he undertook was to visit the local prison. He was asked to see three Chinese criminals who were there under sentence of death. He was told that they were understandably in deep distress. The execution of the sentence was delayed because the area Governor was away, which meant that Burns had almost daily opportunities of visiting and speaking with the three. Burns found out that they had actually been pirates. 'They were very anxious,' recorded Burns, 'to hear of the way of salvation through Jesus and evidently strove to understand my broken Chinese.' On several occasions he read Christian books with them and would

104

pray in Chinese with them too. He would also constantly point to such texts in his Chinese Bible as 'God so loved the world'. As one contemporary writer said, 'the success of his efforts there can only be known in that great day'.

One of the first westerners that Burns met in Hong Kong was Dr Dill, and he would become a close friend. On remembering their first meeting, Dill records:

> The holiness of his general demeanour, as well as his conversation, arrested me at once, and now, after a period of more than twenty years, I can say I never met a man who seemed to walk in such close communion and fellowship with God.... During the year that he was studying the Canton dialect, he preached to us regularly. Sometimes his utterances were most powerful and heart-searching, while a sense of the preacher's manifestly-felt nearness to God communicated a solemn awe, such as one rarely feels, and which could only be expressed in such words as Jacob's – 'truly God is in this place.'

Dill and others asked Burns to form a Church, following the form of Scotland. Burns agreed to minister to the congregation that existed, but said that he had come to the Chinese, and that he would preach there as long as he could. The congregation met in an old bungalow, and the numbers attending at first were not large, but his hope and prayer was that it might form 'the beginning of that which shall issue in important results, both among the Chinese and amongst our own countrymen'. He was happy enough to be thus employed, but from the first and in everything, his heart yearned to reach the native Chinese. It has been well said that 'to the Chinese he became as a Chinese that he might gain the Chinese'. In fact, the one ruling principle of his missionary endeavours was that he might become as one of them, that he might live in their world, think their thoughts and speak their words. This actually was the reason why Burns left the Powers' comfortable home to take a rented house in the midst of the Chinese.

We learn too, not from Burns but from others, that his standard of living was very low, even in the eyes of his humble neighbours. There was a disturbance in his neighbourhood after a petty robbery had occurred and an excited crowd was running past Burns' house in heated pursuit of the suspect. When someone wondered whether they should look in there, the crowd responded, 'Oh! you need not look there, *it is only a poor foreigner.*'

In January 1848 he began to feel the need of the assistance of a native Chinese speaker, that he might succeed better with the proper intonation of the language. A fellow missionary soon found Burns just such a man. He was from Canton and began work at the end of that same month. Burns then took a further step, and rented a different house, one with accommodation that he could use for a small Chinese school. His own Chinese teacher would also act as the teacher for the Chinese school. Burns' intention was that by living with and working around none but Chinese, he would, by necessity, have to speak only Chinese. The house was found in February. The lower level, which had been a chemist's shop, would be used as the school room and Burns would live above.

As soon as the 'school' was opened, there were twelve to fifteen boys regularly attending. Three of them were actually taken in by Burns, as they had nowhere else to live. It was in this patient, unobtrusive, yet faithful way that Burns spent his first fourteen months in Hong Kong. But he was now becoming restless. His proficiency in Cantonese was now sufficient to enable him, at least intelligibly, to declare publicly the good news about Jesus. Part of that restlessness too probably stemmed from the fact that the shores of mainland China, with her mass of villages and towns and cities, lay clearly before him across the bay, and he was now more than ever longing to be labouring for his Master in the midst of such a vast harvest-field.

In a letter written to his brother at this time, William said:

You desired in one of your letters, that three doors might be opened to me, – the door of entrance into the language, the door of access into the country, and the door of admittance for the Lord's truth into men's hearts. The first of these has been opened in an encouraging degree already; and it now remains to seek by prayer and actual trial that the other two doors may be opened also.

Burns announced accordingly the end both of his Sunday English services and of the Chinese school, and then he steadfastly turned his face towards the 'regions beyond'.

'This latter course I have felt it my duty to adopt', he wrote later, knowing full well however, that this new course of action would be 'accompanied with many difficulties and dangers of different kinds'. He then said that he would have 'special need of special prayer to be made in my behalf, and in behalf of the people among whom I may be led from time to time. China is not only forbidden ground to a foreigner, but it is a land of idols and a land without a Sabbath. How great then must be that power which can alone open up my way and make it successful!'

So it was that he set out to preach from village to village, stopping wherever people would listen. He was, in fact, generally well received and the hardships that he had been led to expect, he said were actually much less, so much so that he sent back to Hong Kong a heavy cloak which he had taken with him, together with a revealing message that 'he did not need to sleep on the hills'.

In reality, the chief danger to which he was exposed came from the unfair reputation that attached itself to all foreigners, that they possessed and would be travelling with great wealth. This of course made Burns and others something of an easy target to would-be Chinese robbers. This made Burns wary of anything upon his person that might possess an attractive shape or the appearance especially of gold. Some time later, Burns was given a small pocket-Bible to replace a much treasured one that he had lost. His one objection to this gift, however, was that it had a gilt clasp. He suspected, and rightly as it later turned out, that it could well attract the unwanted attention of a Chinese thief. Soon afterwards, this Bible was stolen.

It is obvious from his journals, that Burns began travelling around areas of China in much the same way as he had done in Scotland. In some places he would spend less than a day and in others, where the door was clearly open, he would stay for more prolonged periods. In April for example, he wrote home from the area of Pan-Seen, which was about 85 miles north of Hong Kong, and all his travelling would be done on foot. He wrote:

We were some time ago invited to come to the village where we now are; and not only do we here enjoy the fullest external liberty to speak to the people, but there are some who receive us with much cordiality, and seem to manifest some interest in our message. One man in particular who this evening worshipped with us seems as if his mind were opening to the truth. But ah! when I speak thus, you must not judge of such a case as if it were similar to those which we remember at Kilsyth, Dundee and Perth, in days that are past! There is among this people no Sabbath, no Bible, no distinct knowledge even of the existence of one only living and true God.

He closed his letter by saying that were it not his abiding conviction that it was the Lord who had indeed sent him to China, and that his grace is sufficient in all circumstances, that 'I would sometimes be overwhelmed when regarding the state of this blinded people, and the danger to which my own soul is exposed in dwelling among them'. At each village his method of approach would usually follow the same general pattern. On reaching a village, he would begin to read the Bible aloud, sometimes under the shade of a tree. When the villagers began to gather, he would then explain to them the way of salvation. More often than not, he would be asked where he was to eat and that person would usually become his host for however long he remained in that village.

As time passed though, Burns began to encounter some degree of opposition, and when, in May 1849, it got quite dangerous for him to continue, he returned to Hong Kong. He remained there for the next eight months, perfecting his Chinese and working amongst the sick and suffering in the mission hospital. In fact the night he landed in Hong Kong, he was less than half a mile from another passenger boat when it was attacked by pirates and robbed, with the loss of several lives. Burns actually said that the firing was so loud, that he took it to be an English warship in pursuit of the pirates. Such were the dangers of the time, and yet, 'no evil was allowed to come nigh to us.'

In November 1849, Burns attempted a resumption of his evangelistic work on the mainland, but he encountered even more and greater obstacles than on the last occasion, and returned again to Hong Kong, robbed and stripped of everything, except the few clothes he was wearing. The work in Hong Kong however closed soon after this, and on the last day of February 1850, Burns sailed with Dr Young, another missionary, for Canton. Dr Young sailed on from Canton to the island of Amoy, which lay four hundred miles north-east from Hong Kong. Amoy is only about seven miles long, by two and one half miles wide, and yet it had, in 1851, a population of 250,000, and with it a massive opium problem. Though it was not a place of very great commercial importance, it was, by its position and relatively easy means of communication, a very good centre for potential missionary operations.

Dr Young soon became the head of two native schools and a hospital. Burns followed Young to Amoy in the following year, moving into the upper rooms above the school, to begin learning the Amoy dialect. The effort to learn Amoy Chinese did not prove as arduous as Burns expected and he was soon able to speak in public and be understood. He wrote home, 'we generally addressed five or six meetings in the course of the day, and in all must have made known something of the truth to at least two or three thousand people.'

In March, he crossed over to the mainland opposite Amoy, and in the course of one week preached in as many as thirty villages. He was welcomed kindly and listened to by many with great attention. In each place too it was his constant experience that he would be given free board and lodging. What is little known, however, is that such was his sense of how promising this harvest-field appeared, and of the urgent need of additional workers to be sent to help, that he gave back two hundred and fifty pounds sterling to the Mission Committee, a whole year's salary, to encourage them to respond practically to the great need. 'Surely,' said the Committee's Convenor when giving the next report, 'that field is ripe unto harvest, when the reaper sends home his own wages to fetch out another labourer.'

The following year, 1853, saw Burns' evangelizing efforts taking in a wider area, including what was known then as the great city of Chang-chow. He spent over one week in April there, preaching to large audiences both inside and outside the city walls. To avoid conflict with the authorities, he lived on the river, in the same boat which transported him the forty miles to the city.

I do not think, upon the whole, that I have spent so interesting a season, or enjoyed so fine an opportunity of preaching the Word of Life since I came to China, as during these nine days. The people were everywhere urgent in requesting that a place might be opened for the regular preaching of the gospel among them; and I am glad to say that the American Mission here have already sent two of the members of the native church to open an out-station in this important and very promising locality.

As time passed and as Burns lived and moved and preached more and more amongst the Chinese people, it became clear just how much he was gaining not only their confidence, but also their respect. Someone who knew him and his work in China well said that during the period when there were uprisings in Amoy, when no other European could venture out among the rebels, Burns 'was free to go where he liked'. The people everywhere would say, 'that's the man of the Book; he must not be touched.' But on one particular occasion, when Burns did not return from a preaching-tour for three weeks, his friends did become especially worried. However, as they were beginning to imagine the worst, Burns turned up quite well; in fact he was a little fatter than he had been when he left. He later recounted what had happened. He had arrived in a certain area and had begun speaking to the people. They were so taken with him and his message, that they fed him and looked after him, but would not let him go!

On 10 March 1853, Burns completed the last revision of the first part of his translation of *Pilgrim's Progress* into Chinese. He had begun his translation in the June of the previous year, and it had become a real labour of love for him. He showed the work to a number of others and later said that it benefited by a number of their suggestions. One hour after finishing the last sheet in the form in which it would be printed, he received from Shanghai a copy of *Pilgrim's Progress* also in Chinese, printed two years earlier by Mr Muirhead of the London Mission Society, chiefly for the use of pupils, the main difference between the two works was that Muirhead's was not a continuous translation as Burns' was.

Another similar task that Burns worked on at the same time was the editing of a collection of hymns for Chinese worship. It soon became a great favourite, especially with children, and since its first publication it has appeared in improved and enlarged editions. Burns delighted to talk about how young and fervent Chinese converts would sing or recite these hymns with great ardour. One favourite example of Burns is included here:

1.   Strait is the gate, and rough the way
   That leads to heaven and endless day;
   Few enter in, and very few
   Their journey to the end pursue.

2.   For we with sin's desires must fight,
   Mouth, ears, and eyes must guard aright,
   In all we do must act by rule,
   Rein in the heart nor play the fool.

3.   We must not covet sordid pelf,
   Nor injure men to profit self,
   Must careful be to speak the truth,
   And far must flee from lusts of youth.

4.   We must not cast an envious eye
   on those whose earthly place is high,
   Nor look with proud and scornful thought
   on those who fill the meanest lot.

5.   This heart of pride must be laid low,
   We must love men, though hate they show;
   Serve God, though to our worldly loss,
   Believe in Christ, and bear his Cross.

6.   Alas! weak men, devoid of grace,
   How can we run this holy race?
   Jesus, from heaven thy Spirit send
   To guide and help us to the end!

What was also a real blessing to Burns was that as he returned from his preaching expeditions on an evening, one of the first things he would often hear would be the singing of these hymns from gardens and even roof tops.

In January 1854, Burns left Amoy on another preaching tour, taking with him as usual as his companions and assistants two native evangelists who had been converted through the American mission. Their first stop was at Pechuia (White-water camp), a market-town of about 3,000 people. They expected to stay there for maybe a few days at the most and then to press on, but they soon found out that God had a very different plan. God did great things in that place, and they actually remained in Pechuia for two months. From the very first time they began preaching, several people showed real interest and became earnest listeners. Burns rented a small building, again the idea being that he would live on the upper floor, whilst the lower level would be used for preaching. Many came to hear and worship services were regularly held in the building. Very soon, several people began renouncing their idols, burning and destroying them, whilst others brought their idols to Burns for him to deal with them.

In March, Burns and his two companions set out on a journey even further inland, visiting places to which they had been earnestly invited by persons who had travelled to Pechuia to hear them. While they were gone, moreover, God raised up two other native Chinese to continue the work in Pechuia. Burns and the others preached in more than fifty villages on their tour. Burns reckoned that there were about twenty people in Pechuia who responded to the claims of Christ. One of these, a young man of twenty years old, took his 'god' and put it into the fire. However, when his mother later discovered a part of its head among the ashes, both mother and father together beat their son very severely. Some others of those who had been at Burns' meetings went to comfort the man and speak with his parents. Miraculously, the parents' eyes too were opened to the beauty of Christ, and within two days they together with their four other sons brought out their idols and ancestral tablets and publicly destroyed them in full sight of everyone.

Burns also described the interesting case of the family who lived in the adjoining house to his. They are 'literally divided', he said, 'two against three and three against two'. The elder brother and his wife opposed Burns' preaching, making their living by creating paper images used in idolatrous processions and for burning in sacrifice to the dead. The mother and two other sons were on the other hand very much on the side of the gospel. These sons formerly made similar images with their elder brother, but they gave up their trade, and began a general business in one half of the shop which the family had in common. It was very curious, said Burns, to notice that on the Lord's day for example, the younger brothers' side of the shop was closed, while the elder brother's side remained open!

Very soon after, Burns wrote 'mightily grew the Word of God and prevailed'. 'I have not witnessed,' he went on to add, 'the same state of things in China before.' There were many conversions and many of these converts went on to be baptized. In that March for example, after several examinations, ten were admitted to baptism that month. Two of these were women, one aged 68 and the other 47. The men were aged from 20 to 64 years old. This wonderful move of God was not limited either, for the London Mission Society was also a major beneficiary of what God was now doing.

It was in the midst of this that Burns' valued colleague, Dr Young, needed to return to Britain through ill health. Someone was required to travel with him, and it was decided that Burns would return with his friend. A female Chinese Christian nurse, Boo-a, also travelled with them to Scotland, which was very apt, for Boo-a was one of the first-fruits of Dr Young's faithful ministry in China. She had been baptized the previous year, along with her own son and fifteen others at Amoy. She is believed to have been the first converted Chinese woman in Scotland, and when Burns later asked her whether she missed China because of her difficulty in understanding English, her reply was simply this: 'Here where I can speak so little to man, I speak the more to God!'

Burns used his few months in Scotland to try and arouse interest and support for God's work in China. He especially returned to those amongst whom he had seen God move in mighty ways in previous years. But when he visited those places, the people were shocked at his appearance. The effects of the Chinese climate, combined with his increasing labour there, had taken a massive toll upon his body, which the rigours of that previous Canadian winter had already partially broken. He looked to them a full twenty years older, rather than five or six, as they might justly have expected. Even his spirit, many said, had become more mellow. His brother describes the change in him, as making him appear 'more genial, more loving, more freely communicative and companionable, less restrained and austere, than in former days. There was less fire perhaps, but even more fervour; less of the Baptist – more of the Christ.'

His preaching too, was quite different, and the frequent illustrations from China constantly reminded his hearers that the evangelist had become the missionary. How true this is can be seen from the following: while in Scotland he received a letter from the infant church at Pechuia, which addressed him as their spiritual father. At Kilsyth, amongst members of his family, he deciphered and explained the precious letter's mysterious characters. It is a wonderful letter:

We, who have received the grace of Jesus Christ, send a letter to pastor Wm. Burns, (lit. shepherd – teacher Pin-ui-lim). We wish that God our Father and the Lord Jesus Christ may give to all the holy disciples in the church grace and peace. Now we wish you to know that you are to pray to God for us; for you came to our market-town, and unfolded the gracious command of God, causing us to obtain the grace of God. Now, as we have a number of things to say, we must send this communication. We wish you deeply to thank God for us, that in the intercalary seventh month and thirteenth day, pastor Johnston (lit. shepherd – teacher Jin-sin) established a free school here; there are twelve attending it. Formerly, in the third month, a man, whose name is Chun-sim, belonging to the village of Chieng-choan (pure fount village), heard you preaching in the village of Hui-tsau (pottery village). Many thanks to the Holy Spirit who opened his blinded heart, so that in the seventh month he sent a communication to the church at Amoy, praying the brethren to go to the village. They went and spoke for several days, and all the villagers with delighted heart listened. Also in the town of Chioh-bey, the Holy Spirit is powerfully working; the people generally desire to hear the gospel. The brethren and missionaries have gone together several times; and now, in the village of Ka-lang, there are two men, Ch'eng-soan and Sui-mui, who are joining heart with the brethren in prayers. Teacher!

we, in this place, with united heart, pray, and bitterly (i.e. earnestly) beg of God to give you a level plain (i.e. prosperous journey) to go home, and beg of God again to give you a level plain (good journey) quickly to come. Teacher! you know that our faith is thin (i.e. weak) and in danger. Many thanks to our Lord and God, who defends us as the apple of the eye. Teacher! from the time that we parted with you in the seventh month, we have been meditating on our Lord Jesus' love to sinners, in giving up his life for them; also thinking of your benevolence and good conduct, your faith in the Lord, and compassion for us. We have heard the gospel but a few months; our faith is not yet firm (lit. hard, solid). Teacher! You know that we are like sheep that have lost their shepherd, or an infant that has lost its milk. Many thanks to the Holy Spirit, our Lord, who morning and evening (i.e. continually), comforts our hearts, [and gives us] peace. And in the seventh month, the twenty-fourth day, the brethren with united heart prayed, and shedding tears, bitterly begged of God again to send a number of pastors, quickly to come, again to teach the gospel. We wish that God our Father may grant this prayer, which is exactly that which the heart desires (i.e. Amen).

The letter was then signed by all the nine Chinese members of the Pechuia Church. Burns later learnt that they had written one sentence of the letter and then prayed, followed by the next sentence and more prayer, until the letter was completed. It was a real labour of love. Burns received a further letter from China, informing him of the success of the spread of the gospel into other areas since he had been away. He was told that similarly to what God had done in Pechuia, he was now so working in Chioh-bey, yet it was all happening through the instrumentality of native Chinese. Daily, and in fact, almost hourly, the Word was being preached, such was the demand to hear. There was scarcely any stop, day or night, those preaching taking turns, and in consequence of the prolonged hours they were becoming almost voiceless. Again there were many decisions for Christ.

Burns returned to China on 9 March, 1855 on the *Challenger*, along with Rev. Carstairs Douglas, who was travelling as the Free Church of Scotland's missionary to China. Instead of immediately resuming his work at Pechuia, Burns headed north, his intention being, if possible, to reach the headquarters of the Taeping rebels at Nanking. This would be a difficult and dangerous journey, but he was determined to at least try his best to get there. The ultimate goal he never did achieve, but the Lord was able to use the journey to reach many people. Burns set out with one Chinese servant at the beginning of August, 1855, ten days after reaching Shanghai from England.

They travelled in a woo-sung boat up the Yang-tse-Kiang and had to pass through several mandarin checkpoints. When they later found out that the way to Nanking was closed, they turned around and began their homeward journey. Travelling down a canal near the city of Tan-yang, they were soon surrounded by a large crowd, eager to look at 'the foreigner', and also to receive some of the books that they were handing out. They anchored there for the night, and in the morning Burns took some books and went onto the shore. Very soon however he was stopped by a policeman, who said that the magistrate wished to know what Burns was doing in that area. Burns answered by saying that he would like to meet the magistrate, and so the two men set out for that office.

Even as he waited in an outer office area, great numbers of people came to see Burns, so he used even that opportunity to carry on handing out his literature and speaking a few words about Christ to them. Burns was eventually taken to see an assistant magistrate, who was seated very regally in full legal dress. He gestured for Burns to be seated at his left-hand, the place of honour, and he began to ask Burns' companion about this foreigner and why he had come. After hearing something about Jesus and the gospel, the magistrate told Burns that in case of further trouble, an escort would go with them and that they had full liberty to distribute their books and leaflets.

They then headed back for their boat, and when they got on board people were so desperate for their books, that several at a time would swim from the bank to the boat. When the swimmer was given his 'prize', he would place it on his head and make it secure there as he swam back to shore by tying his long pony-tail of hair around his head!

For the next six months, Burns made his base at Shanghai, and from there he made frequent and sometimes extensive journeys into the towns and villages of the area. For most of the time he lived on the boat, using it both as his home and his means of transportation. By river and canal he was able to cover a wide area, spreading the gospel-seed in ever increasing areas. On one occasion at this time, Burns' boat halted for the night at Chung-too-Keaon (Passage-for-all-Bridge), where there were only a few houses and little hope of finding a congregation. However, as it turned out, they had only been there a little while when they heard many voices. They found out that there was an immoral stage-play being performed there, which had just ended. Burns began preaching to the dispersing crowd, some of whom had lingered to gamble. The people were panic-stricken, and being overtaken by such a message, they 'listened with a fixed and serious interest. I called on them to join with us in prayer to the true God, in the name of the Saviour of sinners, that he would deliver them from their sins, and save them from the punishment which sin was preparing for them. At the beginning of the address to God's throne there was some noise of voices, but towards the close all was breathless stillness. My companion and I were encouraged by this meeting, as if by God's special guidance, with opportunities of declaring his truth and calling fellow-sinners to repentance.'

Not long after this, on 26 January 1856, Burns wrote home of the friendship he now had with 'an excellent young English missionary, Mr Taylor, of the Chinese Evangelisation Society'. Burns and Taylor became very good friends, and for several months they lived and travelled together. In fact though, one would often find Taylor travelling in his boat and Burns in his, as they each had their own transport. Taylor was never slow in voicing his respect, love and admiration for William Burns: 'Such a friendship is beyond price. William Burns is better to me than a college course with all its advantages, because right here in China is lived out before me all that I long to be as a missionary.'

Several months earlier, Taylor had made the switch to wearing Chinese dress, and Burns quickly became convinced from his example that it brought real benefits in preaching and in freedom of travel. Burns made the change too, and for the first time he also dressed as a Chinese man on 29 December 1856. Years later, we find that when Hudson Taylor was informed of his friend's death, he felt the loss very deeply. Taylor wrote, 'His holy and reverential life and constant communings with God made fellowship with him satisfying to the deep cravings of my heart.' As Broomhall perceptively states, 'Burns' unsparing devotion to the Chinese and to the spreading of the gospel had also made him a man after Hudson Taylor's own heart.... To soldier on without the support of Burns' prayers and wisdom was painful to Hudson Taylor. Another ally had been removed.'

Each week, a weekly missionary prayer meeting was held in Shanghai for all who would pray about missions in China. There was one week when a Captain Bowers was there, a Christian whose ship was in harbour. He had just travelled from Swatow and was burdened greatly with its sin. It was both a centre of the opium trade and of an horrific traffic in human beings, the so-called 'coolie trade'. It was not just that there was no Christian witness in the city, though there wasn't, but there was not even any known Christian living within 150 miles of the city. The Captain made a very challenging case for Swatow to become a base for missionary outreach, his argument being, too, that 'if traders of all nationalities can live there, why should not ministers of the gospel?' But he was very honest too, and he warned them that any missionary who considered going to Swatow would have to be of the right material, for Swatow was composed of what he called the offscourings of Chinese society.

Burns and Taylor both walked silently back to their respective boats. Taylor had been convicted of the need of Swatow, but yearned to remain with Burns that he might continue to learn. A few days later, Taylor told his friend that God was calling him to Swatow, but that he had not yet obeyed because he feared leaving his friend and teacher. How must Burns' heart have leapt when he heard this, for his immediate reply to Taylor was, 'this very night I have accepted the call to Swatow, my only regret being that I realized that it would mean that we must part.'

The following morning, 6 March 1857, it was the same Captain Bowers who provided free passage for them both to Swatow. Only two weeks later, they were able to move into lodgings, ready to begin evangelization of that area too. They were to discover very quickly that it was indeed a very dangerous area, for in only one week, a Malay sailor was murdered in a quarrel; a Chinese woman too was murdered; and then, only a few days later, another Malay sailor was stabbed, possibly with fatal consequences, and this time by a British sailor. In some ways therefore, it was an ideal base for reaching out with the good news of Jesus, and this is what the two missionary-friends did. In fact, the area where their lodgings were to be found was a district that boasted it was 'without Emperor, without rulers and without law'. For six months, the two men worked side by side for Christ, and when the mandarin of Swatow fell ill, Taylor was able to provide treatment that helped greatly.

In July, however, Taylor had to leave Swatow for health reasons, fully intending, if God willed it, that he would return in a few weeks with more medical supplies, that he might minister even more among the Chinese people. The two men were never to meet again.

Burns continued to preach, hand out literature and minister among the people, even when rumours of war between the Chinese and the British began to circulate. He was travelling with his two native assistants when he wrote home that they had 'just been visited by robbers, who have taken all but the clothes we wear, without, however, doing us any injury. This is a new call to pity and to pray for this poor people, sunk so low in darkness and sin.' The idea they decided upon was that one of the assistants would return to Swatow and return with a small supply of money and books, whilst Burns and the other moved on to another town to await his return.

Proceeding on his journey the next day, Burns says:

We were without money, but God provided support for us in a way that was new to me. The people who took our books gladly contributed small sums of cash for our support, and the first day we thus collected enough to keep us for two days. A countryman, also, going the same road, volunteered to carry our bag of books for us. It was heavy for our shoulders, but easy for his, and he said he wanted no money, but only a book.

At the large city of Chaou-Chow-foo, which they next visited, the authorities became alarmed, and the small band was arrested and imprisoned. After examination, it was proved to be a false report. But while they were in the city, there was a great demand for their books and they had many wonderful opportunities for sharing the gospel with the people.

In early 1858, Burns received an offer from Lord Panmure to become Chaplain to the British Forces that were stationed in his area. The offer made clear that Burns would be given the rank and salary of a Major in the British Army. Burns wisely declined the approach, chiefly, he said, on the grounds that his connection with an invading army would be remembered always by the Chinese. There then followed another interesting incident, when Lord Elgin arrived in Swatow during an important mission to the Court of Peking. Burns was invited to breakfast with him, on board HMS *Furious*. Burns spoke at length with Lord Elgin, and ever after Burns would always speak with the greatest respect about him.

Dr Taylor never did return to Swatow, but in his place came Dr De la Porte, who worked with Burns as a medical missionary for two years. The doctor returned to Hong Kong in June 1858, and this meant that Burns' work in Swatow would also probably come to an end. But it was just at that time that he received several urgent invitations to return to Amoy. After much hesitation, he took this as being the next God-given step, although he agreed only on condition that a young missionary, Rev. George Smith, would take his place at Swatow. Burns could then count not one single decided convert in Swatow – the place in which he had ministered for so long. But the seed had been sown, and Burns was obviously concerned that the harvest be reaped and not lost. With the agreement thus reached, Burns sailed for, and reached, Amoy in October 1858.

After arriving in Amoy, Burns learnt that after he had left Amoy years earlier, God had abundantly blessed the area, and many Chinese were saved. The numbers of both converts and inquirers rose year on year, and Burns later described what had taken place as being like a fire spreading out from the central point, Pechuia. 'For several years after this port was opened,' Burns said, 'the labours seemed almost in vain', and even when drops from heaven began to fall, 'they were very few'. But then God opened the windows of heaven somewhat wider, 'and now the number of living adult members is:

> London Missionary Society 150;
> American Mission 100;
> At Chioh-bey 22;
> At Pechuia 25.'

In addition to these, there were about 15 native Chinese Christians employed as evangelists by the various missions. They helped conduct worship services, they went out distributing tracts and Bibles, and they would also preach and speak with those they met. There were also several young men who were under training for this work, who also would assist in the missions. In addition to this, there were several more Chinese people who wanted to help in the outreach in whatever ways they could. 'Oh! that Christians at home,' cried Burns, 'would go and do likewise – go everywhere, in streets, and lanes, and villages preaching the Word, and the Lord would certainly be with them, and his power be present to heal.' Burns acted as the director of this company of preachers, which was at work in every direction and area around Amoy. Hardly a month passed when there were not some inquirers to be instructed, and converts to be baptized. But in the midst of this success, Burns received word from Scotland, that only a few weeks after retiring from the ministry, his father had died quite suddenly.

Six months later, Burns was again on the move. His desire, as always, was to take the gospel to pioneer regions, and so his next stop would be the capital city of the Amoy province, Fuh-chow. Burns spent most of 1860 in this city, and he made rapid progress in acquiring the dialect. He prepared a hymn-book for the use of the infant church, and spent long hours spreading God's Word. Rev. C. Hartwell, one of the oldest missionaries of the American Board at Fuh-chow, said that Burns would always help at whatever mission stations he could, regardless of denominational affiliation. In fact, at one time Burns had been troubled by the arrival in Hong

Kong of a number of Roman Catholic priests, and on the following Sabbath, in speaking from 1 John 2:28 on the words, 'abide in him', he said, 'it matters not what external Church you belong to, whether the English, or the Scottish, or the Romish, if you are not in Christ; these are only externals; the one thing needful is to abide in Christ.'

Burns was seen as being of particular benefit by the 'excellent influence' he was seen to exert upon the native Chinese mission assistants. 'Our helpers', recorded Rev. Hartwell,

> soon learned to feel a great regard for Mr Burns, and their piety was quickened and deepened apparently through his influence. His power over them arose from his own deep piety; his accurate knowledge of the Chinese language; the great fund of Christian knowledge at his command; and the singleness of purpose which he ever manifested. We felt it to be a privilege to have our native preachers under his influence and instruction.

After Burns went to be with his Lord, Hartwell also recorded, that 'the savour of his name is still fragrant at Fuh-chow'. What a wonderful legacy to leave behind! Also at Fuh-chow was the Rev. Dr M'Lay, a missionary with the American Methodist Episcopal Church. He too provides us with a testimony concerning Burns: 'The memory of Mr Burns is very tenderly cherished by those who became acquainted with him during his residence in Fuh-chow, and among all the native Christians his name is as ointment poured forth.'

We have majored on the fact that, on the whole, Burns and others were treated with a fair hearing. This was not always the response, and in fact there was often a great deal of suspicion and sometimes actual physical aggression against the Chinese Christians by their own countrymen. At times, Burns had to intervene with the authorities to try and secure more peaceful relations through better understanding. He also pleaded with the authorities for the confiscated and stolen property of Christians to be returned. He was often quite successful, but the persecution only usually abated for a few weeks or months, and then would begin again. This resulted in Burns leaving Amoy, that he might head for Peking and there have a meeting on this matter with Sir Frederick Bruce. He arrived in the capital in October 1863, and this actually heralded what would be his last period of ministry.

Burns' aim in meeting Bruce was to obtain the same recognition of the civil rights of Protestants that Catholics were already enjoying. Burns did see Bruce, and the latter later declared that Burns 'was one of the most fascinating men he had ever met'. Burns remained in Peking for the next three years, living in one room, and his servant in the adjoining room. All that Burns had consisted of two chairs, a table and a small heater. Apart from the time spent in preaching, he also occupied himself in writing hymns and further translation work. He translated Scottish hymns as well as hymns used in the south of China. He then translated *Peep of Day* in fifty chapters. This book became widely circulated and served as a very good introduction to the gospel story. Burns then worked on another version of *Pilgrim's Progress*. At Amoy he had translated it into a simple style; he now sought to translate it into the Peking dialect. This he finished, and then he began a translation of the Psalms, directly from Hebrew into Chinese. This too he was able to complete, and it was published in 1867, only one year before his untimely death.

The Rev. Joseph Edkins of the London Missionary Society gave a quite lengthy tribute to his valuable friend and co-worker in Peking. Edkins praised how Burns worked with any and all mission agencies in China, that the gospel might be made known by all available means. 'He was at home with all Protestant Christians, and was greatly loved by all his brethren. His manly character, his sober views, his practical good sense, his kindly sociality, his mental strength, his moral decision, and his consistent and unaffected piety made him a friend greatly valued by us all.'

Burns held very distinct and decided views of the most appropriate word in the Chinese language for 'God' in the Christian sense, and even in this he had some influence. He held that the *Shang-ti* of the Chinese classics was the most appropriate term to be used, on account of its being the most correct, distinct, noble and unmistakable word to be found. When in Peking, an attempt was made to unite all Protestant Christians in China in the use of one term for God, and it was to be the Roman Catholic term, *Tien-chu* (Lord of heaven), Burns withheld his consent and was at the time the only Protestant missionary in Peking who did so. As it transpired, it was the *Shang-ti* of Burns which was later adopted by the British and Foreign Bible Society!

In late 1867, Burns left Peking for Tientsin in Nieu-chwang, urged forward as ever by the call upon him of preaching as much as possible in pioneer areas. A house on the outskirts was found, and daily services were held right from the start, with many people coming to listen. In the *Sunday at Home* periodical, a Christian sailor's recollections were printed. The sailor had arrived in Nieu-chwang on 6 October 1867, and upon hearing that there was a service in the town, he went along. 'A Mr Burns took the service,' he wrote. 'It was no formal ceremony, nor with enticing words of man's wisdom, but very earnest and very faithful, warning them to attend to the salvation of their souls, and commending godliness as profitable in all things.' He later went to see Burns.

> I landed at the appointed time, and was conducted accordingly to the missionary I had never seen. I shall not soon forget it, for we seemed to meet as friends that had been acquainted for a long time. I felt perfectly at home with him. Mr Burns walked up and down the yard of his house arm-in-arm with me, and talked to me as a friend, brother, or father, in the most kind and familiar manner.... He told me about how the Lord had guided him to that place. He had many friends, he said, where he had been staying for four years before, and was very comfortable; but he wanted to come to Nieu-chwang because there was no one labouring there. He said we must not study comfort: they that go to the front of the battle get the blessing; the skulkers get no blessing. I have often thought of that since.

Soon after this, sadly, Burns became quite ill. It began with a cold, which then turned into fever, and from that he never recovered. But it was a fever which made Burns linger quite helpless for months, leaving him in great weakness. When people visited him, Burns would speak both of life and death: when he spoke of life, he said what he would do if he had the energy; when he spoke of death, however, he prayed that others might be found to continue the work that God had begun through him. 'I am very happy,' Burns told Joseph Edkins of the London Missionary Society, 'I am very happy. I do not fear death. After death there is unspeakable happiness to be hoped for. Do not think I am sad at the thought of dying. I am not at all so. God's promises are true, and I fear not. My work has been little, but I have not knowingly disobeyed God's commands.'

Even as he lay close to death, several anxious Chinese who wanted to know more about Burns' God, came to see him. As they entered his room, Burns said:

You see in me proof that the Christian doctrine is true. I am well supported now, and this strength which is given me, not to shrink at the approach of death, you can take as proof that what I believe is true; my illness, my decaying body are also a testimony to the truth of the Bible. When I am gone you will have no missionary here. You must therefore pray much and think and read much that you may understand well. I have left friends and home to come here for the sake of this gospel that now supports me. I rely on God now. Listen you to him, and let us resolve all to meet in heaven. Hope for this. Live for this.

Burns suffered in his illness for upwards of six weeks. One of his great delights during this period was to hear worship emanating from the adjoining room, worship that testified to Burns that the work his beloved Master had called him to would certainly continue. On one particular bad day during his illness, he lay as if asleep, but those present in the room suddenly heard him talking. One of his friends present asked him what he was saying. Burns replied, 'Ah! Did you hear? I was saying over the 121st Psalm. I was speaking with God, not with you.' A few days later, Burns was heard laughing. His friend Mr Edkins asked him what it was he found funny. Burns told him that, 'God was speaking with me, and this made my heart glad.'

Two days after this incident, Burns said to that same friend, 'God tells me to go. I have some things to say to you. As to my burial, I wish to have no new clothes bought, but to be buried in these.' Burns then added, 'Do not let the funeral be on Sunday. At the burial read 1 Corinthians 15th chapter. Pray with the inquirers. Tell them to be sure to come and see me again in the place to which I am going. Do not weep after my death. Do not pray for me, but pray for the living. Diligently pray, and God will certainly send you a missionary.'

On 4 April 1868, during one of his visits to see Burns, Rev. A. Williamson read some Scripture, but as he was reading Psalm 23, Williamson hesitated at the words, 'Yea though I walk through the valley of the shadow of death....' Burns immediately carried on where his embarrassed friend left off, and read to the end. John 14 was also read, 'Let not your heart be troubled.' Their time together would have been concluded with the Lord's Prayer, but as Burns spoke his beloved Master's prayer he suddenly became quite emphatic, and repeated the close of the prayer with great power and certainty: 'For thine is the Kingdom, and the Power and the Glory.'

William Burns spoke only very little after this and soon left to join his Lord. He was buried in the land which had become both his field of labour and his home. Burns died of dysentery at Yingkou (Nieu-chwang), on 4 April 1868; he was only 53. The following year, Donald Matheson told Lord Clarendon that Burns' name was 'honoured wherever foreigners are known in China'.

Very soon after, Rev. Charles wrote to Burns' mother concerning the death of her son:

China and its labours, far from the ear and eye of man, was his sphere. He had literally *buried* himself in that vast land; a noble, living burial! No doubt, also, his system was spent. He had done his work (not a short one, be it remembered) in such a manner that even *his* robust constitution was undermined. And so things have just reached their natural close.

William Burns' modest head-stone bears the following words:

TO THE MEMORY
OF THE
REV. WILLIAM C. BURNS M.A.,
MISSIONARY TO THE CHINESE,

From the Presbyterian Church in England,
Born at Dun, Scotland, April 1st, 1815.
Arrived in China, November 1847.
Died at Port of Nieu-chwang,
4th April, 1868.
II CORINTHIANS, CHAP. V.

Burns had possessed little in the way of earthly treasures; the very room he died in was furnished with only a table, two chairs, two bookcases and a small stove, and even the room itself was very small. But how much spiritual treasure had he laid up for himself! As for his mission work in China, 'God', he said, 'will carry on the good work, I have no fears for that.' The account of the return of Burns' trunk to his family in Scotland has become legendary, whilst at the same time it remains true nevertheless. When his family opened it, they were able to see exactly how many belongings William Burns had left behind: there were a few sheets of Chinese printed pages; one Chinese and one English Bible; an old writing case; two small books; a Chinese dress; and the blue flag of the 'Gospel Boat'. As the contents were handled and examined almost reverently in silence, 'Surely', said one of the children present, 'he must have been *very* poor.'

In all that one reads about William Burns, there are two characteristics that particularly mark his life and ministry: faithfulness and prayer. But it is the latter feature which struck those who met or knew him above all others. As one friend wrote of Burns: 'No matter what he did, or had to do, whether of importance or of a nature you might call trivial, he made it a matter of prayer. This prayerfulness of his seems to me to be the outstanding feature of his Christian life and missionary work.'

Another testimony of this aspect of Burns comes from an article in the *Sunday at Home* periodical:

Mr Burns was a man of prayer. No one could be long in his company without discovering that. All the week long 'he filled the fountains of his spirit with prayer', and on Sabbath the full fountain gave forth its abundant treasures. There was a freshness, a simplicity, a scriptural force and directness in his prayers, that formed the best of all preparations for the discourse that was to follow. Out of doors, we have often felt, as we heard him preach, that the opening prayer of the service was like the ploughing up of the field, it so opened the heart, and quickened and informed the conscience; the sermon that followed was the sowing of the seed in the prepared soil; and the concluding prayer was like the after harrowing of the ground, fixing down the seed that had been sown.

In fact, it is not accurate to say that prayer was a characteristic of Burns, even if we add that it was a major characteristic of him. We would really need to agree with his brother's view of William if we wanted to remain true to the facts: 'his whole life,' wrote Islay, 'was literally a life of prayer, and his whole ministry a series of battles fought at the mercy-seat.'

I want to close this biography with the Memorial poem that was written by Grattan Guinness about William Burns and which concluded the original biography that was written by William's brother, Islay.

IN MEMORIAM
By H. Grattan Guinness

As gazed the prophet on the ascending car,
Swept by its fiery steeds away and far,
So, with the burning tear and flashing eye,
I trace thy glorious pathway to the sky.
Lone like the Tishbite, as the Baptist bold,
Cast in a rare and apostolic mould;
Earnest, unselfish, consecrated, true,
With nothing but the noblest end in view.
Choosing to toil in distant fields unsown,
Contented to be poor and little known,
Faithful to death, O man of God, well done!
Thy fight is ended, and thy crown is won.

God shall have all the glory! Only GRACE
Made thee to differ. Let us man abase!
With deep, emphatic tone thy dying word,
Thy last, was this – 'Thine is the kingdom, Lord,

The power, and glory!' Thus the final flame
Of the burnt-offering to Jehovah's name
Ascended from the altar! Life thus given
To God, must have its secret springs in Heaven.

O WILLIAM BURNS! we will not call thee dead,
Though lies thy body in its narrow bed
In far-off China. Though Manchuria keeps
Thy dust, which in the Lord securely sleeps,
Thy spirit lives with Jesus: and where He,
Thy Master, dwells, 'tis meet that thou shouldst be.
There is no death in his divine embrace!
    There is no life but where they see His face!

And now, Lord, let thy servant's mantle fall
Upon another! Since thy solemn call
To preach the truth in China has been heard,
Grant that a double portion be conferred
Of the same spirit on the gentler head
Of some Elisha, who may raise the dead.
And fill the widow's cruse, and heal the spring,
And make the desolate of heart to sing;
and stand, though feeble, fearless, since he knows
Thy host angelic guards him from his foes;
Whose life an image fairer still might be
Of Christ of Nazareth and Galilee –
Of thine, O spotless Lamb of Calvary!

China, I breathe for thee a brother's prayer:
Unnumbered are thy millions. Father, hear
The groans we cannot! Oh! Thine arm make bare,
And reap thy harvest of salvation there.
The fullness of the Gentiles, like a sea
Immense, O God, be gathered unto Thee!
Then Israel save; and with his saintly train,
Send us Immanuel over all to reign!

Conclusion

The aim of this book is not to glorify man, but instead to be that which every biography of a godly individual seeks to be, a challenge to the people of God in the present day. In 1869, M. F. Barbour compiled a selection of William Burns' sermons and published them under the title, *Notes and Addresses by William C. Burns*. In the preface to that small volume, Barbour prayed that it might 'please the Master a second time to bless these comments on his own Word [Burns' sermons], and to stir up believers....' That is precisely the aim of this present volume, that God might be glorified by stirring up his people to earnestly seek his face and to genuinely live for him in their generation.

I will close here with a tribute that was paid posthumously to Burns by Rev. James Johnston, a fellow-worker with Burns in China, when he spoke at a meeting of the China Mission. I believe this testimony sums up wonderfully the example Burns can and should be to each and every believer:

> From the nature of the work for which he was specially qualified, and to which he entirely gave himself, that of a pioneer or evangelist – he could not expect to reap the fruit himself. His work was to break up the ground and sow the seed, not to gather the harvest. No man in this age, so far as we know, has so entirely devoted himself to this self-denying work.
>
> Again and again has our departed brother laboured for years in some dark and unpromising field, and just when the first streak of dawn appeared on the horizon, he would leave another to enjoy the glorious sun-rise, while he buried himself in some other region sunk in heathen darkness. Again and again have we seen him thus, in prayers and tears, sowing the precious seed, and as soon as he saw the green shoots appear above the dark soil, he would leave to others the arduous yet happy task of reaping the harvest, and begin his appointed work in breaking up the fallow ground. The full extent of his great life-work will not be known until that day, when 'he that soweth and he that reapeth shall rejoice together'.

The faith and patience of this devoted servant of God is an example to the church, and to every labourer in the Lord's vineyard, teaching us not to live upon the stimulus of the present success, even in the conversion of souls. No man enjoyed so great success as he did, or thirsted for the salvation of sinners with more intense longing than he, yet have we seen him labouring for seven years, according to his own testimony, without seeing one soul brought to Christ; yet labouring on only with increased diligence and prayer, until he saw, as he shortly did, the awakening at Peh-Chuia, which reminded him of Kilsyth. His influence in this way has been extended over a larger field; and with his strongly marked individuality, he left the impress of his character and piety wherever he went. Missionaries felt it, and blessed God for even a casual acquaintance with William Burns; converts felt it, and have been heard to say, that they got their idea of what the Saviour was on earth, from the holy calm, and warm love, and earnest zeal of Mr Burns' walk with God. We bow to our Father's will in his removal on the 4th of April.

The little mound [his grave in Manchuria] casts its shadow over many lands, for where is Burns not loved and mourned? But his life is the church's legacy, and loudly calls to self-sacrifice and devotion to the cause of Christ, and especially the cause of missions. His indomitable spirit beckons us to the field of conflict and of victory, while his four last converts, the conquest of his death-bed, stand like sentinels by his grave, and long for the advance of the church's hosts.

Extracts from the Journals
of
William Chalmers Burns

Journal Extracts Introduction

The Journals which William Chalmers Burns kept, often in great detail, provide a rich source for a look into the life and spirituality of a wonderful servant of God. They were originally published by his brother Islay in his *Memoir of the Rev WC Burns MA*, which appeared in the 19th Century. This can be a very difficult book to locate and this present volume draws heavily on Islay's edited extracts. One of the values of the entries is the actual compass of the Journals; they cover most of his adult life, from pre-conversion memories to those incidents he recorded close to his death. In addition to the biography, these words taken directly from Burns' Journals should be very challenging to all believers. They should challenge our claim to walk with God, for here in these extracts one sees just what a close walk with God really consists of. Burns' words should also challenge our level of commitment, for here, with no embellishment, we see a man whose very breath was committed to his Saviour. Burns was not perfect and he would be the first to acknowledge that, but he practiced, for all to see, the words of Scripture in his own life, especially that if one really followed Christ then Jesus would make that follower a fisher of men. Burns' words should also challenge our present-day views of evangelism and missions. We are very much mistaken if we believe that bringing a soul to a saving knowledge of Christ is primarily the result of programmes and techniques. God blesses the work of His servants, those who live for His glory and for that alone. No one can read the life and words of Burns without acknowledging that this was his 'secret'.

Inverness, Wednesday, September 19, 1838

Here, if God spare my life, I intend to record from time to time the most memorable incidents in my life and in the experience of my heart before God, my Judge. Grant me, O my covenant God and Father in Christ Jesus, that it may be, through the light and guidance of the Holy Spirit within me, a faithful copy of the truth; and that I may be enabled to look on its contents with those judgments and feelings which a sight of the unerring record of thy book of remembrance will produce within my soul in the day of the Lord Jesus. Amen.

This day I had the great pleasure and profit of meeting at breakfast in his lodgings Mr Davidson of the Training School, Inverness, a singularly advanced and amiable Christian, whose labours have been remarkably honoured of the Lord in the Island of Coll, and for the last twenty years in his present situation.

I have done very little today, but I have seen, I trust, through the light of the Spirit, that I am especially deficient in the knowledge of the *love* of Christ, and am mournfully defective even in attempting to set this before the unconverted. Yet surely this is *the* truth, the exhibition of which is of all most fitted to beget the confidence of an appropriating faith, and to manifest the glory of the Lord's justice in visiting with a more awful damnation those who perish with Christ in their offer. O Lord! teach *thou* me to grow daily and hourly in the apprehension of thy unspeakable and sovereign love to me, a miserable sinner, that I may be constrained, out of the abundance of an overflowing heart, continually to commend thee to others who need thy love as much as I, and deserve it just as little.

Edinburgh, Friday, September 21, 1838

These two days have been spent much as usual, and with nothing very remarkable, except that which is most extraordinary because most uniform when we notice it least, the continued and unchanging love of God in my preservation and support under an hourly increasing load of hell-kindling guilt. How needful to be daily plunged anew under the crimson tide of Emmanuel's blood, that I may walk in the light as God is in the light! I have studied Hebrew chiefly today, which Mr Duncan teaches with great skill and activity. WM's and W's lessons take a long time at present. I saw Mr S's brother, a spirit-seller in Calton, in bed; conversed and prayed with him. He seemed very ignorant of sin. May the Spirit convince him! None other can awaken truly either him or any other. The work of grace is indeed God's from beginning to end, and all the glory will be his. To his blessed name be praise, through Christ Jesus. Amen.

Edinburgh, Sabbath, September 23, 1838
This morning rose at 20 minutes to 7 and met my young men's class from 8 to 9. The attendance is increasing, and the prospect interesting. Mr Duncan lectured in the forenoon on James 2:12. Afternoon I addressed Mr Patrick's little flock in St Enoch's school, from John 3:14, 15 and may well learn several important lessons from my experience. Last time I addressed the same meeting, a fortnight ago, I had made mere mental preparation, but, as I thought, was in some degree supported, and spoke with some force and fullness from Hebrews 10:19-22. Encouraged by this imagined success, I was content with a similar preparation today, and if the former case encouraged presumption, this does not less favour despondency. I felt little alive to the subject, my faith almost failed, and I was left devoid of conscious love to Christ and compassion for perishing souls, the affections which would have given fresh interest to the subject in my mind, and have stimulated me to go through with its exposition and enforcement; as it was, I lost heart after discoursing for some time on our state as dying under the poison of the serpent's sting, and I stammered out some other scraps upon the remaining glorious topics of the subject, and came to an end, concluding the whole service in an hour and a quarter, instead of the two hours of the preceding day. Oh! it is indeed an arduous thing to preach from supernatural views of divine, supernatural truths. The *Lord* must give these, or they cannot be attained. Yet notwithstanding, arduous preparation, in dependence on his power, in the closet and study is, I am more fully than ever convinced from today's experience, absolutely indispensable, at least for me, to prevent contempt being thrown upon glorious truths from

circumstantials of looseness and superficiality which are easily avoided by accurate composition.

My classes in the evening were fully as pleasant as usual. In explaining to my young class the first three verses of John 16, and to the more advanced one the subject of divine providence from the catechism, I felt more than usually my faith realizing the truth, and in particular experienced something like freedom in discoursing of the love of Christ and the freeness of the gospel, the subjects which I think I am least of all acquainted with, but which it is most important to understand exactly, and discourse on with fullness and affection. I speak of knowing something of the love of Christ; where is that knowledge now? Now, when my soul seems to sink back into unbelief and carnal ease? Oh Holy Spirit, who dwellest in me, if indeed I am a child of God, awaken my soul, and keep thou it awake! Manifest the Lord Jesus Christ within me, and grant that his love may continually constrain me to live henceforth *no more* to myself but to him who died for me, and rose again. Amen.

Glasgow, October 25, 1838

(Glasgow sacrament and fast-day). Since last date I have had considerable varieties of outward circumstances and of inward spiritual experience. The dealings of the Lord's providence have been uniformly prosperous, and demand the most fervent and unceasing gratitude, which alas! I have not given, and cannot give, till I receive it of his infinite and sovereign grace. I have few remarkable discoveries by the Spirit, either of myself or of 'the glory of God in the face of Jesus Christ', but I think I have still had some advancement, displaying itself in a more staid waiting upon God, and finding the mysteries of the gospel more natural to my soul in worship, and in teaching my classes. Today I have been in some degree waiting for the manifestations of God, but with little enlargement of spirit in prayer, either for myself or others. At worship I was enabled to speak more fully, boldly, and sweetly for the Lord than usual; but where again is that experience now? It is gone! alas! the fogs of unbelief and carnal affection seem to be gendered almost by the beams of divine glory coming into contact with the marshy, putrid soil of corrupted nature. That which is born of the flesh is flesh, that alone which is born of the Spirit is spirit. I am dependent for every acting of gracious affection on the power of the Spirit, as well as for the first production of the new nature. How sovereign then, and uncaused by anything in me, is the ineffably gracious and blessed love of the Godhead! My classes appear (especially the young women's) to be in rather a hopeful state, but ah! where is my travailing in birth till Christ be formed in them? Grant me this, O Lord, and then bestow a blessing above all that I can ask or think, to the praise of the glory of thy grace in Jesus the beloved. Amen.

Dundee, Fast-day, April 18, 1839
In coming from the evening discourse I was met by the father of James Wallace, Paton's Lane, a boy of twelve, whom I had previously called to see, and found, on my entrance, to my astonishment and delight, such a specimen (if all signs do not deceive me) of the work of the Holy Spirit as I have I think never before witnessed on a sick-bed, except in the case of —, Rothesay. James was lying placidly on his couch, but his eye beaming with intelligence and inexpressible joy. He told me at once that he had been afflicted for his profit. I asked him what he needed from Christ. He said, 'Redemption.'

Question, Tell me some of the particular things you need.

Answer, A new heart and right spirit, and deliverance from temptations, the world, and the devil.

Q. Can Christ give you these great things?

A. Yes.

Q. Why can he do so?

A. He is the Saviour of sinners.

I then led him back to the pre-existent state of Christ as the eternal Son of God, and then,

Q. What did he become?

A. A Man.

Q. What did he do?

A. He suffered persecution, he sweated great drops of blood, he was nailed to the cross that he might redeem sinners.

This, I said, was wondrous love.

A. Yes.

138

Q. Do you love Christ?

A. Yes.

Q. Why?

A. Because he loved me.

Q. When did you get these views of Christ?

A. Since I lay down here.

Q. Who has taught you?

A. The Holy Spirit.

Q. Did you seek him first, or did he seek you?

A. He sought me; 'I am found of them that sought me not.'

Q. Can you ever praise Christ enough?

A. No.

Q. Would you like to sing his praise in heaven?

A. Yes, for ever.

I said, There is a song which they sing in heaven: 'Holy, holy, holy is the Lord of hosts, the whole earth is full of his glory;' and they say also, 'Worthy is the Lamb'.

A. Yes; that's the four beasts.

Q. What do you chiefly desire; is it to get better?

A. No; to depart and be with Christ, which is far better.

Q. What would you wish for all those about you?

A. That they should know Christ, and love Christ, for he teaches us to desire that all should know him.

Q. Do you pray much?

A. Yes; he commands us to pray always.

Q. Can we pray ourselves?

A. No; the Holy Spirit helpeth our infirmities, with groanings which cannot be uttered.

Q. Would you like us to pray?

A. Yes, very much.

When we had done, I said I would come soon again. He said, 'Yes; he has promised that where two or three are gathered together in his name, there he will be in the midst of them to bless them and do them good.'

These are a few of the precious and spiritual sayings of this dearly beloved boy, not in the order in which they were uttered, for that I cannot recall. He also said of himself, that out of the mouths of babes and sucklings God gets perfect praise. He said he had heard Mr McCheyne with great pleasure; and that his father had one day told him something that he had said, 'When water is spilt upon the ground, it cannot be gathered up again, and yet the sun gathers it up; and so Christ draws sinners to himself when they are lost.'

I came away mingled with astonishment at the work of the Spirit, and desires for gratitude to him for his wondrous love in calling me to behold his marvellous works.... I went from this to Mr M'Cheyne's, and spent a few minutes with Mr Moody, who goes off tomorrow at 7. Came home tired; had worship, and went to bed at eleven. Unspeakable mercies, unspeakable unfruitfulness and ingratitude. The glory will be all the Lord's, for the mercy and the grace are his. 'Bless the Lord, O my soul, and forget not all his benefits.' Amen.

Dundee, Monday, April 24, 1839
Warned by Mrs P. against the danger to which young ministers are exposed; home to my studies at a quarter-past eight; got some humiliation, or rather some discovery of pride in prayer. The Lord is indeed infinite in mercy when he bears with me; to his name shall be the praise.

Home at a quarter past eight; studies till a quarter past ten, interesting and profitable, especially reading from Fleming's remarkable and precious *Fulfilling of the Scripture* regarding the strength afforded to God's saints under trials and for difficult duties. Praise the Lord. But O for a revival of that experimental deep-laid religion which Fleming valued and exemplifies so fully in his pages! 'Awake, awake, O arm of the Lord! awake as in the ancient days, in the generations of old!'

Dundee, April 30, 1839
Called on ML, in distress since the time of the cholera; she is reading Rutherford's *Letters*. Seems a really experienced child of God; said many striking things: e.g. 'The ways of God are strange; we maun just wait to see what airt he taks.' She said among other

things, 'Ministers shudna use big words, they micht as weel speak Erse [Gaelic] or Latin; it's weel we dinna need sic big words at a throne o' grace.'

Dundee, May 21, 1839

I composed and committed two discourses on Matthew 11:27, first clause, and was more than ever supported in the pulpit, especially in the afternoon, when I was enabled to plead with sinners to submit to the King of Zion. In the evening I visited JW, where I met KB, the woman who sits in the pulpit stair. She said all head-learning could not enable a man to feed the lambs; there must be first repentance, as in the case of Peter. She exhorted me with spiritual earnestness to watch for individual souls, saying, 'You may lose a jewel from your crown; though you do not lose your crown, you may lose a jewel from it.' She appeared to recognize the work of God in my soul, and spoke with great pleasure of the discourses of that day. Praise all to God! I am vile, vile, vile. O that the Lord would give me the skill of a Brainerd or a Dickson, for my present difficult and most precious duties! 'Establish the work of our hands; yea, the work of our hands do thou establish it.' How various are God's ways of dealing with the soul; how much does he display his sovereign hand in bringing souls under conviction and into the Peace of believing. One of the class came upon Monday night when we were dismissing, and asked if I could tell her anything she could do for Christ. O what a precious question, when put in the spirit of Paul, What wilt thou have me to do? Among other things I told her to be sure to ask the Lord himself, and to leave the matter in his hands.

[When he heard that one had been awakened under his sermon on Psalm 71:16, he recorded this entry]: O marvellous grace, that the Lord should regard at all my carnal, self seeking ministry; to him be the glory eternally! Lord Jesus, the good Shepherd, lead this wandering sheep to thy fold; even now do thou fan into a flame by the quickening breath of thy Spirit that smoking flax which thou hast touched with the heavenly fire of thy matchless grace, and give me grace, the grace of the indwelling Spirit, to fit me for feeding the lambs and tending the sheep. Thy blood and obedience freely offered to sinners of the deepest dye are all my pleas with the Father. Come, Lord Jesus, come quickly, and cause many to say with hearts smitten with the rod of thy strength, 'We would see Jesus.' Amen.

On Sabbath I preached in the forenoon from Matthew 18:3, 'Except ye be converted', etc. and in the evening from Psalm 110:3, 'Thy people shall be willing in the day of thy power,' when a collection of £8. 10s. 6d. was made to assist in establishing a parochial library. I was more than usually assisted of the Lord all day. O how much I would wonder and adore his long-suffering and grace in bearing with me, and in still prevenient me with his tender mercies. It is all to the praise of the glory of his grace. 'Not for your sake do I this.' Truth, Lord. 'The wages of sin is death, but eternal life is the gift of God through Jesus Christ our Lord.'

On Monday Mrs T, Mrs L and ML called and presented me with a Bible, Eusebius' *History,* and Dr Duff's *Missions the Chief End of the Christian Church*, from my female class. I returned thanks with them on my knees. I am vile, vile, vile, and feel myself most so when thanked for serving him. May he return their kindness in enabling me to give them back, with 'demonstration of the Spirit and power' the Word contained in the blessed volume they have given me. It is Bagster's English Polyglot, with index and concordance, and is finely bound in morocco.

I had a sweet note the other day from WU, in which he asks me, 'How is it with your soul? Is the glory of God ever in your view? Do you desire above all things to glorify him upon earth? Is this the grand centre-point in all your wishes?' Thanks to God for these questions thus faithfully put by his dear young servant.

Dundee, June 6, 1839
AM came with joy to tell me that she had found her own case all opened up the last two Sabbaths, and that she now found herself as under Mr M'Cheyne's ministry. I told her not to cast sparks from hell into my inflammable heart, to give thanks to God, and to beware of commending man. On Monday I had a visit from an interesting old woman, Jean D, who in her youth was a parishioner of my father's at Dun, while servant with Mr M, Somershill, and whose mother, Jean M, lived at Arat's Mill, and was often visited by my

father in her last illness. She told me many interesting facts, among others the following:

While a servant with Mr M, my father came round and catechized her, and she told me the questions he put, and the kind manner he spoke to her. She requested to be allowed to attend his Sabbath-class; he objected that she was too old; but she was so anxious, that though twenty-five, she was admitted. Her parents were both godly people, who prayed much, and on the Sabbath afternoons they used to sit in the summer time upon a green, and go over all that had been said. She said then more would have been got over at such a time than now was learned in a year, when people left almost all behind them at the church. Her father, when he could not through sickness rise to pray with them, knelt and prayed in his bed. She had a brother who went to Brechin to learn a trade, and went astray, but was hurt, became ill, and then came home and was brought under convictions of sin. He had very dark and despairing views of himself for a long time, and would often cry like a child. One day he had been a good while out of sight, and her mother said to Jean, 'Where is your brother?' He soon after appeared, rising from the green where he had been, as she thought, at prayer, and came into the house with a smiling countenance. They were amazed, and asked the reason; he said, 'O mother, I see that there is more merit in the blood of Jesus than there is guilt in my sins, and why should I fear?' This brought tears of joy into all their eyes. He afterwards died in great peace, the peace of God in believing the gospel.

This woman told me many interesting facts regarding Mr Coutts and our uncle at Brechin, what were their texts, particularly at communion seasons, and many things that they said. Regarding her later history also, since she came to this neighbourhood, she gave me a full account, in many respects remarkable. One of her sons now comes regularly to St Peter's from Longforgan, a distance of five miles. The origin of this is very remarkable. One day in winter, he and another man were working in a quarry, and happened to be beside a fire, when a person came up on a pony and, for what reason they did not know, came off, and went up to them. He entered into conversation on the state of their souls, drawing some alarming truths from the blazing fire. The men were surprised, and said, 'Ye're nae common man.' 'Oh yes,' says he, 'just a common man.' One of the men, however, recognized him as Mr M'Cheyne, and they were so much impressed that Jean D's son resolved, as soon as the weather would allow, to come in to hear him. The consequence has been, that he has continued to come regularly. She hopes that he is really a converted man, and told me that he has been for some time a member of a prayer-meeting. What a striking lesson to be 'instant in season and out of season'.

Dundee, July 2, 1839

My manifold engagements have prevented me from recording the multiplied and wonderful doings of God towards me in this book which have occurred during the past month. I can now only note a few. I went to Edinburgh on the 8th of June, at Mr Moody's request, and preached for him on Sabbath afternoon, from Matthew 18:3, 'Except ye be converted.' On the Saturday I saw Mr Candlish and other friends relative to the mission to Aden. That day the Lord directed me most marvellously to meet with several remarkable saints whom I had not before seen. On my way home I called on Mr M'Cheyne, and finding that they were dividing a sheet among them, and sending a letter to Constantinople for Mr R. M. M'Cheyne, I was kindly allowed to occupy part of the remaining space.

This was a wonderful day to my soul, a day fitted to humble me very low before him under whose teaching I have so little profited in comparison to many others, and to exalt in my eyes more than ever the riches and sovereignty of the grace of a redeeming God. Since I came home, three Sabbaths have elapsed. On the first (June 16), I preached all day from Matthew 11:28. Owing to my many engagements I had nothing written but a few sentences of the forenoon sermon; but thanks be to Jesus, on whose strength I was enabled in some degree to rely, I never, perhaps, preached with greater liberty and power. Next Sabbath (23rd) I was upon the following two verses. In the forenoon I was considerably deserted of God, and was much weighed down in the interval owing to my having nothing written for the afternoon, and my fears that God was about to make me ashamed before the congregation that I might thenceforward prepare more carefully. I cried to the Lord in my distress, and he heard me, and in the afternoon, as soon as I began to speak upon these words, 'I will give rest to your souls, for my yoke is easy and my burden is light', I felt most sensibly the quickening breath of the Holy Ghost upon my soul, and was enabled to preach in a way more affectionate, full, and earnest, than almost ever before. I resolved, however, in future to prepare more carefully if possible. Last Sabbath (30th) I began in the forenoon to lecture through the Colossians, taking the inscription and salutation as the first subject, and in the afternoon I commenced a series of discourses on Psalm 130, taking the help of the great Owen. I was much supported all day, and had nearer views of the holiness of Jehovah than ever before in the pulpit. There are some favourable symptoms of the presence of God among the flock. Two prayer-meetings have been among the young women; those among the older people are becoming larger and more lively.

July 1839
Retrospective Journal entry for July 1839
Having a spare hour, it has occurred to my mind that it may be for the glory of God that I should at last record my recollections of the marvellous commencement of the Lord's glorious work in this place in the month of July 1839, and I entreat the special aid of the Holy Ghost, that I may write according to his own will and for the divine glory regarding these wonders of the Lord Jehovah.

During the first four months of my ministry, which were spent at Dundee, I enjoyed much of the Lord's presence in my own soul, and laid in large stores of divine knowledge in preparing from week to week for my pulpit services in St Peter's Church. But though I endeavoured to speak the truth fully, and to press it earnestly on the souls of the people, there was still a defect in my preaching at that time which I have since learned to correct, viz. that, partly from unbelieving doubts regarding the truth in all its infinite magnitude, and partly from a tendency to shrink back from speaking in such a way as visibly and generally to alarm the people,

I never came, as it were, to throw down the gauntlet to the enemy by the unreserved declaration and urgent application of the divine testimony regarding the state of fallen man and the necessity for an unreserved surrender to the Lord Jesus in all his offices in order that he may be saved.

However, I was gradually approaching to this point, which I had had in my eye as the grand means of success in converting souls from the first time I entered the pulpit, and even from the day of my own remarkable conversion, of which I trust the Lord may enable me to leave some record behind on this earth for the glory of his own infinite, sovereign, and everlasting love in Christ.

During the last three Sabbaths that I was at Dundee, before coming to Kilsyth, I was led in a great measure to preach without writing, not because I neglected to study, but in order that I might study and pray for a longer time; and in preaching on the subjects which I had thus prepared, I was more than usually sensible of the divine support. The people also seemed to feel more deeply solemnised, and I was told of some who were shedding silent tears under the Word of the Lord.

I was to have preached on the evening of the fast-day at Kilsyth, July 18th, but the burial of my dear brother-in-law, George Moody, at Paisley was fixed for that day and I was of course obliged to be present thereat. His death was accompanied with a blessing from Jehovah to my soul. I never enjoyed, I think, sweeter realizations of the glory and love of Jesus, and of the certainty and blessedness of his eternal kingdom, than when at Paisley on this solemn occasion. The beautifully consistent and holy walk of our dear departed brother, with the sweet divine serenity that marked the closing scene of his life, made his death very affecting, and eminently fitted to draw away the heart of the believer after him to Jesus in the heavenly glory. This was its effect on my soul through the Lord's power. On the way to the grave I wept with joy, and could have praised the Lord aloud for his love in allowing me to assist in carrying to the bed of rest a member of his 'own body, of his flesh, and of his bones'; and when I looked for the last time on the coffined body in its narrow, low, solitary, cold resting-place, I had a glorious anticipation of the Second Coming of the Lord, when he would himself raise up in glory everlasting that dear body which he had appointed us to bury in its corruption and decay.

I have taken this retrospect of circumstances in my own history previous to the time of my coming to Kilsyth, as they bore very powerfully upon my own state of mind, and were among the means by which the Lord finished my preparation, a preparation which he had begun even in my infancy, for being employed as his poor and despised but yet honoured instrument in beginning, and in assisting to carry on, the wonderful work that followed. I was appointed to preach at Kilsyth on Friday evening. I did so from Psalm 130:1, 2, a subject I had lately handled in Dundee after studying Owen's treatise on this psalm. I believe I preached with considerable solemnity, and in a manner in some degree fitted to alarm unconverted sinners and sleeping saints. I remember that some of the people of God seemed to respond with great fullness of heart to many of my petitions in public prayer, that while I was preaching there was a deep solemnity upon the audience, and that some of the Lord's people met me as I retired, apparently much affected and testifying that the Lord had been among us. On Saturday I preached at Banton from Psalm 130:3, with considerable assistance, as far as I can recollect.

My uncle, Dr Burns of Paisley, seemed to feel as if the Lord was with me, and kindly asked me to take his place at Kilsyth on Sabbath evening, leaving him to fill mine on Monday forenoon. He spoke also, I remember, in the family of its not being my duty to go abroad as I was on the eve of doing, but that I should be a home missionary in Scotland.

I myself did not speculate anxiously about the future, but desired to be an instrument of advancing his work at the present time. In the evening of Saturday I met with one or two persons under deep distress of soul; and one of these, who is now a consistent follower of Jesus, seemed to enter into the peace of God while I was praying with her. This brought the work of the Spirit before me in a more remarkable and glorious form than I had before witnessed it, and served at once to quicken my desires after and encourage my anticipations of seeing some glorious manifestation of the Lord's saving strength. On Sabbath everything went on as usual until the conclusion of the third table service, if I remember right, when Dr Burns kindly shortened his own address and introduced me to the people, that I might give a short address not only to the communicants but to all present in the church. I had no precise subject in view on which to speak, but when rising was led to John 20, if I mistake not, simply by its opening to me and appearing suitable. This subject I tried to generalize as depicting the experience of a saint in seeking communion with Jesus, and the manner in which Jesus often deals with such. I had much assistance, and was especially enabled to charge hundreds of the communicants with betraying Christ at his table. I heard afterwards of some that were much moved at this time, and in particular of one woman who was then first apprehended by the Spirit and has been to all appearance converted.

In the evening I preached from Matthew 11:28, but, as far as I can recollect, with no remarkable assistance or remarkable effects. At the close, however, I felt such a yearning of heart over the poor people among whom I had spent so many of my youthful years in sin, that I intimated I would again address them before bidding them farewell, it might be never to meet again on earth; and that I would do so in the market-place, in order to reach the many who absented themselves from the house of God, and after whom I longed in the bowels of Jesus Christ. This meeting was fixed for Tuesday at 10 a.m., as I intended that day to leave Kilsyth on my return to Dundee.

On Monday evening we had a meeting of the Missionary Society. Dr Burns preached an excellent sermon from Isaiah 52:1, in which some things were said upon Christ's wedding garment which touched my heart. In speaking I felt the case of the heathen lying nearer my heart than I think ever before or since, and was enabled, though without any previous idea of what I was to say, to speak with liberty and power of the Holy Ghost.

This and all other similar facts I would testify as in the sight of Jehovah, and as being obliged to do so for his glory. May he enable me to give the glory all to him, and take none of it all to my own cursed flesh! The people seemed much impressed. The meeting, however, was not very large.

I can hardly recall the feelings with which I went to preach on Tuesday morning – a morning fixed from all eternity in Jehovah's counsels as an era in the history of redemption. May the Holy Ghost breathe upon my soul and revive in my memory, too faithless, alas! to the records of the Lord's wondrous works, the recollection of the marvellous scene which was displayed before the wondering eyes of many favoured sinners in this place. Though I cannot speak with precision of the frame of soul in which I went to the Lord's work on that memorable day, yet I remember in general that I had an intense longing for the conversion of souls and the glory of Emmanuel, that I mourned under a sense of the awful state of sinners without Christ, their guilt in rejecting him as freely offered to their acceptance, my own total inability to help them by anything that I could do, and my complete unfitness and unworthiness to be an instrument in the hands of the Holy Ghost in saving their souls; while at the same time my eyes were fixed on the Lord as the God of salvation with a sweet hope of his glorious appearing.

I have since heard that some of the people of God in Kilsyth who had been longing and wrestling for a time of refreshing from the Lord's presence, and who had during much of the previous night been travailing in birth for souls, came to the meeting not only with the hope, but with well-nigh the certain anticipation of God's glorious appearing, from the impressions they had had upon their own souls of Jehovah's approaching glory and majesty, especially when pleading at his footstool. The morning proved very unfavourable for our assembling in the open air, and this seems to have been a wise providential arrangement; for while, on the one hand, it was necessary that our meeting should be intimated for the open air, in order to collect the great multitude; on the other hand, it was very needful, in order to the right management of so glorious a work as that which followed, that we should be assembled within doors. At 10 o'clock I went down to the middle of the town, and with some others drove up before us some stragglers who were remaining behind the crowd. When I entered the pulpit, I saw before me an immense multitude from the town and neighbourhood filling the seats, stairs, passages and porches, all in their ordinary clothes, and including many of the most abandoned of our population. I began, I think, by singing Psalm 102, and was affected deeply when in reading it I came to these lines:

> Her time for favour which was set,
> Behold, is now come to an end.

That word, 'now' touched my heart as with divine power, and encouraged the sweet hope that the set time was really now at hand. I read without comment, but with solemn feelings, the account of the conversion of the three thousand on the day of Pentecost; and this account, I am told, affected some of the people considerably. When we had prayed a second time, specially imploring that the Lord would open on us the windows of heaven, I preached from the words in Psalm 110:3, 'Thy people shall be willing in the day of thy power.' This subject I had studied and preached on at Dundee without any remarkable effect; and though I was so much enlarged on this occasion in discoursing from it, I have not been able to treat it in the same manner, or with the same effects, at any subsequent time.

I was led to allude to some of the most remarkable outpourings of the Spirit that have been granted to the Church, beginning from the day of Pentecost; and in surveying this galaxy of Divine wonders, I had come to notice the glorious revelation of Jehovah's right hand which was given at the Kirk of Shotts in 1630, while John Livingstone was preaching from Ezekiel 36:26ff., when it pleased the Sovereign God of grace to make bare his holy arm in the midst of us, and to perform a work in many souls resembling that of which I had been speaking, in majesty and glory!

In referring to this wonderful work of the Spirit, I mentioned the fact that when Mr Livingstone was on the point of closing his discourse, a few drops of rain began to fall, and that when the people began to put on their coverings, he asked them if they had any shelter from the drops of Divine wrath, and was thus led to enlarge for nearly another hour in exhorting them to flee to Christ, with so much of the power of God that about five hundred persons were converted. And just when I was speaking of the occasion and the nature of this wonderful address, I felt my own soul moved in a manner so remarkable that I was led, like Mr Livingstone, to plead with the unconverted before me instantly to close with God's offers of mercy, and continued to do so until the power of the Lord's Spirit became so mighty upon their souls as to carry all before it, like the rushing mighty wind of Pentecost!

During the whole of the time that I was speaking, the people listened with the most riveted and solemn attention, and with many silent tears and inward groanings of the spirit; but at the last their feelings became too strong for all ordinary restraints, and broke forth simultaneously in weeping and wailing, tears and groans, intermingled with shouts of joy and praise from some of the people of God. The appearance of a great part of the people from the pulpit gave me an awfully vivid picture of the state of the ungodly in the day of Christ's coming to judgment. Some were screaming out in agony; others, and among these strong men, fell to the ground as if they had been dead; and such was the general commotion, that after repeating for some time the most free and urgent invitations of the Lord to sinners (as Isa. 55, Rev. 22:11), I was obliged to give out a psalm, which was soon joined in by a considerable number, our voices being mingled with the mourning groans of many prisoners sighing for deliverance.

After Dr Burns and my father had spoken for a little and prayed, the meeting was closed at 3 o'clock, intimation having been given that we would meet again at six. To my own astonishment during the progress of this wonderful scene, when almost all present were overpowered, it pleased the Lord to keep my soul perfectly calm. Along with the awful and affecting realization which I obtained of the state of the unconverted, I had such a view of the glory redounding to God, and the blessings conferred on poor sinners, by the work that was advancing, as to fill my soul with tranquil joy and praise. Indeed I was so composed, that when, with the view of recruiting my strength for the labours still in view, I stretched myself on my bed on going home, I enjoyed an hour of the most refreshing sleep, and rose as vigorous in mind and body as before.

Dundee, August 24, 1839

I ought to have been daily recording the wonders of the Lord's love in this book, had they not been so many that I could not find time to speak of them all. I shall now however try to do so regularly, though in the briefest form.

Since the 20th, many notable things have occurred. The church has been crowded every night, and many have been forced to go away without getting in. Mr Reid assisted me on Wednesday, preaching in a very searching manner on regeneration from John 3, and Mr Bonar from Kelso followed him on Job 22:21. I then myself prayed and spoke till near 11 p.m. on Joel 2:28-32. On Thursday James Hamilton from Abernyte lectured on the young man, Mark 10:17, after which I read and commented on a passage from Robe's narrative. Last night Mr Baxter preached with much solemnity and more of the freeness of the gospel than usual, from Jeremiah 15:15, after which I read another passage from Robe, and before pronouncing the blessing was led to speak particularly to Roman Catholics, and of our duty towards them. Mr Roxburgh was there last night. Indeed we have daily not a few of the ministers in town and from a distance among the audience.

On Thursday I was called to visit a Roman Catholic family, the mother very ill; they had been visited by the priest, but were not satisfied, and seemed to welcome me. I hear daily many interesting evidences that the work of the Lord is going on through his own mighty power. Some of the greatest drunkards have been abstaining from day to day from their cup of poison that they may attend our meetings, and they appear to be daily receiving deeper impressions. O Lord! grant that these may at last prove saving. I was told of a man last night who, though previously ungodly, had been so much impressed by attending the meetings, that his wife, a godly woman, missing him the other morning at the breakfast hour, found him in the other room on his knees, and again awaking at four in the morning and missing him from his bed, she rising found him in the same room with his Bible in his hand.

Dundee, August 28, 1839

On Saturday evening the congregation was large. I preached with very considerable assistance from God on Psalm 32, particularly with reference to the day of fasting, humiliation and prayer, which by the recommendation of the session I was to intimate for Tuesday, the fair-day. On Sabbath forenoon I preached with much of God's presence and power from John 4:10 and in the afternoon with still greater liberty from Romans 8:34. In the forenoon the church was densely crowded and in the afternoon every corner was filled, so that I could not, without much difficulty, force my way to the pulpit; hundreds were forced to be excluded. I never felt so powerfully as in the afternoon the absolute certainty of the believer's acceptance as righteous through Jesus and the people appeared to be much impressed; although I have not yet heard of any new cases of awakening or conversion.

In the evening I thought it better not to preach, in order to save my bodily strength for preaching, as I had intimated I would, in the Meadows; but being told that a great crowd was assembled, I ran up to renew the charge on Satan's hosts, and was told that Mr Miller, a preacher from Edinburgh, who had filled Mr Lewis' pulpit during the day, and was come along to be a hearer, would gladly assist me. When however I went up, the multitude had dispersed, and we would have given up thoughts of preaching had not a few pressed us to go on. Mr Miller accordingly preached from John 3:8 to a considerable number, which was rapidly increasing when we dismissed. On Monday night Mr Macalister preached a truly admirable gospel sermon from John 12:21, after which I intimated the fast for Tuesday, with remarks as I was enabled to make on the subject. We particularly agreed to keep from 10 to 11 in secret prayer by concert.

On coming home I found a letter from the magistrates interdicting the preaching in the Meadows for Tuesday, which did not surprise me, but led me to meditate solemnly on that approaching conflict with the world and Satan in which many will probably be called to die for the name of Jesus. O Lord, may Jesus Christ be magnified in me, whether by life or by death!

I immediately was led to see the propriety of exchanging the

Meadows for St Peter's Churchyard, and accordingly next day, at the hour appointed, Mr Baxter, Mr Miller and myself, after intimating the will of the magistrates in the Meadows, walked, accompanied by a great number, from thence to the churchyard, where many were already assembled.

Mr Baxter began the services by praise and prayer, and I was then called after prayer to preach. I had however no enlargement, and after speaking about the usual time under great conscious desertion of the Spirit, I came to a close. Mr Miller concluded with prayer and praise. In the evening Mr Miller preached an interesting sermon from 1 Corinthians 10:31, after whom Mr Walker from Edinburgh gave us a precious discourse on Psalm 89:15. I think the Spirit of God was much among the people of God on this occasion, filling them with joy and wonder at the free and infinite love of Jehovah.

This evening Mr Walker preached an excellent sermon from 2 Corinthians 7:5, after which I began to read Robe, where, finding an allusion to the Spirit convincing usually of particular sins, in the first place, I was led to speak in very plain terms of many prevailing sins, and especially of the peculiar sins of the fair-day. I had great liberty from the Spirit of God, I believe, to tell all I knew of the truth on these points, and O! may the Lord greatly bless for his own glory all his own truth which any of his servants have spoken, and pardon through the blood of Jesus all that we have said of our own invention, according to the darkness and folly of carnal reason.

Dundee, September 2, 1839
In the evening Mr Macalister preached an excellent sermon on Song of Solomon 2:16, after which I read Robe's narrative, and engaged in prayer more than once for the outpouring of the Spirit, which I think we received more signally perhaps than on any former night, if we except the very first meetings. There were many crying bitterly, one fell down, and when near the end, I stopped and sat down in silent prayer for five minutes, that all might be brought to the point of embracing Jesus, the feeling was intense, though most calm and solemn, and to believers very sweet.

Dundee, September 4, 1839

I had this forenoon a call from Mr Morgan of Belfast, who had heard of the extraordinary movement among us when in Ireland, and being in Scotland felt induced to come and see its true character. He and I, with Mr Kirkcaldy and Mr Fairweather the preacher, walked together a long time on the river side, conversing on the subject of the work at Kilsyth and here, after which we came into my lodgings and engaged together in Divine worship, Mr Morgan officiating with great suitableness to our present state.

Before parting he kindly agreed to preach this evening, which he accordingly did at the usual hour. His text was Romans 5:20, 21. He treated the subject with great clearness and scriptural accuracy, and added many very useful directions suited to our present circumstances. He also told me of an interesting work of God going on during the last three months in Tipperary under Mr Trench. He had called on his people to pray specially for the unconverted, and in consequence many were awakened, and already between one and two hundred had been to all appearance savingly converted to God. Mr Morgan is a very interesting and most judicious man, and we wonder at the marvellous goodness of our God in sending him among us. It is, like all his other blessings towards us, to the everlasting praise of the glory of his grace. After he had concluded I read as usual a quotation from Robe and made a few remarks upon it.

Dundee, September 13, 1839

I went at two o'clock to M'Kenzie's Square and preached to one or two hundred, many of whom, alas! were from other quarters. I spoke from the words, 1 Corinthians 15:55-57, at first with great want of faith and power, but after I had stopped and prayed, with very considerable liberty. When I was just going to begin the last prayer, two gentlemen came near, whom I supposed to be one of our physicians and a friend, who had been passing accidentally and been attracted by the sound; but after I had done, one of them, a reverend-looking oldish man, was gone and the other came up and told me that this was Caesar Malan from Geneva, and that he was Robert Haldane, WS, Edinburgh. He told me that Malan was desirous to preach this evening, which I intimated with joy to the people as they were dispersing. How marvellous are the Lord's ways towards me and his people here! He is sending his servants to us from east and west and north and south! Surely he has some great work of his glorious grace to do among us. All the glory shall be his!

Went to the church, where I met Malan, Mr Baxter, and Mr M'Leod, just translated from the Gaelic chapel, Edinburgh. Malan, after solemnly engaging in prayer, went to the pulpit, where he again knelt down and prayed for a minute or two in silence. He then prayed aloud shortly, sang, and then prayed sweetly at greater length. He read John 14, and preached from the verse 27. His heads were that the peace of Jesus was, first, a sovereign peace; second, a just peace; third, an all-ruling peace; fourth, a glorious peace. His great design appeared to be to press on believers, in the name of Jesus, the duty of believing that they are saved.

His teaching seemed to me to differ from that which is common among our best ministers, not in holding that assurance is of the essence of faith, which he seemed plainly not to do; nor in anything at variance with particular redemption, which he seemed also to hold distinctly, speaking always of Jesus dying for 'his beloved church', etc.; but in pressing us very specially to believe in the name of Jesus as the Son of God with adoration and love, and again pressing all who do so to believe that they are saved, because God says so, not seeming to notice or to suppose the case of those who do not know whether they believe or not.

He illustrated the effect of true faith in the witness of God by the following anecdote:

One day when Bonaparte was reviewing some troops, the bridle of his horse slipped from his hand and his horse galloped off. A common soldier ran and laying hold of the bridle brought back the horse to the emperor's hand, when he addressed him and said, 'Well done, captain.' The soldier inquired, 'Of what regiment, sire?' 'Of the guards,' answered Napoleon, pleased with his instant belief in his word. The emperor rode off, the soldier threw down his musket, and though he had no epaulets on his shoulders, no sword by his side, nor any other mark of advancement than the word of the emperor, he ran and joined the staff of commanding officers. They laughed at him and said, 'What have you to do here?' He replied, 'I am captain of the guards.' They were amazed but he said, 'The emperor has said so, and therefore I am.'

In like manner, through the Word of God 'he that believeth hath everlasting life' is not confirmed by the feelings of the believer, he ought to take the Word of God as true because he has said it, and thus honour him as a God of truth, and rejoice with joy unspeakable. He told us plainly that we ought not to pray for the beginning of faith in Jesus in ourselves, though we might pray for its increase, but that we must believe and pray in faith.

He seems to fear all excitement in divine worship, going to the very opposite extreme from the Methodists, saying as he did to me, that this leads men away from the simple testimony of God; and he told me he thought I had far too much when he heard me speak a few words and pray in the afternoon. I cannot, however, agree with him altogether, and I think many facts in regard to the preaching which has been most honoured in this land prove that that which is accompanied with the deepest impression of the truth on the speaker's soul, and consequently most affects the hearers, is in general most blessed for leading men to flee from the wrath to come.

Dundee, September 14, 1839
I called at the Ms and found these sisters rejoicing with solemn delight in the death of their beloved sister with all its remarkable circumstances, which so clearly mark the hand of the gracious Lord who has called her to his kingdom and glory! [Elizabeth Miller, who died very suddenly, but in the perfect peace of God, while conversing with him in the vestry of St Peter's Church, September 13, 1839.]

They told me many interesting and affecting facts regarding her last days. She appears to have fed with remarkable relish upon Christ in the Word during her last days, and especially the night and morning before her departure. I prayed with them, and felt drawn uncommonly near to the divine presence of our Father in heaven. We entreated earnestly that as the Lord had not allowed her to manifest her love to him in the world, he might show his love to her by making her death the means of quickening many souls. O Lord Jesus, hear this prayer, and answer it abundantly tomorrow, yea, tonight! Coming home at six I found many gathered together praying and singing praises. I went in and prayed with the young men and women in the other room.

I had much nearness to God with unspeakable composure of soul, which, praise be to the Lord, has never been ruffled during these remarkable days; though many of them were very much affected, and all seemed to realize eternity and the preciousness of Jesus! It was indeed a sweet season. WL came and joined the meeting with great joy, which broke in upon him with such power at the meeting last night, that he went home in transporting ecstasy. This is a sweet youth. Lord, make him a minister of thy gospel.

Burns closes the week of incessant labour with these words:
Twenty minutes to twelve; when this week is expiring I would again, with praises which must echo through all the arches of heaven, set up my Ebenezer and say, Hitherto hath the Lord helped me! O what a week of mercy and grace and love! Last week was wonderful, this is much more so; what will the next be? Perhaps it may be with Jesus in glory! O that it may at least be with Jesus, and that it may redound to the eternal glory of his grace in me and many thousands of redeemed souls! Come, Lord Jesus, come quickly! O scatter the clouds and mists of unbelief which exhale afresh from the stagnant marshes in my natural heart, the habitation of dragons, and pour afresh upon my ransomed soul a full flood of thy divine light and love and joy, in the effulgence of which all sin dies, and all the graces of the Spirit bloom and breathe their fragrance! Nor do I pray for myself alone, but for all my dear friends, and for my father, mother, brothers and sisters, and for all the people here; and for all the ministers of every name whom Jesus hath called to preach his gospel, and for all who shall tomorrow hear or read the glad tidings of great joy which shall yet be to all people! Lord, hasten the latter-day glory! Come quickly, and reign without bounds and without end! And now wash me in thy blood, whose price I cannot tell, but need to cleanse me, so

great a transgressor am I. Glory be to thee, O Lamb of God, and to thee, O Father, and to thee, O Holy Ghost, eternal and undivided! Amen!

Kilsyth, Saturday, September 21,1839
I stayed at Mr Guthrie's all night, and started at 7.00 a.m. by the boat for Kilsyth. The boat was nearly filled in the cabin by dear brothers and sisters in Christ going to the communion at Kilsyth. We had much blessed converse together, and engaged twice in prayer and once in praise.

We arrived at a quarter to one, and found that I was expected to officiate at half-past two o'clock. I accordingly preached to about a thousand from Romans 10:4, with much assistance. On Sabbath, after Mr Rose had preached at the tent, I was called on to follow him and accordingly preached for about two hours from Isaiah 54:5, to a congregation which, according to a calculation founded on the extent of the ground which it occupied, is thought to have been little short of ten thousand.

They were very solemn and attentive, hardly one removing during the sermon, and though I did not notice many under visible impression, I was told that not a few were in tears, young men as well as others. After leaving the tent I went to the communion table, which was addressed in a most interesting way upon the love of Christ by Mr Rose.

After Dr Dewar, Mr Middleton of Strathmiglo, and Mr Somerville had preached at the tent, I was called again to preach the evening sermon there at seven o'clock, while Mr Rose did so in the church. The subject was Isaiah 54:10, 'The mountains shall depart'; and I was so much assisted both in exposition and exhortation, that there was visible among the people a far greater awakening than during any part of the day.

We continued together till between nine and ten, the moon being full and the sky unclouded, though the mist began to settle in the hollow in which the tent was placed. After we had gone home, my father and Mr Rose not having yet come in, it struck me, while at tea, that we ought to have a meeting still in the church, and continue all night in prayer to God for the outpouring of the Spirit.

Some objected, but Charles Brown was completely on my side, saying that he was put in mind of that occasion on which the friends of Jesus sought to lay hold of him, saying, 'He is beside himself;' and accordingly we again repaired to the church, where many were already assembled joining in prayer with Mr Martin of Bathgate and Mr Middleton, and after the bell had been rung and the church was filled, Charles J. Brown sang and spoke upon a part of Psalm 122, and then prayed.

When he had concluded, Mr Martin spoke on Psalm 14 to those still unawakened, and engaged in prayer according to concert specially for the same class. Mr Somerville then addressed the awakened but not yet converted, from the account of the conversion of Saul, and afterwards prayed for them as Mr Martin had done for the others. I was then called in conclusion to speak more generally to all, and did so at considerable length and very calmly from the first four verses of the 116th Psalm, which having been sung, the whole was concluded with prayer.

We separated from this most precious meeting, in which not a few were awakened at 3.00 a.m. of Monday, and after leaving the church, Mr Somerville and I were forced to remain in the Session house with the distressed, instructing and praying till between 5.00 and 6.00, when we went home to rest. The cases in the Session house were numerous and very interesting.

Kilsyth, September 23, 1839
Having arisen from a refreshing sleep at twelve noon, I was told that I was expected to preach the second sermon about two at the tent. I was counselled by my mother to beware of harsh expressions in preaching and prayer, and told by J that she thought there was a danger of my losing the former sweetness, as she said, of my manner in preaching for an unpleasant sternness. I thanked the Lord for this counsel, and was told by her afterwards that I had been enabled to correct the fault. There were an immense number of ministers and preachers at the tent on Monday and I went down under some anxiety, as I had no special preparation.

However, I was enabled in private and public prayer to cast myself on the Lord, and he did not prove a wilderness to me, a land of darkness, but aided me beyond all my expectations. The text from which I spoke was Ezekiel 36:26, 'A new heart also will I give you', and I found so much laid to my hand, both in expounding and applying the subject, that I could hardly get done.

There was great attention among the audience, which might amount to two thousand, and blessed be God, some of the ministers present seemed to be convinced that the Lord had helped me to be faithful; Charles J. Brown and John Duncan spoke particularly in this way.

In the evening Charles J. Brown preached a most excellent discourse in the church at eight o'clock, from the words in Matthew, 'What do ye more than others?' After he had concluded I felt deeply impressed with the desirableness of continuing in prayer to God, especially with and for the unconverted, whom we were, alas! to leave at the close of this blessed season farther in many cases from Jesus than before. I accordingly proposed to Charles J. Brown that I should ask the unconverted to stay behind, not excluding others who might also desire to do so. He said I should do as I thought best, and accordingly after the praise was ended, I asked those who knew that they were still unconverted to remain, coming down into the front seats below to be addressed and prayed for.

My thus assigning them particular seats rather alarmed and staggered Mr Brown and, as I afterwards found, my father also and many other of the ministers present; but as no remonstrance was at the time made, and after so many had come forward that the seats were fully occupied, and even ... (a young gentleman from Glasgow whom I had been conversing with a little before under considerable concern about his soul) went into them with a younger brother also much affected, as I noticed, during the sermon, when the love of Christ was spoken of, Mr Brown's doubts appeared to vanish, and I proceeded, after singing and long-continued prayer, to exhort at great length those in the seats and also the congregation at large to an immediate closing with Christ.

In this work I was assisted, I think, as much as ever before in my life, having a degree of tenderness and affection which my hard, hard heart is rarely privileged to feel, and in prayer I was favoured with peculiar nearness to God, inasmuch that at one time

I felt as if really in contact with the Divine presence, and could hardly go on; while at the same blessed season there seemed to be a general and sweet melting of heart among the audience, and many of the unconverted were weeping bitterly aloud, though I spoke throughout with perfect calmness and solemnity. We separated between 1 and 2 o'clock from this the last, and I think, without doubt, the most eminently blessed part of the whole communion season, at least in as far as I was a witness to it.

After the meeting had broken up many went to the session-house, where my father had been with not a few in distress during the greater part of the meeting, and then he and Mr Rose continued for several hours longer, witnessing, as they told us when they came home, the most wonderful displays of the Holy Spirit's work.

Dundee, Tuesday, September 24, 1839
In the afternoon, when on my way to Paisley, I had hardly seated myself in the Glasgow boat when an acquaintance (John Marshall, Auchinsterrie) said to me, 'You should have worship here.' 'Of course if it is agreeable to all it will be agreeable to me.' All seemed anxious for this, and the next minute the Captain came saying, 'Will you allow me to open the steerage door as the passengers there would like to hear?' This of course we gladly agreed to, and in a few minutes I found myself, to my own joyful astonishment, standing at the partition door and praying with the whole company. We also sang more than once, and I would have expounded a passage, but I had a little hoarseness and did not see it to be my duty to expose myself when I had so much of the most important work before me.

Dundee, Sabbath, October 6, 1839
I rose at a quarter-past nine, and felt very strong even after the incessant duties of Saturday, so wonderfully does the Lord refresh me with sweet sleep. In the forenoon I preached with much comfort, though not with much depth of experience or present feeling of the truth, from Romans 3:20, 21. In the afternoon I preached from 1 John 1:3 last clause, and was much more assisted than in the forenoon, getting a nearer view of Jehovah, and a firmer hold of

the truth and also of men's consciences. The congregation seemed much solemnized. I saw some young converts rejoicing greatly, and during the last Psalm a young woman was so deeply wounded that she could not restrain her feelings, and cried aloud for mercy from the Lord.

In the evening I preached in Hilltown church from Job 33:23, 24. At first, and especially when I should have spoken of the Lord's terrors from the words 'going down to the pit', I was much deserted, and was forced to be both bare and brief; but when I came to speak of the Lord's love and mercy I got such an insight into the subject that its glorious grace almost overcame me; the tears were flowing from my eyes, and I was enabled to speak with some degree of tenderness both in expounding the truth and in afterwards applying it to men's hearts. I could not but thank the Lord for restraining me from too much terror, and giving me on this occasion a message of love, perhaps, to some of the gainsayers. The crowd was most dense, and many hundreds were standing without or obliged to go away. A blessed Sabbath.

Dundee, October 16, 1839

This forenoon I visited, after seeing several cases privately, the Orphan Hospital, under the government of my dear friend McDougall, with whom I, one dark evening, prayed in Bute upon some lonely rocks by the sea-shore, and a pious matron, Mrs. Dickson. In the governor's room I saw a fine picture of Whitefield, who was a great favourer of this institution, and when I went into the little pulpit of the chapel, saw the dear orphans so neatly clad and so beautifully arranged before me, and began to read Psalm 103, 'Such pity as a father hath...', I felt quite overpowered with sympathy for these dear children in their orphan state, mingled with grateful wonder at the love of God in dealing so kindly with them.

In prayer also I had considerable enlargement, but particularly in speaking from 2 Corinthians 8:9, and telling them some anecdotes, I felt unusually melted myself, and yearned over them, I think, in the bowels of Jesus Christ. Some of the boys and girls were crying, and when I bade them farewell, they unwillingly and with many tears withdrew. O Lord, think upon each of these dear children, convert them all to thyself through Jesus, and raise up from among the boys a great band of holy and devoted ministers and missionaries of Jesus! It was with peculiarly affecting feelings that I hurriedly bade adieu to this most interesting institution, running to be in time to visit, as I had promised, the Greenside Female School, under the conduct of Miss Haldane and other pious ladies.

Dundee, Friday, November 15, 1839
Had a letter from dear Mr M'Cheyne, written in a spirit of joy for the work of the Lord, which shows a great triumph, I think, of divine grace over the natural jealousy of the human heart. O Lord, I would praise thee with all my heart for this, and would entreat that when thy dear servant, the pastor of this people, is restored to them, he may be honoured a hundredfold more in winning souls to Christ than I have been in thine infinite and sovereign mercy. Amen.

Dundee, Sabbath, November 17, 1839
In applying the subject I was remarkably aided, and just as I was concluding it came into my mind that though I might probably preach to the people again, yet now I had reached the termination of my ministry, and this gave me an affecting topic from which to press home the message more urgently (subject 'Union to Christ,' John 15). The season was indeed one that I shall never forget. Before me there was a crowd of immortal souls all hastening to eternity, some to heaven, and many I fear to hell, and I was called to speak to them, as it were, for the last time, to press Jesus on them, and to beseech them to be reconciled to God by the death of his Son.

After I had intimated that Mr M'Cheyne was expected to be here on Thursday, I spoke a few words on my leaving them, but I was so much affected that I could say but little, and I felt that it was a cause of praise that the Lord hid from me so much of what is affecting in my present circumstances, though I believe it were good both for the people and myself to feel this much more. The people retired very slowly when we had dismissed about five o'clock, and many waited in the passage and in the gallery until I retired, who wept much when I was passing along, and obliged me to pray with them in the passage again. When I came out I met with many of the same affecting tokens of the reality of my approaching separation from a people among whom the Lord, in his sovereign and infinite mercy, has shown me the most marvellous proofs of his covenant love, and from among whom, I trust, he has taken, during my continuance among them, not a few jewels to shine for ever in the crown of Emmanuel the Redeemer! 'Glory to the Lamb that was slain!'

Dundee, Friday, November 22, 1839

I got safely home at four o'clock (from Dunfermline), and after dining with Mr Thomas at five I met Mr McCheyne at his own house at half-past six, and had a sweet season of prayer with him before the hour of the evening meeting. We went both into the pulpit and after he had sung and prayed shortly, I conducted the remaining services, speaking from 2 Samuel 23:1-5 and concluding at ten. We went to his house together and conversed a considerable time about many things connected with the work of God, and his and my own future plans and prospects.

I find he preached to a densely crowded audience on Thursday night, and with a very deep impression, from 'I am determined to know nothing among you'. He seems in but weak health, and not very sanguine about ever resuming the full duties of a parish minister. O Lord, spare thy servant, if it be for the glory of thy name, and restore his full strength that he may yet be the means of winning many souls for Jesus. Amen.

Perth, Friday, November 29, 1839

I had intended to leave Perth this morning by ten o'clock, but was prevailed on by Miss M, whom I saw at the Bridge of Earn, to think of remaining till four p.m., and then I thought I might as well stay all night and preach among them; accordingly I came to Perth at one o'clock, and having met Andrew Gray at Mrs M's, where I took up my lodging, it was agreed that I should preach in his church at seven o'clock. Some men were accordingly sent round to give intimation, and short and partial as the notice was, the church was crowded, and hundreds went away who could not get admittance. I preached from Job 33:24, and had unusual liberty throughout. We did not separate till near eleven, and I am persuaded that had I had time to wait there were not a few who were in deep anxiety about their souls; as it was, two men and four or five women came up after me to the vestry under deep concern.

Perth, Saturday, November 30, 1839

I this morning met at breakfast Andrew Gray and Mr Milne, who has just been settled in St Leonard's Church, and with them I walked about on the quay for a considerable time waiting for the boat which was considerably behind her time owing to the flood in the river, and had much interesting conversation. Both of those dear friends, but especially Mr Milne, seem deeply anxious for a stirring among the dry bones in poor Perth, where they are very many and very dry, and both kindly pressed me to come back to them soon.

Sabbath, December 1, 1839

I preached in the forenoon for Mr Robb at Strathkinnes, text John 15. During the first prayer I had great nearness to God. Riding straight home I went almost immediately to the parish church, and there preached to an immense audience, including Drs Haldane and Buist, Professor Jackson of the divinity chair, Sir D. Brewster and Mr Gillespie, etc. Before all these learned men, blessed be the Lord, I was not allowed to feel in the least abashed, but testified the gospel of the grace of God to them all with as much plainness and liberty as on most other occasions; subject, Job 33:24. I preached to a most densely crowded audience in the evening in the Secession Church, with more enlargement than during the day, from Isaiah 54:5. At half-past nine I went home, feeling less fatigued than in the morning, though I had spoken for between seven and eight hours.

Dundee, Monday, December 2, 1839

This morning I preached to the inquirers in Mr Lothian's church at eleven o'clock, from Psalm 51, upon repentance. It was a solemn season. At two o'clock I met the fishermen in the Secession Church, and preached to them in as nautical a mode as I could command, feeling much supported. At eight o'clock I lectured to a crowded audience in the Secession Church from Luke 7:36-52. It was an affecting subject, and not a few of the people as well as myself appeared to be in a very tender frame. On coming down from the pulpit many came to bid me farewell, with whom I was led by circumstances to stand and speak for a considerable time. Many at this time were weeping profusely, and I hope the Holy Spirit was sealing some souls to the day of redemption.

Kilsyth, Thursday, December 5, 1839

I this day went by coach from Dundee to Cumbernauld. At Cumbernauld I left the coach, after giving tracts to all on it and in it (a practice which I intend to follow wherever I go, as eminently calculated to advance the salvation of souls), and walked over the hill towards Kilsyth. I first made up to two boys going home from school who seemed very ignorant of Jesus. I spoke to them, gave them tracts, and shortly prayed with them on the road. I next met Mr Lusk going home, with whom I also prayed on the road. At the Craigmarloch Bridge I met widow Mitchell and her daughter Agnes, an old school companion of my own. With them I prayed, going for a little into the house. At home I found all well, my father absent at the presbytery, and expected to return in the evening with some minister to officiate in the evening meeting. This duty, however, was devolved upon me.

I preached from Ephesians 5:1, chiefly seeking the edification of those lately converted to the Lord. During the service my father and Dr Smyth of Glasgow came in. It was delightful indeed for me to meet, after the congregation dismissed, with many of the dear lambs of Jesus' fold, who appeared to be growing in faith and love both towards Jesus and towards each other. All the road home was strewed with little groups of these dear believers waiting to welcome me back among them and receive some word of exhortation.

Port Glasgow, Saturday, December 7, 1839
In the afternoon I sailed down the Clyde, but was in a very dead
frame of soul, and could hardly bring myself to speak for Jesus to
any of the passengers. Indeed, though it is always duty to be doing
the work of an evangelist, it is a duty entirely dependent upon the
prior one of 'living in the Spirit'.

It is a fearful sin to be going through the world with a light
kindled by the Holy Ghost to guide sinners to Jesus, and yet to
carry this as a dark lantern which can give no benefit to any one.
But ah! how vain is it, on the other hand, to hold up a lamp to one
when the light is almost out, and the oil is nearly done! May I
always be like a lamp full of oil (the Holy Spirit), burning brightly
with the love of Christ, and guiding those that are in darkness to
the strait gate and narrow way that leadeth unto life!

Before I left the boat I spoke to a young woman from Gourock,
whom I saw in mourning, and who had lost within the last six
years her father and mother, and her uncle and aunt, with whom she
went to live after her parents died. She seemed anxious, but in great
danger of settling on the quicksands of legality. I gave her a copy
of Ralph Erskine's sermon on the Harmony of the Divine Attributes.

At Port-Glasgow I found the Simpsons all well, and was
delighted to find that I had indeed come opportunely, and according
to a marvellous dispensation of the Lord's providence. Mr Kennedy,
expecting my brother I[slay] to preach his first sermon in his church
on Sabbath, had agreed to go to Greenock on that day, and fill Mr
Smith's pulpit in his absence at Rutherglen communion, but, to
his dismay, on Saturday morning he got a letter from I[slay] saying
that he could not come, and that Mr K was mistaken in supposing
that he had ever given a promise to do so. Mr K was just sitting
with the letter in his hand, and hardly knowing what to say or do,
when Mr Simpson came in and showed him my letter from
Glasgow, which I had written without any concert with I[slay],
intimating that I would be in Port-Glasgow on Sabbath, and that I
would wish him if possible to secure Mr Smith of Greenock's pulpit
for me one half of the day – the very pulpit which Mr K had agreed
to fill. It was accordingly fixed that I should preach forenoon and
evening in Port-Glasgow, and afternoon in Greenock.

Kilsyth, Tuesday, December 10, 1839
Preached to the dear Kilsyth flock in the evening from John 15:1, 2. I had in the afternoon of this day several very interesting conversations with particular individuals, as widow Miller, a remarkable old woman, who was converted on Monday evening, July 29th, in the meal-market, while I was speaking after Mr Somerville had concluded. She appears to be making marvellous progress in the knowledge and love of Emmanuel, and being naturally of a superior cast of mind, she makes the most beautiful and striking remarks; she said, for instance, 'Oh ! you must rouse them, you must rouse them tonight, just as a mason drives his chisel with his mell upon the stones; and are we not all stones, rough stones, till God hew and polish us? You roused them before, just as if you were to put a cold hand on a man's warm face.' She said also to a poor old beggar, 'Oh! you must be made new Robby; it's old Robby with you yet. I was old Betty, but I am new Betty now, and you must pour out your old heart before the Lord and get a new one.'

Perth, Sabbath, December 29, 1839
Forenoon. Preached in East Church, Dr Esdaile's. I was not left to myself, I hope. Subject, Isaiah 42:21; time too short to allow of sufficient fullness; church full, the gay people of Perth, the magistrates present.

Afternoon. St Leonard's, great crowd; subject, conversion, Matthew 18:3; more aided than ever before on this text, I think; solemnity deep. Inquirers invited to meet at 7.00 in the evening, and at 1.00 p.m. on Monday.

Evening: About 150 were present. The Lord was very near. We had to continue till about 11.00 p.m.. This was a meeting very similar to some of the Lord's most gracious visits at Kilsyth and Dundee. Praise and glory to his matchless name!

Perth, Monday, December 30, 1839
From 200 to 300 were present at one o'clock; a solemn season; separated about four.

Evening: an immensely crowded audience in the Gaelic Church, subject, Isaiah 54:5, first clause. I was much aided, there was great solemnity and some in tears.

After the blessing spoke a little to some that lingered; much affected. I was impressed by them to go into the Session-house. It was over-flowing; all in tears nearly. Sang, read, spoke and prayed for an hour. They would not go. Mr Stewart concluded with prayer, the tears were standing in his eyes; indeed it was an affecting scene!

Perth, December 31, 1839
Forenoon. Meeting at one, a few hundreds present. Mr Cumming, who had promptly answered our call for aid, began. I then followed upon Psalm 110:3; a solemn meeting. When it was ended the vestry was filled with weepers, with whom we had to pray and sing a long time.

Evening in Mr Turnbull's church, at seven o'clock; subject, Matthew 11:28; dense crowd. Meeting at ten o'clock in St Leonard's Church, to bring in the New Year. We all took part in the service, Mr Cumming first, Mr Milne second, and myself third; we separated about one o'clock on the New Year's morning; a sweet season. I never brought in the New Year so sweetly before.

Perth, Wednesday, January 1, 1840
Meeting in the forenoon in Kinnoul Street Church, Mr Bonar of Collace present, and officiated along with Mr Milne, Mr Turnbull and myself. We met with many interesting cases in the vestry. I went off to Dundee at four o'clock, and left Mr Bonar to officiate in the evening. He preached to a most densely crowded audience in St Leonard's Church, from the Ethiopian eunuch; Mr Milne also spoke, and it is said to have been a most solemn season, not a few in tears.

Perth, Sabbath, January 5, 1840
Forenoon. Sat in St Leonard's, Mr Milne on the barren fig-tree. Afternoon, I preached in Mr Gray's on Ezekiel 36:26, 1st clause. Evening, in Dr Findlay's immense church, from 2 Corinthians 5:21; very much aided in exposition and application; densely crowded; thousands went away, I am told, without getting in. Glory to the Lamb!

Perth, Friday, January 10, 1840
In the evening I spoke from Romans 5:1, but felt much straitened, and was so filled with self complacency, vain elation, and spiritual blindness, that I had to stop in a very short time and felt called on to tell the people that I believed, and had been made to feel for some days, that unless we were humbled under God's mighty hand and the people ceased from their idolatrous confidence in instruments and looked more to God alone, I was convinced his work would not go on.

Perth, Saturday, January 11, 1840
I was alone during the greater part of the day seeking humiliation before the Lord, and began through grace to discover how far, alas! I have fallen from that contrition of soul for sin which I once enjoyed. Lord, I am indeed set in slippery places. Lord, humble me and keep me from falling into the snare of the devil!

Perth, Sabbath, January 12, 1840
Afternoon. Preached in Mr Gray's from Romans 12:1, with some degree of brokenness of heart and comfort in the Lord.

Evening, preached in Dr Findlay's from Ephesians 4:30, on the work of the Holy Spirit. It was a solemn season, an immense assembly. I had great liberty, especially in pressing sinners not to resist the Holy Ghost. Dr Findlay was with me in the pulpit.

Perth, January 16, 1840
In the evening I met a great many young men in the vestry, and found among them a great number of interesting cases. At eight o'clock I visited the prayer-meeting of females in Miss Ramsay's, which was very full and interesting. Coming out I saw behind a public-house some men and women sporting themselves, and went up and said, 'You are making work for the day of judgment.' They all ran in except one young man, a son of the house-keeper; he was subdued. I asked him if he would allow me to go in and pray. I got into a large room; many assembled, and we had a very solemn meeting. They all promised to come out to the meetings at parting.

Perth, January 30, 1840
When I went home, Mr Milne told me he had heard that Mr L, the public-house keeper, in whose house I was so remarkably led in God's providence to hold a meeting, had given intimation to his landlord that he was going to give up his shop at the next term, and to leave the spirit-trade. Praise to the Lord!

Perth, Sabbath, February 9, 1840
Afternoon. Preached in Mr Turnbull's to a crowded audience, from John 3:14, 15. I felt under the bonds of unbelief during the chief part of the discourse, but towards the close was enabled by the Lord fairly to break loose and speak with some degree of faith and joy in Emmanuel, especially when insisting on the stronger grounds for faith in our case than in the case of the Israelites. They were called to look to a piece of brass as a saviour, and thus their looking was an act simply based on the divine Word; but we are called by the same divine Word to look for life not to an object of no intrinsic power or value, but to the most glorious Object in the universe, the Son of God purchasing the church on the cross with his own blood. I saw several persons in tears; I was weeping myself, and found this a blessed time. Praise to the Lord!

Evening: the crowd was so great seeking to get into St Leonard's Church that it was supposed there were more collected in the street an hour before the time than would have several times filled the church. The press was so great when the doors were opened, that several persons were somewhat injured. I preached from Romans 10:4, and felt considerably aided; though to myself the season was not quite so sweet as in the afternoon. We prayed particularly for the raising up of Jewish missionaries, according to the call of the Jewish Committee by circular, and prayed that some of those present, if it were the Lord's will, might be called to this glorious work.

Perth, Monday, February 10, 1840
The day of Queen Victoria's marriage. Last night about eleven o'clock Agnes S, Miss R, and two other females, called to express their regret that no advantage had been taken of the cessation from

labour on this day for advancing the glory of Jesus. I had amid so many engrossing duties never thought that this was the day, and it had escaped Mr Milne also. We prayed together on the subject. I met the people of God and many inquirers at half-past twelve, and we continued together till three. I spoke upon Colossians 3. I met with several people during the day; walked with Mr Milne distributing many tracts, and having many interesting conversations with persons on the road.

Evening: there was to be a grand display of fireworks on the Inch, and we hardly thought that the church would be anything like filled. However, it was quite full, and after a time not a few were standing. I spoke upon the 45th Psalm, commenting on the glory of the Bridegroom Emmanuel, and the privileges of the Bride, the Lamb's wife, and thus enforcing the divine call, 'Hearken, O daughter, and consider.' I felt much of the Lord's presence, and had a full persuasion from the frame of the hearers that some, if not many, were in the act of being betrothed to Christ for ever in righteousness, and judgment, and loving-kindness, Hosea 2. And while we were thus celebrating in the British dominions the marriage of our beloved sovereign, I trust there was joy in the presence of the angels of God over sinners espoused to the Lamb. How infinitely does the one event transcend the other in importance and glory! and yet, alas! this poor world, blinded by Satan, extols the one and despises the other. Awake, O gracious Lord, awake this sleeping world! Amen.

Perth, Tuesday, February 18, 1840
Forenoon. In closet wrote several letters, drove out to Stanley in gig, gave tracts to all by the way; well received. Afternoon, with Mr Mather the minister; and chiefly in closet; a humbling season. Evening, immense crowd in the spacious church, (a thousand people work in the mills) subject Luke 24:47; more aided than ever on the same subject. A very solemn season; many met me deeply affected as I retired. Walked home to Perth seven miles, arriving at half past twelve, accompanied by nearly twenty from Perth; men, women, and children seemed all very solemn and heavenly in their demeanour; prayed before we parted.

Perth, February 25, 1840
I drove out to Balbeggie to preach in the Secession Church. The man who drove me seems very like a Christian, and told me that of late, especially since our meetings began, there had been an astonishing change on the face of the country around in point of morality and anxiety about religion. On the way out all the people came to their doors with a great appearance of anxiety, and I gave away many tracts. The hour of meeting was six; the people were many of them assembled at two o'clock, and at half-past four, when I went, the church was full. I preached on Psalm 110:3, and had considerable assistance, feeling much joy in my own soul.

Perth, February 28, 1840
We had a very large and solemn meeting. I concluded the exposition of Hosea 14, and then spoke of the nature of the duties for tomorrow (appointed among us along with some of the people at Dundee, Kilsyth, Dunfermline, and Stanley, as a day of fasting, humiliation, and prayer), and also of the reasons for the appointment of this day.

Perth, March 1, 1840
We had this day a solemn fast, kept by many I have no doubt very strictly, as far as the duty of abstinence is concerned. We met at two o'clock p.m.. and I spoke upon the exercises appropriate to this day:

1. Self examination in order to the discovery of sin, of the heart and nature as well as of the tongue and life, by the law and the Spirit of Jehovah.
2. Humbling the soul before God under sins discovered.
3. Confession of sin, full and particular, free and filial.
4. Penitent turning from all sin.
5. Entering into the covenant of grace by the receiving of Emmanuel and the surrender of the soul to him and to God through him.
6. Special prayer for the outpouring of the Holy Spirit upon this city, and the other places united with us in this fast, the great end designed in its appointment. There was very great solemnity.

Evening: we met again in Mr Turnbull's church, Kinnoul Street, and concluded the subject. I had at this time more melting of heart under a sense of the love of God than ever I remember to have had in the pulpit, and I think shed more tears than ever before in preaching. The people also seemed in an unusually tender and solemn frame. Glory to the Lamb!

Perth, March 10, 1840

Morning. Alone, and writing letters, especially to the young people attending Miss Haldane's Greenside School. While writing this letter, and speaking of the interposition of Jehovah-Jesus between the wrath of God and sinners, I got a view of the glory of this mystery surpassing anything I had ever enjoyed before, and the tears fell plentifully from my dry eyes.

Perth, March 19, 1840

(Returning from Auchtergaven) We made up on the way to the Stanley people, a great crowd, and I knelt down with them at the roadside under the bright moon and prayed. Their love and deep solemnity put me much in mind of the first Christians. After singing and pronouncing the blessing, we parted in affecting silence!

Perth, Sabbath, March 22, 1840

I rose this morning strong in body, but with much conscious deadness of soul, and awfully assaulted, as I often am, by doubts regarding every truth of God in his Word. I preached in the church from Matthew 11:28, and had little enlargement in the exposition of the text, feeling still an inward struggle with infidelity. However, after I had closed the Bible, and was concluding with a few words of exhortation, the Lord gave me the victory over unbelief, and I had such an impressive realization of the state of the unconverted, that I was enabled to speak very closely to their consciences, and beseech them with all my heart to awake from the sleep of death and flee to Jesus for refuge. I saw the tears starting from the eyes of some men advanced in years, and felt that the Lord was indeed present. The meeting lasted three hours and a half. After dinner, Mr Maclagan, who was very kind, pressed me to come again, saying that a number of his people had been benefited by our meetings in Perth.

I drove home, praying all the way, and after an hour alone I went to the church (St Leonard's) at six with clear direction to Deuteronomy 32:35 as my subject. The church was as usual a solid mass of living beings.

I availed myself of many hints in Edwards' sermon proceeding in the following order:

I took the whole verse as my subject and considered:

I. What was meant by vengeance, recompense, and calamity, the things that are coming on the wicked which, copying Edwards in his application, I opened up in three particulars:

1st. It is the wrath of Jehovah.

2nd. The fierceness of his wrath.

3rd. The fierceness of Jehovah's wrath for eternity.

II. In the second place, I put the question, What is it that defers this wrath till the due time? In other words, what is it that keeps an unconverted sinner a moment out of hell? To this it was answered, Negatively,

1st. It is not divine justice. This has already sentenced the sinner to eternal wrath.

2nd. It is not that God is pleased with the sinner; on the contrary, he is awfully angry with him, and in many cases more angry than with many that are already in hell.

3rd. It is not on account of anything that the sinner has done, or is doing, or intends to do.

4th. It is not on account of a good bodily constitution or great care to preserve life on the part of the sinner or other persons on his behalf.

5th. It is not on account of any promise given by God to the unconverted.

But, positively, sinners are kept out of hell from moment to moment only by the long-suffering of God, who 'endures with much long-suffering'. I then came to apply the subject to the case of the unconverted, and went on to point out that they were suspended by the hand of a long-suffering God over the pit of hell, and were yet madly hating and resisting that God, and provoking him to let them go and fall into the flames, especially by rejecting Jesus, his unspeakable gift.

These statements appeared to be accompanied with an extraordinary measure of the Holy Ghost, and the feeling of the hearers became so intense that when one man in the gallery passage audibly exclaimed, 'Lord Jesus, come and save me,' the great mass of the congregation gave audible expression to their emotion in a universal wailing. I immediately changed the theme, and began, as at Kilsyth, to repeat such invitations as Isaiah 53, pressing Jesus on all as God's free gift. After a few minutes the great multitude became more composed, but as I went on particularly addressing those who continued impenitent spectators, the feeling became again as deep and general as before. To me, looking from the pulpit, the whole body of the people seemed bathed in tears, old as well as young, men equally with women.

This second display of feeling continued a few minutes and I gradually ended, a few only here and there throughout the church continuing in great and visible distress of soul. When the impression became so deep and overpowering, many that did not like, or did not understand, such a glorious manifestation of the divine power, were offended, and one man came up the stair of the pulpit and asked me to dismiss the people!

After I had prayed and sung with the people a considerable time beyond the usual period, with brief addresses interspersed, I pronounced the blessing, and asked them to disperse, promising to meet with any who might wish further prayer and direction in a school-house.

Hardly any, however, would go away, and even after all the lights in the church but two had been one by one extinguished, a few hundreds still remained in the church, who would not, and in some cases could not, retire. Mr Milne arrived when it was nearly ten o'clock and we found it necessary again to sing and pray. After we had done so we at last got the people away. I went down to Miss Ramsay's school, and there met with as many as the house and passage would contain, both men and women, though chiefly the latter, all in deep distress about their souls and in most cases in tears. I remained for an hour, and then left them all to pray and sing together, which they continued to do for some time longer.

This glorious night seemed to me at the time and appears from all I have since heard to have been perhaps the most wonderful that I have ever seen, with the exception perhaps of the first Tuesday at Kilsyth. There was this difference chiefly between the two occasions, that a great many of those affected at this time had been convinced or converted during the previous weeks, while at Kilsyth almost all but the established children of God were awakened for the first time. Glory to the Lamb! This is the last Sabbath of the first year of my ministry as an ambassador of Christ! To the praise and glory of infinite, eternal, free and sovereign mercy and grace. Praise the Lord!

Perth, March 28, 1840
When during this day I tried to be grateful to the Lord for all the marvellous work that I have seen during the year that was closing, I felt my soul almost overwhelmed, and could only think with joy on the subject, when I remembered that I had an eternity to spend in praising and blessing God. Praise to the Lamb! Infinite, eternal praise; mercy sovereign, infinite, unchangeable, everlasting! The Father electing, the Son redeeming, the Spirit renewing.

> To Father, Son, and Holy Ghost,
> The God whom I adore,
> Be glory, as it was, and is,
> And shall be evermore!

Perth, Wednesday, April 1, 1840
This day begins my 26th year. I would act for the Lord Jesus henceforth as if I had hitherto done absolutely nothing in his service. May he enable me. I spent the morning alone and in fasting. The Lord, I trust, was near, though I cannot say that I spent the season in a manner befitting such an occasion. Indeed, I can hardly dare to think of God's dealings with me. They overwhelm my soul with astonishment. I wait for eternity to study and admire and extol them.

Aberdeen, April 26

In the evening I preached in Castle Street to an immense audience, chiefly men, on the willingness of Jesus to save the chief of sinners, from the 'thief on the cross'. I felt more of the divine presence than on any former occasion in Aberdeen, and laboured to pull sinners out of the fire. The impression was very deep, many weeping, some screaming and one or two quite overpowered. At 8 o'clock we adjourned to the North Church, where Mr Wilson from Belfast was preaching, and when he had concluded we remained with a crowded audience for another hour in exhortation, prayer and praise. After this we dismissed the people, but a great many were so deeply moved that we could not get away, and accordingly I returned with Mr Murray, who addressed along with me about 400 from the precentor's desk. After prayer and singing, we dismissed about 10 o'clock.

Getting with difficulty out of the crowd, I went down to Albion Street, and addressed in a school-room about 70 of the poorest and vilest of the people in that degraded district. They were very solemn and interested to all appearance. We separated about 11.00 p.m. Though this was a day of uncommon toil, yet praise to the Lord! I was not worn out, but felt strong as ever on my way home.

I may here record that none of the ministers were in favour of the street-preaching but Mr Parker. He and his session all went to Castle Street, though I felt that I did not need human countenance, having so clear a conviction of the duty, and being so conscious of the divine support in this effort to advance the glory of Jesus.

Aberdeen, April 27, 1840,

When walking on the links in the afternoon I met some poor lads, with whom I prayed among the sand-banks. They were very serious for the time, and one of them said he had been in Albion Street school the night before. He said that many were praying for the first time, and he among the rest, after I went away.

Aberdeen, Tuesday, April 28, 1840

In the evening I preached to an immense audience at the foot of the Barrack Hill, including multitudes of the worst people in the town. I was hoarse and the situation was very unfavourable, owing to its vicinity to the public road; yet with all these disadvantages the audience were most fixed and solemn in their attention, and I was encouraged to intimate a similar meeting in the same vicinity for Thursday night, though I had previously proposed to leave Aberdeen on the afternoon of that day. This afternoon I had also at half-past five a meeting in the barracks with about thirty of the soldiers. They seemed much impressed, and some of them shed tears when I came away.

Aberdeen, Wednesday, April 29, 1840
I preached in the evening in Holborn Church; an immense audience, the result of the outdoor preaching, as Mr Mitchell granted with good-will, his mind seeming to be a good deal changed on this point. Mr M, Mr Parker, and Dr Dewar all took part in the services.

Aberdeen, Thursday, April 30, 1840
I was again at the barracks in the afternoon; appearances just such as on the former day. I preached thereafter at the foot of the Barrack Hill to an immense audience. I had been thinking on the subject of conversion, but I was led in the time of the opening prayer to think of Matthew 11:28, and I preached on it with perhaps more of the divine assistance than I had done at any time before. Towards the end especially, many were screaming and in tears. I felt as if I could pull men out of the fire; indeed, I never had more of this feeling than this evening, and on Sabbath evening in Castle Street. In order to escape the crowd I slipped into the barracks, and after walking up and down in concealment a little, I went up to some of the men and spoke to them of Jesus and salvation. I got a good many of them to come and have a last prayer-meeting before our parting, which we had accordingly. When going up to the room I met dear JC standing with streaming eyes, alone. He had run up Union Street, thinking to overtake me, but not seeing me, and being obliged to be in by nine o'clock, he returned disconsolate, thinking that he might never see me again, the regiment being to leave Aberdeen for Paisley on Tuesday first. Our meeting was sweet indeed, and our parting affecting, but full of the hope of meeting in the presence of the Lamb. Glory to his matchless name!

Aberdeen, Friday, May 1, 1840

I am now come to the end of my sojourn in Aberdeen, and must notice a few general features in what met my eye and ear. We had meetings every morning to the end in Bon-Accord Church, which were very sweet and solemn, and increased in size towards the end. I also continued to meet almost every afternoon, from one to three, with anxious inquirers. Many that came to these meetings, as well as many that called at the house, seemed in a most promising state, and altogether, upon a review of all I saw of this kind in Aberdeen, there seemed to be very hopeful symptoms of an extensive awakening.

And now, Lord Jesus, grant me and all thy people there, the Holy Ghost as a Spirit of praise for all the tokens of thy glorious and gracious presence there; and may those who were impressed by thy power not be left to fall back into their former security beneath the abiding wrath of God, but be brought to wash in thy blood, and put on the glorious wedding-garment of thy righteousness, and adorn the doctrine of God their Saviour by a life and conversation becoming the gospel; and to thee be all the glory! Amen.

Kilsyth, 1 July, 1840

I spent the day chiefly alone, seeking personal holiness, the fundamental prerequisite in order to a successful ministry. I was in Burleigh Castle for an hour on the first floor, which is arched and entire, having climbed up by a broken part of the wall. Before me I had to the right Queen Mary's Island in Lochleven, and to the left the Lomonds, where the Covenanters hid themselves from their persecutors, and I stood amid the ruins of the castle of one of their leaders. The scene was solemn and affecting, and I trust the everlasting Emmanuel was with me. O that I had a martyr's heart, if not a martyr's death and a martyr's crown!

Inverarnan, Friday, August 14, 1840

I travelled to Inverarnan, at the head of Lochlomond, where I slept. Nothing particular occurred by the way, except that I spoke to one or two of my fellow-travellers, wandering in quest of pleasure, and was generally in such a dead frame of soul that I had to remain below, and could not dare to open my mouth in the Lord's name. At Inverarnan I spent much of the afternoon in wandering about and admiring the grandeur of the Lord's works in this mouth of the highlands of Perthshire. I noticed two things among the people as affording an index to the nature of the privileges they had enjoyed. Some seemed to have full knowledge of a kind that is only to be got by hearing the most spiritual and systematic of our Scottish preachers, and one woman I met on the road who seemed to me a perfect specimen of a groaning hypocrite (perhaps I am doing her injustice, the Lord pardon me if I am); as soon as I began to speak to her, she wrung her hands and twisted her features as if trying to manufacture the symptoms of repentance. This agreed well with what I know had been the Lord's dealings with this part of the country. They have had under some ministers the very best of preaching, and some of the people retain not only the mould of the doctrine taught them, but the recollection of the deep and overpowering emotions which it produced in the hand of the Spirit upon many minds at a former period; particularly about 20 years ago, when Breadalbane was signally blessed of the Lord, under the preaching of Mr M'Donald and other godly ministers.

Evening. I had a meeting in the toll-house adjoining the inn, with about twenty persons, chiefly men, who seemed solemnized. The innkeeper was not very anxious for this meeting when I spoke of it to him. He had much scriptural knowledge, and many of his expressions put me in mind of Mr M'Donald's phraseology, but his attachment to his trade seemed stronger than his theology. His family I was much interested in, and they upon the whole received me well, though I did not spare the publicans' trade even when Mrs. M'Callum was present. I this forenoon travelled by the Dunkeld coach from Inverarnan to Lawers, up Glen Falloch, down Glen Dochart, and by Killin along the side of Loch Tay, a splendid route for a great part of the way. I did little on the way but sigh occasionally over the poor people whom we passed, and to wish them an interest in Emmanuel. I also gave away one or two little books to Highland boys in their kilt, who hung upon the coach from time to time. Dear boys, they looked surprised and pleased!

At Killin I breakfasted along with two young gentlemen on a fishing excursion, who seemed to eye me suspiciously with my black clothes and white neck-cloth, and took care to allow me to begin breakfast before them, I thought, in order that I might not ask a blessing aloud. When leaving them I said, 'I am a fisher too.' They looked grave, and one of them said, 'Oh! a fisher of men, I suppose.' 'Yes,' I said, 'but like other fishers, we have often to complain of a bad fishing season.' They smiled, and so we parted. I arrived at Lawers at one p.m., and found Mr Campbell a truly pious and very kind man. His partner equally so.

Evening, I walked up the hill, and prayed for the outpouring of the Holy Ghost. I had, however, to walk by faith and not by sense.

Lawers, Sabbath, August 16, 1840

A congregation of, I suppose, fifteen hundred assembled, though the day was unfavourable, at the tent by twelve o'clock, to whom I preached, but with little assistance, speaking comparatively, from Luke 14:16. At the end I told them that I had got no message for them from the Lord, but that I was not therefore led to despair of yet getting a blessing among them, as I generally found that when the Lord meant to pour out his Spirit, he first made both preacher and people sensible that without him they could do nothing. A godly man has since that time told me that he felt an unusual fullness of heart that morning at family worship, and thought there would be something unusual done.

Evening, we met in the church, which holds five hundred sitters, and was crowded. I preached from the parable of the barren fig-tree, and had much more assistance. A good many were in tears, and one cried aloud as we were dismissing them.

Lawers, Monday, August 17, 1840

We met for public worship at twelve o'clock. The church was crowded, though the day was very stormy. I spoke from the 51st and 32nd Psalms, particularly upon confession of sin, and the people seemed very solemnly impressed, some, perhaps many, being in tears. When I had done, Mr Campbell came up and spoke a little very solemnly in Gaelic, and the people became much more visibly moved. When the blessing was pronounced, a great many remained in their seats, and some of them began to cry out vehemently that they were lost. We in consequence continued praying and speaking to them until about five o'clock, when we thought it good to let them remain alone, seeing that we were to have public worship again at six o'clock; at half-past six Mr Campbell of Glen Lyon preached in Gaelic from Matthew 25:10, and gave some account at the close of the wonderful work of the Lord at Tarbat in Ross-shire. When I went into the church near the close, I heard some persons groaning, and when we were separating one woman cried out bitterly. We parted about half-past eight, as we were to meet next day at twelve again. A great day!

Lawers, Tuesday, August 18, 1840
We had a prayer-meeting at twelve, when the church was three-fourths filled. Mr M'Kenzie began and was followed by Mr Campbell, both in Gaelic. This occupied nearly two hours, and when I went to the pulpit I found it my duty to dismiss the people without detaining them any longer, offering, however, to converse with any individuals who might desire it. From one hundred and fifty to two hundred waited about the door, and with these I engaged in prayer. During the prayer the Spirit of God was mightily at work among us, so that almost all were deeply moved, and one man cried aloud. Mr M'Kenzie said that he almost never felt in the same way as at this time. After prayer I addressed the people in a series of miscellaneous remarks tending to bring them immediately to surrender to Jesus. Many I saw in tears, and among these a number of fine stout young Highlanders. We then prayed again, when the impression continued, and concluded by singing Psalm 31:5.

This day at a quarter to one conversed with the following anxious inquirers:

1. MC, aged 17, East Lawers, 'Oh! I am in deep, deep in sin.' She got her eyes opened on the Sabbath night in the church. 'I saw that I was utterly lost.' 'I have not found Christ yet.' 'Who can lead you to Christ?' 'The Holy Spirit.' Deeply affected.

2. CC, above 20, West Lawers. Concerned three years ago,

particularly from a sermon of Mr Campbell's of Glen Lyon, on 'How shall we escape?' He said that if they went away from the church neglecting Christ, they would be trampling on his bosom. It was this that affected her. She has been more deeply affected during these days past.

3. CR, aged twenty, West Lawers. 'I can get no rest nor peace, my heart is seeking after something which I cannot get. This began when I came into the church on Monday morning and heard you praying. I felt as if my heart would come out. I have been seeking Christ, but I have not got near to him yet.' Deeply and tenderly affected.

4. RM, servant to Mr Campbell, came with them from Benbecula (about eighteen years); was awakened on Saturday night at worship in this room: the first meeting that I had after arriving. 'I felt as if something were gripping my heart in the inside, and could get no rest since that time.' Seems deeply and habitually concerned. This we see, as she lives in the house.

5. JL, West Lawers (about twenty years): 'A word of Mr Campbell's of Glen Lyon, which he had at the sacrament (ten weeks ago), always keepit wee me. He said that Rebekah's brother asked her, "Will you go with this man?" and so he said we were to go with Christ. This keepit we me, and when Mr Campbell came into the pulpit on Monday night, I first thought, "I have not yet gone with Christ," and when he spoke of the door being shut, and we being out for ever, I saw that I would be out. I have got no rest since. (She cried out in agony that night.) I often was concerned before, but it always went away when I came out: If the Lord had not been merciful, I would have been in the place where his mercy is gone for ever long ago, to be sure.'

6. B M'G, four miles west (aged twenty-one years). Was a little touched at the Glen Lyon sacrament (ten weeks ago), when Mr Campbell's brother was preaching, especially by his saying, 'If you are missing the Spirit, it will be ill for you.' 'I did not go on however at that time until Sabbath, when I felt something at my heart, I did not know what, and I got worse and worse every day. I heard my conscience crying I was guilty in everything.'

7. CC, aged fifteen, a cousin of MC, stays at East Lawers;

awakened on Monday forenoon; can make little out of her, she has so little English.

8. C M'G, aged fourteen, awakened yesterday forenoon at Struan. She has little English, and I had to question her, through Mr Campbell, in Gaelic; yet she understood enough to reach her heart, and told me in Gaelic that I had said their hearts were as hard as steel, and how when a sheep was lost they would all go out one this way, and one that way, and the shepherd would go to the hill till they found it, and then they would be satisfied.

In the evening I preached at six o'clock to a crowded and most solemn audience from Isaiah 45:22, and enjoyed some degree of assistance, I think. We concluded about nine o'clock, but just as the people were going away 'a woman that is a sinner' cried out vehemently, and we had to stay and pray again. Many of the people were in tears, and among these some stout hardy men. Praise to the Lord! It is sweet to see how the people show their kindness when their hearts are opened to Jesus. During these few days there have been four fat lambs sent as presents, some to Mr Campbell and some to me, with many other articles, such as butter.

Breadalbane, Fortingall, Friday, August 21, 1840
In the Lord's wonderful providence, the minister of this dead parish consented to my preaching there this day at twelve noon, and accordingly we went; this morning I felt such an entire vacancy of mind and heart, that it seemed impossible that I could preach. However, in secret prayer before leaving the manse I had hopes of a good day. The people were met at the tent, but the wind being high we adjourned to the church. I spoke with assistance at the outset from Psalm 72:16-18, and had considerable enlargement in prayer.

The subject was conversion; text Matthew 18:3, and in discoursing upon this I experienced more assistance in attempting to speak home to the very marrow of men's souls than at almost any other time (a few occasions excepted). Two wicked men could not stand it, as we supposed, and retired from their seats. Many others, and among these the stoutest men, were in tears. At the conclusion, when I had pronounced the blessing I sat down in the pulpit in secret prayer as usual, but to my amazement I heard nobody moving; and waiting a full minute I rose and saw them all standing or sitting, with their eyes in many cases filled with tears, and all fixed on the pulpit. It was indeed a solemn moment, the most solemn Mr M'Kenzie and Mr Campbell said they had ever seen. I asked them what they were waiting for, and whether they were waiting for Christ. I prayed again, when there was the utmost solemnity, and then spoke a little from a Psalm which we sung, and then parted at four p.m.

The people retired slowly and most of them in tears. We dined at the manse, when all were very serious, and came away immediately in order to hold a meeting in this parish at six o'clock. As we came along the road we overtook some men and women in deep distress, as their tears and sober countenances indicated, and their iron grasp when we shook hands with them. Many also came to their doors and recognized us with evident concern. At six we had a meeting for an hour and a half in a house at the east end of this parish, when about a hundred were present. Praise to the Lamb!

In the evening I walked up the side of Ben Lawers, until I could command a view from the head of Glen Dochart to Dunkeld, having Loch Tay in the centre from Kenmore to Killin. It was a beautiful evening, and the scene was magnificent. However, all my thoughts of external scenery were well-nigh absorbed in the thought of the wonderful works of Jehovah which I had witnessed during the week that was closing among the poor inhabitants of this splendid theatre of the Lord's creation. I could have supposed that I had been in Breadalbane for a month instead of a week; the events that had passed before me were so remarkable and so rapid in succession. It has been indeed a resurrection of the dead, sudden and momentous as the resurrection of the last day, nay, far more momentous than it to the individuals concerned. After coming home, I was alone, and felt much my need of a broken and grateful heart. Mr Campbell was telling me of some very noted sinners among his people whom he had met with, and who seemed to be genuine penitents.

Breadalbane, Ardeonaig, Sabbath, August 23, 1840
This morning I crossed the loch at a quarter past eleven, along with hundreds of the people, to preach at the missionary station of Ardeonaig, under the charge of a most primitive Christian minister, Mr M'Kenzie, a nephew of Lachlan M'Kenzie, late minister of Loch Carron, a very remarkable and eminently honoured minister of Jesus. The tent was placed on the hill-side behind the manse, very nearly on the spot where it stood in the days of the former Revival under Mr M'Donald of Urquhart, and the minister who then was placed here, the eminently godly Mr Findlater, whose memory is sweet in this neighbourhood.

There was an immense assembly, collected from a circuit of from 12 to 20 miles, which could not amount to less than 3,000. Mr M'Kenzie began in Gaelic at eleven. I succeeded him in English at one, preaching from Ezekiel 33:11. I felt a great uplifting of the heart in pride before God, and though I was enabled so far to get over this as to be able to speak boldly and strongly upon the 'evil ways' of men from which they are called to turn, yet I could make nothing of the display of Jehovah's love which is made in the words, 'As I live, I have no pleasure'; and though I stopped and prayed with the people for assistance, yet I had to conclude abruptly, having nothing to say but what would profane and degrade in the eyes of the hearers these marvellous words. I came into the house at four o'clock, much cast down on account of the reigning vanity and pride, and self seeking, of my desperately wicked heart, and was driven to my knees, when I found the Lord very gracious, and had a sweet anticipation given me of the Lord's presence in the evening, when we were to meet in the church.

Accordingly we met at six o'clock. I did not discourse on any set subject, but was led to speak upon the Psalm which we were to sing (Psalm 102:11-14), and in this I felt so much enlarged, that both people and preacher were tenderly moved with a view of Emmanuel's love. After we had prayed I made a few additional remarks of a miscellaneous kind, which seemed also to come home to the heart. When we were separating, some individuals began to cry aloud. I tried to quiet them, as I am always afraid that they are in danger of drawing the attention of many who are less affected away from considering the state of their own souls. However, they could not be composed, and when I went up to the gallery, where the most of them were, I found to my joy that they were persons from Fortingall who had, I suppose, been impressed on Friday. We took them along with a number of other persons in the same state into the manse, and after prayer sent them away, though not in the best state for going to so great a distance. Praise! I saw a number of men in the church much affected, but they did not come so prominently forward, being better able to restrain their feelings.

Breadalbane, Ardeonaig, Monday, August 24, 1840
During the greater part of the day my soul was in a light and easy frame, for which I was rebuked in speaking with Mr M'Kenzie; and from this time till the hour of meeting I was under a humbling sense of pride and impious profanity of heart in the work of God, inasmuch that it seemed to me almost beyond hope that I should be supported of the Lord in his public service. I could fix on no passage to speak from, but was led to study with personal reference Ezekiel 36:25-27.

After I had sung and prayed in the church, I was thinking of speaking on this passage, but not having very clear direction to it I thought it better to sing again that I might have further opportunity to cry to the Lord for guidance. I opened the psalm-book and my eye rested on Psalm 69:29. The suitableness of the words to my own spiritual state attracted me, and I began to make a few remarks in consequence upon them. I soon however got so much divine light and assistance in commenting on them, that I spoke from them I suppose for an hour, much affected in my own soul, and to an audience in general similarly moved. Mr M'Kenzie seemed much affected, and said when we came into the manse that I had not had such an hour in Breadalbane before. Oh! how wonderful are the Lord's dealings! How fitted to humble the pride of all flesh, and teach us a childlike and entire dependence on him for all blessings! We were hardly in the manse until a number of men and women came in after us, in deep distress of soul, with whom we had to pray again.

Lawers, Tuesday, August 25, 1840
We had a meeting here at one o'clock of thanksgiving to Jehovah for his glorious work in the souls of the people here during the past days. It was conducted chiefly in Gaelic by Mr Campbell and Mr M'Kenzie. I spoke a few words at the end, from Psalm 149:1-4. The people seemed in a very solemn frame. As we came from the ferry-boat, we looked into the old church on the lochside, now used as a barn, and joined in giving the Lord praise for the marvellous displays of his saving grace made in it to many who are now in heaven!

Evening, we had a public meeting at six. The evening was fine, and the audience could not be much under 700, I think. Many had come a distance of 8 miles. I was, as yesterday, brought under a deep sense of my inability to say anything to the Lord's glory previous to our assembling, but I was aided in my extremity in no less a degree. I read Mark 9:41-50, and preached from Luke 16:16. I believe I never spoke more faithfully in the pulpit than at this time from these three particulars:

He that presses into the kingdom of God,
I. Sets his whole heart on Christ.
II. He gives up all that would prevent his following the Lord fully.
III. He fights his way to heaven through the opposition of his enemies.
    1. The Devil.
    2. The world.
    3. The old man.

There was very little visible emotion among the people, but the most affecting solemnity and most riveted attention. It was as if the veil that hides eternity had become transparent, and its momentous realities were seen appearing to the awe-struck eyes of sinners.

We parted at a quarter-past nine, after pressing on the people to retire directly home to the throne of grace. I am told today (Wednesday) by Mr Campbell, that for a quarter of a mile from the church every covered retreat was occupied by awakened souls pouring out the heart to God. He seems to think, from all that he saw and has heard to-day, that last night was the most solemn season that we have had at this time. Praise, praise! O humble me, Good Shepherd, and be thou exalted over all! Amen.

Lawers, Friday, August 28, 1840
We rode home by Fortingall, passing down to the foot of Glen Lyon, through some of the most sublime scenery that I ever witnessed. I felt awfully the power of corruption in my heart by the way, and when we were within a mile of the foot of the glen, I went out and getting down among the rocks by the river side, where the voice was lost in the noise of the gushing flood, I was enabled to cry aloud for help to the Lord. The Lord heard me I think, though, alas! I neither then, nor almost at any time, can get so near to him as I did in former times; I come rather as a minister than as a sinner. Lord, help me!

At Fortingall I met GG, formerly in the 79th regiment, in which he served at eight storms and twelve general engagements, and yet escaped with a single wound. He is known in the country as an awful drunkard and a discontented radical, and yet, to the astonishment of many, he was so much affected when I was at Fortingall that he has been with us at all our meetings since. He said, 'There is an impression on my soul, and I am determined to follow it out.'

I could not see that he had got a full view of his sins, but it was sweet to see him even inquiring. I could not believe, when on the way home, that it was possible for me to address in the evening a public meeting at Kiltire, four miles west from Lawers, but when going to the place of meeting I felt that humiliation under God's gracious hand which filled me with hope. The house was crowded, and many were outside at the windows. There must have been 250 in all. I spoke from John 10:27, and had my closed lips again opened, to my own astonishment. The people were deeply solemnized and tenderly moved.

It was our last meeting, and I know that many would have wished to shake hands at parting; yet I rejoiced to see that they seemed so solemnly engaged about the truth, that few sought after this and went rapidly off in solemn silence. Indeed, I think I never had so pleasing a separation from any people. Glory to the Lord! In walking home I overtook a few of the people. They said nothing, but walked in thoughtful silence, and in some cases wept. In looking back upon this work from the beginning till now, it appears to me more clearly the fruit of the sovereign operations of God's Spirit than almost any other that I have seen.

We have never needed to have any of those after-meetings which I have found so necessary and useful in other places, the people were so deeply moved under the ordinary services. I never saw so many of the old affected as in this case. The number of those affected are greater in proportion to the population than I have ever seen, and there has been far less appearance of mere animal excitement than in most of the cases that I have been acquainted with. Perhaps most of these advantages are to be traced to the excellent ministry under which they have been, and to their universal acquaintance with conversion as a necessary change, and one that some of their fathers underwent.

Lawers, Saturday, August 29, 1840
I left my dear and kind friends at half-past twelve by the coach, after visiting a young man on his sick-bed, a son of the Baptist minister. Many of the people recognized me as we went along. Mrs M'N or Mary M'G, who was on the road, burst into tears and threw herself down upon the dike. We had a delightful drive. At Kenmore a gentleman in clerical dress, who had been on the front of the coach, addressed me and said, 'You have very affectionate hearers; I am glad to see it. I am a minister of the Church of England, and have under my care fifteen thousand souls in the heart of London.'

Another English gentleman who was standing at the inn said to me, 'That is one of the excellent of the earth, his name is Mr W. He was a missionary, but had to come home from bad health, and is now travelling from the same cause.' He had a livery servant with him. He left us at Aberfeldy, and I went down and spoke to him while the horses were changing. He seemed a sweet, humble Christian man. 'Oh!' he said, 'that is a heavenly scene, if we had only a heaven within; at least I want that.' We parted with Christian salutations. The Lord's people are indeed one in him, though separated in the world.

Moulin, Tuesday, September 8, 1840

This morning I rode with Mr C to Straloch, in this parish, through Glen Brirachan, and then preached to about five hundred in the open air at twelve o'clock. I was under a heavy load of conscience all the way to the place of meeting. I got a little relief during the time that Mr Drummond of Kirkmichael, who had come to meet us, prayed in an adjoining house before I began; but still I was in such bondage of spirit that I could hardly speak to the people, feeling as if they were seeing the infidelity and hypocrisy of my heart from my countenance, and so being unable to look them directly in the face. My text was Isaiah 32:2, first clause, in which I considered, 1st, Why we needed a covert; 2nd, What was meant by the wind and tempest; 3rd, Who the 'man' spoken of is; 4th, How he becomes a hiding-place.

After some introductory remarks on the text I prayed, and then got considerable liberty in speaking of the evil of sin, and its deserving the wind and tempest of divine wrath. However, when I proceeded to the second head, this assistance was withdrawn, and I was so dark and dead that I had to draw quickly to a close. I prayed, and gave out a concluding psalm, during which Mr Campbell came and pressed me to say a few words more, as there were people there who in all likelihood would not be got at again. This affected me, yet I could get no greater liberty to speak and told him that I could not speak at that time for the whole world.

I intimated, when I had pronounced the blessing, that I desired to speak further to them, and that I was persuaded there must be some cause, either in me or in some of them, for the withdrawal of the Spirit of God; but that though I had no message for them at that time, I would rejoice to remain with any who were really desiring a blessing to their souls, and join in crying to the Lord for his help. No-one went away. We joined in prayer, the people with far greater solemnity, and I with some degree of liberty; and after I had ended, I felt so carried above the power of my enemies that I began at once upon the topics I had left; and throwing down the gauntlet to the enemies of Jesus, I spoke for a long time with such assistance that I felt as if I could have shaken the globe to pieces through the views I got of the glory of the divine person of Christ, and of his atoning sacrifice to rescue sinners from eternal death.

The people were bent down beneath the Word like corn under the breeze, and many a stout sinner wept bitterly. We separated about four o'clock, and I felt myself called, in consequence of what I had seen and felt, to agree to Mr Drummond's request that I should go to Kirkmichael on Sabbath week instead of to Grandtully, as I had intended. Glory to the Lord! We had some of the gentry there in tears!

Moulin, Wednesday, September 9, 1840

I rode up in the forenoon to B, the property of Mr S of Perth, where he and his family at present are, with the view of preaching at Tenandry church, near which they are. The scene is the most sublime that I have almost ever seen, including the pass of Killiecrankie, but I have no time, even had I the power, to describe the grandeur of the Lord's works in nature. I felt the temptation to be unfaithful to the 'rich man' with whom I was called to live and through this compliance unfaithful also to the poorer classes around. If we are unfaithful to the rich and great, all our faithfulness to others must be more or less hypocritical.

This I felt, and being made to cry to the Lord for help, I got so completely over it that when preaching in the evening at Tenandry, with the S's, Mrs H of S, the builder of the church present, I spoke boldly and openly of many things that the rich alone could understand, and which they would find it hard to bear unless they would unreservedly submit to Christ and his cross. We met at five o'clock; I spoke from Hebrews 4:7. At first I had assistance enough to expound, but not enough to reach the conscience with keen exhortation and reproof. However, after praying, got this for a considerable time, and the people were so much affected that all were riveted in their looks and some were weeping audibly. The plan followed was this:

1. Considered the meaning of,
    1st. Hearing God's voice.
    2nd. Hardening the heart.
    3rd. The arguments against this sin.

(a) Our losing the promised rest;

(b) Our having been long called already, 'after so long a time';

(c) Our being called 'today'.

After I had prayed I sought to improve these truths by selecting a few passages of God's Word such as, 'Ye must be born again', 'Come now and let us reason together', and pressed the people by the arguments of the text to hear and obey these immediately as the voice of God. It was this part that seemed to come chiefly home. We had an after-meeting with the anxious, who seemed to be numerous.

Logierait, Saturday, September 12, 1840

At 6 p.m. I left Moulin manse, and had a very solemn and affecting parting from this family. The servants I conversed with individually during the day, and all, but particularly three of them, were deeply affected, as they had previously been in church at several of the meetings. Leaving Moulin by Mr C's gig, I drove down the strath to Logierait, where I was kindly received by Mr Buchanan (another Moderate minister) and his sister. I spent the evening for the most part alone and in conversation with Mr B, who is a man of superior talents and attainments in knowledge, and seems to have a good disposition towards those remarkable outpourings of the Holy Spirit in Scotland against which so many are arrayed in open enmity.

Logierait, Sabbath, September 13, 1840

The morning was fine and an immense congregation assembled at twelve o'clock in the churchyard, with whom I continued uninterruptedly until five p.m., singing, praying, and preaching the Word of life. The subject was 2 Corinthians 5:19–6:2. The people were very solemnly affected, indeed more visibly than on any previous Sabbath that I have been in the Highlands; at one time many were crying aloud in agony, and tears were flowing plentifully throughout the audience. One of the addresses that seemed most signally blessed originated in a somewhat remarkable way.

As I was about to engage in prayer at the middle of the service,

I noticed two young gentlemen looking down upon the audience from a little eminence a few hundred yards distant from us, and feeling a strong desire to say something that might arrest them in their carelessness at so awfully solemn a time, I called on the people of God to join me in praying for them, and spoke so loud that they could easily hear me. When I was doing this a third young man ascended to my view, and joined his companions. The three put me in mind of the three young men who were so remarkably converted at the Kirk of Shotts, when going to Edinburgh to be present at some scenes of public amusement.

I told this anecdote, enlarging upon many things which it suggested with much liberty, and the impression seemed to be deeply affecting. The young men in my view, as soon as they heard me speaking of them, and had the eyes of the congregation turned upon them, withdrew from their position and came near, concealing themselves behind the church, where they no doubt heard what was said. The rich people, with very few exceptions, remained to the end, and some of them I thought seemed solemnly affected, at least for the time. Some of the most pointed appeals were addressed specially to them. Mr B seemed satisfied, and gave me encouragement to come to him again. Both he and Mr C of Moulin expressed themselves as agreeably disappointed, having expected to hear something very exciting, and not solid and sober.

Logierait, Monday, September 14, 1840
This day I spent chiefly alone, in letter-writing, etc., having no meeting in the evening. Oh! how sweet and profitable to my soul I find a day on which I have no public duty! Would that I had more such, if it were the Lord's holy will! In ordinary cases they would be absolutely indispensable, but when the Lord moves in so mighty and sovereign a manner as he is doing now, the mountains become a plain.

Logierait, Tuesday, September 15, 1840
Mr B left today to be absent from home for a fortnight, and parted with me, expressing regret that we could not meet again in public, and pressing me kindly to make all the use I could of his house,

etc., in his absence. This I did. We joined solemnly in prayer before parting. The Lord bless him!

Evening: I went down three-and-a-half miles toward Dunkeld and preached at Dowally. The subject I forget. The season was pleasant but in no respect remarkable. I went home again to Logierait at night.

Grandtully, Wednesday, September 16, 1840

Being tired last night, and having told the servant that she need not awaken me in the morning, I slept until past ten a.m., and got up, fearing to be too late for the Lochlomond coach, which passed up to Grandtully on the other side of the Tay at eleven o'clock, and trembling at the thought of being hurried so quickly through my secret duties. I got hastily ready, and without taking any breakfast got my luggage ready and set off. On reaching the ferry-boat I learned to my grief that the coach had passed fully a quarter before the usual time, and was already out of sight, and that thus I was left to walk a distance of six miles.

I went on with my bag in my hand, thinking that the Lord might have some design of a gracious kind concealed under this frowning occurrence, and when I had gone about one-and-a-half miles, and was passing through the little village of Balnaguard, I discovered one which fully explained his mysterious intention. For after I had passed a great number of people engaged under the burning sun in cutting down and also in gathering in the plenteous fruits of the earth, two men in the prime of life came running to meet me, evidently under concern about their state, and pointing to a school-house beside us, the shutters of which were shut in consequence of it being the harvest season, pressed me to meet the people there though it were but for half an hour.

I went in, and in the course of not more than seven minutes the room was crowded to the door by people of all ages, from the child of seven to the grandfather of seventy. We prayed; I read the 70th Psalm in the metrical version, and made a few remarks on the last eight lines; we then prayed again, and I came away leaving these dear people in as solemn a frame, to all appearance, as I have ever witnessed any audience.

There could not be fewer than 120 present, and among these I hardly saw one that was not shedding tears. The wonderful providence by which we had been brought together affected us much, and I was so much struck with the dealing of God in this and in the state of the people, that I intimated another prayer-meeting among them for Friday forenoon, when I expected to pass them on my way to visit Dowally a second time. During the time of our meeting I noticed a farmer of the name of M'G of H, of Grandtully, come in and stand listening with the most riveted attention to what was said. He was a rough-looking man, and one whom I noticed in this character the first night that I was at Grandtully, saying to myself, 'How wonderful it would be to see that man brought under conviction of sin.' From his appearance at Logierait on Sabbath, and now at this meeting, I entertained a hope that this might be the case.

When I came out and met him, my hope was agreeably confirmed. Having to go from home on business, and being anxious to be at our meeting at Grandtully in the evening, he had set out very early and was now returning in the utmost haste. When he heard that I was at Balnaguard he sent home his horse that he might be present and accompany me home. We accordingly had a good deal of solemn converse on the way. He seemed under deep concern, and pressed me to go in, though my time was nearly gone, and pray with them. I did so, and hardly had I entered when the room was filled with old and young, collected from the harvest-field. Without saying a word we joined in prayer, and so remarkably was the presence of God granted that all were in tears, and some cried aloud.

After prayer I left this scene, which was certainly one that displayed the finger of God as much as any one in which I ever was, and walked home in company with RD, a stepson of M'G's, and the boy who cried out in the church at Grandtully on the first night that I was there. He seems to continue under deep concern, and has got some comfort since that time. He went, dear boy, with me to carry my bag. When we had got to a considerable distance, a number of those who had been affected in the house came running across the fields to meet us again, weeping bitterly, but I did not encourage this, and sent them to secret prayer.

I arrived at Grandtully by five o'clock, and hardly conscious of fatigue. 'The Lord will give strength to his people.' 'As thy days, so shall thy strength be!'

Aberdeen, October 22, 1840
In the evening I preached in Trinity Church at seven to a full church, from the Pharisee and the publican. The impression was solemn. At an after-meeting a great many remained, and the impression became deeper, many being in tears. We parted at ten, but as we were leaving the session-house many crowded round us, and one mill-girl cried aloud, so that I had to return to the session-house with the concourse. The place was filled in a few moments, and almost all fell on their knees and began to pray to the Lord. I continued to pray and sing and speak with these until after twelve o'clock, having frequently offered to let them go, but finding that they would not move, and feeling in my own soul that the Lord was indeed in the midst of us. This was the most glorious season, I think, that I have yet seen in Aberdeen. Many poor sinners lay weeping all the night on their knees in prayer, and some of the Lord's people present seemed to be filled with joy.

Aberdeen, October 23, 1840
In the evening I met from three to four hundred in the Albion Street school, chiefly mill-girls, and spoke chiefly from the beginning of Luke 15. I was enabled to speak very awfully of the lost state of sinners, and the enormity of many sins abounding among us at one particular time, and the impression was so great that almost all were in tears, and many cried aloud. This impression seemed so deep and genuine, that it continued the whole evening afterwards, and though I dismissed them three or four times, hardly any would go away, the greater part crying aloud at the mention of dispersing. Accordingly we remained until after eleven, and even then the greater part remained behind me, and the beadle could not get some of them away for a long time after this. It was indeed to all appearance a night of the Lord's power, and I trust a night of salvation to some.

Aberdeen, October 28, 1840
Evening. I met with anxious inquirers in the North Church session-house, but so many came (they could not be fewer than two hundred and fifty) that we had to go to the church; of these two-thirds were mill-girls. After speaking to them all together until half-past nine, I kept the mill-girls behind and took down about half of their names. Some of them seemed in the deep waters, and a great many were weeping silently. A few only seemed unmoved. I found that there were individuals among them from all the mills in town, as far as I am aware. Surely the Lord is dealing with some of these souls. I would not doubt it, though my past experience of the deceitfulness of almost all appearances makes me hesitate in regard to individual cases. At the Saturday evening meeting a good man who works in Hadden's mill told me that he had seen that day what he never saw before: a number of the workers bringing their Bibles with them to their work! Sweet token!

Aberdeen, November 19, 1840
At eight, Albion Street school; full attendance, though I did not intimate at the mills. What a sweet contrast the meeting presented at the time I came in, to the appearance of these dear young people when we first met in this place! Glory to the Lord! The subject, 'Behold what manner of love.' I desired to speak in an awakening way, which is my natural bent, but could not, and was enabled in some degree to speak for the comfort, examination, and instruction of those who are under concern. Many wept tenderly during the whole meeting. There was great solemnity and earnestness in prayer, and when we dismissed at a quarter past ten many were almost unable to go away. Indeed, a great number went into the lower school-room, in the dark, and remained there for a considerable time in prayer, Miss C, the excellent teacher of the infant school, being with them. I was told today by Mrs M. that a person had said to her, though he was not particularly favourable, 'I am persuaded there is much good doing.' It is said that now on a Saturday night there is not one for ten that there used to be of these young women walking in the streets! Praise!

Aberdeen, November 22, 1840

Evening. I preached for Mr Foote in the East Church at six o'clock: a collection for his infant school. The sermon was therefore advertised. The church was choked as soon as opened. There could not be fewer than two thousand five hundred, a great number of whom were men. I preached from Romans 2:4, 5. At eight o'clock, I had to divide the subject in order to allow those to retire who needed. As many nearly came in as went out, and we continued till nine. I saw no men go away. There was a fixed and solemn attention to plain and momentous truths throughout, and some girls cried out. Praise to the Lord!

When I came out I heard a young man in the street, with a curse, saying, 'There is the rascal himself.' I went and spoke kindly to him, saying he did me no ill, but himself a great deal. He went along with me and spoke a little more seriously, saying, 'Perhaps I'll turn to God too.' Turn him and he shall be turned. Praise!

Aberdeen, November 23, 1840

Evening. At eight we met in the church Bon-accord with anxious inquirers, but in consequence of the movement so publicly seen on Saturday night, there were so many came as nearly to crowd the church, and among these many gentlemen drawn by curiosity. I read the 12th of Zechariah beginning with verse 9, and spoke upon it at first more textually, and afterwards with greater variety and latitude, and I obtained so great liberty that I spoke in a manner I have hardly ever done before. We remained speaking and praying until half-past eleven p.m., and hardly one even of the scoffers went away; many, even gentlemen, remained riveted to the spot, evidently having a witness in their consciences to the truth. There were some avowed infidels present! Glory to the Lord! There would have been a great outcry among the young people, had I not at the beginning, and frequently as I went on, debarred them from crying out that others might hear and be benefited. Many sighed and wept aloud.

Aberdeen, Wednesday, November 25, 1840
Heard that the Dudhope Church is open to me at Dundee. At the prayer-meeting spoke on the last chapter of 1st Thessalonians. Tender weeping among many, nay almost all, when I intimated my proposed departure. We fixed Friday for a day of fasting. Oh! may it be indeed so. Many shook hands with me, young and old, rich ('not many') and poor, when I came out, with tender weeping. Praise! Praise! Oh! may the week that remains to me here be pentecostal! Come Jesus! Amen.

Aberdeen, Saturday, December 5, 1840
Though I was very late up last night (this morning), and had but a short time for sleep, I awoke of my own accord at the proper time quite refreshed, and set out at twenty minutes to seven with the Dundee Mail. A number of my young friends had found out the time of my departure, and stood by on the pavement in tears. The mockery of many around made our tongues silent: we looked at each other, with Jesus in our hearts' eye I hope, and wept.

Newcastle, Thursday, September 23, 1841
During the day I was very weak in body, and was tempted to think of neglecting an opportunity of doing good at the cattle-show, which is held here this day. But the passage turned up, 'If thou say, Behold, I knew it not', and I was compelled to go. I found that there was no opportunity for preaching, as the show was within a park, and the people outside were staying but a few minutes. Alas! perhaps it may be found in the day of God that there was opportunity. Certainly the showmen found an opportunity of attracting many. However, I only gave away tracts, spoke to the people here and there, and intimated that I would preach in the cloth-market in the evening, which is at the end of the corn-market, the place where, at three p.m., about 1000 were to dine together. The tracts were received by high and low.

After dinner I felt my strength of body renewed, and had hope of something being done of God in the evening. A little after six we went to the scene of action, and found a great crowd around the place, many of them trying to see in through the windows, and multitudes waiting for the music at interval. I thought of heaven lighted with the brightness of a thousand suns, and of poor lost souls longing to be in when it is too late, and forced to hear from afar the joyful praises of the redeemed, loud as the noise of many waters. We had no sooner begun than an immense crowd gathered round.

Some of the enemies were enraged and urged the police to interfere, crying, 'Down with him, down with him.' The policeman told me that the people were disturbed by us within, but this was so absurd that he did not insist on it, and as he could not find us guilty of a breach of the peace, he soon went away. But although the enemy could not oppose us by legal force, they did not cease to show their deadly hatred of what was said and done. Once a stone was thrown, again a quantity of manure, which espattered my clothes.

Afterwards, in the time of prayer, when we were prevailing against them without hand, they raised a burst of horrid laughter, and pushed the crowd at the side on me with the view of overthrowing the pulpit. At this time I had to pause in the prayer, and when I began to tell them that they could do nothing without the Lord's permission, and that all they did would promote his cause, they were quieted for a time, and I was led out to speak with greater power, perhaps, than ever before in Newcastle, putting the sword into the very heart and bowels of the town's iniquities. At this time, and ever after it until ten o'clock, when we parted, there was the greatest solemnity, and a deep impression, and though I was frequently interrupted with questions, they all tended to bring out in a marvellous way the truth of God, so that they who put them were silenced and the people rejoiced.

During the first hour and a half we were obliged to contend, at intervals, with a tumult of people all around the music in the Corn-market, and the movements of a travelling show taking up its encampment close to us. Even amid those trials, although increased by the contradiction of sinners, I was enabled not to waver nor faint; afterward, however, the meeting in the market broke up, the show people were quiet, the streets were nearly empty, and we worshipped the Lord amid solemn silence for another hour and half. At this time the singing was truly sublime, and the whole scene, when contrasted with what it had lately been, was fitted to deepen the impression of the Word in the hand of the Spirit. I did not speak on any text, but used the various circumstances of the feast so near as to set off by way of comparison and contrast the feast of fat things on Mount Zion. I did not proceed regularly, but from time to time noticed such topics as these:

That feast is for the body, this is for the soul; that is one of which you easily take too much, in this you cannot exceed; that is soon over, this will last eternally; that would tire and nauseate if often repeated, this becomes sweeter every day; that is only open to those who can pay for a place, this is provided freely for the poor: it is made free not because it is of little value, but because it is so costly that no money can buy it, and in order that it may be a feast for all; that is made on bullocks and fatlings, but this, oh! wonder of wonders, is made on the body and blood of God's own Son; the greatest sinners are welcome to it now, and the greater they have been, they will sit nearer the head of the table as honoured guests, in order that the more the grace and mercy of Jehovah may be displayed to view!

Newcastle, Friday, September 24, 1841
Sometimes when we think we are much assisted, there may be less divine power attending the word than when we are ready to conclude nothing has been done. I trust, however, that the Lord is bringing me nearer to the town, and that soon his own artillery may be opening fire with effect on its central towers and carrying alarm into its citadel! It is not at once that we can come into close conflict with such an enemy, and time is needed to study the enemy's position and weak points, that the fire may take full effect. The Captain of the Lord's hosts is all-wise to direct, and all-powerful to execute. He will work, and who shall let it? Who art thou, oh great mountain? Before Zerubbabel thou shalt become a plain! And he shall bring forth the top stone with shoutings of grace, grace unto it.

Oh! how glorious a sight to behold this town awakened from its deep sleep, and calling upon God with the whole heart! 'The waste cities shall be filled with flocks of men!' Be it unto us according to thy Word. Amen.

Newcastle, Sabbath, September 26, 1841
At five I went out to preach at the Spittal, as a man having no strength, yea, as a worm and no man, saying to Mr S, I never was so low as this. If it were so that I were truly humbled, it would be different, but I am dead, and that is all. I could not fix upon a text; indeed, every door of hope seemed closed, and I knew that God, and he only, could grant deliverance. I found many already assembled, and in the course of a very short time the crowd became much greater than on any former day, and continued so, and even increasing to the end. I thought of preaching on, 'Seeing, therefore, that we have a great high-priest,' but when I opened the Bible after prayer, my eye rested on Revelation 20:15, and this I fixed on, with dawnings of hope that the Lord would again speak by my unclean lips. I began from these sublime and awful words, 'And I saw a great white throne, and him that sat on it', making some simple remarks on the throne, its greatness, its whiteness, etc.

After prayer, I resumed, and spoke a little with an increasing sense of the divine presence and power on the rising of the dead, our individual rising and appearing at the dread bar of judgment. We then prayed again, and in doing so I felt more, perhaps, than since I came to Newcastle, as if a direct communication were opened between my soul and the Divine Mind. My heart was truly drawn out and up to God for the advancement of Emmanuel's glory, even more than for the salvation of guilty worms, as a heart-satisfying end. After this I got closer still to the people, and was enabled in a way quite new to me here, to open up the sins of the town, their deformity, their dreadful working, and inconceivably awful issues in eternity. I also found myself in an agony to compel sinners to come to Jesus now, and not even the next hour, which I felt was not man's but God's.

Indeed, I felt so much that I could almost have torn the pulpit to pieces, and the audience seemed to sympathize throughout. Oh! it was a glorious, an awfully glorious scene! The fleecy clouds were showing here and there bright stars, and the harvest moon was diffusing a sombre peaceful light upon the quiet world around us. We dying, and yet immortal creatures, were contemplating the eternity before us, looking to the appearance of the Son of Man in the clouds, conceiving ourselves placed at his bar, wondering and thinking what would be our sentence, and whether we would rise with him to heaven, or be drawn from him into hell; some were, I hope, opening their eyes to their awful destiny as sinners, and on the very point of seeking refuge for eternity from the wrath of God in the cleft Rock of Ages. I trust that some were saved, I have no doubt that God was with us of a truth.

At a quarter to nine we closed, and as we had remained so long in the open air, I thought it better not to meet in the church as we intended, but to retire direct to our closets. After I had been a few minutes in the house, two friends came to me from the church, and told me that it was nearly full with a congregation entirely different from what I had had in the open air, and that they had been waiting for me since seven o'clock. I had again, accordingly, to go out in the Lord's name, and I spoke on the same as in the open air, though by no means with the same consciousness of the divine presence. We came out after a solemn meeting at a quarter to ten.

Edinburgh, Tuesday, November 16, 1841
Today I was chiefly occupied, as far as business is concerned, in preparing for the press, the letters I sent some time ago to the Greenside Place School.

In taking the air I walked over the scenes which were indeed fitted to speak aloud of mercy to my favoured soul. I walked along York Place, and looked up to the windows of the room (No. 41, west side, upper flat) where, when reading Pike's *Early Piety* on a Sabbath afternoon, I think about the middle of December, 1831, an arrow from the quiver of the King of Zion was shot by his Almighty sovereign hand through my heart, though it was hard enough to resist all inferior means of salvation.

Who can understand the feelings with which I again revisited the spot. Alas! the windows in the roof above met my eye, as the place where a few months afterwards (in 1832) poor Uncle Alexander died in one day of cholera! Oh! what a contrast between the scenes of mercy and judgment exhibited by God in places so near each other!

From this I walked down and revisited my old lodgings, No. 69 Broughton Place, where my earliest days as a child of grace were spent, and where first the Spirit of God shone with full light upon the glory of Jesus as a Saviour for such as I was. This was, I think, about the 7th of January, 1832.

Although it was then, I remember, that the light of God first shone fully and transportingly on his Word, and into my heart, I was never from the beginning, three weeks before, in utter darkness, but felt that God had always been willing to save me, that I was a self-murderer, and that now he was in his own sovereignty touching my heart and drawing me to himself for his own glory; and again, though about the time mentioned, I remembered to have beheld transporting wonders in God's law, yet my peace following on from this was far different indeed from a settled quiet frame of mind. I had many fears and many awful struggles with sin and Satan, and many sleepless nights of mingling joy and fear, and faith and hope, and love. Ebenezer! Hallelujah! Hallelujah! Amen.

Edinburgh, Wednesday, November 17, 1841
In many ways God prepared the way for me, but as yet I am fully conscious that my heart was spiritually dead. However, the set time came. I sat down, with solemn impressions arising from the causes now mentioned, to read a part of Pike's *Early Piety*, which my dear father had given me at leaving home (Ah! little did he know what use God was to make of it; little did the author of that solemn treatise know one of the purposes for which he wrote it), and in one moment, while gazing on a solemn passage in it, my inmost soul was in one instant pierced as with a dart. God had apprehended me. I felt the conviction of my lost estate rushing through me with restless power.

I left the room and retired to a bedroom, there to pour out my heart for the first time with many tears in a genuine heart-rending cry for mercy. From the first moment of this wonderful experience I had the inspiring hope of being saved by a sovereign and infinitely gracious God. and in the same instant almost I felt that I must leave my present occupation, and devote myself to Jesus in the ministry of that glorious gospel by which I had been saved.

From that day to this, blessed be Jehovah, I have been conscious more or less deeply of the possession of a new and holy principle, leading me to live by the faith of Jesus to the glory of God, and in the communion of the Holy Ghost. Salvation unto our God, who sitteth on the throne, and unto the Lamb!

Monday, April 8, 1844. At Rev. W. B. Kirkpatrick's, 34 Wellington Street, Dublin

On Saturday, after being here an hour or two, I thought of going to preach in the open air, but on going through the streets thought it better to wait a little until my way should open more gradually. Yesterday I preached for Mr Kirkpatrick at twelve, on 'Go ye into all the world', and in the evening in Adelaide Road Church, on John 3, regeneration. I had assistance on both occasions, and in coming home at night spoke to numbers. I found them a very engaging people, very open and frank, and accessible to kindness. O that Jesus may be glorified among them!

This evening I felt the hand of the Lord laid upon me so powerfully that I could not but go forth to attempt entering fairly on his work. I went down to the quay to look out for a suitable place to preach, and having found one I tried to begin, urged by his word, 'Preach the Word'. The enmity which even the attempt to open my mouth provoked showed what I may look for if I do the Lord's will. When I asked some sailors if they would attend they seemed disposed, but shrunk away, saying, 'This is a bad part of the world, for there are too many on the other side of the house.' In coming away to the meeting in the chapel, I asked the Lord to direct me to some true child of God, not a minister, who might go with me when I next attempt this work, and as soon as I got to the church I was introduced to one of the elders, who seems the very person. After the meeting, again I met with another, who seems equally desirable. The meeting was very sweet. I spoke a little on the account of Hagar and her son, Genesis 21, prayed, and was followed by Mr K in prayer. He is a man of genuine piety and very considerable power.

Dublin, Tuesday, April 9, 1844
During this day my path has opened a little, or rather not a little, farther. During the former part of the day I wrote letters to Scotland. Was alone with the Lord, and also traversed the city that I might get a full view of its character, naturally and morally, which is always most easily done before you become known. I conversed with Mr Drysdale, the elder to whom I alluded above as a man of God. I spent an hour with him in his workshop alone. He gave me an awful account of the difficulties of outdoor preaching in Dublin, but after much converse I felt that I must make the attempt. He would gladly have gone with me, but was engaged this evening at the great meeting in connection with the Presbyterian marriage question, and thus I was left quite alone.

However, I went, looking to the Lord, and took up my position on the open ground to the west of the custom-house, laid my hat on the ground, and standing a few paces from the footpath began to read, 'It is appointed unto men once to die.' I had soon a large and most interesting assembly, but, as usual, the Romanists introduced their questions, and when the answers came too near them they began to make a rush with the view of putting me down. A police officer also came and advised me to remove. I said I believed that I was trespassing no law, that that was the ground where Father Matthew spoke, and that I would not remove unless he had authority to stop me. He seemed to be a Romanist, and was evidently set on putting me down, so that after throwing the responsibility on him, and telling the people where I would preach tomorrow, I came away with a disburdened conscience. Dear people! they seemed intent on hearing, and followed me far on my way home despite of all I could do.

Dublin, Friday, April 12, 1844
Half-past one o'clock this morning I awoke under a powerful assault of despondency and unbelief, tempted to say, Let me sit still and take things in the ordinary way. However, at worship, the fifth chapter of Hebrews, read by Mr K, particularly the words, 'Be followers of them who through faith and patience are now inheriting the promises,' quickened me again. We had some interesting

conversation on the need of perseverance, in this taking a lesson from O'Connell, and at half-past nine I went down in the name of Jesus to the scene of last night's meeting. I asked one captain to give me his ship to preach in, but he refused.

I was then standing in doubt to what ship to go to next, when I saw some poor Romanists, emigrants, I suppose, on board another vessel, who seemed to know me, and were mocking. I asked them how they were so unwilling to hear the Word of God; they said they loved it, but not from me, that I could not preach it, etc. This opened the way. With all their confidence they mingled many oaths, which I told them certainly showed that they were not on the right way. A crowd gathered, and I had the best hour among them that I have had in Dublin. I was greatly aided in gaining their confidence.

They threatened to throw me into the river at first, but I told them I did not mind that: they treated my Master worse. One asked me for my commission; I pointed to 'Let him that heareth say, Come'. One said something vile; I said, 'You know that when you go to confession you must confess that as a sin.' Another, hearing of confession, and thinking that I was speaking against it, said, 'What do you know about confession?' I said, 'Not much; but I am saying no more than I know,' and repeated what he had said. He was pleased. One said, 'You must be saved by prayer and fasting'; I affirmed it, but showed the infinitely higher place of the blood of Jesus. One pressed me to prove that the Bible was the Word of God, wishing to bring me under church authority; I said I would do so if he denied it, but that as we both admitted this, why should I prove it, and so we got to more practical and personal matters. I was so full of God's joy in all this that I could not but smile, or rather laugh, in speaking to them; they wondered at this and said, 'he is a good man, we cannot make him angry.' I told them I would come back again at the dinner-hour and speak again; and so we parted. This was a good beginning.

At twelve we had a very good prayer-meeting, and all that seems needful is faith, and patience, and prayer. I am just about to return again to the field; but ah! I must go deeper this time, and be prepared for the worst that the enemy can devise or execute. 'They overcame him by the blood of the Lamb and by the word of their testimony;

and they loved not their lives unto the death.' Oh! to be enabled thus to fight and overcome!

Evening. The public duty of the day is now over, and I have abundant cause to sing of mercy. At the dinner-hour I got a good many to hear, and had increasing assistance. In the evening I got free of all controversies, and spoke with divine relish on the love of God: 'God commendeth his love toward us.' We met with some opposition; among other things, some one threw a pailful of water at me from a ship's side, but it did not harm me. The impression was greater than before, and though the policeman who first put me down came near, he did not interfere. They are a very interesting people, and if I be faithful to the Lord's call I doubt not to see some or many of them obeying the gospel. It is now near to the end of my first week in Ireland, and I have indeed cause to thank the Lord that so soon I should be within sight of so full and blessed a work.

August, 1844. On board ship heading for Canada.
In every circumstance, even to the least, I have seen infinite grace towards me on this occasion. The ship in which I am is an excellent one. As there is no cabin passenger but myself, I have the cabin as quiet as my own study could be, and a state-room in which to meet with God. The means provided for me by the Lord have so exactly met my wants, that I go forth truly 'without purse', having only two shillings remaining in the world; and yet I am infinitely rich, 'having nothing, and yet possessing all things'.

September 2, 1844. On board ship heading for Canada.
This morning beautifully clear; a gentle north-east breeze, wafting us to our desired haven, brought us in sight of American land, after a delightful run of 23 days. Our seasons of divine worship have been increasingly pleasant of late, although I see no mark of a divine work of grace in any one around. Part of my daily work has been to teach the ship-boys to read. One of them is an interesting black from Africa. Oh that my heart were enlarged in pleading for the ingathering of all nations to Emmanuel!

Quebec, September 10, 1844
In God's great mercy we arrived here yesterday, after a delightful passage of 36 days. As it was the day of holy rest, I did not go ashore, but had worship on board, and spoke on the 22nd chapter of Revelation. In the evening I was put on shore, and after looking a little at the aspect of the town, I took up my position alone, and yet not alone, at the market-place, close to the river, and began to repeat the fifty-fifth of Isaiah. A crowd of Canadians and of British sailors soon gathered, who at first seemed mute with astonishment, but soon showed me that the offence of the cross had not ceased by their mocking and threatened violence.

However, I got a good opportunity of witness-bearing for God and his Christ, and when I left them had some interesting conversation with some individuals who followed me. When I came down again, at half-past eight, to the place where the ship's boat was to meet me, I got into conversation with a company of young sailors, two of whom remembered well having heard me at Newcastle at the quay and in the corn-market. Some of our poor soldiers and sailors were going about intoxicated. Though it were only to reach these two classes of degraded men, it would be to me a reward for crossing the great ocean. Who knoweth what may be the fruit of this evening's testimony among the wondering crowd!

I have had on board the ship a time for solemn observation of the character and ways of the unconverted, which I trust will be profitable. The only book I have had with me beside the book of God is Owen on the Glory of Christ, which I find precious indeed. I have had some seasons of great nearness to the God and Father of our Lord Jesus Christ, and have found his Word full of power and refreshment.

1844. At Montreal Harbour.
When we came into the harbour two Christian gentlemen, Mr Orr and Mr M'Kay, came on board, and before leaving my little cabin we had sweet communion at the mercy-seat together. I live with Mr and Mrs. Orr, a godly couple from Greenock, in a delightful situation at the head of the town. Truly goodness and mercy are heaped on me.

Before leaving Scotland I observed that the 93rd Regiment, the depot of which I laboured among at Aberdeen in autumn 1840, had removed from Kingston to Montreal, and I trusted that somehow I might get in among them; but what was my joy and wonder to be told that there were about thirty godly men among sergeants and privates who have a hired room near the barracks in which some of them teach a daily school for poor children gathered from the streets, as well as a Sabbath-school, and in which they meet for social prayer every Friday from six to half-past eight. This is the Sutherland regiment, of which in its early days the Rev. Ronald Bayne, an eminent man of God, afterwards at Inverness and then at Elgin, was chaplain; and that enjoyed until lately the command of Colonel M'Gregor, a distinguished Christian officer, now at the head of the constabulary force of Dublin.

I had hardly arrived when I was told they were looking with desire to my coming, and that they wished me to attend their prayer-meeting, and to preach to them next Sabbath. I accordingly went last night, in company with two pious Scotsmen. When we got to the place I found such a scene as I never before saw: a room crowded with soldiers, wives, and children, who were met not to hear a man speak, but to wait upon Jehovah, as their custom was. It put me in mind of the centurion of old. I enjoyed the meeting exceedingly, speaking upon Moses at the burning bush. One of the soldiers prayed, as well as Mr M'Intosh and myself. In the soldier's prayer I was struck by the petition that they might cherish such expectations of good through my instrumentality as were warranted by his Word, and were according to his mind. They seemed all to feel too that nothing but the presence of God himself would be of any avail. I found it very affecting to them and me to allude to the church of our fathers in the furnace, and to the people of Ross and Sutherland, from among whom the regiment was at first raised.

Montreal, Saturday, September 14, 1844
During the present week my work has gone on as before, but in addition my conflicts in soul about it have been deeper than before, and several new doors have been opened.

1. 250 of the 71st Regiment have come to the cavalry barracks, whom I visited on Tuesday and Friday, and whom I am to see again on Tuesday, if the Lord will. It seems very remarkable that the 93rd and 71st Regiments are the only ones whose depots I visited in Scotland, and that the whole of the 93rd and so many of the 71st should now be here. I have met with a number of the 71st whom I knew well in Dundee, and this prepares my way among them.

2. I have got liberty and more than liberty from the commanding officer of the 89th (Irish) Regiment to meet with the men in their school-room from week to week. This seemed so unlikely, as he is said to be a Romanist, that I had given up thoughts of applying, but one of the men in the hospital wanted me to ask a favour for him, and this gave me an introduction.

3. We have got most wonderfully the use of a large room exactly opposite the French church for holding meetings in, both in French and English, all for nothing, the owner being a friend of the gospel, a hearer of Dr Carruthers the Independent, whose church met for a long time in this very place. This seems a remarkable arrangement, as it is the very best place in the city for reaching the people.

Montreal, Tuesday, September 24, 1844
Evening at seven in open air in Place d'Armes in the centre of the city, in front of the great Romish cathedral. The proposal of this tried some spirits among us. When I went, a considerable number had assembled, and among them a band of the 93rd. I had a fine opportunity, and felt the power of the living God with us. Towards the end our enemies made a commotion. The mayor of the city, a Roman Catholic, came to stop me, but was restrained by God. As we retired about half-past nine we were mobbed, chiefly as usual through the excessive fears of friends seeking to guard me from violence. The mayor offered his protection, but I said to the people in his presence, 'No one will harm me, it is my own friends who are creating groundless alarm. I would ask all to go quietly home, and if any one is my enemy he will give me his arm and we will go together.' They quietly moved away. I put my hand on my white neckcloth and moved on unknown to the multitude. If the kingdom

of Satan is to be disturbed here, this is but the shadow of what will yet come, and then shall many be offended.

Montreal, Friday, September 27, 1844
At half-past five in Place d'Armes, awfully mocked and pelted, though with nothing deadly, yet got much truth delivered both while here and after going to an adjoining street, where a gentleman walking with me was struck on the back. While in the Place d'Armes, one of the magistrates, evidently, I think, a Romanist, came and ordered me to remove, threatening me with the exercise of his power if I did not. I said I was doing no harm, and would continue, and that he might take me to prison if he pleased; I was ready. He shrunk away and left me to go on. I feel that standing thus in the breach, though it may have no other effect, invigorates my own faith, lifts a testimony honouring to God, and sets me on a high vantage-ground in preaching in the churches.

Montreal, Saturday, September 28, 1844
This evening I was again in the field about six o'clock. A great number assembled, and, in contrast with the previous night, they seemed to have ears given them to hear. This continued for some time, but afterwards they began to throw gravel, and to jostle me in the crowd. Little evil might have come of this, had not some who befriended me as a Scotsman sought to save me from danger, and thus my back being turned the crowd rushed on me, and I got away without my hat and one of the tails of my coat containing a handkerchief and Bible. Their enmity was so great that I believe the Bible was torn to pieces as well as the rest, the hat only being recovered. I got into a shop, where many who trembled for me would have had me to remain, but I was quite above all fear, and went out again alone among the people, and got much opportunity of declaring the truth on the way home. Surely these displays of enmity are a token that the Prince of darkness is in some degree afraid!

Wednesday, June 23, 1847. At sea heading for China.
It is now a fortnight since I embarked in this vessel, and thus far God hath graciously prospered our way. For a week after we set sail we were detained by contrary and, in general, stormy winds at the mouth of the British Channel, but since that time the weather has been delightful, and we have been wafted speedily on our way, so that tomorrow morning, if the wind continue favourable, we shall pass by Madeira. During the first few days I was rather sick, but I have been able from the beginning to do a little at my Chinese studies, and during the last few days my progress has been, I think, encouraging. We have had public worship every evening in the public cabin, and today I succeeded in getting it begun also in the morning.

Wednesday, July 28, 1847. At sea heading for China.
At Sea, Lat. 23^0 south, Long. 29^0 west. It is seven weeks this day since I came on board this vessel. Hitherto we have been all mercifully preserved, and have advanced steadily, though not very rapidly, on our voyage. Some of the crew have had illness, but they are again able for their duties. I have suffered a good deal, and still suffer almost daily, from nausea, which abridges my ability for close application to study. I am, however, able to do a little from day to day in acquiring the Chinese, and occasionally I make more rapid advances. The work is pleasant and profitable from the Bible being my text-book, and in consideration of the momentous end which I have in view. Morrison was enabled to accomplish a great work in preparing such a version of the New Testament as that which it is my privilege to study. I have felt much interested by his Memoirs, which I am again reading. He was a spiritual man, as well as a man of strong natural parts, and was thus both naturally and by grace qualified for the work of translation.

I have been graciously permitted hitherto to maintain family worship in the cabin every evening, and generally also in the morning, although with occasional difficulty, the desire not being as yet very great. The illness of one of the seamen opened my way a good deal in the forecastle, and I now have worship there also at least twice a week. On Sabbaths all join with us excepting one or two. When shall the cry be heard among us: 'What shall I do to be saved?' Yesterday afternoon we passed Trinidad, a very picturesque island, uninhabited except by a few goats and swine. It stands quite alone in the midst of this vast ocean. Should our voyage be favourable, we shall not again see land until near the Chinese seas. The Island of St Paul's comes first in sight.

I was glad to find on crossing the line that the heathenish practices which used to be common on shipboard, and of which Dr Morrison gives an account in his journal forty years ago, had no place among us. All went on as usual, with only some passing allusions to the subject. Such changes among our seamen are hopeful.

'Do thou thy glory far advance
Above both sea and land' Psalm 37.

Thursday, July 29, 1847
Written at sea, Lat. 25⁰ 30' south; Lon. 28⁰ 40' west. From this time (July 23rd, 1839) until the Disruption I appeared to have a special work to do in my own country, and having no call to the missionary field I thought no further of it than this, that I did not feel it would be lawful for me to settle at home, but only to comply with present calls of duty to preach the Word. In the year 1843, and still more in 1844, I found my heart very much drawn off from the home field, the days of God's great power with me seeming to be in a great measure past, and ecclesiastical questions having taken so deep a hold on the public mind, that it was not in a state as before to be dealt with simply about the question of conversion. In these circumstances I went at the call of some friends to Dublin in 1844 to try the field there, but finding no great opening, I returned to Scotland, and the way being made very clearly open for my going on a visit to Canada, I sailed for Montreal, August 10.

In Canada I found sufficient evidence that it was indeed the call of God which I obeyed in going to it, but after labouring there for nearly two years, and having gone over the ground which seemed providentially laid out for me, I felt that unless I were to remain there for life, the time was come for my departure. I was confirmed in this view by having had my mind afresh directed towards India by a letter from an acquaintance there, and also by a call from our continental committee to make use of my newly acquired knowledge of French by visiting the continent of Europe. I accordingly sailed from Quebec for Scotland on August 20th 1846, having a deep impression that I should find no special work to do in Scotland that would detain me there longer than a few months, but feeling quite uncertain what would be my ultimate destination.

On my arrival I was asked anew to go to the continent, but against this there were objections. I did not see any prospect of doing much there during a brief visit, and I could not but reflect that at my period of life it must be now decided whether I was to preach from place to place to the end or go to a heathen field, as originally destined. At any rate I felt that I could decide on nothing until I had paid a few visits to those home fields with which I had formerly been connected. The work occupied me during the autumn and the early part of the winter. I might have protracted the period indefinitely, being encompassed with invitations on every hand, but as I did not see or feel any special blessing in this work, I preached no more than I could not avoid doing, and then came the question, What is my duty with reference to the future?

About the end of the year, at the time of the Parsee's ordination in Edinburgh, I arrived at the clear decision that I was not at liberty to labour any longer as hitherto without ascertaining whether our missionary committee would still desire me to fulfil my original intention. I accordingly called on Dr Candlish, and having laid before him my views, and joined with him in imploring divine guidance, he stated that he thought it was clearly my duty to go as I originally destined to the heathen provided that I found no special cause as heretofore to detain me, and said that he would confer with others on the subject. He did so, but found that though no one would object to my going if I wished to do so, yet as the Indian stations were all occupied, there was no special opening for me.

At this very time, and while they were actually conversing on the matter, a letter came to the convenor of the Foreign Mission Committee, Dr James Buchanan, from James Hamilton of Regent Square, London (convenor of the English Presbyterian Church

Missionary Committee), making earnest inquiry whether Dr B[uchanan] could point out any minister or preacher in Scotland who might be suitable to go as their first missionary to China, seeing they had contemplated this mission for more than two years, and had as yet been disappointed in finding suitable agents. This seemed to Dr B[uchanan] a providential coincidence, and without communicating with me, he wrote mentioning a few names and mine among the rest.

Some weeks elapsed without my hearing anything further on the subject, but meanwhile my own experience more and more pointed my thoughts and desires to the foreign field, and at last in the beginning of February a letter came to me from Mr Hamilton, in which, after reminding me of my original design and prospects regarding an eastern mission, he mentioned the position of their own missionary scheme, and asked what my views in regard to embarking in such an undertaking now were. As he wished a speedy answer, I could only reply that the matter was too varied in its bearings and of too momentous a character to be at once decided on, but that it would be the subject of prayer and consideration, as well as of conference with the servants of God around me.

On receipt of my letter, their missionary committee instructed Mr Hamilton to send me an express and earnest call to become their church's first missionary to China. I received this, but still found myself unable to arrive at a final decision. Regarding the importance of the work there could be no doubt; but when I considered on the one hand the manner in which God had hitherto called me to labour, and the many calls at home and abroad which I still had to preach the Word as heretofore; and on the other considered the uncertainty of my being suited to the peculiarities of the Chinese field, I felt embarrassed, and though I wrote a letter of acceptance, I could not send it off, but rather suspended the case by letting them know my difficulties and my need of delay. With a view of getting further light I also urged them in the interval to look out for others, and mentioned two ministers to whom they might apply.

Another ten days elapsed, during which I was in Edinburgh, as I had been for some time previously, preaching in St Luke's, etc., and now also assisting Dr Duncan in his junior Hebrew class, his health being imperfect. The call to China was gradually assuming more and more importance in my view, and though some of God's servants seemed to doubt whether it was a field suitable to my habits, yet the prevailing opinion seemed to be that I ought to go.

Feeling that I must resume communication with the English committee, I went out before doing so to Kilsyth, at the communion season on the first Sabbath of March, that I might sit, it might be for the last time at the table of the Lord Jesus on earth with my beloved parents, and that I might have the aid of their counsel, and that of my cousins David and Charles J. Brown (of Glasgow and Edinburgh), who were expected to be my father's assistants. On the Monday after the communion I wrote to London again to let it be known that I was still weighing the matter brought before me, and that with a view to arrive at a final and satisfactory decision, I would be glad to be furnished with information in regard to the nature of the work in which they would wish or expect me to be engaged, and also to learn what length of time it would require to attain an adequate knowledge of the language with a view to preaching the gospel in it. I also stood generally on the subject,

1st. That I did not make such inquiries as if difficulties would be sufficient to keep me back, were the path of duty in other respects plain, but simply in order that I might have full materials for comparing this call with others that were given me, as from France, etc.

2nd. That as devoted to the missionary work I felt that unless it appeared that God detained me at home by some special call, I must go to some field where Christ had not been named, etc.

In reply to this letter, Mr Hamilton wrote that he believed the difficulties of the Chinese language had been overestimated, but that they expected about the end of March from China Mr Hugh Matheson, one of their committee, who would bring them full and recent information, and that this would be communicated to me. At this time I spent four weeks preaching in Bute and Arran, and on the 10th of April I went to Edinburgh to preach in Mr Moody Stuart's. The impression of my duty now became so strong that I felt I could no longer hesitate about signifying my willingness to go, and on Monday I wrote to that effect. I saw that I would dishonour my profession of the gospel, and thus wound the honour of Jesus, if I seemed to linger any longer, and though I had not heard again from London, I felt that on general ground, and taking even the most discouraging view of the case, it was my duty to go forward.

The committee met on this very day, and so discouraging was the view given by Mr M of the field and of the missions there, as compared with our missions in India, that the committee resolved to recommend to the Synod (about to meet at Sunderland the following Tuesday) to give up thoughts of a mission to China, and begin to place a mission in Hindustan. When I heard of this decision, which the receipt of my letter did not seem to have altered, I was at a loss how to act, but saw that now matters were coming to a crisis and that the issue would be either to shut up my path toward China or set me free from their call altogether. I did not feel any sympathy with their proposal to draw back, and fearing lest they might do so, and thus dishonour the command and promise of the exalted Jesus, I was the more pressed in spirit to go forward, that such a consequence might be avoided. I accordingly resolved to go up to Sunderland on the 20th, and meet the Synod on the matter. I did so, and on Wednesday the 21st I found that the Synod were bent on prosecuting the mission, and so on Thursday I was ordained to the work.

In this manner from step to step my path has been hedged up in this important matter and now I find myself in the midst of the great ocean studying Chinese, and having the prospect, if the Lord will, of spending the rest of my days in that vast empire of heathen darkness. 'The people that walked in darkness have seen a great light, and to them that dwell in the land of the shadow of death, upon them hath the light shined.'

Thursday, August 5, 1847
Lat. 33° south, Lon. 14° west. This morning at half-past four o'clock, Thomas M'Leod, an apprentice in the ship, fell overboard and was drowned. They tried to render him assistance, but all was

vain, as it was dark and rainy, and the wind was changing at the time. He was aged about seventeen, a native of Rothesay, and the son of a widow. The evening before last I had worship in the steerage or half-deck with him and some of the other men, and was led to speak especially of the danger of sudden death to which they were exposed. He seemed attentive, and answered me the question in the Shorter Catechism, 'What is prayer?' I had also conversed and prayed with him previously when sick. This is all I can say of his case. He is, alas! now numbered with those whom 'the sea will give up' at the last day to stand before the great white throne. It is sad to see and feel how little this solemn event seems to affect us. Who can tell but it may be the precursor of other displays of the Lord's righteous hand? May I and others be taught to prepare for the Lord's coming!

I am still enabled to continue worship morning and evening (with occasional interruptions in the morning) in the cabin. In the half-deck and in the forecastle I have the fullest liberty to do all I can for these precious souls. I am sometimes refreshed in these exercises, though I cannot see any special evidences of fruit. 'Let us not be weary in well-doing.' We are now about 1600 miles from the Cape of Good Hope. The weather has been fine hitherto, but this being the winter season in these southern regions, it is now becoming cold, and may be expected to be stormy. I go on pretty regularly with my Chinese, and find it gradually become more familiar, although it is evident from the nature of the language that it must require long practice to render it at all natural to a European mind and tongue.

I occupy myself much in translating the English New Testament into Chinese, and comparing these rude attempts with Morrison's version. This I find an admirable method of mastering the substance of the language, although the peculiar Chinese manner of thought and expression can only be fully attained from studying native authors. This I am also practising to a certain extent.

Thursday, August 26, 1847
Since the previous date we had some very stormy weather, with an intervening calm of some days. The wind however, when strongest,

was favourable and has been therefore less severely felt. On Tuesday 24th it blew almost a hurricane from the north-west. I was standing on the poop when a lofty wave broke over the vessel. By its force and the rolling of the vessel I was lifted from the deck, but having a firm hold I was mercifully preserved. My watch was filled with salt water and the chain snapped. How in a moment the pulse of life might have been thus arrested!

Hong Kong, Tuesday, December 7, 1847
Hong-Kong. After the storm of November 8th we had favourable winds, and anchored in Hong-Kong Bay at midnight on Saturday the 13th. On Monday I came on shore, meeting a very kind and Christian welcome from the friends of the gospel here, and finding such doors of useful labour immediately opened to me, as confirm me in the soundness of those convictions of duty which brought me here. I am most comfortably boarded with a Mr and Mrs Power, close to the mission premises of the London Society. Mr Stevenson has been prevented from coming out to minister to the Presbyterians here, and this gives me a greater hold of my own countrymen, to whom I have opportunity of preaching once every Lord's day in the London Society's chapel.

My progress in Chinese is slow compared with my desires, but still I hope encouraging considered in the view of the difficulties of this very peculiar and hard language. On my arrival I was permitted once more to hear from my beloved parents, who are all well. Our deliverance from the perils of the deep appears now the greater, since we have heard within the last few days that the *Anne and Jane* from London, with which we were in company in the Java Sea, was on the 8th driven on shore near Manila and totally lost. All, however, were saved except one of the crew and a passenger, Mr Rogers from Edinburgh, who were washed off a raft to which they had betaken themselves, and were drowned. Another vessel, also narrowly escaped, getting into Manila with the loss of all her masts.

Hong Kong, January 4, 1848
During the past month I have been making some progress in the Chinese, and have had some opportunities of bringing into use the

measure of knowledge already acquired. A fortnight ago Dr Morrison asked me to go and visit in the prison three Chinese criminals under sentence of death for murder and who were in deep distress and anxious to be visited by the ministers of Christ. Unable to do much, I felt called to do what I could, and as the execution of the sentence was delayed longer than usual in consequence of the absence of the governor, I had almost daily opportunities of meeting these poor men. I generally went alone, but at other times in company with the Chinese preacher Chin-Seen.

They were very anxious to hear of the way of salvation through Jesus, and evidently strove to understand my broken Chinese. Although unable to say much to them I made them read with me Christian books, and on several occasions I even joined with them in prayer, through the medium of their own tongue. They did not speak the Canton dialect, which I am chiefly studying, and this no doubt made my rude attempts less intelligible, yet I felt encouraged, and enjoyed, I think, something of the power of grace in praying with and for them. One of these poor men has received a commutation of his sentence.

Tuesday, February 29th, 1848
Corner of Aberdeen Street, Queen's Road –
During these two months mercy has abounded towards me. May I have grace to bless and glorify the God of my life and salvation! In my work among the British population I have been in some degree encouraged, though not in any manner fitted to show me that they ought to be the principal object of my efforts to promote the kingdom of God. Our meetings on Sabbath continue rather to increase, but on week-days very few attend. Early in January I began to feel my need of having the assistance of some native of this province to read with me, in order that I might get acquainted with the colloquial dialect, and acquire as far as possible the right mode of intonating each word – a point of the greatest importance in order to effective speaking, and one of the greatest difficulty. The Lord has graciously, I trust, guided me in this. A brother missionary spoke of my want to Mr Gutzlaff, who kindly furnished

me with a teacher, a young man from Canton city, whom I have found very suitable. He came to me on January 25th.

After a week or two I found it would be desirable, in order to give full employment to my teacher, and also to open up my way into Chinese society, that I should get him if possible to open a small Chinese school, and I thought it would be well if I could get a house having accommodation for this purpose, and where I might myself live with none but Chinese around me, and so be obliged to speak the language at all times. It is in this view that I have taken the house in which I now am. I entered it a week ago (February 22nd), and found myself alone, with none but my two Chinese servants, to whom, however, I had been providentially directed, and whom I found willing from the first day to come and worship with me. We read and have continued to read together in Matthew's Gospel (Morrison's version), and I pray with them imperfectly. These beginnings have encouraged me. 'Who hath despised the day of small things?'

Yesterday my teacher came to live here, and he expects to be able to open a school in the lower flat of this house, which was formerly a druggist's shop, and is very suitable for this purpose, and also for collecting a small congregation, should the Lord incline them to come, and give fitness to enter on the solemn work in a manner so public.

Shap Pat-Hoeung, February 1849

We went to Cowloon, but they took me to a school-house rented by the London Mission, and after one day's stay among a listless people we were obliged to leave in consequence of the mandarin's remonstrating with the landlord of the house. On Thursday the London missionaries came over, and I went back with them to the Chinese Medical Hospital (Hong-Kong). On Friday we again landed directly opposite at Tseen-Sha-Tein, had good openings and favour among the villages, and lodged in a mat-shed, I eating, as I had the previous day and have done since, with my Chinese companions, but not putting on in the meantime any part of the Chinese dress.

On Saturday we removed to Tseen Wan (Shallow Bay) village,

a distance of perhaps twenty-five Chinese miles; the people very friendly, but generally speaking the Hak-ka, not the Puntee or Canton city dialect. Here we remained until Wednesday (yesterday), when we crossed the hills, a distance of 20 or 25 Chinese miles (probably 7 or 8 English miles) to this valley covered with villages (Shap Pat-Hoeung). Today I have been out, and have had more encouragement in the aspect of the people, and also in my ability to communicate to them the great truths,

(1) That there is but one true God, his character,
(2) That all men are sinners – idolaters, etc.
(3) That there is a Saviour and only one, Jesus the Son of the living God.

Shap-Pat-Woeung

Much encouraged at Pat-Hoeung. Left it on Tuesday the 20th. 21st at Cum-Teen. Many people, attention, at night fear of robbers. 22nd. Came here. Door opened. Many people. Attention.

Shum-Chan, Monday, March 5, 1849

Came here on Friday, after being 6 days here at Shap-Pat-Hoeung, and 3 days at Sin-Teen. People friendly. Arrived on the market-day. Great press to see the foreigner, but all friendly. On Saturday messenger arrived from Hong-Kong, robbed by the way of the money he was bringing. In my own room: not an everyday privilege in this land. Oh! for the Spirit of grace to improve it.

March 29, 1849. Chinese Hospital, Hong-Kong

We stayed at Shum-Chan until Wednesday the 14th, visiting the surrounding villages.
14th. Removed westward to Sheung-Poo-Tan, visiting villages to the west, Kak-Teen, Kong-Ha, Wong-Kong, etc., 8 days.

February 7, 1852

I am now engaged a good deal in the work of spreading the gospel among this people, being in the gracious arrangements of God's providence favoured with the co-operation of professing Christians, both indoors and in the open air. One of these, baptized since I came here by the American missionaries, aids me regularly, and others from time to time. We have meetings in the chapel of Tai-Hang, where Dr Young resides, but get greater numbers in the open air when giving addresses in the open places of the city. During this week I also went to the neighbouring country (on the island) among the villages, spending a night in one of these in the house of my servant, and preaching the word with my companions T and K, in six different villages. The work increases in interest and hopefulness. 'Thy kingdom come!'

March 6, 1852

On Tuesday the 24th February I again set out to visit some villages on the island of Amoy, and returned in much mercy on Tuesday the 2nd, being absent seven nights. The day we set out was the 5th of the first Chinese month, and as at this season the villages are full of people who have not yet returned to their usual employments, we had large audiences everywhere. We generally addressed five or six meetings in the course of the day, and in all must have made known something of the truth to at least two or three thousand people. The people were everywhere friendly and attentive. We distributed a large number of tracts and hand-bill copies of the ten commandments. May the seed of the Word sown spring and bear fruit to the glory of God and the salvation of souls!

March 12, 1853

In the great mercy and by the gracious and constant aid of the Lord and Saviour, I was enabled on the 10th to complete the last revised copy of Bunyan's *Pilgrim* (1st part) in Chinese, which has occupied us from June 1st, 1852 until now, with the exception of a month at the end of last summer, when through feverish sickness I was obliged to lay it aside. The whole has been looked over by Messrs. Doty and A. Stronach with their teachers, and the work has been benefited by a number of their suggestions. One hour after finishing the last sheet in the form in which it will be printed, I received from Shanghai a copy of the *Pilgrim* in Chinese, printed two years ago by Mr Muirhead of the London Society, chiefly for the use of pupils. It is not, however, a continuous translation of the whole.

Amoy, May 16, 1853

Last month I had the privilege of paying a visit to Chang-chow-foo, a large city in this neighbourhood, at the distance of about forty English miles. We left Amoy on the morning of April 13, and returned here on the 26th, being absent about a fortnight, nine days of which were spent at Chang-chow, preaching to large and very interesting audiences both inside and outside the city. A week or two before our going, two native Christians, of the American Mission here, had visited Chang-chow, and preached to crowds for a number of days with much encouragement, and as they were purposing to go again, at the earnest desire especially of one of them, it was arranged that I should also go, although there was some reason to fear that, unless God should graciously open our way, there might be some unwillingness on the part of the authorities to allow a foreigner to pay more than a brief visit, or to preach at large to the people.

To avoid difficulty as far as possible, it was arranged that we should live on the river, in the boat which carried us there, going on shore only to preach. On our arrival we immediately went on shore, and being at once surrounded by many people, we had a fine opportunity, within a few steps of our boat, of preaching the Word of Life fully and without hindrance. We continued thus to preach on the bank of the river for three days, going upwards from our boat in the morning, and downwards in the afternoon, and addressing large companies for three or four hours at a time, until we had exhausted all the suitable stations near the river.

We then went inwards, but still outside the walls, and at the very first station at which we preached, a man came forward and pressed us to go further on, and preach again opposite his house. This man the following morning came and was with us at worship in our boat; and when it began to rain, and our boat was more uncomfortable, the same individual opened his house to us, and here we stayed (making the man a small remuneration) for five days. going on from this as our head-quarters, still inwards, we enjoyed the fullest liberty, both within and without the city, of preaching to large and very much engaged audiences. I do not think, upon the whole, that I have spent so interesting a season, or enjoyed so fine an opportunity of preaching the Word of Life since I came to China, as during these nine days. The people were everywhere urgent in requesting that a place might be opened for the regular preaching of the gospel among them, and I am glad to say that the American Mission here have already sent two of the members of the native church to open an out-station in this important and very promising locality.

Since our return here three individuals have also come here at their own expense, to inquire further into the nature of the gospel. The native Christians with me were the same with whom I went last year in making some visits to the neighbourhood, and I have pleasure in adding that they seem to be moved by love to the Saviour, and to the souls of their fellow-countrymen, in giving themselves to this work.

October 13, 1853

When I wrote in May, I made allusion to an interesting missionary visit which I had paid, in company with members of the native church here, to a large city in this neighbourhood, Chang-chow. I also mentioned that the American Mission here had the view of establishing permanently an out-station there, and were about to send two of their native assistants for that purpose. The sequel to this proposal, which is of a very affecting kind, and very different from what we had looked for, I have not yet mentioned to you.

About the middle of May the native assistant, whom I have alluded to as co-operating with me here, went to Chang-chow along with another belonging to the same mission, and rented, as a place of meeting, the house of the man whom I alluded to in my May letter as having, in April, received us into his house, and taken some interest in our work.

They had gone but two days when the local rebellion broke out in this neighbourhood, and had had in Chang-chow but one Sabbath's services when the insurgents reached that city. The man who had rented them his house took part with the insurgents, which led the native brethren to remove their lodgings to another place, that they might not be involved. When the insurgents had got possession of the city but two days, in consequence of their showing a disposition to rob and plunder, the populace on a sudden rose en masse upon them, and put nearly all who were within the city to an instant death! How little did we suppose when in April preaching the gospel in these streets, that in the course of a short month they were to be flowing with human blood!

At the time of this awful massacre both the native brethren from Amoy were within the city, and as being strangers, from the same part of the country as the insurgents, they were in imminent danger of being reckoned as belonging to them, and sharing in their dreadful end. The one who is now here early saw his danger, and with difficulty made his escape, by dropping from the city walls. The other, a native of Canton province, was more fearless, being in company with some friends engaged in business in Chang-chow. He also did escape at this time, although not without much danger, but having delayed to leave the city, as his companion wished him, and return to Amoy, he was the following morning, on a sudden, arrested by a band of the populace, and, despite all his friends could do, was dragged before the mandarin, and instantly beheaded!

His companion having separated from him the day before this occurred, with great difficulty made his way home to Amoy, and it was several weeks before we heard of the affecting event. Nor was this all; the man who had rented them his house, having openly joined the insurgents, was seized in the street by the populace, and publicly beheaded!

This was the melancholy end of one who, though not a man of good character among his countrymen, had a few weeks before welcomed us in our mission, joined us in all our services, and seemed to have, at least, the joy of a stony-ground hearer, if nothing more. Since that time the people of Chang-chow city have been engaged in almost constant fighting with the insurgent party, and although the insurgents have not been able again to recover the city, yet to the present hour it is so shut up, that almost no communication can be carried on between it and Amoy. The sufferings of its inhabitants have been, and still are, very great. A native of the city who had become interested in the gospel message, and who, as well as other two, came down to Amoy in April on purpose to hear it more fully, was also in great peril of being seized and put to death, like the others. His house was surrounded by armed men, and he only made his escape by getting through the roof, and running along the tops of the houses, with difficulty. After some weeks of wandering, he got here, and has remained under this roof since, it being still unsafe for him to return home.

* * * * *

Retrospective Journal entry in 1855

I see from the *Witness* of May 8th, received today, that in a reference made to a letter from Amoy, it is said, 'Mr B preached for some days to crowds of the gay inhabitants of this city (Soo-chow), on his return from an attempt to reach the patriot camp at Nanking.' This statement is incorrect, as I only passed through the suburbs of the city in a boat, and this under the surveillance of mandarin officers, who did not, however, hinder the distribution of books and tracts as we passed along. As, for important reasons, I forbade at the time any account of this attempt to reach Nanking being published at Shanghae, and when writing home I purposely made the most meagre allusion to it, it is no wonder if misstatements more important than the one above quoted should be made by any one who had occasion to refer to the matter.

It occurs to me that now it may not be without use to take this opportunity of giving some details regarding that journey, as it was one on which, though it failed as regards its primary object, I experienced more than usual marks of the Lord's gracious care and guidance. It was about the beginning of August 1855, ten days after reaching Shanghae from England, that, in company with a Chinese servant from the neighbourhood of Shanghae, and who having gone with a missionary (Mr Milne) to England, returned with Mr Douglas and myself in the *Challenger*, I set out in a woo-sung boat to try whether the way were open to reach the insurgent camp.

I went in my own dress, and had resolved that unless permitted to proceed without disguise or artifice, I should return, or rather confine my efforts in making known divine truth to those whom we should meet on the way, or who should hinder us from going on to the desired destination. After proceeding rather slowly, I think for three days and a half, up the Yang-tze-Kiang, we were on a Saturday favoured with a prosperous wind, which bore us rapidly on against the stream of the river, and brought us early in the afternoon to Tan-Too, a town not far below Chin-keang-foo, and situated at one of the openings of the Great Canal into the Yang-tze-Kiang.

Our getting thus far without impediment was not a little remarkable, for we had already passed two Imperial outposts, and at Tan-Too our boat was lying in the midst of a mandarin encampment. How was this, you will ask? We were just passing the head of a large island in the river, and running with a fresh breeze towards Pagoda Hill (I suppose from ten to twenty miles below Chin-keang-foo), when, at the mouth of a creek on the south side of the river, we met the first trace of the Imperial forces encompassing the insurgents. A number of boats were moored here, and as we approached one of them pushed off to meet us and examine what we were. I felt that now, unless God remarkably favoured us, our journey must at once come to an end, and, hid in the cabin of the boat, I prayed that the Lord would graciously interpose.

The boat pushed out to meet us, waving a flag and calling us to wait and give account of ourselves, but the boatmen, no doubt alarmed, told them they had a foreigner on board, and ran on. The guard-boat, whether satisfied or not, saw that it was too late to overtake us, and, no doubt reporting that all was right, returned to their station. Shortly after this, in consequence of a bend in the river at Pagoda Hill, the boat made a tack towards the north bank, and this course I saw would directly bring us to a mandarin encampment with a guard-ship anchored in front of it. I might have told the boatman to make his course short and try to keep clear of further inquiries, but I felt this would have been a subterfuge, and so running straight on, I soon heard the cry of voices inquiring what we were. The boatmen also were calling loudly that I should come out and take the responsibility on myself.

I now expected we should be boarded and detained, but coming out I found that there was no small boat near, but only a company of twenty or thirty persons looking on us from the mandarin vessel. I almost involuntarily bowed to them; they graciously returned the salutation; the boat was put about, and we were gone again upon our course without remark or hindrance! Our character was now of course established, by having passed successfully these outer guards, and about three p.m. we took up our place at Tan-Too, without inquiry made, among the boats of the Imperial soldiers. As the day was Saturday, I resolved to spend the Sabbath at Tan-Too, and here my companion and myself (he was then considerably interested in the gospel, and is now a professing Christian and assistant-preacher in the hospital of the London Mission at Shanghae) on Saturday afternoon and the whole of Sabbath had a full opportunity of making known the truth and distributing books both among the inhabitants of the town and the mandarin soldiers, who were congregated to the number of some thousands in it.

No-one seemed to wonder at our visit, or to suspect that we had any design of going among the insurgents. Indeed the people were afraid to allude to the insurgent party at all. The town had been already in their hands and might soon be so again. Our boatmen, who had been prevailed on to come thus far, now obstinately refused to proceed farther. We had often reasoned with them on the subject, but, to cut the matter short, the head-man (there were three boat-men), on our getting moored at Tan-Too said, somewhat curtly, 'Now, if you want to go to Nanking, you can get out and walk.' No offer of reward would induce them to go a step further. They said it was just possible that we might get to Nanking alive, but that I, and still more they, could not hope to return. Their boat would be lost. But it was said, 'You will be remunerated.' They replied, 'Of what use will money be when we have lost our lives?' Finding them thus decided, and seeing no other way open consistent with truth and integrity, I arrived unwillingly at the conclusion that, if after the Sabbath was past, circumstances wore the same aspect, this attempt to reach the insurgents must be abandoned.

I had asked the boatmen where they would propose to go in case of not proceeding farther towards Nanking. They replied, 'We will return to Shanghae by the Great Canal' (literally, as they call it, 'Transport-provision-River'). This course recommended itself as second best, if the original one must be abandoned, and so, early on Monday morning, finding the way to Nanking closed, we passed through Tan-Too into the Great Canal on our homeward route. In entering the canal we had to pass a custom-house, but a bow to the officials from our boat, coupled no doubt with the thought that if we had come too far from home, we were at any rate now turning the head homewards – this sufficed to gain us a free entrance. We now went on to the district city of Tan-yang, distant about twenty miles.

We were examined at the custom-house as we arrived, and such a visit from a foreigner seemed to excite surprise. We were however going, as every one could see, in the right direction (Shanghae), and had come from an unsuspected quarter, Tan-Too; thus we were allowed to pass, and a present of books was received with politeness. After passing a little farther along the canal, which skirts I believe the south and east of the city, we were brought to near the south gate, and from the boats and the population on shore were soon surrounded by a large crowd, eager to look at the foreigner (an uncommon sight in these parts), and also to get possession of the books we were distributing. At this time I had but an imperfect knowledge of the Shanghae colloquial, and that would but poorly serve here, owing to a difference of dialect. Still I could say a few things which they understood, their anxiety to comprehend no doubt quickening their apprehension.

I would have got on to all appearance well in this work, but a drawback arose through the uninvited assistance of a number of Canton men, soldiers or followers of military officers from the south. Having some greater acquaintance with foreigners than the natives of the locality, and finding I could converse with them in their own dialect, they were too officious in their friendship to me, as well as harsh and overbearing to the crowds who pressed forward to get books. To avoid the crowd, they almost forced me on board one of their mandarin boats, but I had hardly got on board until the crowd pressed after us down the sloping bank, and by the pressure behind, those next to the water were in danger of getting a plunge.

One man went down, and on seeing this I rushed on shore, and with some effort regained a position on the level ground. Perhaps it was on account of this little confusion, that when I got to our boat, I found that some people had been there from the mandarin's office requesting that we should remove farther off from the city. The boat-men wished to get quite away, but after moving on to near the east gate, they consented to bring to there for the night. The following morning I went on shore with books, and walked along the bank of the canal by the foot of the city wall towards the south gate, where we had been the previous day. Here I was met by a kind of policeman, who asked me what my object was in coming, and said the district magistrate wished to know.

Having had little previous acquaintance with Chinese mandarins, and having a good supply of books, I said that if the mandarin wished to make any inquiries about me, I would be happy to go in person with him to his office. He said this would be still better, and so we walked on, in by the gate, through streets and fields, and at last to the office. I did not see the magistrate, but great numbers of people collected, both officials and people from the town, and to them, while in waiting, I had opportunity of giving books and saying a few words in regard to the first principles of divine truth.

After some delay, one or two of the magistrate's assistants came out to inspect me, and having asked through the policeman who brought me there, whether I was willing to leave their city, the same policeman conducted me through the city by another route to the east gate, and so back to our boat. It seemed for the moment that the matter was ended, and that we had nothing to do but to go on our way peaceably, but after a short time the original policeman and one or two more came and asked my companion (he had not been with me in the city: I was alone) to go on shore as they wanted to speak to him.

He was about to go, when I became alarmed, and said to them that if any one was to be beaten (signing to that effect) it was I and not he, and that if he went, I must go also. They said there was no fear of that, and that if I went also it would be better. I got some books and we went ashore outside the east gate. In a small hall we found an assistant magistrate seated in full dress waiting for us. We were called to sit together at his left hand, the place of honour, and he proceeded to ask my companion about me and our objects in coming. In answer to the inquiry who I was, we put down in writing that I was a disciple of Jesus and a publisher of [his] religion. He saw I was a foreigner, but never thought of asking to what particular country I belonged, and in writing we did not think of making reference to this.

He said with Chinese politeness, that as on the way to Shanghae people might give us trouble, an escort would be sent with us! and that they would very soon be ready to set out. I expressed the hope that they would not prevent us from distributing our books. He said that full liberty would be given us to do this. We then returned to our boat, the original policeman and another remaining on board to see that we did not get out of sight. We would have remained here until our escort was ready, but people were so clamorous for books that the ire of the old policeman was aroused, and at last, when all other means failed, he ordered the boatman to move on for about a mile or so from the city.

All the way we were followed on the banks by earnest applicants for books, and it was truly amazing to see the policeman at one time chiding and remonstrating with the people for thus following us, and then once or twice when his eye fell on an acquaintance among the applicants, his zeal for his office was forgotten, and he came in to get from us a large book for his friend!

At last when we had got to a considerable distance from the city, the evening was falling, and as we had neither wine nor opium for the policeman, he thought of going back to the city, got his arms full of books for his friends and left us. Poor man! he had not gone far, we were told, until the people mobbed him and took his books from him. The sight of this poor people, so eager to get our books, but alas! so little able to understand them, was fitted to affect the heart. May the day soon come when the Christian teacher shall have liberty to go and make known to them fully the love of

God in the gift of his Son for sinners, and the power of the blood of Jesus to cleanse from all sin.

After the policeman left us we had still many applicants for books. Our boatmen moved on, and in their eagerness to gain their object, several applicants from time to time went into the water and swam to our boat (a distance of only a yard or two). But how could you give a book to a man who had to swim with it to shore? The book, one would think, must get wet. But nay, the Chinese are in many things singular; here was a new expedient. The swimmer got his book, placed it on his brow, made it firm there by his tail tied round his head and swam to the bank!

As it was becoming dark we reached a market-town extending for some distance on both sides of the canal, and here no sooner had we arrived than our coming became known (I know not how), and from that moment onward until our stock of books was more than two-thirds exhausted, we were beset by crowds of applicants, and among them a larger number than usual of respectable people, and even several Buddhist priests. It was well nigh midnight when our escort, two retainers of the mandarin's office, made up to us here in their boat.

They seemed alarmed lest we should have got beyond their reach, and were proportionally glad to find us here quietly waiting them. We were glad also that our book distribution had advanced so rapidly during the short respite allowed us. Our escort were intelligent men, and conversed with us at length in our boat before going to rest in their own. Next day we moved on to the inferior department city of C'hang-chow, where our escort was changed, those from Tan-yang returning home, and two from C'hang-chow accompanying us to the next city, viz. the district city of Woo-seih, like C'hang-chow situated on the banks of the Great Canal.

Here again our conductors gave place to others, or rather, I think, to one only, who the following day accompanied us to the famed city of Soo-chow, the allusion to which in the newspaper you have sent me has given occasion for this unusually long narrative. The stage from Woo-seih to Soo-chow was rather longer than usual, and the afternoon was so advanced when we reached one of the principal city gates, that our escort was just in time to get in before the gate was shut. In the former times of China's peace, and Soo-chow's famed grandeur, the gates would not shut so early as now, when the sound of rebellion is heard so near as at Nanking and Chin-keang. It was in passing through a long suburb on our way to the city gate that we had an opportunity of witnessing, in the many gaily decorated pleasure-boats we passed, evidence at once of the wealth and the moral pollution of this famed city.

It was during this transit, too, that in this crowded street of 'Vanity Fair' we distributed the word of life in the form of tracts and copies of the Scripture. Our escort, on this occasion an old man, not so lettered as some of his predecessors, was most diligent in this work, aiding us in it as if for this alone he had been sent. Some came in boats to get books, and some reached out with bamboo basket-hooks from their doors and windows opening to the canal. (These basket-hooks they use for picking up things from the water.) This, alas! was all that we were able to do at Soo-chow; others have been able to make a somewhat longer stay, and to do more, and the time is coming fast, we trust, when Soo-chow, like Corinth, will receive the gospel, and many of its people exchange their luxuries for higher and more enduring pleasures, being 'washed and sanctified and justified in the name of the Lord Jesus, and by the Spirit of our God'.

Here I might close this narrative, but as the sequel embraces some circumstances possessed of a certain interest, and which I have never till now alluded to in writing, I shall proceed with the remainder as briefly as I can. As I have mentioned above, our escort reached Soo-chow just in time to get into the city before the gates closed. It was perhaps on this account that some delay had taken place in appointing those who were to succeed, and next morning, when the usual hour for starting had passed, no escort appeared. Our boatmen did not think it needful to wait any longer, and moved on leaving them to follow.

We felt the rather freer to do this as the day was Saturday, and on the previous day we had told our escort that on the following day, the Christian Sabbath, we would not travel, but rest at K'wan-shan, the next city on our way, and the only other we had to pass before reaching Shanghae. Moving on, we arrived at Kwan-shan early in the afternoon, and spent the remainder of the day, and also the whole of the Sabbath, in preaching and book distribution outside two of the city gates. No escort appeared, (we did not regret their absence) and on Monday morning we left for Shanghae, where we arrived on Tuesday with no other event than that on the night previous we had a visit from thieves, who, at the place where we had to bring to, frequently take advantage of the shallowness of the water to pilfer from boats.

The head boatman knew our danger, and enjoined on all to sleep wakefully, never proposing however that we should watch in turns. For a while we were wakeful, but then we all slept, and no one awoke until both the boatmen and ourselves had been partly robbed. We had been absent a fortnight from Shanghae, and returned rejoicing in the Lord's mercy throughout our journey, and not least in this, that the mandarin officers had (as we supposed) ceased to follow us, and so permitted us to end it peacefully. Soon after, I again set out to another part of the country, ready to forget the matter as one of the things that were 'behind,' but on returning to Shanghae, I was informed by missionary brethren that the Taow-T'ae, the highest, civil authority, had been in search of me.

He had sent communications to all the foreign consuls complaining of a foreigner who had wandered up in the direction of Chin-keang. The communication sent down about me from Tan-yang was defective in this, that it gave no hint to what nation I belonged. I was described of course by a Chinese name and surname, and this in itself could to a foreign consul give almost no clue to the party intended; besides, I had been but a few days in Shanghae when I set out, and the English consul neither knew of my being in Shanghae, nor of my having gone on this journey, and to crown all, the escort, trusting I suppose to the papers they carried for my discovery, had failed to conduct me to Shanghae, and knew nothing as to where I lodged.

There was no clue to the real person, and all the consuls answered that they knew of no such person as the one spoken of. Where was he? Let the Taow-T'ae point him out. After this answer had been given and the matter was over, the British consul learned from one of the missionaries who was the person intended, and I received through the same channel a verbal message to be wary about going to such places in these times of rebellion. Here the matter secured to end, but it was not yet so. I had again gone into the country, and on my return was surprised to be told, by Mr Wylie of the London Mission Press, that a few days before, two men had been seeking me, and that they wished my aid in getting out of prison the son of one of them, who with another police-runner had been put in prison at K'wan-shan for failing to conduct me to Shanghae.

The matter evidently stood thus: The Taow-T'ae having failed in his efforts to discover who I was, had given orders for the arrest of the men whose duty it was to come with me to Shanghae and to know where I could be found. With a view to their release, the father of one of them came to Shanghae, and through a native printer who was acquainted with Mr Wylie, inquired of him whether he knew anything of the person alluded to. 'Yes,' said Mr Wylie, 'He stays here when he is in Shanghae, but at present he is in the country.' On learning this from Mr Wylie, we at once sent for the printer. He was absent from the city at the time, but when he returned he found me out in the boat in which I had then located myself, sometimes being at Shanghae, and sometimes at other places. He said that in order to the release of those in confinement, it was necessary that I should be found, and be conducted, he supposed, as I originally should have been, to the English consul's office.

It seemed now as if I must be brought into trouble from which I had thought that I had most mercifully escaped. I felt however that there was no course open but the one suggested, and accordingly, in company with the father of the prisoner and the printer, his friend, I went directly to the office of the Taow-T'ae.

My companions went in to make known the matter, and soon returned to say that they had been told that this was not the place for a foreigner to come to, and that if I had anything to say I must go to the English consul. In reply to this, I informed them that I had no business at the consul's, as he now knew who I was, and where I was to be found, and that our coming here was no matter of mine, but concerned solely the men in confinement, in order to whose release it was supposed that I must be found and made over to the English consul. I was now on the spot to go with them, if it was desired, to the consul.

They agreed to the justness of this view of the case, and said that the proper parties would go with me as soon as the papers necessary in the case had been got ready. While these were getting ready I had to wait for a long time in a side room, and here among many of the sub-officials I had a good opportunity of distributing Christian books, and speaking of the gospel message. At last, the delay was so long that I saw it would soon be too late to find the consul in his office, and I returned to my boat, having agreed that next morning they should call for me on the way. I had however reached my boat but a short time, when the printer came with sorrow to tell me that he found my going to the consul's would be of no use, that as usual, what was wanted was money, and that when this was forthcoming, the men would be released, but not sooner!

His friend, the brother of one of the men, was now going home to try and make up the sum needed. He made no application to me for aid, and since then I have heard nothing more of the matter. Thus ended my attempt to reach the insurgent camp at Nanking. To me, in how much mercy, but, alas! not without suffering brought upon others on my account. It was a signal mercy in the case that the Sabbath had intervened, and that we had spent it not in journeying but in preaching publicly at K'wan-shan. Had it been otherwise, it might have been said with some appearance of truth that we had purposely eluded the mandarin escort, and so brought trouble on them which belonged of right to ourselves.

December 13, 1855

I write these lines on board a river boat, which has been my principal habitation during the past three months, and in which I returned to this place on Monday last, after an absence in the surrounding country of twenty-six days. I was accompanied by a native professing Christian, received into the visible church during the present year, and now employed to circulate the Scriptures in connection with the Million Testament scheme.

We visited several market towns, the names of which I need hardly trouble you with, remaining one or two days at places of smaller importance, and for a full week at one place, Fung-king (or Maple-tree Creek), where a foreigner had hardly been seen, and where the interest felt in our message was rather greater than usual. Two or three came to our boat to pray with us, and at one time I almost hoped that the anxiety of the people would have detained us for a longer time.

We spent a few days also at the city of Tung-keang, about thirty miles from Shanghae, and frequently visited by missionaries, as well as by the foreign community generally. Here we found but little encouragement, and the rabble were even inclined to use us a little unceremoniously. The last place we visited was a market-town, Min-hang, about halfway between Hun-keang and Shanghae, and here we were prepared to meet with less attention than usual, as the place is often trodden by foreign feet, and there are few among the missionaries, I suppose, who have not been there.

However, in this case our fears were disappointed and our hopes much more than exceeded, for during the Saturday and Sabbath which we spent at this place, we had unusually large and attentive audiences, and on the Sabbath evening, when it was getting dark, we still continued to preach to an engaged audience, with whom at the close I felt at liberty to join in public prayer to the living and true God in the name of Jesus. It is not generally our custom thus to pray with the people, preaching as we do in the public street, and alas! too frequently to a people not prepared to join in spirit with us.

Swatow, March 31, 1856.
When I last wrote I was on the point of leaving Shanghae for this place in company with Mr Taylor of the Chinese Evangelization Society. We left on the 6th of March, and, after a favourable passage of six days, arrived here on the 12th. We were very averse to the thought of being located even temporarily on the island (Double Island), on which some of our countrymen have, by compact with the local magistrates, taken up their headquarters, but were anxious, if possible, to find a location in the Chinese town of Swatow, which is on a promontory of the mainland, five English miles further up, at the mouth of the river Han.

We were apprehensive lest we should not be permitted thus to locate ourselves, but in the gracious and all-governing providence of our God and Saviour, we found favour and assistance from those whom we least expected to aid us, viz., the Canton merchants here, who are the agents or correspondents of the foreigners (our countrymen) down the river, and two days after our arrival we were, to our own surprise and joy, enabled to take possession of the lodging which we have since been occupying unmolested. Our lodging is not indeed large, being only a small upper flat of a house occupied below as a shop, but it is sufficient for our present wants, and we are the more thankful for it as of vacant houses here there are almost none. Swatow is not a very large place, but it is growing at present very rapidly, and has all the appearance of being in a few years a place of great importance.

During the first ten days after our arrival, the *Geelong* lay at anchor along with another ship off the town discharging cargo, and Captain Bowers continued to show us the same Christian kindness which he had manifested in bringing us here free of charge. On the two Sabbaths that occurred during these days, I preached on board his ship, and on week-day evenings also generally met for worship with him and his crew. For the last week they have been down at Double Island, and on Saturday (29th) I went down, and yesterday preached twice in his ship to such of our countrymen as chose to attend. The number of ships at anchor there was, as usual, nearly a dozen, and among their captains and crews were an unusual number of Scotsmen, who, along with others, came very readily not only to the forenoon service, but in nearly equal numbers to a second meeting in the evening.

I felt it a great privilege to be allowed to preach the gospel in a place where it has been, as far as we know, seldom before proclaimed. Originally there seems to have been almost no population in Double Island, but since first the opium-ship captains, and afterwards some other foreign merchants, began to build houses and to occupy it, there has sprung up also a small Chinese town, consisting of those who live by business which the presence of the foreigners creates, or are occupied, alas! I am forced to add, in pandering to their unholy lusts. Yesterday week (on the Lord's day) a Malay sailor was murdered in a quarrel there, and yesterday a Chinese woman was also murdered, and another Malay sailor stabbed dangerously, if not fatally. The latter crime was the work, I understand, of a British sailor.

Mr Taylor and I are thankful indeed that we are permitted to live apart from a place where such tragedies are enacted, and where pollution and debauchery seem to stalk abroad without shame; but at the same time I shall feel it at once a duty and privilege to take every opportunity of preaching there either on ship-board or on shore while we remain in the neighbourhood. Mr Taylor and myself came here quite undecided whether we should be able to attempt more than simply to make a running visit for the purpose of scripture and tract distribution to the open parts of the country, but now that we see more fully the importance of this region as a vast and unoccupied scene for missionary labour, we are anxious, before going further, to prepare ourselves for the purpose of teaching the people orally by acquiring some knowledge of their dialect.

This is a comparatively easy work in my case, the dialect spoken here being, as I formerly mentioned, very similar to that spoken at Amoy. We have as yet done very little in the way of active labour among this people, but would pray that our zeal may increase with our ability to improve the openings for usefulness that may be afforded us. We have much need, as every one must see who considers our present position, of special grace to support and render us useful. For this grace may many be led to pray, that for the gift bestowed on us by means of many persons, thanks may be afterwards given by many in our behalf, should it please the God of grace to preserve us in his truth and love, and make us a means of blessing to some of these dying millions.

July 16, 1856. At Nan-Yang, 10 miles from Swatow
During the last fortnight I have been moving from place to place, making known the gospel message and distributing tracts, etc., in company with two professing Christians, natives of this district, who came up from Hong-Kong fully a month ago, sent by Mr Johnson, an American missionary, to co-operate with us. Previously to their coming, I had been out on a missionary tour accompanied

by a servant only. Mr Taylor, having occupied himself in learning the dialect of this district since our arrival at Swatow, left us a fortnight ago for Shanghae, intending, if the Lord will, to return in the course of a month or two, and bringing with him his medical apparatus [to] use his knowledge of medicine for the purpose of opening a door for more regular missionary operations among the people.

Had we obtained a place suitable for indoor preaching at Swatow, I would not have ventured at this hot season to go about in the country. Difficulties, however, have been thrown in the way of our obtaining such a place, and so no other course has been left open but the one we are now following. We have met as yet with but little decided encouragement, but still something is done to spread an incipient knowledge of the truth, and in a field which has been so little cultivated we must not be discouraged if we meet not with immediate success.

Swatow, June 3, 1857

Oh! that they were as anxious for the salvation of the soul as for the healing of the body. Alas! the gospel pool does not yet seem here to be visited by the angel to trouble the waters. All is sin and death around us.

Swatow, August 5, 1857

Whatever change we can mark is in the way of progress. The medical work brings an increasing number of persons about us, to whom we seek to make known the truth, and gives us, in connection with our efforts to diffuse the truths of the gospel, a very favourable position in the eyes of the community. There is a district of country, Phoo-ning, at a distance varying from thirty to fifty English miles, from which we have had of late an unusual number of visitors, both men and women.

They have taken lodgings near us for a succession of days, and not only have seemed to value the medical aid for which they came, but have very generally attended all our daily religious services, and have shown a more than common interest in our message. That district of country seems particularly afflicted with a species of leprosy, and some persons suffering from this and other diseases having received benefit, the poor people form parties and come out, at no inconsiderable trouble and expense to themselves. Those that come to us from this and other quarters we generally make the bearers of tracts and Scriptures to their villages, and sometimes when we neglect to supply them, they apply of their own accord....

I am resuming my pen after being below at our usual evening worship. We had with us, from the opposite house where they are lodging, seven or eight sick persons who have come a distance of from thirty to forty miles for medical aid, and must wait until Friday, when Dr De la Porte comes. These sick people come thus sometimes as many as thirty or forty at once, and while they are here, as well as merely on the patient-seeing days, they have a good opportunity of hearing the glorious gospel. A week or two ago a large party of women thus came, having hired a boat for themselves, and many of them seemed a good deal interested in our message.

One old matron of seventy-three I was specially interested with. Staying opposite, she was often below stairs. She came generally to worship, and by her serious and intelligent look one might hope that she understood something of what was taught her. One evening, after she retired from worship, I heard her, across the street, mentioning the Saviour's name, and she appeared to be attempting to pray.

Have you any prayer-meeting now in which China is specially remembered? We need much prayer on our behalf, and on behalf of China at this time, when new treaties may be made with foreign powers, either very favourable to the entrance of the gospel or the opposite.

Swatow, September 15, 1858
Within the last month I am glad to be able to mention that we have obtained an additional standing-point for missionary labour at the large town of Tat-haw-poe, distant about four or five miles from Double Island. I had often wished to visit this place, but delayed in consequence of being tied down, through the medical work, to Swatow, and being thus unable to follow up any favourable opening that might be given.

Four weeks ago, after the assistants and I had specially sought the divine direction, we determined that two of them should go direct to Tat-haw-poe from Swatow, and that the following day, August 17th, one of them should join me at Double Island, and conduct me from there to Tat-haw-poe. He failed to come for me on the day appointed, and next morning came to say that, at Tat-haw-poe had just been posted up a Canton proclamation, warning the people from having anything to do with the English, and that it was a question I must myself decide whether I would venture to go or not.

There was some reason to fear that no one would give me lodging, but I thought it my duty to go, and wonderful to say, just as we were about to conclude addressing the people, a man of respectability invited us into his hong, gave us a kind welcome, asked where I was to lodge, and when he found that there was but poor accommodation in the shop where my assistants were staying, he pressed us to come to him, leading me from room to room, and desiring me to take which one I preferred. Finally he put me into his own room, and one of the assistants into the adjoining, and there I remained for several days. Though passing the night in this gentleman's hong, we continued to take our meals in the shop where the assistants had been lodging, until on Saturday morning, August 21st, the shop-man informed us that his landlord had, on the previous night, given him notice that he must on no account admit foreigners into his shop, and that therefore I must cease to come.

On this we went and made known the matter to our host, asking him whether he shared in the fears of this man. He made no account of the matter at all, and said that though, from the near approach of a Chinese term, he was a good deal occupied, and could not attend to us as he wished, if I would come again in a few days, he would give us an unoccupied part of his house to stay in as long as we liked.

In this he was not deceiving us, for while I returned back to Double Island on that day, one of the assistants continued to remain in his house, and yesterday, September 14th, I returned from a second visit of six days, and have now a room waiting me whenever I am able to go.

Amoy, November 25, 1858
I am sitting in the room formerly occupied by our dear and respected brother and fellow-labourer who is now no more with us, but has, like his divine master, left us an example that we should follow his steps, in order that we may overcome like him at last through the blood of the Lamb and the word of his testimony! [Burns is here speaking of the devoted and greatly beloved David Sandeman, who died of cholera, at Amoy, July 31, 1858.] On the occasion of his so sudden removal from us, I felt unable in any suitable manner to write to any of his kindred, although I took the pen in hand more than once to do so.

On coming up here four weeks ago, I went to see the spot where his mortal remains are laid. It is as yet marked by no monumental stone, but is side by side with the graves of not a few members, old and young, of the missionary circle, and with many of them we trust he will rise in glory at the Lord's coming. What a lesson to us, and to all! When little more than a year ago I visited Amoy, I had much sweet intercourse with him, and as the vessel that conveyed me back to Swatow left the harbour, he stood on the balcony above, and waved to me until we were out of sight. Now we may imagine him from a higher elevation, beckoning us to follow on in the Christian race, laying aside every weight, and running that we may reach the prize – the crown of life, which we believe has been already given to him by his Saviour and Lord.

Letters
from
William Chalmers Burns

Letters Introduction

There can be substitute in seeking to understand a person, than to read his own words, his personal and sometimes relatively private words. Another real value of this present volume therefore, is that it contains not only an account of William Chalmers Burns' life and works, but that it sets aside a good deal of space to Burns' own writings. These include extracts from his Journals, a number of previously unpublished sermons and then this section too, a collection of assorted letters, many of which have never appeared in print before, letters which give us a deeper insight into his actions, thoughts and spirituality. The letters which many will find to be of unique value, will be the letters I have included which Burns wrote to Robert Murray M'Cheyne of St Peter's Church of Scotland in Dundee. It is these letters which are being made available in print for the first time, for the manuscript letters were discovered in the Special Collections Section of Edinburgh University's New College Library in Scotland. The letters as they appear here in this volume, are printed directly as transcribed from the original letters. Robert Murray M'Cheyne obviously regarded these letters from his Godly friend as valuable enough to keep safely. It was an action with very great foresight.

Details of recipients:
Letters to Burns' sister Jane: pp. 253; 254; 255; 256; 259; 260
Letters to Robert Murray M'Cheyne: pp. 261; 263; 264; 265; 267; 268; 269; 271; 272; 273; 275; 278; 279; 280; 281; 282; 283; 284; 287; 288; 289; 290; 291.
Letter to St Peter's Church, Dundee, p. 285.
Letter on page 311: recipient unknown apart from the details Burns gives.
All other letters are to the recipients Burns addresses.

Edinburgh, February 20th, 1832

My Dear Sisters,

I feel it often a great encouragement to me to persevere in that life upon which I have entered, that I do not *make for heaven alone*; but though there be few that find 'the strait gate' and the 'narrow way', yet that my nearest and dearest friends upon earth are my fellow-pilgrims to the 'heavenly Canaan'. Let us encourage and exhort one another in following and trusting in the Lamb who was slain, who now intercedes for all who trust in him, at the right hand of the Father.

I have been apt, as is I believe the case with many young Christians, to make my safety depend upon my feelings, and consequently to feel miserable when not engaged in religious exercises, and to despise in some degree the ordinary business of life; but I have for some time past been coming to juster and more stable views.

I had another conversation with Mr Bruce about a week ago; I was as much as on the former occasion delighted with him, and I trust edified. He had two admirable discourses last Sabbath (yesterday), the one a lecture from the 7th and 8th verses of the 6th of Matthew, and the other from Ephesians, 3rd chapter and 12th verse, 'In whom we have boldness.' They were both very much suited to my state, and I trust I was much benefited by them.... Mr Moody and I are on the most intimate terms; he is one of the few that *live near* to God.

If the Lord spare us all, I look forward to the happiest meeting that ever we have had. We are now, my dearest sisters, linked together by a new tie, being members of the same body, and the children of the Almighty, our Father in heaven: but till then let us pray daily to him for one another, and seek a nearer communion with him to whom we have access with confidence by the blood of Jesus.

Let not the question be with us, 'How near must we be to him in order to insure our safety?' but 'how much communion can we possibly attain to while here on earth?' This is not our home, 'for we are dead, and our life is hid with Christ in God.' 'When he who is our life shall appear, then shall we also appear with him in glory.' What a hope is this, that our eyes shall see him, and that we shall dwell with him for ever and ever! He now makes intercession for us at the Father's right hand. May we be 'kept by the power of God through faith unto salvation'. Let us have but one object in view, the kingdom of heaven, and all other necessary things shall be added unto us. All things shall work together for the eternal good of them that love God, and we must wait upon the Lord that he may give us this love.

There is no object in this world, the contemplation of which is an adequate employment for that immortal and divine principle in us, 'the soul', except the character of the 'Lord of hosts'; with the contemplation of which, although we were to devote our entire lives, yet would we be compelled to exclaim, 'Thou art past finding out'; and this is the God to whom we approach with so little humility and contrition of soul.

How wonderful that he should not only listen to us when we call on him, but condescend to work in us by his Holy Spirit, exciting us to draw near unto him. We ought to strive to bring our fellow-creatures to a knowledge of their state, and of the mercy that is freely offered them: it is truly an awful thought, that any one to whom the gospel is proclaimed should go down to that lake *that burneth with fire and brimstone for ever.*

People are apt to think themselves independent creatures, and that none has a right to their services, but if we do not take God's mercy in Christ Jesus, we must take his wrath. I pity most of all those whom we call decent people, who, although they will hardly believe it, are in as unsafe a state as the openly profligate, as they do not build on Christ as the foundation....

The cholera is going on here though slowly, and I hope we may all be mercifully spared, but let us endeavour to say from the heart, 'The will of the Lord be done.' I have a letter to ——— ready, which I expect to have an opportunity of forwarding this week. Let us pray earnestly for him, that the Lord would open his heart to the truth; that we may go all on together to that blessed country to which Christ has purchased an admittance for all who trust in and follow him. I cannot tell you all nor any of my thoughts on paper, but wait for a meeting with you, if the Lord will. Till then farewell.

I remain,
my dearest sisters,
your truly affectionate brother,
William C. Burns

Friday, November 16, 1832. Aberdeen

Dear Jane,

In regard to my own state of mind, I can say little that is pleasing. When I came here my spiritual state was very low, but I hoped that the necessity which I knew there was of my walking carefully would, by God's blessing, have had a beneficial effect, making me seek nearness to him and strength for all my emergencies; but I lament to say, I have been disappointed. During the first few days after my arrival, I am sensible of having been guilty of much hypocrisy, striving to make it appear that I was indeed converted, while I felt myself to be far from God, and acting I fear rather for the upholding of my own reputation than with a view to the glory of God. I might say much on this subject, but feel at this moment that although my entering on it is calculated to be beneficial to me, in bringing it more immediately before my own mind, and calling forth your earnest prayers in my behalf; yet the very feeling of having expressed my mind upon this subject may prove a snare to me, leading me to suppose that I have retraced my steps to the Cross of Christ, while I remain in reality unwilling to become his *wholly* and his *only*. May the Lord in his great mercy teach me my real character, and lead me to some just conception of his perfect holiness and hatred of sin, that I may prize as I ought that salvation which he has provided, and be made to count all things but loss for the excellency of the knowledge of Christ Jesus! The counsel and sympathy of dear friends are then especially effective when they are absent; for as we delight to think of again meeting after being for a time separated, our views are directed to that blessed abode where alone there is a security of our dwelling in sweet and uninterrupted communion.

I remain,
my dear sister,
your truly affectionate brother,
William C. Burns

1838

My Dear Jane,

I am sorry, as usual, to be obliged to despatch the basket in so great a hurry as to prevent me answering as I could have wished your very pleasing note. It is indeed hard to be truly serious and interesting, while it is easy to be morose and dull in the service of God; yet still, we must not desist from an ardent pursuit of our high and holy calling, because of the difficulties which, from an utterly depraved heart and blinded understanding, it is encompassed with. Let us in this as in all things commit in humble but earnest faith our way to the Lord, and he will direct our steps – not thinking on the one hand that we can have too deep an impression of the value of immortal souls, and the danger in which we all naturally are, if it is counterbalanced on the other by a view of the glorious remedy, and the fullness and certainty of the Christian's inheritance. O that we might live nearer to God, and then indeed if our manner may appear for a little less natural, it will become at length naturally serious and heavenly!

I have had a very dull and unfruitful week, have been conscious of more heart-atheism than I remember of feeling, but am now, I trust, desiring in some measure that this discovery of my utter depravity may by God's sovereign and precious grace be blessed to make me more humble and more grateful to the adorable Redeemer, who for such vile creatures as we, descended so infinitely low and bore so much.

I think highly of your scheme of Sabbath teaching, and hope that you will be greatly honoured and supported in it.

Your affectionate brother,
Wm C. Burns

Rothesay, Thursday, 1838

My Dear Jane,

I have from various causes delayed till this time writing home, in expectation, before ———'s arrival, of every day seeing some of you; and since then, waiting the opportunity of his return home. And now when the time has arrived, I am disappointed to find that, owing partly to other engagements in the evening, and partly to a doubt whether or not ——— would go tomorrow morning, I must take to my desk when I should retire to rest.

I cannot however think of allowing him to go without some little supplement to the intelligence which I have no doubt he will retail among you for days to come.

I have been enjoying Rothesay, since I saw you, in an unusual degree, the weather being so fine, and my health, in the great kindness of God, unimpaired. Nor can I reckon among the least of the present sources of pleasure the duties in which of course my time is a good deal occupied.

I have an interesting little charge here, and one which I think I have increasing cause to feel at once responsible and engaging. I have this season the privileges obtained by request from Mr ——— of joining with my pupils in the morning exercise of reading a portion of Scripture and prayer, which gives a new facility for bringing to bear on their minds and hearts the religious influence which God may enable me to employ, and accustoms them by practice to a duty which, imperative and fundamental as it is, they are unfortunately not yet otherwise acquainted with.

I have many pleasing tokens, had I time to enter into particulars, of such an interest in all my pupils in those truths which must decide their eternity, as hang one between hope and fear on their account, and demand on my part a diligence and prayerfulness, which, now that I record this truth before grace to occupy my present little talent, instead of looking forward to a larger sphere, for when may I expect to be faithful if not now, and may I not here be privileged in Jehovah's infinite lovingkindness, if ever I shall be so honoured, to tend the lambs of the fold of Jesus?

It is unbelief and not faith, I find, that discourages the ambition. Let us provoke one another, my dear sister, to love and to good works; let us be steadfast in our efforts and instant in our prayers, and never forget, for your encouragement in the service of our Divine Master, that if I have ever yet known the precious faith of God's elect, it was a letter from you and Margaret, in which I remember you spoke of being 'pilgrims to a better country', that was first blessed to rouse me from the unconcern of an ungodly state.

I wrote to ――― some time ago and have had a letter in reply. His circumstances appear, from his account, in many respects very favourable for his improvement. ――― appears to have enjoyed his short stay with me exceedingly, and we have been very happy together. He is a boy of very warm heart, solid and in the main thoughtful; a hopeful subject of grace he appears to me, when I contrast his character and impressions of truth, as far as I can see these, with my own at a similar age. May the Lord make him his own, and prepare him, if it be his holy will, for important service in the advancement of his cause!

We have been thinking of you in the enjoyment of your New Testament feast. In the strength of this food may you have grace to go many days.

And now farewell, my dear Jane, and give my cordial and brotherly regards to all at home and at Croy.

Ever yours,
Wm C. Burns

Wednesday, 26th September, 1838

My Dear Jane,

I hope you will not misinterpret my conduct in not answering your note on Saturday. The subject to which it referred was of too important and solemn a nature to be lightly and hastily noticed, and I desired, first, to give special thanks to the Lord for his inviting us to correspondence on such topics; and, next, to seek by prayer and fasting to obtain light from his Word, expounded by the Holy Spirit, to guide me in regard to them.

The time to write you has arrived, and my conscious deadness and spiritual blindness form a new argument to convince me of the need I have of using more vigorous and regular means for obtaining that advancement in the knowledge of Christ which can alone fit me to be an instrument in his hand for the advancement of his kingdom in the world.

I am almost afraid to speak of some things, which, I believe in common with yourself, my convictions have for some time approved of as indispensable means of our growth in grace – my practice of these has been so irregular, and, at best, so far behind even my own dark and partial views regarding them. Yet it is the spirit of pride and legal hope, I am aware, that makes me shrink from these as if from a broken covenant, instead of casting myself again as an undone transgressor on the free covenant of promise, that in me henceforth Christ may live, and regulate all things according to his own good pleasure, and for his own glory!

The great fundamental error then, as far as I can see, in the economy of the Christian life, which many, and alas! I for one commit, is that of having too few and too short periods of solemn retirement with our gracious Father and his adorable Son Jesus Christ. It is, we well know, when meditating in secret on his Word, when examining our hearts in his holy and omniscient but fatherly and gracious presence, when pouring out our complaint before him, and seeking to utter the praises of his glorious character and works – it is in these exercises that we come to know, through the teaching of the Spirit, our natural darkness, depravity, and vileness, and that the glorious Sun of Righteousness arises upon our souls with healing in his wings, giving light to us who sit in darkness and in the region and shadow of death. The communion of the saints in Christian converse is indeed important, nay, indispensable to the growth of the new man when it can be obtained, but when is it sweet and soul-reviving but when each brings out into the common store something of the heavenly food which he has been gathering in the closet? Whenever the holy, heavenly light of a Christian deportment is seen in any one, when we hear him bringing forth from a full heart some of the glorious things of the kingdom, we ought then to learn the lesson that 'he has been with Jesus', and to go in like manner to him that we too may obtain this living water to be in us as a well of water springing up unto everlasting life.

I have alluded to this subject in connection with your proposal, which I would hail with joy, for 'united prayer', because it strikes me from what I have felt that our object will be best attained by our stimulating each other to greatly increased fidelity in these regular and acknowledged means, instead of first adopting any special measures which is only a burden and an impediment, except when it is like an additional channel dug for the conveyance of the waters which are overflowing their ordinary banks.

O that our private and personal covenanting with the Lord were more frequent and regular! This would form some basis for united efforts in his service; but without it I fear we are in danger of neglecting the Lord's own ordinance for means of our own devising.

For myself then, dear Jane, I intend tomorrow, D.V., solemnly to review my duty in the private exercises of God's worship, in the light of his Word; and may he grant it, of his Holy Spirit, that I may, by his promised grace, be humbled before him for past neglect of his blessed appointments, and resolve, in his strength, henceforth 'to keep his statutes', not as a servant for his wages, but as a son from love to his father's presence and his father's laws.

It will serve the end of these lines, dear sister, if they be a link in a chain of correspondence between us regarding the work of God in our own hearts, and around us. Such a correspondence I much desire, and much more need; and I am satisfied that had I been earlier thus engaged, I would have been more fruitful in the glorious work of the Lord, and have written, not as now I do to my shame about the things of God with so ignorant a mind and so cold a heart.

O may the love of Christ constrain us to live no more as our own, but as manifestly his! This is the motive that will carry us with a rejoicing heart through tribulations and distresses for his name's sake; and make us count all things but loss that we may win Christ and be found in him, clothed upon with his spotless righteousness, and filled with his Holy Spirit.

And now, desiring that the Lord Jesus may manifest himself to you in his surpassing beauty and matchless grace and love,

I remain your affectionate brother,
Wm C. Burns

P.S.

I expect to hear from you soon. Let us be free, faithful and affectionate, and seek to taste the excellence of living habitually what we write from time to time.
WCB

30th September, 1838

My Dear Jane,

I would not write you so paltry a note, were it not that writing to ——— has exhausted my time, and I cannot let another opportunity pass without thanking you for your kind and interesting letter, which I have not yet acknowledged; and expressing my desire that your midday period of solemn retirement may be specially regarded of the Lord, and that you may obtain new and remarkable communications of the Holy Spirit in all his vivifying and comforting power. I enjoyed my late visit very much, though, had we been alone, it might have been spent in closer intercourse on the things of the Spirit, and in special approaches to the throne of divine grace, and thus have been rendered more stimulating to us all. Mr Denniston, I hope, will see you on Friday, and I hope that, through the presence of the Lord, his parting visit may be eminently blessed to your growth in the excellent knowledge of Christ.

I am asking, though alas! with little becoming solicitude, whether the present is to be added to the list of our almost Christless sacraments. Would that the Lord would pour out on us the Spirit as in former days, and bring his saints into close and ravishing fellowship with himself! 'Whither is our beloved gone?' 'Why tarry the wheels of his chariot?' 'Wilt thou not revive us again, that thy people may rejoice in thee?'

In earnest expectation of his coming, let us wait day and night, and he will at last arrive to our infinite amazement and eternal rejoicing.

My love in Christ Jesus to dear Charlotte, and believe me,
your affectionate brother,
William C. Burns

Wednesday 17th, 1838

My Dear Jane,

I would have sent the basket sooner, but could not find the time necessary for despatching it; and I hope that we shall get it returned not later than this day week.

None of us have been able to get out to Paisley as yet, but I heard of them yesterday. They are all, it would seem, well, with the exception of Aunt ———, who I hear is confined to bed with cold, and is still troubled with her arm, which does not seem to mend rapidly. I paid a most delightful visit to Uncle Islay's the other evening, when Mr ———, their new minister was there, and expounded in a manner remarkably interesting and impressive. He seems indeed a very uncommon Christian, and has made me feel in some degree my own miserable ignorance in the excellent knowledge of the Son of God. O that I might know him, and the power of his resurrection, and the fellowship of his sufferings, being made conformable to his death! God forbid that we should glory save in the Cross of the Lord Jesus Christ, by whom the world is crucified to us, and we to the world!

I trust, my dear sister, that you are obtaining some advancement in the knowledge of your own vileness and misery, and of the glorious righteousness and atonement of Emmanuel, our elder brother. Of such precious knowledge I can say little, but I would desire, I trust by the grace of the Holy Spirit, to fix the eye continually on Jesus, who is the finisher as well as the author of faith, and who as he is the faithful God, will perfect for his own glory that which concerneth us. I am approaching, as you know, an era of my history, if we except the time of conversion, the most important that can occur to a human being in this world. Soon must I offer myself, miserable as I am, to the Church of God as a candidate for the work of an evangelist; and still more, that Church must decide, so great is the honour I have in prospect, whether in this land or among the perishing heathen it shall be my lot to preach to sinners the unsearchable riches of Christ crucified.

In the meantime, O pray for me, and our dear brother ----, as I now again resolve to pray for you, that, in our present respective spheres, we may be always living epistles of Christ, that may be known and read of all men, and be even now the means, in the hand of the Spirit of the Lord, of converting sinners and edifying believers! Especially for our dear brother ——— let us plead unitedly, that he may be speedily given to the Church of God, and thus preserved safe into the heavenly kingdom from those sins and snares of youth which have drowned so many in destruction and perdition!

We had the privilege of being lately addressed in our missionary society by Dr Kalley of Kilmarnock, 'a good physician', who is leaving his present practice, which I understand is excellent, to consecrate his medical skill to the promotion of the cause of Christ in China, a channel which seems at present almost the only one open among that benighted people, so puffed up by their imagined knowledge in almost every branch of science and religion. Though a member of our own church, he goes out supported by the London Missionary Society, as the Committee of the General Assembly did not judge it expedient to extend the field of their operations farther east than India. He appears a most superior man, calm, but resolved and eager; and being one who I am informed was converted some years ago from a life of vanity, he seems, especially in prayer, to have obtained peculiarly deep views of man's sin, and of the glorious grace of God.

But I am forced abruptly to conclude,
and am, I trust,
your affectionate brother in Christ,
Wm C. Burns

March 2nd, 1839
Glasgow, 28 North Portland Street

My Dear Sir,

I have just received your letter, and hasten to pen a few words in reply to your important and interesting proposal, though as I expect, D.V., to visit Edinburgh on Wednesday next, I shall leave all detail in the views which occur to me on the subject until then. Indeed, I would not trouble you with a letter at all, were it not that I received yesterday a communication from Mr Dunlop, informing one of the unfavourable decision of the India Mission's acting committee, relating to N. Brunswick, and enquiring whether it was agreeable to me that he should bring the subject before the General Committee on Monday 1st; and that I have written him to the effect that I am perfectly passive in the matter, and leave him and his colleagues to prosecute the business as they may judge to be best for the interests of the Redeemer's Kingdom, provided that on conversing with him or with other members of the Committee, they should be led to desist from any further steps regarding my going to N. Brunswick, and provided that I am not called, which appears to be at least possible, to go to Ceylon in the absence of any other call.

As for the gracious and unexpected call to come to Dundee, it will not be a little beneficial especially with reference to my ultimate desires, to have an opportunity so favourable of making proof of the ministry of Christ among my dear countrymen who are either still ignorant of Jesus, or who have been brought into the glorious, and holy fellowship of the Father and the Son.

I am indeed unfit, as I am unworthy to engage in this arduous, but most noble embassage. I am darkness. I am deadness. I am carnal, sold under sin! But what then? Glory be to Jesus, his grace is sufficient for me, for his strength is made perfect in weakness. I am afraid to speak or to think of his incomprehensible and most free love in opening up so many prospects of labour in his service to me, and especially, should he call me, (for he will arrange the matter!) to enter for a time into your labours and watch for the souls over which the Holy Ghost hath made you overseer. I do rejoice in the thought of being connected so closely with yourself and others of his chosen people, and, in the fruits of which may thence ensue, in my increased preparedness for that fight of faith in India to which he has led me to look with hope.

With the earnest prayer that God may greatly increase your faith, and hope, and love; and order all the circumstances of your outward lot for his own glory.

I am, dear sir,
Your brother in Christ,
Wm C. Burns

Glasgow, 28 North Portland Street
March 11th, 1839

My Dear Sir,

I have been endeavouring since I saw you, to discern, by deliberation and the advice of friends, accompanied by special prayer for the light and guidance of the Holy Spirit, the will of God in regard to the important proposal made to me by you. And now as far as I can discern my path, it appears to me to be this, that I am bound to leave myself at your disposal, and, in case you shall still see cause for asking me to enter on your sphere of duty during your absence, to cast myself on that grace promised in the Covenant which is sufficient to fit the weakest instruments for accomplishing the work he gives, which yields a service of glory to God.

I confess I am afraid to speak in such terms as these, for though it be true that God can fit even me for such a mighty work as this which is proposed, yet I have too much reason to fear that the work of the Spirit is making little progress, or even going back, in my own soul, and thus I am in the greatest danger of entertaining the language of dependency, while the reality of this precious grace is so much awanting.

I hope that you have been directed to some other in whose hands you would prefer to leave the weighty charge of your people's souls. If however, you still desire that I should attempt this work, I dare not refuse from any inability which the Lord, who calleth me to his service, is able and willing to remove.

I have been calculating that in all probability I will not be able to preach before the 1st Sabbath of April, and if it did not cause any serious inconvenience, it would be desirable that I should enjoy the Sacrament here on that day, and preach on the following one at Kilsyth. If, however, this will not suit your views, I must first proceed at once to the field of labour, and make a commencement there. Regarding this and all other arrangements, you will, I hope, be able to give me the necessary information soon that I may proceed accordingly. I would like also to know what opportunities of consulting theological works, especially commentaries, I might hope to enjoy at Dundee, as there are certain works of that kind which I must procure for myself, if they cannot be otherwise consulted.

I must now conclude, as I have written these lines in the greatest haste, to be in time for this forenoon's post.

And I remain, dear sir,
Your brother in Christ,
Wm C. Burns

Glasgow, 28 North Portland Street
March 16th, 1839

My Dear Sir,

Your delightful letter, for the contents of which I desire to give continual praise to God, I have delayed answering with the view of having an opportunity today of consulting my friends at Kilsyth in regard to some things which it contains. It has, however, just occurred to me that on every thing of real importance to be immediately answered, I have at present sufficient means of coming to a decision, and that I ought not to delay communicating what is necessary for enabling you as soon as possible to make arrangements necessary before your departure.

Regarding anything else in your letter, I have not time to say a word, as I am hurrying to be in time for this forenoon's post. I cannot, however, omit to say that I am at any rate a sufficiently good economist to be most comfortably supported at the rate which you propose, and consider it a much more ample provision than in my circumstances I had any reason to look for.

For my guidance perhaps you could tell me, along with other things, at what periods my temporal provision might be expected to be received, that I may know how far it is necessary to draw for a time on the resources of my friend before leaving home; and it would be well also to know to whom I could write in case anything unforeseen should prevent my being at Dundee on the day I have spoken of, to obtain supply for your pulpit in my absence.

I trust you will excuse these hurried, but necessary, lines, that all arrangements will go well.

I remain, dear sir,
Your brother in Christ
Wm C. Burns

June 18, 1839

Dear Aunt,

I am afraid that I must decline the kind invitation to come to St Andrews and preach there, for the people here are in that interesting state of hopeful movement and inquiry, in which it is least of all the duty of their appointed teacher to be absent from them.

It is my earnest desire and prayer, dear aunt, that the Lord may look down in his infinite mercy and grace on St Andrews, which in ancient times he so highly honoured, but from which, alas! is not his glorious presence greatly withdrawn? Oh! for a Rutherford or a Halyburton to awaken slumbering sinners at ease under the wrath of an angry God, and to stir up the true people of God to abound in the love and in the praise of Jesus! 'Wilt thou not revive us again, that thy people may rejoice in thee.' Oh! may the Lord grant to that remnant that serve him in the Spirit to be 'zealous, and strengthen the things which remain, and are ready to die', to plead, yea, to besiege the throne of grace with their unceasing and importunate pleadings, that he may appear in his glory, and build up Zion, giving ear to the prayer of the destitute and the groaning of the prisoners. Oh! what a plea is the name of Jesus! How omnipotent to move the heart of the Father, who loveth the Son, and hath given all things into his hands! None of God's people have yet proved the power of that matchless name in the presence of Jehovah. Let us henceforth do so in the strength of Jesus, and we may yet see, before we leave the kingdom of grace for the kingdom of glory, such a plenteous rain as will refresh God's heritage which is weary. The time is short! Behold! the judge standeth before the door. Come, Lord Jesus, come quickly!

Your loving nephew,
Wm C. Burns

Perth: at Revd. Mr Milne's
December 30th, 1839

Dear Brother in Jesus,

I intended fully to have returned to Dundee, on Wednesday 1st January 1840, in time if required to have officiated in the evening in St Peter's Church, but the appearances of the presence of the Lord Emmanuel in his ordinances here (particularly last night where I remained in a meeting till 11 o'clock in St Leonard's Church, along with Mr Mylne the minister) make it seem to us all very desirable that, if possible, I should remain a few days longer, and aid my dear brethren in the Lord's glorious work of salvation.

I therefore write this note, that you may let me know by return of post whether there appears to be any stronger reason for returning to Dundee on Wednesday than there is, as you may be able to understand, for my remaining here. If you think I need to come, you will write in time to reach me on Wednesday morning, and I will come, D.V., by the evening coach in time for any public duty in the church. If you think that I may stay here, in that case also it will be better to send a line and let me know this. I will conclude, if I hear nothing, that you have not got this letter in time, and that I must first come home as I intended when I left Dundee. Truly the Lord is doing great and marvellous works in Zion at this time!

At Dunfermline I have seen the clearest tokens of his mighty working, and last night the work was so glorious that hardly one out of about 150 seemed free from deep impressions of the Word and Spirit of Jesus, and many were evidently pricked in their hearts, whilst some heavy-laden souls emerged into the glorious liberty of the children of God. This forenoon again, from 200–300 came to the Church between 1 o'clock to 3 o'clock, to converse about their state, with whom we had a united meeting of the most blessed kind.

Before I left Dundee, I pressed on the Lord's dear children there the duty of praying for me while absent and I am convinced their prayers have been heard. Oh! Will not what others have been receiving provoke the unconverted in Dundee to jealousy! Would you, dear brother, press on the Lord's children at the meeting tomorrow evening (Tuesday) the case of Perth. It is still as a city in Satan's hands, but now it may be taken if they join us in giving the Lord no rest in its behalf.

Is not the furnace heating for the trial of the Church of Christ, and do not we see that the Lord is preparing gold for its fires? I pray for you dear brother, whom I love in the Lord. I know you do the same much more for me. Oh! Increase your prayers for me at this time, that so the Lord may be greatly glorified.

Yours in Christ,
Wm C. Burns

P.S. Tell me if I can be absent on Sabbath first. It would be desirable. Please make James bring up my letters that are waiting me and send them with yours in one by post.

Collessie, Fife
June 4th, 1840

My Dear Brother,

I am sorry that your note came too late to be of any use, having only arrived this morning. I can only relieve my anxiety about supply by casting the case on the Lord. May you return to your dear people with a double measure of the Holy Spirit, and see the vineyards flourishing.

I am now, praised be the Lord, quite well, though I fear the end of God's grace in my sanctification are not yet answered. I am doing a little from day to day in Collessie and Monimail, where I am to be tonight, but I do not yet see the hearts of men beginning to move, yet I have hope in the Lord. Next week, if spared, I propose visiting Perth, which I much long to do, and the following one, if the Lord will, I intend to visit you for a day in Dundee, spending the intermediate Sabbaths at Monkston (in the open-air) and remember 'poor wretched' Fife. It is the valley of the shadow of death.

Your note contained the first intimation to me of dear brother Macdonald's marriage. I seek to pray that the union may be for the glory of the Lord in them both.

In haste I am,
Your affectionate brother,
Wm C. Burns

Kinness Manse
July 2nd, 1840

My Dear Brother,

I was very sorry that it was quite out of my power to remain in Dundee and supply your pulpit when I passed through on my way to Kilconquhar. This, however, was impossible, as my visit to Kilconquhar was so long arranged, and so fully known. I spent ten days in that quarter, preaching in Kilconquhar, Methil, Largo, St Monance and Anstruther. Dr Finie and his son (indeed all the ministers, but these in particular), received me with astonishing kindness. They not only allowed me the liberty of meeting privately with anxious enquirers among their people, but actually pressed me to this most important part of the work of Christ's ambassadors. Many seemed to be anxious at Kilconquhar, and perhaps a greater number at Anstruther, where the labours of Mr Wright and the Independents seem to have been blessed during the last twelve months for the conversion of souls, and where I was supported by the wrestling prayer of God's people of every name. It was to many of us very affecting and delightful to see the whole population of Anstruther, with many from surrounding places, assembled together during the afternoon and evening at the Tent in the Churchyard: the dissenting bodies having of their own accord shut up their own places of worship. The Lord's people did indeed seem to be 'all one' in Christ. Praise to the Name of the Lord, who only doeth wondrous things!

Remember Dr Finie and his son in your prayers with me. They are both very anxious apparently to be useful among their people. May the Lord fill them both with the fullness of the Holy Ghost, that Jesus may be glorified mightily. Remember me also, dear brother, my own soul I mean, which is in the utmost peril I am convinced, and the spiritual health of which is so intimately connected with my official success, as an Ambassador of Christ.

Would you favour me by giving Mr Morrison the teacher my warmest regards, that when the bookcase which they were making for me is ready, I would like it packed up and forwarded by one of the Glasgow packets to Kilsyth, as I have already got all my books sent home. The address is: 'Revd. Wm C. Burns, Manse Kilsyth.

To be left at Auchensterry.' If any letters come to you for me, they may be directed to Kilsyth until you hear from me again.

I trust the Lord's work is going on among your dear people, with increasing purity and power. This is the burden of my daily prayers. Oh! That the Lord would shake the foundations of Satan's Kingdom in poor Dundee, and gather tens of thousands of its God-defying inhabitants to the feet of Jesus.

May the Lord's own people keep their garments lest they walk naked and they shall soon be admitted to walk with Jesus in white, being found worthy.

Your affectionate brother in Jesus,

Wm C. Burns

Drop me a note soon, which may do me good.

Perth, July 11th, 1840

Dear Brother in Jesus,

I had to thank the Lord, though alas with a cold and ungrateful heart, for the counsel which he sent me through you the day we last met in Dundee. I have indeed need of much grace to keep me standing, and much more to keep me fighting at present, and I have been led to think that I will not be much blessed in the Lord's work again, until he has abased me in my own sight, and taught me, if not the people also to whom I preach in his holy name, that I am indeed all vile, and that all the glory is his alone. Oh! Pray that this may not be shown by my fall, but by my being chastened and humbled in the way that his infinite wisdom and love may choose.

We have had, I am persuaded, some drops from the Lord's gracious and holy presence, but as far as I can see, the work, in as far as it is truly Divine, is of comparatively small extent and though there are many who seem to have a degree of interest, it seems insufficient to bring them to enquire about Christ even in private. They are not under genuine spiritual conviction of sin, and there are even some who show such a lightness of demeanour, which I felt it proper to rebuke even from the pulpit.

Last night I was greatly straitened in preaching and was only able to tell the people, after I had sung a Psalm and prayed, that unless they ceased to look to man, and began really and directly to deal with God in Christ, trembling themselves in his sight, I felt that I neither would nor could any longer preach among them. I trust that this dispensation is a hopeful indication that the Lord intends to abase in his sight, and thus prepare the way for his appearing in glory and building up Zion in answer to the prayer of the destitute. I have had a little humbling of soul today I trust by the Holy Spirit, from which I would desire to praise his matchless Name, but oh! I am still 'proud knowing nothing', and ready to fall into the snare of the devil. 'Lord Jesus, save me or I perish!'

In answer to your welcome note, which I have been too long in answering, I have to say that next week I do not see how I can come down to Dundee sooner than Saturday, as we intend to have further meetings on Monday, Wednesday and Friday, and in the present state of this city, I cannot see that I can be absent on the least of these days, having engaged some time ago to be at Mr Walker's last day on Wednesday 1st. The state of matters here is simply this: Dense crowds came out from night to night to our meetings in St Leonard's Church, and as many came in the forenoons to converse privately about their state. Some of them seemed to be deeply convinced of sin, and others who seem to be the children of God being evidently refreshed and quickened in their devotedness to the Lord Jesus.

A great many prayer meetings are in the course of being formed, the people of God appear to be getting acquainted with each other, and to be increasing in the love of the brethren, and the people of the world who are standing by are madly saying with their tongues against our proceedings, and ready to rejoice in the thought of our meetings coming to an end, and the town being allowed to sink back into its former ease – oh! fearful! – under the wrath of the Almighty God! In these circumstances I seem called to remain here for a few days longer at least. Though much saving work may not yet have been done, yet the Lord has been, I am assured, visiting some poor prisoners, and the ministers are in some cases beginning to become more alive to the awful state of spiritual death in which Perth as a city is lying.

Oh! that I had a heart and a tongue to give the Lord praise, for he is good, his mercy endureth forever. I fully agree with you in your sad reflection upon the state of your own dear flock, and though, alas! I cannot with truth say that I pray much for them, yet I know their case in grave measure and desire to labour and pray for their everlasting emancipation from the cruel hold over them by Satan and sin.

If I am spared, I will be with you on Saturday, probably though not certainly by the morning coach, and I will be ready as the Lord may give preparation for any needed services on Sabbath and also for any duty that may devolve on me upon Monday or Tuesday.

I will conclude in order that I may have more time to pray for you and your dear people, whom I desire to long after in the bowels of Jesus Christ, and whom I pray that He may signally visit with his salvation on this blessed occasion to the glory of the Father's grace for ever and ever.

Yours in Jesus,
Wm C. Burns

Dundee, July 21st, 1840

Dear Brother,

I send this hurried note simply to say that I ask you to be home in time for the next Thursday prayer meeting. I suppose this is your intention, but as I did not hear you say anything, I thought it best to make sure of avoiding any mistake. We had a sacred meeting last night and are to have a prayer meeting in the schoolhouse this evening, in which Mr Bonar with his people and yourself shall have a chief place.

The work of the Lord appears to be progressing from day to day in Perth and the neighbourhood and I entreat a very special interest in your prayers and in those of dear Mr Bonar, whom I love in the Lord, for that very important neighbourhood.

I must conclude, not having a moment to spare, and am dear brother,

Yours in Jesus,
Wm C. Burns

Perth, July 24th, 1840

Dear Brother in Jesus,

Should I not wait until I receive answer from Dr Driver about my call through him to go to Keith before answering with a yea or nay your kind letter just received? And even if he should release me, whether it is my duty to take your place in St Peter's on the Sabbaths or Mr Lewis in St David's, as I have for some time requested to do, during his absence at Huntly? I shall leave you to think of this in connection with your own duty towards Dundee when there is certainly at present a special call for 'all hands to work', which neither you nor I should overlook until I see or hear from you. You know I expect to be with you on Tuesday to preach, D.V., in the evening.

The work of the Lord continues to extend and deepen here. I had about 30 young men with me last night seeking conversion and prayer, whose cases were very interesting and certainly the fruit of the present work. I cannot add a word more, as after having written two other letters, I find I am too late for prayer meeting in the Church.

Dear Brother, I can never thank you for all your very Christian and kind wishes towards me. Do not think that I tire of your counsel. If you want my love in Christ, oh! be faithful to me, that I may not fall into the snare of the devil.

In haste,
Yours in Emmanuel,
Wm C. Burns

Perth, July 26th, 1840

Dear Brother,

I purposed to have preached as usual in St Peter's on Tuesday next, but I find since I returned that it is too late to alter a conditional arrangement which I had made to be at the Bridge of Earn on that day, Mr Cumming having already intimated the meeting in some of the neighbouring parishes, and therefore it is impossible to be with your dear people as they had expected when we last parted. If you think it desirable and were willing to take the Tuesday yourself and leave to me the Thursday, I should be very happy to come down on that day instead of Tuesday. You will judge of this and let me know.

When I was in Dundee I made agreement in conversation with some of the godly among your people for a day of solemn fasting and prayer, which the godly who attend our meetings here intended to observe soon, and we agreed in thinking it very desirable that the Lord's people with you should join us and cry unitedly with solemn humiliation at the foot of the cross for all those sins which have hitherto obstructed the progress of the Lord's work, for an abundant outpouring of the Holy Ghost upon the church and especially on these two cities with the adjacent country.

We have fixed on Saturday first for this purpose, intending to spend the day as far as we can *alone*, and in the Private Prayer meeting; having perhaps a season of humiliation and prayer in the church some time in the evening. Would you think it proper to call on all who choose to join us in this solemn and at present, especially, most necessary duty? If so I would like to have a note saying that you care to join us. It is not unlikely that the people at Kilsyth will join us and also some in other places. You might also give us any hints that occur to you regarding special cause for observing such a season and the most profitable manner of conducting our exercises upon it. I have not a moment to spare.

The Lord's work goes on here
and am Dear Brother,
Yours in Emmanuel,
William C. Burns

Thanks for your letter. Praise for the good news in it!

Grandtully Manse, Aberfeldy
August 31st, 1840

My Dear Brother,
It is unwillingly that I am so great a stranger to you, but I am so completely engaged day after day in the Lord's work, that I need every spare minute and would need many more for the study and

the closet. As I am writing letters today I cannot, however, longer refrain from dropping you a line. I rejoiced to hear from more than one of my correspondents at Dundee, that you have lately had some interesting cases of awakening, though I am grieved at the same time to hear that some have proved wavering and unsettled in principle of where better things were expected. Oh! how mightily Satan, the World and the old man, are to delude and destroy our poor souls. The Almighty Emmanuel is our only hope and how wonderful, how infinitely gracious it is, that he does not give us all up to be filled with our own devices. Glory to his Name, he will have mercy.

You were, I rejoiced to hear, seeking in the strength of the Lord to make the Fair-Day in Dundee, a fair-day indeed. Oh! how fearful to see on such a day thousands rushing headlong into the fearful pit. Praise to the Lord, we are not all left to follow them.

Write, when you can, a note and let me know your affairs and how you do. Send me also Denniston's letter which I left with you, that I may at length answer it. Could you soon write to me a few lines. Oh! do so, I would value them much! Give to Mr Morrison the teacher, and to my other kind friends, my thanks that my bookcase arrived at Kilsyth safely and in due time. The Lord reward them for their kindness. Oh! remember me at the Throne of Mercy and send me faithful counsel. We have had good appearances in Breadalbane during the last two weeks. I shall remain so long as the Lord seems to have work for me to do in this quarter. We had upwards of perhaps 5,000 yesterday here. Moulin next Sabbath etc., etc.

Commend me to the prayers of the Lord's people
and I am yours ever in Jesus,
Wm C. Burns

Kirkmichael Manse
September 21st, 1840

My Dear Brother,

Your precious note was a cordial sent by the Lord to my fainting soul yesterday morning before I went to the Tent here. May all its faithful counsels be blessed to my soul, and may the fruit appear many days hence. As my time is the shortest possible, I must tell you somewhat of that which is going on in this part of the country. May I be enabled to record it only for the Lord's glory. The six weeks just concluded, have been among the most remarkable that I have ever enjoyed in a public capacity. I have been at Lawers and Ardonaig on Loch Tay side, at Fortingall, Aberfeldy, Dowally and Kirkmichael, and in hardly any of these places have we been left without evident tokens of the Lord's gracious Presence.

In Breadalbane, the work has been as remarkable a move as any of the other places. During the first week that I was there, it seemed, as Mr Campbell of Lawers said, to be like a resurrection, the work of the Spirit was so intended, powerful and evidently independent of the means employed.

I never saw God moving more evidently in a sovereign manner than there. In many cases, I have found it eminently necessary and much blessed to ask those anxious to wait at the close of a public meeting, in order to get their attention and bring them to a stand as to the offer of free salvation. And there this was not needed. The Lord carried on his work mightily among the ordinary services, and I always found it most desirable to leave the people instantly after the blessing was pronounced and send them to search a meeting with the Lord. Many were awakened and among these a great number of men, some of them the hardest hearts and some the most openly wicked. During the fortnight that I remained in that part of the country, all things seemed to promise well for a harvest of souls, and within these last few days, I have seen Mr Campbell of Lawers and have heard that there is no appearance of going back, but that on the contrary, a number of new cases of awakening have occurred since I left them, under his own ministry. They had an entire day last week (Wednesday) devoted to public thanksgiving for the Lord's mercy toward them. The people were all present, and the scene I am told, was in the highest degree solemn.

Some of the people are now getting great comfort from the Lord, or as a woman from that place described it, 'the people in Breadalbane are greatly recovered now'. And so great has been the effect of the Lord's presence upon the people, that last Thursday the market at Kenmore (Tay Mouth), which used to be a resort of all the thoughtless and giddy among the young, passed over without a single individual of this description attending it.

If I was telling these things to any other than such as you, I might speak of the likelihood of many of these interesting appearances coming to a speedy end, but I need not guard you against thinking that Mr Campbell or I expect that every blossom will end in fruit. There is much to fear, but there is much also to hope and much to form a sound of praise to the Almighty Lord, who saveth with his right hand. It would need twenty sheets to give you an outline of all that my eyes have seen of the Lord's mighty working in this district. There is a time coming when it may be to go, for the Lord's glory.

Is it not remarkable, and does it not show the wonderful hand of God, that I have been welcomed into the Parishes and pulpits of a number of moderate ministers in this part of the country? For instance, Mr Buchanan of Logierait, with whom I was last Sabbath (the 13th), Mr Campbell of Moulin, with whom I was throughout the week previous to that day, and Mr McDonald of Fortingall, in whose church I have already been in a week day, and expect to be again, if the Lord will, on Sabbath next. There are other moderate pulpits also I hear, which have been hitherto shut, but which the voice of the people and the example of brethren is beginning to open. Yesterday week at Logierait, we were at the Tent without interruption during five hours and the power of the Word in the hand of the Spirit was so great that hundreds were in tears and many cried aloud and yet Mr Buchanan seemed very friendly and very serious. I feel a great interest in him and in Mr Campbell of Moulin. Oh! join me in wrestling with the Lord, that he may pour out the fulness of his Spirit upon their souls and make them mighty instruments in saving others.

You have sent me to a sweet duty, but one that compels me to be egotistical. May the Lord save me from the accompanying danger to my own poor soul and do you pardon me and pray for me, more and more, that I may lie as clay in the hands of the potter, at the feet of Emmanuel.

I am relieved by hearing that the unreadiness among some of your dear people which Mr Thoms alluded to, is of the kind you mention, and that the Lord seems to be overruling it for good. There are good accounts from Perth. Our dear brother Milne says, September 15th, 'You will be glad to hear my firm conviction, founded on a pretty extensive observation in visiting, that the number of those who have been permanently, and I trust savingly, benefited by the winter meetings is very great. I meet with them in all quarters, especially among the poor and the young. They are a peculiar people, keeping much by themselves and among themselves. They have been left in a great degree as sheep without a shepherd, but I have a hope that the Lord is preparing for us a season of revival and quickening. There is much prayer among the people, especially on Sabbath mornings, and for a week or two I think I have experienced the benefit of it.'

Oh! pray for dear brother Milne whose words I have quoted. I have good hopes that the Lord is preparing him for some greater work than he has yet been employed in. He was in a desponding kind of frame last winter at times, but the Lord has, I trust, been showing him his condition in the deep, and is now bringing him forth into the light. I judge this from what I have heard from him through others and also from the whole tenor of his last letter, as well as particular impressions in it. For instance, he says (I write in confidence), 'I cannot help feeling that the Lord is beginning to give me a more sensible deliverance from the fear of man.' Oh! let us give glory to the Lord who only doeth wondrous things!

Drop a note to our dear brother Denniston. His letter affected me much when I read it over again last night. How interesting it is to see him attending to the young Jew of whose confession of Christ we heard in the Missionary Record, in the following words: 'I have just heard this evening of a young Jew seeking my acquaintance from being impressed on Sabbath by a sermon on the Temptation. This is all but it tends to hope that the hand of God is in it'!!!

Oh! do send him a few lines if you have not already done it. He loves you much and it will be as cold water to a thirsty soul for him even to see your hand.

I go, D.V., to Aberdeen for Sabbath October 1st.

Yours with affection in the Lord Jesus,

Wm C. Burns

Enclosed is one pound to the Jews from a labouring man per Wm C. B.

Aberdeen at Mr Murray's
October 17th, 1840

My Dear Brother,

It is remarkable that I had a strong desire to get free from coming to Dundee at the time that I would have needed to do so in order to preach in Dudhope Church, and so your letter has come to me as an answer to prayer from the Lord. This is not because I would not rejoice when he calls me to labour in Dundee again, but because I have had a pressing invitation to go to Forglen, Banff, and a number of other Parishes in that quarter, after leaving Aberdeen, and this season is thought particularly suitable for reaching the population in these places. Indeed, when you were writing the note I have just got, Morton of Forglen and I were praying that if it were for his glory I might get free from Dundee and be at liberty to go to the north.

From what I have said, you will see that it will not be in my power, however much I might desire it, to be with you and your dear flock at the great solemnity. I shall however, if spared, be with you I trust in Spirit, praying that Emmanuel may unveil his hidden and matchless glory to many sinners and saints. While the Lord of Hosts is making for you on Mount Zion a feast of fat things, may he also 'destroy by his Spirit' the face of the covering that is spread on the face of the people, and give many to behold with open face the glory of the Lord, and so to be changed into his image from glory to glory! May you, dear brother, enjoy the presence of the King of Saints on this occasion in a far greater degree and in a more excellent and glorious manner than at any former season of Communion.

In regard to the state of the Lord's Kingdom here, I can say but little that is good, though still there is room for prayerful hope. The mass of church-going professors seem to be almost stereotyped, and little impression seems to be made upon them. Mr McDonald of Urquhart for instance, though coming from a scene where the power of the Lord has been and still continues to be marvellously displayed, left Aberdeen without, I believe, seeing any appearance of remarkable impression among those to whom he preached. I have found it the same as others, and after continuing during these ten days past to preach, as Dr Chalmers would say, on the principle of 'attraction', to such as chose to come, I last night adopted the plan of assembling the poor and abandoned in a schoolhouse. I've seemed to have more of the Lord's presence there than at the meetings in Church, and this afternoon I had the privilege of meeting a number of mill-workers at the same place at 5 o'clock.

When leaving the meeting last night and thinking of the different way in which the ignorant, profane, dead professors receive the gospel, the passage, 'I will move them to jealousy' (Deuteronomy 32:21), struck me very forcibly and also the parable of the Marriage Feast (Luke 14). Oh! entreat, dear brother, that the Lord would glorify Jesus in a Christ-crucifying city which seems to be at ease under the wrath of God.

When you can find time, do send me a few lines of information regarding the progress of things with you and also of godly counsel.

Yours in Jesus,
Wm C. Burns

Aberdeen, Revd J. Murray's
October 30th, 1840

My Dear Brother,
I drop these few lines to let you know that I am still in Aberdeen and have the prospect of remaining here D.V. for a few days longer at least; and also that I may ask you to tell me what you think is

likely to be the final result of the application that has been made from the Dudhope district in response to my occupying for a time the new Church there. It is of importance that I should see the end of this as soon as possible, as upon it depends in a great degree my future movements.

Should I be called to come to Dudhope at the end of this month, I would not go too far north at present, whereas if I am left free from this engagement, I might leave this place soon for Forglen.

Of the state of the Lord's work in Aberdeen as a whole, I can say little that is favourable. I have, however, reason to think that while the generality of the people are fast asleep in their sins, and at ease under the wrath of God, the Lord is beginning to work among the poorer and more neglected. I have for the last fortnight been meeting almost exclusively in school houses with the mill population and on some occasions there seemed to be a very general, and in some cases I hope, a saving impression. On Wednesday night last I had a meeting on King Street which was crowded (from 300 to 400) and from the impression that seemed to be made upon them by the Word of the Lord, I hope favourably, though I dare not say much more at present. My chief object in attending to these things is to entreat you as you have opportunity to stir up the Lord's people to remember Aberdeen, and yourself to bear unceasingly on your heart in the holiest of all. I trust you have had a glorious Communion season and that there is a vehement desire among the people of God to see still greater things.

I was trying to remember you all, though alas, as usual with a stupid and dead heart. Good news from Breadalbane. The Lord's work is going wonderfully on!

Your affectionate Brother in the Lord,
Wm C. Burns

Aberdeen
November 25th, 1840

My Dear Brother,
It is out of my power to come to Dundee sooner than in time to occupy Dudhope Church on the 1st Sabbath of December. May my coming be indeed ordained of God for his glory, and may I be

guided by the meekness of wisdom, and speaking the truth in love. I cannot add more as I have but a minute to write before the first hour. There are increasing evidences of the Lord's presence here, and I hope that the remaining week may be indeed Pentecostal.

We had a day of fasting lately and we are to have another on Friday first. Remember me as I do try to remember you.

Yours always in the Lord,

Wm C. Burns

February 14th, 1841

My Dear Brother,

I have corrected, though I fear in some cases in my way rather than yours, your interesting Tract. I am sorry that on the first page the ink shines through, so as to seem to make changes where none were intended. May its republication be eminently conducive to the advancement of the Divine glory.

I will not, I fear, be able to undertake the first Sabbath of March in St Peter's, as I have all but resolved it as my duty to go to the Communion at Kilsyth. I am doing little here, and there seems little prospect meantime of my doing more. My Popery Lecture is beginning to engulf all my thoughts, and this I hope with advantage to myself and it may be future advantage to some others. May we have a season of great nearness to the Lord tomorrow at the time and in the exercises agreed on.

Yours ever,

Wm C. Burns

My going to Kilsyth is uncertain as yet.

Kilsyth, April 19th, 1841

My Dear Brother,

As I have been called in the Lord's Providence to meet the Aberdeen Committee on Revivals on Thursday the 29th Inst., I have the prospect of passing through Dundee on Tuesday the 27th, and have written to Mr Kerr, one of the Dudhope managers, offering to preach to the people that evening. This will release me from the duty of writing to the people who were concerned about their souls, and be a sweet opportunity of meeting all my friends in the Lord again.

Should you be away to Ireland before that time, I wish you would leave out my manuscript volumes which I may probably need. I was trying to remember you all in connection with the Communion Season, and hope it has been a blessed season, and one of great glory to the Lord. I cannot thank you as I ought for the kind charge you have taken of the precious souls who seemed anxious about an interest in Emmanuel, but the Lord's free favour is an infinite reward. If you are away before I arrive, perhaps you may leave me a few lines today of what appearances you have seen among them.

I have had a few days rest here, though having gone to Glasgow in the coach, I was forced to preach five times there. I am now, blessed be the gracious Lord, strong in body and also stronger in mind than I was. Oh! pray that I may be strengthened with all might by the Spirit in the inner man, that I may be able to comprehend with all saints what is the breadth and length and depth and height of the *love of Christ* which passeth knowledge, and be filled with *all* the *fullness of God*!

Commend me to the prayers of the people in the view of appearing for God's work in the presence of the Presbytery. May this greatly redound to the Lord's glory.

In haste I am Dear Brother,
Yours in eternal bonds
(Glory to the Lord!)
William C. Burns

Perth, May 7th, 1841

My Dear Brother,

I hoped to have had the privilege of meeting you here on your way to Dundee, and also to have got from you my mss volume which you took to Ireland. It is not improbable that I may be called by the Aberdeen Presbytery to give a statement of all that I have seen of the Lord's glorious work during these past years, and I must have my volumes at hand in case this is needed. At Dundee I felt somewhat supported, both when at Dudhope on my way to Aberdeen, and also on Wednesday evening last in your pulpit. Surely Jehovah has been doing something in the souls of a number. Oh! watch over them for Jesus' sake, and let us do all we can at the Throne of Grace and otherwise to get Dudhope filled with a man of God.

Let me hear from you at your leisure your opinion more particularly of the general aspect of that concern which you have found among the Dudhope people. I intended to have gone today to Kilsyth, but could not get away from Perth and am to remain over the Sabbath here. Let us remember each other more and more. I hope the Lord stood by you and was magnified in you when in Ireland. Thanks to his Name for all his infinite love.

Great good will result from the Aberdeen investigation. Next Monday the Presbytery meet to discuss the subject, many are engaged in prayer and I have no doubt that the work of the Holy Ghost is going on. I was delighted unspeakably by what I saw and heard when there.

Would you favour me by sending up the mss volume I have spoken of on Monday by the boat, giving it in special charge to the Captain?

I am in haste
Yours always in Jesus,
Wm C. Burns

Kilsyth, July 29th, 1841

My Dear Brother,

I hope you have written engaging to visit Milnathort next week. I long after these dear people, and shall pray that you may have many among them for a crown of joy in the Great Day. I have to thank you for your kind note and I do thank you from the heart for the precious and, alas! much needed advice with which you end. My soul is indeed in peril. Oh! continue to pray for me, and, when you write, ask a word as much in season as the last I hope was.

I am to be at Kilmarnock on Sabbath and after preaching in one or two other places, I have the view of going to the south by

Newcastle, Kelso, etc. I trust you and many in Dundee will wrestle for us. Give me your advice in regard to the letters which I have been led to print. May Fleming's letter is to be reprinted at the desire of many, but I have first to ask you with a trembling heart whether she walks through grace in such a manner as to leave no objection to this: if otherwise, drop a note to Middleton immediately and he will not proceed.

What is come of your pastoral letters? Should you not put them out revised and one by one as I have done? You would in this way get them much more intensively read I think. Middleton would manage them well. If I can do anything in the way of correcting points etc., as before, I shall be glad. I would like you to tell me when you have any news about Dudhope. Remember me to all who seek the way to Zion,

and I am Yours ever,

Wm C. Burns

92 Pilgrim Street, Newcastle on Tyne
September 9th, 1841

Dear Brother,

Your Tract is excellent. May it be an arrow in the quiver of Zion's King. One remark I may with deference make for consideration in future. The Tracts have the aspect of being general in their application, but when we read them, they are found to be properly addressed to your own people. Might it not be well, either to write for the public or directly to address the people of your own charge, e.g. you close the present tract with a request that parents would send their children to your Sabbath Schools, while the body of the address is general in its form. Pardon the hint if you think it groundless.

I send with this a few lines addressed to the Children of God among your people, to entreat their supplication in behalf of Newcastle. It is an awfully wicked place, but there is the more room for grace to work if the Lord is pleased to visit us with the arm of his strength. The people's ears are beginning to be open, but one only can open their hearts for himself. He openeth and no man shutteth. The enclosed will give you some idea of our proceedings. Mr Nile on the Sabbath had produced a very great sensation, and I am told that the pleasure trip which last summer made a large sum of money, was this year a failure and that a gloom hung over all their proceedings! The chief public defenders of this fearful iniquity are the Socialists, who have a Bill on the walls saying that they have been at Hell, and found no room there except for me and some of the 'Newcastle saints'. It is put out 'in the name of the devil', as the other was, 'in the Name of God'!!

It is well when Satan puts his name to his own work. We had large and solemn audiences yesterday in the open air at 7.00 a.m. and 5.00 p.m., also in the church at 7.00 p.m. And this week we are proposing to speak particularly to the little flock of Christ on the subject of Humiliation and Fasting, with a view to a season of this kind in concert. Are you keeping in view 'the General Concert for Prayer', in the beginning of October? I fear many will forget it. Should we not use special efforts to prepare the people of God for it? Would not a few lines in print on the nature and importance of the Concerts recommended be seasonal? Oh! when should we lie in the dust and seek for hidden sins and idols if not now, when the Church of Scotland, a strong buttress in the Lord's walls, is shaking? I have just had Wm Bowman with me. It was sweet to meet with one who brought St Peter's Parish so near the eye. He sails to and from Newcastle almost every week. Oh! pray for me, and let us seek to be full of the Holy Ghost and faith.

Your brother,
Wm C. Burns

Newcastle on Tyne
92 Pilgrim Street

Beloved Brethren,
Your number I fear is still small, and perhaps smaller than we think, but you are precious and powerful. Precious, because bought with divine blood, and powerful because you can say, 'Jehovah is my strength.'

I send these lines to you in remembrance of all that we have seen and tasted together at the hand of our God and Father, and to entreat you for the glory of God to remember without ceasing in your prayers the cause of the Lord Jesus here. This town is like Sodom, abandoned to utter ungodliness and enormous wickedness. Satan's trenches are deep and wide, his walls are strong and high, his garrison is great and fearless, and all that man can do is but like arrows shot against a Tower of brass! Oh! what is to be done?

Beloved, I do not need to tell you. You have known that God the Spirit is omnipotent, and can with a touch of his finger make his enemies quail and raze their fortresses to the ground. Oh! how simple to him that the walls of Jericho should fall at the blast of a ram's horn! That the mountains should be ground to dust and fanned into the air by a worm! Come believers, let us look to the Lord. Let us stand still in an agony of desire and hope that we may see the Lord's salvation. The ears of many base are beginning to be engaged. Oh! cry to Jehovah that he would open their hearts and enter in. The battle is beginning, the enemy will not give way without a dread struggle. Hold up your hands, give the Lord no rest and look for news of victory in due time. We have not yet resisted unto blood striving against sin. Oh! shall Britain drain the hearts of thousands before the gates of its enemies, and shall the Lord's soldiers shrink at the sight of blood in following the Son of God to eternal life and glory? Oh! plead mightily that the Lord may be magnified. Lie low in the dust and look at Jesus reigning above all, with the keys of Death and Hell in his hand!

I rejoice to pray for you and to hear of your welfare, and that from time to time one more is filling up the place of those who have fallen asleep. Oh! that thousands in Dundee would come in at the eleventh hour. If they do not move speedily, there will be tens of thousands damned. Sinners awake out of sleep! Believers work while it is Day, for the night is at hand!

Yours ever in the adorable Jesus,
Wm C. Burns

To the Children of God in Dundee, to whom this may come.

Newcastle on Tyne
September 21, 1841

Dear Brother,

Oh! stir up the people to plead for us here. There is progress, though as yet slow. We are, I hope, coming to the crisis of the work and I have hope that something great may yet be done by him who only doeth wondrous things.

I was much refreshed by your 28 Meditations, which I have seen (at least the greater part of them) in the Christian's Daily Companion. I like these better than anything I have seen from your pen. May they be the means of winning many souls and of refreshing the Church of God.

Should not the enclosed to the Carlisle Railway Directors be put in the *Warden*? Mr Chapman who signs it as a Banker here and a large shareholder, means to leave the Company unless they grant at least some decided concession. Praise.

Yours
Wm C. Burns

Would you get a proof of a letter of mine now printing at Middleton's and send me your suggestions?

Newcastle on Tyne
September 29th, 1841

Dear Brother,

I thank you for your kind suggestions, which I have in part improved at present and shall remember again. You are right in regard to the absence of divinity in this Letter, but I feel again that something lighter and less didactic is needed to accompany such a series as that, of which 'The Knowledge of sin' forms one. I have put the 'Plain Sentences' before the other, and this will, in part, prepare the reader for the brief points which follow.

I do not know that I can say anything particular about the Union for Prayer, but I seek to pray that it may be generally and solemnly observed. I do not know whether daily public meetings are desirable or not, unless they are accompanied with special efforts in behalf of the unconverted. Particular circumstances must determine our duty. I should think we have had some very solemn and impressive meetings here, particularly last sabbath, and I would entreat increased prayer in behalf of our circumstances, which are eminently critical.

In haste,

Yours in love,

Wm C. Burns

Have you been honoured with D.D.? I was afraid to ask this until I heard from yourself.

Edinburgh, 53 North Frederick Street
December 1st, 1841

My Dear Brother,

Excuse a very brief reply to your welcome letter. I shall see what I can do about Mr Edgar, although I confess that there seems to be a difficulty in bringing the matter about without his being made aware in some degree of the object in view. I shall see however, and write you again on the subject. I go to Newcastle and Sunderland on Monday, returning on Saturday again D.V.

Since I came here I have been cultivating privacy a good deal for the purpose of study and renewal of spiritual life. Alas! I fear it has been to little purpose as yet.

No. III I have been trying to write, but I make so little progress, the subject is so vast and so glorious. I do not think I can make it without a new measure of grace, and this seems to be in the meantime withheld, for holy reasons. I am indeed a worm of the ground and I am awfully insensible to the knowledge of it. After my return from England, I must return to full labour as a matter of duty, preaching one or two days each week in the surrounding country when I have openings, as well as in St Luke's at usual seasons. In regard to what God will do, I am in the dark. He can work by any means that he chooses. This is my hope.

I have seen Miss Dunbar (at Mr Gardner's 51 North Frederick Street) next door, and shall see her again if the Lord will. How little can be made of the dying! It is surely with the healthy that we have chiefly to deal; still strangers are chosen in the furnace of affliction. I would be afraid to speak for a little at least of the exchange you mention, however much I might personally desire it. Let us wait to see the Lord's way. How dark the times are growing. Truly open persecution to all who follow the Lamb is near at hand. Oh! to be prepared for suffering with him, that we may reign with him. I hope to be at Perth on the 1st Sabbath of the year and may perhaps see you about that time. Meantime pray for me as I for you, though with a stupid heart. Your counsels are always seasonal and sometimes blessed I would hope.

Your brother,
Wm C. Burns

Edinburgh, January 4th, 1842

My Dear Brother,

I have been enquiring after Mr Edgar, but could hear little about him that could aid you in forming a judgment, and I did not find it easy to get him to preach or indeed to get him to preach at all, except on the ground of your desire to know his character, and this was a matter of considerable delicacy. Might you not ask him to preach for you at Dundee? I know that there are objections to this, but there seem to be nearly as many to my asking him to preach here. I shall still however try to ascertain more about him, and as I am to be at the meeting of the Missionary Day in the College on Saturday morning, I may perhaps find some among the students who know him. I shall write soon on this if anything may transpire.

I trust you had a blessed Communion season at Dundee. My thoughts, if not my heart, have been with you in part, although I confess I have been a good deal engrossed by constant labour here and at Leith. In the latter place there is much encouragement to labour at present. During last week I preached 6 times in the open air as well as on several evenings, and much power seemed to attend the Word. On Saturday (New Year's Day), we were three and a half hours in the open air, and the impression was so great that we could have continued much longer together. On Sabbath also, as Dr Gordon had agreed to take the afternoon in St Luke's at the time that I thought of being at Perth, I went down between the forenoon and evening services (there was an evening service to children) and preached at the head of the pier to a great crowd of

Sabbath-breakers for nearly three hours. It was affecting to see so many young men drawn together to hear the Word in such circumstances, and I hope it was not in vain. Tonight I am to be in the North Leith Church and tomorrow evening in the Mariner's again. Today I am keeping much alone that I may enjoy a renewal of life within.

I enclose a letter from a precious man in Newcastle on Tyne, who is secretary of the Lord's Day Observance Society there, and has been ever the mainspring of all its movements. He is truly a precious man and though an Episcopalian, yet a thoroughly enlightened Christian, and a hater of Puseyism in all its workings. He would be much delighted for a few lines from you and would rejoice to give you information which you might make great use of. His address is: Thomas George Bull Esq., Land Surveyor, Newcastle on Tyne.

What do you think of the Railway-Abstinence Pledge? It involves far more than many are aware of and I fear that few are reckoning on keeping to their purpose, should the effort not succeed. Such conduct would do infinite evil and I am therefore in doubt what to do. Advise us, for some of the members of the Session feel as I do.

As to the Communion here, you know well the persons whom I would like to assist you, the Bonars, Somerville, Cumming, etc. Make your own choice. Your proposal of my taking your place may be considered especially, as I will need, no doubt, to visit Perth soon. Oh! for light from on high! I am afraid prematurely to fix, as I sometimes see cause to change such arrangements.

Yours ever,

Wm C. Burns

Thanks to the Lord for Horace Bonar etc.

Edinburgh, March 8th, 1842

Dear Brother,

Take care to whom you give such notes as the enclosed, for I am afraid they are made bad use of. Poor William Moore, to whom you gave it, has been, I fear, practising deceit among us, and I am truly glad that I got this out of his hands. Of course I said that I would return it to him if you thought proper, but I shall not advise you. At the same time I do not throw him quite away lest he go from bad to worse, but give him still parts to tell.

There is a young friend of mine in Glasgow lately licensed, John Adam, whom I should like well to come and aid you in Dundee if he is not fixed on, as is likely, to succeed Morrison at Dunipace. You may look after him, if you still want such, for he is the best I know, and promises well with excellent points and outlook: able or rather improvable disposition.

It is likely that Railway shall be opened here next Sabbath morning at 7. If the Lord enable me, I am to be there in good time to give tracts to all comers and preach at their very gates after the train is off. This I intend to continue as long as I remain here. I pray that in this you and the people of God will remember me.

I need not tell you that if Jehovah reveal his arm in Edinburgh there will be greater enmity and opposition than perhaps in any other city in the land. Let them come on! One thousand shall flee at the rebuke of one – two shall put ten thousand to flight! I wish you were here to aid, but it is all one with him to help, whether with many or with them who have no strength.

In haste,
yours ever,
William C. Burns

'Feed the Church of God which he hath purchased with *his own blood*.'

Edinburgh, June 13th, 1842

Dear Brother,

You might object were I to send anything for the purpose we spoke of when together, but you cannot refuse the enclosed (out of much that is sent to me) to be a help in giving away your Tracts as you have opportunity. My chief reason in now sending these lines is to suggest the great importance of a No. VI from St Peter's Dundee on 'Fasting', with an especial view to the Day of Humiliation throughout the Church. Of course you will ask counsel from on High, but the thing has occurred to me as very important. Boston's book would afford good help and such a Tract is much wanted. I have often thought of attempting one, but in this as in regard to No. III, I could not satisfy myself.

I go off, if the Lord be pleased so to order it, on Wednesday morning for Newcastle, and I hope that you will stir up the people to remember us, specially next Sabbath and the following week, when in all likelihood we will be meeting the enemy on his own ground – the Race Course.

I was at Logie etc., etc., last week and would press on you to pay that place and Leuchars an early visit. It is a dry ground, but there is hope. Entreating a large place in your prayers.

I am in haste,
Your brother,
Wm C. Burns

My address will be 92 Pilgrim Street, Newcastle on Tyne as before.

Largs Manse
December 16th, 1842

Dear Brother,

I am become as a stranger to one than whom none is nearer my heart amid duty and at the Throne of our Father and God, and I much wish that you would drop me a few lines in return for these, to open again our intercourse. I rejoice to see you among the honoured ministers who are professing to regard the will of the Lord Jesus as more powerful to guide their conduct than the authority of this world, principalities, or the interest of this world's wealth. I am more and more assured that you are following the way which the glory of Emmanuel demands whatever may be the issues, and alas! As far as I can see these, they will be awfully disastrous to this poor land whose cup of iniquity is, it may be, nearly full. How great need have all God's professing witnesses to be broken down in humiliation before Him on account of personal and public sin. Many would rather do the first works than begin by remembering whence we have fallen and repenting. Are you not

292

thinking of putting out a Tract on the present duty of God's children in the Church of Scotland? It is surely much needed, and when the discussion on the ground of human nature is now so nearly at an end, and the field of battle is to be removed to the ground of the divine testimony simply, is it not the time for such as your coming in to the field with Scriptural and practical views of the matter, which may suit the minds and reach the hearts of the less learned?

What are you thinking also in regard to a more general diffusion of the Gospel over the land by evangelistic labours? Is the Lord, do you think, preparing you for this either in outward circumstances or in inward bias? Whatever is to be done in this way must it not be done speedily? For when ministers leave their churches, especially in the country parts, we cannot hope that liberty will long be given to any of us to interfere with the peace – accursed peace of their successors. In the meantime, everyday is precious. I felt this so much that I could not keep from itinerating even in this inclement part of the season, nor have I had reason to doubt the propriety of my decision.

I have been now an exact month in Fife and during that time have had my hands more than full, and that in a district where I know of only *one* whose name is with yours on the Resolutions. The pulpit even of Mr. Milligan at Elie has been twice open to me on week-nights, on the latter of which as the opportunity was rare I did not vacate it for five hours! Happily he was from home and could not interfere.

Next Sabbath I am to be here D.V. in Mr. Brown's pulpit, who is on the right side as you know. On the 25th again, I am to preach in the pulpit at Crail, at present occupied by Mr. Merson, a thorough moderate. You will wonder how I get in to such places, I wonder not less, but the hand of God is visible, opening the way through the wishes of the people. I trust also that as the door is great, it is not altogether ineffectual. The power of the Lord the Spirit is indeed not so evidently mighty as at some times we have seen, but many of the meetings are deeply solemn as well as crowded, and I hear of not a few who are under some anxiety about their state. I preach in all kinds of churches: Independent, Secession, Relief, and the union of heart among God's true people is sweet indeed. The scattered brood must gather under the mother's wing when the night is coming on and she summons them with a peculiar note which they can understand! *Remember me in prayer – commend our case to the prayers of God's children* in dear St Peter's Church and let me hear from you when your time allows.

Ever dear Brother
Yours in Jesus
Wm C Burns

Oh! that you and a few more of our brethren were sent forth by the Lord to the field in which I am favoured to be. The people are waiting in the market-place until someone call them in the name of Jesus. Support will be given, no fear of that, to body as well as soul. One of my trials is to be *too* well treated. In many cases it might be best to go two and two, although an individual gets in to some places more easily than a greater number could. I often wish I was labouring along with you from place to place. Doubtless those ministers who are going out will be glad to get all that is possible done while they have the key in their hand, and when one Parish is moved, the neighbouring ones follow. May Jehovah give us counsel. Weigh these hints in His presence, which though put down in haste, are the result of many and of recurring thoughts. I found when I left Edinburgh that the people of God entered so fully into the view which I had taken of the path of duty, that I had actually to restrain them from giving of their means to aid me and ever since I came to Fife, resolved to refuse all aid. I have been forced to accept of eight pounds, besides other sums which I succeeded in refusing. This will not always last, but we shall always get the "bread" and the "water", which are in the promise, "Thy bread shall be given thee, and thy water shall be done."

Oh! the fields are white. Why should St Peter's or any other Parish, have shower upon shower, when many districts have not a drop! The time is short. Come away to the help of the Lord, the help of the Lord God the Mighty!

If your answer comes about the middle of next week, direct to Kilconquhar House, where I am to live again when in that quarter, as I did before. They are Episcopalians but Lady Bethune is a subject of Zion I hope, and he also is thinking. Oh! pray for him. He asked me specially to do so when I was leaving them on the former occasion. Some of the servants are anxious, no restriction is laid on me at morning and evening worship, and we dine at 2, that all may go to the evening meeting in the Church.

I must however, put a close to this extended postscript,

And am yours with much love

W C B

I am afraid dear brother Milne of Perth may wonder at my not writing to him. If you see him you might let him know my need of his prayers and my constant remembrance of him at the Footstool. Remember me also to A Bonar, whom I love in the Lord.

Do not forget Crail on the 25th and with a view to it. If the work is not done in one day, I shall not likely get in again. The case of thousands demands intercession. Oh! pity them. *Lord Jesus have pity!*

Farnham, Lower Canada, April 21st, 1845

My Dear Friends,

When I last wrote to Mr Milne about a month ago, I was at the French Canadian Missionary House at St Re, twenty-three miles from where I now am. I returned to Montreal shortly after, and had the great pleasure of receiving on my arrival your welcome letter. I desire to thank you for your great kindness in ministering to my temporal wants, but much more, as you yourselves say, for seeking to bear me on your hearts at the throne of grace. My temporal wants are few, and Canada can easily supply them all, but my spiritual necessities are very great, and I dwell indeed in a dry and parched land, where no water is. Yet I cannot deny that I find by experience that the God of Israel is everywhere present with his poor people, and that his presence is not excluded from the recesses of a Canadian forest. I could not but remark that your season for specially remembering me was very nearly one when I needed very special support, and when I saw the Lord very clearly leading me in a path that I knew not. On the second day after I received your letter (28th March) I again left Montreal, with the view of visiting some desolate settlements of Protestants (chiefly Scotch and Irish) in the quarter where I still am, and also desiring to find some opening among the poor French Canadians, who are the principal inhabitants here and around.

One of my fellow-travellers was a young Canadian student at the French college of St Hyacinthe, with whom I had some conversation. He said, if I were at their college, they would soon convince me that I was in error. The opening was too favourable to be neglected, and I said that if I was in the neighbourhood I would certainly call upon him. In consequence of this, the following Wednesday (April 2nd) I set out for Yamaska, the seat of the college. The thaw here was so rapid at that time that most of the bridges were swept away by the breaking up of the ice, which till then, as you may suppose, had formed so strong a covering that the heaviest wagons could pass and repass upon the rivers. In consequence, I found that the stage could not proceed, and that I must either go on foot or return. I felt it my duty to go on, and though the distance was considerable (eighteen miles) in deep roads, I easily made it out, and reached the college on Thursday at seven o'clock.

I must also mention a circumstance which happened by the way, which was remarkable when connected with what it led to. When I was about half-way I was a little fatigued, and was wishing to find some house where I might rest a little, but the houses were all French, and I saw no appearance of a public inn. However, the Lord directed me. Beside the road I saw a sheep which had got into a muddy ditch, and seemed to be unable to get out. I of course laid hold of it and pulled it out, thinking of the parable of Jesus. The people in the nearest house came out, and we got into conversation about the lost sheep in the gospel. I asked them if there was any house where I could refresh myself; they invited me in with them.

I told them on entering who I was; that if they wished it I might pass on, or if otherwise, that I might speak to them the more freely. They did not object to receive me as a Protestant and a Scotch minister of the gospel, and when we began to converse about the nature of my religion as compared with theirs, they were so engaged that it was difficult to get away from them. After remaining with them a full hour and a half, they asked me to remain during the night, as they said that with such roads I could not reach my destination. However, as I was obliged to return from Yamaska the following day (Friday) in order to fulfil another engagement, I resolved to go forward, and bade them adieu.

I got easily forward, being supported by a strong sense of duty, and by the presence, I trust, of the great Master himself, and on arriving called for the young man I have alluded to. He seemed more careless than before, and was evidently afraid to show to any of those around him any mark of anxiety. He said, 'If you wish to see any of the priests I will let them know.' 'No,' I replied, 'I have no such desire on my own account, as I have no doubt that they are in deadly error, and that this book (the Bible) contains the truth of God. It is for your benefit that I am come, and if you have any desire to be instructed, you must ask them to converse on the subject in your presence.' He hesitated at this, but said, 'If you be here tomorrow, you may call at twelve o'clock, when it will be more convenient than now.' I spent the night in a French inn, and the object of my visit becoming known, occasioned a good deal of conversation, and led in particular two strangers to ask me to converse with them on the subject. At the hour appointed I went to the college, and found the young man of the same mind as before. However, he said, 'I will go and see what the priests say.' He returned after some time to tell me that they absolutely refused to speak with me on these things unless I met them entirely alone.

Of course I had no wish for this, as it might have been turned to a bad purpose, and after warning a number of the young men of the awful danger of allowing themselves to be blindly led by those who feared the light, I came away, and set out on my journey. These young men told me they were not allowed to see the Bible, although not younger than seventeen. As I came along the street in front of the French church, thinking that I had seen the end of my visit, to my surprise I met the man in whose house I had been the previous day, and whom some business had brought to the village.

On learning the result of my visit to the college, he said, 'Come, we will go to the curé (parish priest) and converse with him.' I told him I was willing, provided he understood that it was on his account that we went. He entered, and after a little returned and invited me in. I there met three priests and a number of their poor parishioners, and after explaining the circumstances which led to our meeting, we had a solemn and interesting interview for some time, during which I had an opportunity of stating some important truths which may yet be blessed, and of bringing before them the question of their own personal salvation. I have indeed cause to wonder at the strength given me on this occasion, and also, that though our intercourse was altogether in a foreign tongue, I felt scarcely more difficulty than in English.

Since that time I have been preaching among the Protestants exclusively, although now and then I find an opportunity of meeting a few Canadians. Their spiritual sleep is indeed deep, and such as no power but that of God can break, even so far as to lead them to hear the truth. Their leaders cause them to err, and the poor people love to have it so. I have seen nothing very remarkable of a spiritual nature among our countrymen since I came to Canada, but our meetings are often very solemn, and during these past days I have seen as much appearance of impression as since I came to this land.

It is my intention to return soon to Montreal for a time, and it may be that when this reaches you I shall be attempting again to reach the multitude there in the open air, and that in both languages. You will then see what need we have of your prayers. My heart is often among you, and I do often plead for your salvation, and the advancement of Emmanuel's glory in you. I close these lines with the words I spoke on here yesterday evening: 'The grace of God that bringeth salvation hath appeared to all men, teaching us that denying ungodliness and worldly lusts, we should live soberly, righteously, and godly in this present world; looking for that blessed hope, and the glorious appearing of the great God and our Saviour Jesus Christ, who gave himself for us, that he might redeem us from all iniquity, and purify unto himself a peculiar people, zealous of good works.'

May these glorious ends be accomplished in you and me to his name's glory!

Commending you to God and to the word of his grace, which is able to build you up, and to give you an inheritance among all them that are sanctified,

I am ever yours in the bonds of the gospel,

W. C. Burns

*On board the 'Mary Bannatyne', off Portsmouth
June 9th, 1847, 11.30 p.m.*

My Dear Mother,

My embarkation has been at the last, as I will tell in detail, rather sudden and hurried. I expected not to leave London until tomorrow morning, but the ship got quickly round to Portsmouth, and last night when entering the door of Mr Thomson's church at Woolwich to preach, a messenger from London met me to say that I must get to Portsmouth without losing an hour lest the ship should be gone. I endeavoured accordingly to leave London by the last train, but was too late, and happily so, for in case I had got away I would not have seen I[slay]; but as it was graciously arranged, I came away at seven a.m., and had J[ane], I[slay], and Mrs I[slay] to the station, and I all the way. He was on board during most of the day, and left us in the evening. My heart was too full to put pen to paper at that time, and I left as I thought all news for him to give, but since he went away I find that by our pilot I may still send a few lines, which I cannot omit the duty of attempting.

I have now entered on a new sphere of duty and trial, I mean on board ship. Much fidelity and wisdom are needed to be a witness for the Lord in such circumstances, and I have in this matter, as well as with reference to ulterior designs, much need of fervent believing prayer. Do not forget us. May all that sail with us be given to Jesus. We have already begun worship in the cuddy, and I hope it may be continued throughout, if possible, morning and evening. I felt it a great privilege to have I[slay] with me at the last. May this separation for the gospel be to each of us a blessing.

Ah! what grace is manifested in such a separation! Why am I not, as many, going forth in search of mammon; or put to sea, as some are, because they are unprofitable even in man's account on land? Who maketh thee to differ? O! to live under the full influence of Christ's constraining love! To us to live will thus be Christ, and to us to die will be gain. We know not the progress nor the end of this voyage, nor what news may reach us from Britain should we reach our destination. Yet I rejoice to go. I feel that I am where it is the Lord's gracious will that I should be, and I would join with all his people in praying, 'Thy will be done on earth as it is in heaven.' All the ends of the earth shall yet remember and turn to the Lord; and all the kindreds of the people shall do homage unto him; for the kingdom is the LORD'S, and he is the Governor among the nations. On his vesture and on his thigh there is a name written, King of kings and Lord of lords!

Now may the God of peace sanctify you wholly, and I pray God your whole spirit and soul and body be preserved blameless unto the coming of our Lord Jesus Christ. Faithful is he that calleth you, who also will do it. Brethren, pray for us! Salute all the brethren for us.

Thus in haste again writes,
dearest mother,
your affectionate son,
Wm C. Burns

March 28th, 1848

My Dear Mother,

After having had worship with my Chinese family (two servants, a teacher, and three boys), I take up my pen to endeavour to hold some kind of communication, from this distant region of the earth, with those who are dearest to me on it. I feel, as I did last time, the want of hearing from any of you, but I have been comforted in some degree by the absence of any bad news, whether by the papers or by Mrs K's letters. May the living and true God be the God and Redeemer and portion of each of my beloved friends, and be more and more gracious to and more and more glorious in the eyes of my beloved parents as they advance to the borders of the unseen and eternal world!

May you be enabled to say with the divine Psalmist, 'Whom have I in heaven but thee? and there is none upon the earth whom I desire besides thee: my flesh and my heart faileth, but God is the strength of my heart and my portion for ever!' 'As for me I shall behold thy face in righteousness; I shall be satisfied when I awake with thy likeness.'

May your faith be as the shining light, shining more and more unto the perfect day! Oh! that I might hear in this far land of those of our dear kindred that as yet love not Jesus, having the eye divinely opened to behold his beauty and preciousness! For myself I am here in the midst of a people of a strange language, and who know not the true God nor Jesus Christ whom he hath sent to be the light and life of men, and yet I cannot say that I am solitary or forsaken. I feel indeed more at home here than I did when I was last among you in Scotland, when the weight of that call which I believe I obeyed in coming here was resting upon me, and making me as a stranger among my own kindred.

When I last wrote I had newly taken up my abode here with my Chinese domestics, and had been encouraged by feeling able to read and pray with them (though feebly) in their own tongue. My teacher had not then joined me, and I was uncertain whether he would succeed in getting a school formed on the principles of the gospel.

In this, however, I have been encouraged beyond my expectation. He got a few boys to come from a little distance of his own acquaintance, and as soon as he opened the school others came from the neighbourhood of their own accord, so that for the last fortnight he has had regularly from twelve to fifteen scholars. Were we to make any effort I believe we could get more, but in the first instance I want to go on gradually until the character of the school becomes fixed on right principles, and see that it really promises to accomplish more than that which I sought for it at the outset, viz. bringing me into such intercourse with the people as might enable me to acquire the language as they speak it, and might open up the way for preaching the Word among them when I am able to do this. Three of the boys stay with us in the house, and all of them come regularly to worship in the morning, when we have a little meeting of seventeen or eighteen persons in all. The school is of course shut up on Sabbath, but the last two Sabbaths most of the boys have been with us most of the day learning a Christian book, and have also attended Chinese worship of their own accord at the chapel of the London Society, where a native at present officiates.

Soon after the school was opened, it was interesting to me one morning about six o'clock, and before any one was on foot but myself, to see a Chinese woman with a little boy of eleven or twelve knocking to be admitted to the school. I thought of that blessed time approaching when the mothers of China will bring their children to the feet of Jesus that he may bless them. The Chinese are diligent in learning after their own manner. They begin with the morning light and continue to con over their insipid task (insipid, as we would reckon it) until evening. They are an intelligent and interesting race, and when the gospel takes hold of them in elevating and saving power, they will be interesting in another manner.

I am, dear mother,
your affectionate son,
Wm C. Burns

January 29, 1849

My Dear Mother,
The routine of my work hitherto has been in learning the Chinese language, with the important accompaniment of preaching from week to week among my own countrymen. Now, however, I am entering as far as can be foreseen on a new sphere and mode of labour, being about to discontinue my temporary position both among the Chinese and English, and go forth among the people of these shores with the Word of eternal life in my hands, and gradually also on my tongue.

Yesterday (Sabbath, 28th) I intimated the discontinuance of my English preaching, and today I have given warning to my servants, etc., that the school, which is at present interrupted by the Chinese New Year, will not be again reopened. To this decision I have been clearly led, as we have yet no prospect of any minister from Scotland, nor of any other missionary who might take up the educational part of the work among the Chinese, and I had but one alternative before me, viz. that of either proceeding to form a church and locating myself among my countrymen and in my Chinese school; or that of leaving both, and going forth into the field at large in order at once to attain in a proper manner the spoken language, and to spread abroad the gospel of salvation among these unsaved millions. This latter course I have felt it my duty to adopt, although it is one accompanied with many difficulties and dangers of different kinds. But the work must be done, and I am enabled joyfully to say, 'Lord, here am I, send me.'

The young man who has been teaching the school and myself will not, I think, return to me, but the other two assistants will go forth, I trust, with me, and perhaps others also. Certainly my past habits and experience fit me above most preachers for attempting this mode of missionary work, but whether, and how far, I may succeed in it is with the Lord, at whose command alone I go forth. I need not add that in these circumstances I shall have special need of special prayer to be made on my behalf, and on behalf of the people among whom I may be led from time to time. China is not only forbidden ground to a foreigner, but it is a land of idols and a land without a Sabbath. How great then must be that power which can alone open up my way and make it successful!

But JESUS hath said, 'All power is given unto me in heaven and on earth'; and JEHOVAH hath said to the Son, 'Ask of me and I will give thee the heathen for thine inheritance, and the uttermost parts of the earth for thy possession.' Let the weak then say, I am strong!

I shall not add more by coming down to matters of lesser moment. May the souls of God's people among you prosper and be in health, and may many be brought nigh who are now far off in heart from the living God!

With love to all who love the Lord and seek his face,

I am, dear mother,

your affectionate son,

Wm C. Burns

At Shap-Pat-Hoeung (or Eighteen Villages)
February 26th, 1849

My Dear Mother,

I have had the privilege of again hearing from you, and this privilege has been even greater than usual, from the fact which the date of this letter intimates, that I am now no more among our countrymen, but am dwelling among this heathen people alone, were it not for the presence of a covenant God and Saviour. In following out the purpose intimated in my last, I left Hong-Kong on Wednesday the 7th current for the opposite continent of China, and have been, since that time, going from place to place with my Chinese assistants and one servant, much as I used to do in Scotland in days that are past. In some places I have spent only one day; in others I have remained for a longer time, the population being large and the door open. As yet I have been furthered and prospered far beyond what I looked for, and although the difficulties are many, even of an outward kind, yet I do not despond in looking to the future.

One of our difficulties arises from the constant fear the people are in of robbers, who suppose, though in my case without cause, that foreigners have much money with them; and again in places where there are mandarins a foreigner is likely to be dislodged at once. This was my experience at first setting out; for I had spent only one night at Cowloon, opposite to Hong-Kong, when I was warned to remove, and so had to retreat for the time. The people also at present are in constant apprehension of war with England, and this makes them more suspicious of foreigners who come into their borders. But with all this I have hitherto had great liberty of access to the population, and as far as I have been able to declare my message I have found attentive, and in some cases earnestly attentive hearers.

The valley I am now in is full of villages, as its name intimates. It is also the seat of a market held nearly every third day, to which the people of the surrounding country resort, and this makes it an important centre of operations. Yesterday, the Christian Sabbath, was the market-day here. I was out among the people about three hours, and had much support from God. What need have I of the presence of the Lord of the Sabbath in a land like this, that I may not lose my own soul in seeking to save the souls of others! I shall probably need to leave this place soon, as the master of the house I am now in does not promise us lodgings even for another night. But the Lord will provide. 'They shall not be ashamed that wait for me.'

Thus I write again,
dearest mother,
and remain your affectionate son,
Wm C. Burns

From the village of Pan-Seen about
85 miles to the north of Hong-Kong
April 16, 1849

Dear Mother,

After writing you from Hong-Kong at the end of last month, I remained there a few days longer, to enjoy the advantage of retirement and the privileges of a Christian Sabbath, and on the 4th of the present month returned again to this continent of China. Since coming back I have visited four villages of 1000 to 1500 inhabitants each, remaining generally for a few days, and embracing such opportunities as are given me, both in going out among the people, and in the visits which many pay to us, to make known something of the gospel message.

We were some time ago invited to come to the village where we now are, and not only do we here enjoy the fullest external liberty to speak to the people, but there are some who receive us with much cordiality and seem to manifest some interest in our message. One man in particular who this evening worshipped with us seems as if his mind were opening to the truth. But ah! when I speak thus you must not judge of such a case as if it were similar to those which we remember at Kilsyth, Dundee, and Perth, in days that are past!

There is among this people no Sabbath, no Bible, no distinct knowledge even of the existence of one only living and true God, and in my present circumstances it is not a little encouragement to find tokens even of a distinct and cordial apprehension of the simplest principles of divine truth. How little are many who neglect the great salvation among you aware that they are indebted for all that is pure and elevated in their knowledge to that holy Book which they despise!

Were it not my abiding conviction that the Lord hath sent me here, and that his grace can be made sufficient for us in all circumstances, I would sometimes be overwhelmed when regarding the state of this blinded people, and the danger to which my own soul is exposed in dwelling among them. From day to day I have enjoyed many tokens of the Lord's guiding and supporting hand, but while this is the case, I cannot say that as yet I have seen any clear indications in the state of this people that the day of their spiritual deliverance is at hand. In other days it has been my solemn privilege to enter into the labours of others, and it may be that here I am to labour where others are to reap.

April 17th. This morning I resume my pen in haste to conclude this letter. From morning to morning the Lord's mercies are ever new. Great is his faithfulness. I am about today to remove to a village further on. My messenger waits, and I must in haste conclude.

Praying for all covenant blessings to my beloved parents, kindred, etc., and for grace and peace to all the churches of the living God.

I ever am,
Your loving son,
Wm C. Burns

Chinese Hospital, Hong Kong
June 21st, 1849

My Dear Mother,
My last letter would not prepare you for hearing from me again so soon, and that too from this place. I went on last occasion more to the westward (having already visited a good part of those who speak my dialect to the north), and there we found the people everywhere so averse to the presence of a foreigner, that after sleeping nine successive nights on the water in going from place

306

to place, and not being allowed to lodge on shore, I returned here, where I have again resumed my quiet studies, and where I enjoy opportunities of doing what I can amongst this people, not only in speaking to the patients in the hospital, but in visiting others in the neighbourhood.

The season also at present, both from great rain and great heat, is not so favourable for that mode of life which I have been following for some previous months on the opposite continent. I trust that in due time my path may be further opened, and that it may graciously be made plain by the Lord in what way and in what place I am to be more permanently employed upon these shores. I do not think at present of returning to the continent, but it is possible that my path may be made plain to do so sooner than I can anticipate.

Perhaps you are by this time aware that Dr James Young, a much valued friend here, offered himself some time ago to the Presbyterian Church in England as a missionary. The last mail has brought to him the intimation of his offer of service being accepted, but where and how we may be located and employed on these shores is not yet fully determined; nor can Dr Y leave his present employment until the close of the present year.

It was a great mercy that in my last journey as well as in the two previous ones I was preserved from every danger, although surrounded with perils seen and unseen. The night before I landed here we were not, I suppose, above half a mile from a Macao passage-boat when it was attacked by pirates and robbed with the loss of some lives. The firing was so loud that, in the darkness, we supposed it must be some English war-steamer in pursuit of pirates. I was, at this time, on board the Chinese passage-boat from Canton, and no evil was allowed to come nigh to us.

The person who has charge of the Chinese hospital where I am now lodged is a converted Jew, Dr Hirschberg, connected with the London Missionary Society. I have long enjoyed his friendship, and now for a season I am very favourably situated in lodging with him, both for learning the language and for speaking a little among the patients who come seeking cure to their bodily diseases. It is little indeed, however, that I can add regarding tokens of an encouraging nature among the people. But the day of mercy and deliverance promised will come, and then those ends of the earth shall remember and turn unto the Lord.

You have need to pray for all of us who labour here, that we may be endued with a patient and persevering spirit, for the natural and spiritual difficulties of the field are of no common kind.

Commend me, dear mother, to the prayers of God's people. May you and my father never forget me, when either one or both, you draw near the glorious high throne of our Father in heaven. Jesus is the way. In his blood we have access: in him we are complete.

Your loving and affectionate son,
Wm C. Burns

July 25th, 1849

My Dear Mother,

I take up my pen (not so much used in these days as my Chinese pencil) to write a few lines that you may know something of my present affairs.

During the past month I have been quietly resident here, and while I have thus enjoyed much leisure for study, I have also had daily opportunities of taking part, both as a hearer and as a speaker, in the meetings which are held for the good of the patients and of the household. As I had no present need for my former native assistants who journeyed with me on the mainland, they left me more than a month ago, and I am thus in the meantime alone, and co-operating with others as formerly at home and in my own tongue. This kind of position suits me, and will probably continue to be my position here until at least Dr Young is ready to join me, which is not until the beginning of next year.

Do not cease, dear parents, to pray for me, that I may be still graciously kept and divinely quickened and enlarged in the way of God's testimonies. The removal of such pillars as John M'Donald and also Sir Andrew Agnew would overwhelm the minds of God's people, were it not that they are not man-worshippers, but have their faith stayed on Him who ever liveth, and hath an unchangeable priesthood. While Jesus lives, the Church which is his body shall live also, each member receiving by faith out of his fulness and grace for grace. How securely must the Church of the living God be built, when it can stand unshaken while so many who seemed to be pillars are removed! But in the Church above, those who are 'made' to be pillars 'shall go no more out'. Blessed, holy, glorious society of the redeemed in the presence of God and the Lamb! May our hearts be ever there until amazing grace open the door of that inner sanctuary, and call us to come in!

Oh! when shall the nations on earth – the many millions of these distant Gentiles – hear the call of the Son of God, bringing them into the Church below to be prepared for the Church above! The change will be great indeed when this takes place! May we have grace to pray and labour that the time may be hastened! You will remember me, dear father, to all who ask of my welfare, and engage the praying to pray much and more in our behalf, and that China's gates may be opened to the King of glory!

As ever,

I remain your affectionate son,

Wm C. Burns

Amoy
July 25th, 1851

My Dear Mother,

As you see from the date, I am now at Amoy, having left Canton only a few days after I last wrote you, and having been here already ten days. My expectations of getting the house I had in view at Canton were completely disappointed, and my way seemed hedged up to come here. I embarked accordingly at Whampoa in the English barque *Herald* for Amoy on the evening of June 26th, and after spending the Sabbath and Monday at Hong-Kong by the way, we reached here on the forenoon of July 26th.

The passage was a delightful one, and very refreshing to the bodily frame after sixteen months in Canton. The days I spent in Hong-Kong were pleasant. I had two opportunities of preaching in Chinese, and stayed with my old friend Dr Hirschberg.

I have found a very kind Christian welcome among the

missionary brethren here, English and American, and my expectations are more than exceeded in all I have seen as yet of Amoy as a place and as a missionary station. I stayed for three nights with Mr and Mrs Stronach of the London Missionary Society, members of old in the Albany Street Congregational Church, Edinburgh, and I am now very much to my mind lodged in the middle of the Chinese population, in a little room connected with the school which was made over to Dr Young by an American missionary on his removal here a year ago. Thus settled down amid Chinese voices, and with a Christian native servant (who prays with me; I cannot yet pray with him in his own dialect), and a Chinese teacher who comes daily, I am endeavouring to exchange my Canton for the Amoy Chinese. To speak this new dialect publicly and well may require a good deal of time, but even already I can make myself easily understood about common things, and am able to follow a good deal of what I hear in Chinese preaching.

Dr and Mrs Young are well, and seem to be getting on well through the divine blessing and guidance. I feel it a great privilege to be connected with him as well as with the other missionary brethren here, who all go on in much harmony: and not without tokens of divine encouragement. The people here present a striking contrast to the people of Canton in their feelings and deportment towards foreigners. Here all is quiet and friendly, and although there is here also a great apathy on the subject of the gospel, yet a good many seem to listen with attention, and the missionaries have inquirers who come to be taught.

I was preaching last Sabbath-day (in English of course) from the words: 'Because iniquity shall abound, the love of many shall wax cold' (Matthew 24:12); and, alas! I felt they were solemnly applicable to my own state of heart. Unless the Lord the Spirit continually uphold and quicken, oh! how benumbing is daily contact with heathenism! But the Lord is faithful, and has promised to be 'as rivers of water in a dry place, and as the shadow of a great rock in a weary land'.

May you and all God's professing people in a land more favoured, but alas! also more guilty, experience much of the Lord's own presence, power, and blessing, and when the enemy comes in as a flood, may the Spirit of the Lord – yea, it is said, 'the Spirit of the Lord *shall* – lift up a standard against him'.

Your affectionate and loving son,
Wm C. Burns

Twenty-Five miles from Shanghai
January 26, 1856

My Dear Mother,

Taking advantage of a rainy day which confines me to my boat, I pen a few lines, in addition to a letter to Dundee containing a few particulars which I need not repeat. It is now 41 days since I left Shanghai on this last occasion. An excellent young English missionary, Mr Taylor, of the Chinese Evangelization Society, has been my companion during these weeks, he in his boat and I in mine, and we have experienced much mercy, and on some occasions considerable assistance in our work.

I must once more tell the story I have had to tell already more than once, how four weeks ago, on the 29th of December, I put on the Chinese dress, which I am now wearing. Mr Taylor had made this change a few months before, and I found that he was in consequence so much less incommoded in preaching by the crowd, that I concluded that it was my duty to follow his example. We were at that time more than double the distance from Shanghai that we now are at, and would have been still at as great a distance, had we not met at one place with a band of lawless people, who demanded money and threatened to break our boats if their demands were refused.

The boatmen were very much alarmed, and insisted on returning to some place nearer home. These people had previously broken in violently a part of Mr Taylor's boat because their unreasonable demand for books was not complied with. We have a large, very large field of labour in this region, though it might be difficult in the meantime for one to establish himself in any particular place. The people listen with attention, but we need the power from on high to convince and convert. Is there any spirit of prayer on our behalf among God's people in Kilsyth? Or is there any effort to seek this spirit? How great the need is, and how great the arguments and motives for prayer in this case! The harvest is here indeed great, and the labourers are few and imperfectly fitted without much grace for such a work. And yet grace can make a few and feeble instruments the means of accomplishing great things, things greater than we can even conceive....

Ever your affectionate and loving son,
Wm C. Burns

July 1856

My Dear Mother,

I need perhaps as much as ever I did since I came to China the presence and power of God's quickening Spirit to maintain divine love and compassion for souls in my heart. Are there those who feel for us in this unbroken field of heathenism, and cry to God with spiritual agonizings for the descent of the Spirit in his life-giving and converting power? The God of grace grant to us such helpers, for the glory of his own great name!

The people in this district are, I think, if possible, more blind and hardened in idolatry and sin than in any place (if we except Canton) where I have formerly laboured. Although society presents here the usual features of Chinese civilization, it is coupled with a barbarity in certain circumstances which I have seen or heard of nowhere else in China. The fishermen, boatmen, and people working in the fields, pursue their work in summer in a state of savage nudity, and within the last twenty years I am credibly informed, persons taken prisoners in the clan feuds have not only been cut to pieces, but their *heart* boiled and eaten by their enemies. Such is heathenism in this part of civilized China.

The ravages of opium we meet with here on every hand, and the deterioration of the morals of the people generally cannot but ascribe, in great part, to the use of this ensnaring and destructive drug. When will measures be taken by those in power to lay an arrest on the opium traffic, which is inflicting such indescribable injury on this people, and which threatens in its progress by its direct, and still more by its indirect, effects – poverty and anarchy, to sweep away a great part of this nation from the face of the earth?

How blinded by the love of money are they who seek to enrich themselves by the gains of such a traffic! Oh! what need have we here of gospel labourers, and of the power of God accompanying their words! Where are the volunteers for this service, and where are those who will hold up their hands in this fight?

Your ever loving and affectionate son,

Wm C. Burns

P.S. About two o'clock a.m., or past midnight, July 18th, 1856. We have just been visited by robbers, who have taken all but the clothes we wear, without however doing us any injury. This is a new call to pity, and to pray for this poor people, sunk so low in darkness and sin. One of our number, it is proposed, shall return to Swatow to get a small supply of money and books, while the other Christian and I go on to another town to await his return. We are preserved in much peace, and have just been joining in praise and prayer for this poor people.

Canton
October 10th, 1856

My Dear Sir,

When I last wrote you in the middle of July, I and my companions had just been robbed in our lodgings at a village about sixteen miles from Swatow. The following day one of my companions returned to Swatow with my letters, and to obtain a fresh supply of books and money, while my other Christian companion and I went forward, as we had intended, to the town of Tang-leng, about six miles further on. We were without money, but God provided support for us in a way that was new to me. The people who took our books gladly contributed small sums of cash for our support, and the first day we thus collected enough to keep us for two days; a countryman also, going the same road, volunteered to carry our bag of books for us; it was heavy for our shoulders, but easy for his, and he said he would want no money, but only a book. Thus the Lord helped us in going forward in his work, instead of turning back to Swatow for help.

At Tang-leng we were very well received. In the neighbourhood there are two native Christians, converted in connection with the American Baptist Mission in Siam, and who, though they are left much to themselves, seem to follow the Lord in sincerity. With these we had much pleasure in meeting on the Lord's day and at other times. A heavy and continued fall of rain detained us at Tang-leng for some weeks, without our being able to do much abroad, and at last, on Monday, August 18th, we left this town, intending to return to Swatow. Our course by water leading us to within five or six miles of the Chaon-chow-foo (chief city of the Chaon-chow department), we agreed to pay it a visit, but fearing lest we should give offence to the authorities, we determined, instead of living on shore, to make the boat which conveyed us there our headquarters while we remained.

On Tuesday the 19th we went on shore, and were particularly well received by the people. The demand for our books among persons able to read them, was unusually great. In the meantime, however, an alarming report of the presence of a foreigner outside the city having been carried to the authorities, we were in the evening suddenly arrested in our boat, and, with all our books, etc., taken prisoners into the city. The same night we were examined publicly by the district magistrate, and after the interval of a day we were examined anew by a deputy (I suppose) of Che-Foo, or chief magistrate of the department.

On these occasions my companions and myself had valuable opportunities of making known something of the gospel, and of the character and objects of Christ's disciples in China, and as there was a great demand for our books, the work of many days seemed to be crowded into one or two. The magistrates examined us with great mildness and deliberation, seeming anxious to obtain information rather than to find fault, and on the evening of the 21st, the day of our second examination, a sub-official was deputed to inform us that the magistrates found we had been arrested on a false report, and that if the Canton merchants at Swatow, or any one of them, would stand security for us, we would be allowed to return to that place.

The Canton merchants (through whom the trade in foreign

vessels is carried on at Swatow), on being written to, came forward in the kindest manner with the document required, but in the meantime, it appears, the magistrates had reflected that, having once arrested a foreigner, confined and examined him, they could not, according to law or with safety to themselves, give him up to any other than a foreign consul, and so I was told that I would be sent to Canton. On Saturday the 30th I was put on board a river-boat, and carried about a mile above the city. Here we remained until Tuesday morning, when, being joined by a number of officials, high and low, in all occupying four river boats, and going to Canton, some in connection with my case, and some on other business, we at last commenced our journey.

I was provided with a servant, and with whatever food I wished, at the expense of the government, and had I been well, and had had with me a good supply of Christian books, I might have enjoyed the journey much. As the case was, my books were nearly all gone, and as to my health, a slight cold which I had caught before coming to the city had, through excitement, etc., taken the form of an intermittent fever, with chills (ague), which, violent at first, continued more or less during all my journey.

Our course lay first up the Chaon-chow river against a rapid stream, through Ken-ying-chow, and then, when the river ceased to be navigable, we crossed the country through a hill-pass – a distance of about twenty miles – to where another river, flowing down through Heong-chow to Canton, becomes navigable for boats of considerable size. The first part of the journey was tedious, and (including days on which we halted until our business at the various cities we passed was concluded), we were on the way in all thirty-one days. The news of our arrest, and of my being sent to Canton, had reached Hong Kong, and through the great kindness of many friends who felt anxious for my safety, and could not explain why we should be so long on the way, inquiries were made for us at the office of the native authorities in Canton. It was perhaps owing to this in part, that on reaching Canton on the morning of September 30th, instead of being taken to the mandarin's office, two men were sent by the authorities to conduct me straight from the boat to the office of the British consul.

The consul had had a communication from the governor-general about the case. I did not see it, but the consul informed me that it was conceived in a mild strain, much more so than he had expected, and I am thus wonderfully preserved, and freed from the infliction of any punishment or penalty. I am sorry to add that there is reason to fear my two companions are still confined at Chaon-chow-foo, though the governor-general assures the consul they have been sent to their native districts (in the Chaon-chow department), to be liberated on finding proper security.

You will remember that these two men, though natives of that part of the country, have been for a number of years resident in Hong-Kong, and connected with the American Baptist Mission there. It was Mr Johnson, the American missionary there, who sent them up in the beginning of June to act as colporteurs, and to co-operate with us as far as found desirable. Looking at the lenient view of our case which the native authorities both at Chaon-chow and here seemed led to take, I was disposed, now that my health is graciously restored, to proceed very soon back to Swatow, in the hope of being able to prosecute the missionary work there unmolested, but yesterday, when in the act of making arrangements for going to Hong-Kong, I was met by a message from the British plenipotentiary, conveyed to me by the consul, to the effect that, 'after the representations of the imperial commissioner, he should deem it imprudent and improper that I should return to the district from which I have been sent'.

Met by such a message, from such a quarter, I think it will be my duty to delay making any movement of the kind I contemplated, at least until I hear from Mr Taylor about his plans and prospects, and until the native brethren, as we hope they soon may, be released. Mr Taylor went to Shanghai in the beginning of July, partly for a change during the hot months, and partly intending to bring down his medical apparatus to Swatow. Whether he has already come down, or whether, it may be, hearing at Shanghai of our arrest, he has delayed, I am as yet entirely ignorant. In the meantime, if shut up for a season at Canton, I am in the midst of kind missionary brethren, American and English, and my acquaintance with the Canton dialect now revived, should save me, through the grace of

God, from spending my time unprofitably.

The field is the world, the seed is the Word of God. Most of those who came down with me from Chaon-chow were Canton men; they treated me with much respect and kindness, and with them, in the course of the month we spent together, I had many conversations on the subject of the gospel, which I trust may not prove altogether useless.

Looking back on the whole scene through which I have passed, and contrasting the life and misconstruction and suffering to which we might have been subjected, I cannot but adore the wonderful goodness and power of him to whom the kingdom belongs, and who unceasingly cares even for the most unworthy of his servants. While the people of God have need to pray for us that we may be guided to act aright, and not to rush into danger without cause, they have surely cause to give praise for deliverance vouchsafed, and for opportunities, such as seldom occur, of making known something of the truth of the gospel to men in authority and to many others.

I am glad to learn that at the time you wrote there was a prospect of Mr Sandeman joining the missionary band in China. I trust he may be now on the way, and that he will come to be a blessing to many.

With Christian regards to all friends,

I am,

ever yours,

Wm C. Burns

December 4th, 1856

My Dear Mrs Barbour,

... We thus have some encouragement in our present circumstances, as compared with the past; and were the spirit of grace and supplication granted to some of God's people in Scotland to plead on behalf of us and this people, it would be a sure token that the Lord had special blessings in store for this hitherto so neglected and desolate a part of this inhabited earth. I am glad to hear of such spontaneous offerings to aid us, as that six pounds which you mention. I shall endeavour, when such are forwarded, to dispense them in the way that seems best for the advancing of the Lord's work.

When I was in Scotland lately there were a number of small sums put into my hand, which I did not put into the public mission fund, and which I laid out in printing, at Shanghai and the neighbourhood, about 15,000 copies, in a sheet form, of one or two of Milne's *Village Sermons* (in Chinese). These I found very useful for distribution on certain occasions, when a number of larger tracts could not conveniently be carried. The first contributors to this small fund, or rather the founders of it, were the children at M– manse (Established), a little girl at the A– Free Church manse, and another at a toll-bar to the north of that town. Some of the other sums were also from the north of Perthshire. I hope we have a few in that region, and in some other places, who pray for us and China's conversion to Christ. The harvest here is truly great, and how few the labourers are. May the Lord of the harvest send forth many more labourers, and especially from among China's own children.

Your affectionate friend,
Wm C. Burns

March 31st, 1857

My Dear Mother,

... All things are going on as before in this place. We have outward peace, and an increasing attendance at our meetings, both ordinary and on the days when medical aid is given by Dr De la Porte, but we need the outpouring of the Holy Spirit in Swatow, as in Kilsyth, to turn the souls of sinners from darkness unto light, and from the power of Satan unto God. We need this, and this God has promised to prayer – true prayer. Who among us has the spirit of prayer! They are mighty who have this spirit, and weak who have it not. We need that the Lord would prevent us with his mercy, and quicken when we are brought very low. Help us for the glory of thy name! Deliver us and purge away our sins. Come, Lord Jesus, and take unto thee thy great power and reign! Is there any special prayer among you for China? Perhaps in seeking the awakening and conversion of these perishing millions a blessing may come down on your own borders as well as on us.

Brethren, pray for us, pray without ceasing! I will conclude this note with Christian regards to all who love the Lord Jesus, especially among my own kindred. If any man love not the Lord Jesus Christ, how dreadful the judgment recorded against him! Oh that all may have grace to flee that judgment and to love him who is altogether lovely, who loved us and gave himself for us.

Wishing grace and peace to my beloved parents,

I am ever your affectionate son,

W. C. Burns

P.S. Finished near midnight, entering on April 1st, 1857, the beginning of my forty-third year.

Swatow, February 22nd, 1858

My Dear Sister,

I have to thank you for more than one letter which I have failed until now to acknowledge directly. You know that the use of the tongue is more natural to me than the use of the pen, and this must be my excuse. I am but poorly able to satisfy your inquiries about the people who, during last year, were about us at various times as applicants for medical aid. They were generally from places distant at least two or three days' journey, and of course unless they come again, we lose sight of them. In consequence of the uncertainty of Dr De la Porte's continuance here, and other causes, the medical work was a month or two ago interrupted, and though it has been resumed, and is now carried on, patients have not yet begun to flow upon us in a stream, as was the case six months ago, when many of the poor people, both men and women, flocked to Swatow for medicine with almost the same zeal as they would resort to some famed idol's shrine.

During the past few weeks I have been almost constantly resident, not at the Chinese town of Swatow (my proper station), but at Dr De la Porte's (Double Island). I came down at first for a change of air, but after getting the full benefit of this I am still for a little detained here by superintending some repairs and improvements in the Dr's house. I need to attend to this rather than he, not only because I understand the language, but because, in the view of his going to England, I consented to take his cottage, etc., from him, wishing to hold the situation in behalf of the mission cause generally as well as for present use.

We have the workmen about us, and have some of them always with us at evening worship. Among other things, we are at present engaged, like the patriarchs, in digging a well, and as the position is rather elevated, we need to go deep in order to find 'springing water' such as Isaac found, Genesis 26:19. You allude to the invitation given me to become chaplain to the Presbyterian soldiers in China. I have lately had a very kind acknowledgment from the War Office of my letter declining the appointment. As I had refused on grounds connected with my occupation as a missionary, Lord Panmure will not press the appointment on me. Unless the Lord in his providence should shut me up to such a course of acting, I feel more and more that I could not safely leave for a moment the position I occupy, and had I accepted the appointment, I would have found on the one hand at least, up to the present time, that the troops among whom I was expected to be, had gone to India instead of coming here, and on the other hand would have been in the greatest danger, from knowing Chinese, of being diverted from my proper work, and sinking down into a kind of interpreter about all and sundry matters.

Mr L whom you once wrote to me about after he had been in Glasgow, has lately got into a position somewhat of this kind. He is now at Canton assisting generally the provisional government established there by the English and French until matters are settled at Peking. He about a year ago disagreed somehow with the Chinese Evangelization Society, and became government school (Chinese) inspector in Hong-Kong, and from the newspapers I have just seen that he is gone to Canton in the capacity I have mentioned. This is not the kind of work that would suit me, and I anticipated from the beginning that had I become an army chaplain, it was work that I could have hardly avoided. I was surprised to see from the same paper which contained the notice of Mr L, that my friend and former fellow-labourer here, Mr J. H. Taylor, has just been married at Ningpo to a daughter of a late missionary, Mr Samuel Dyer.

I am almost surprised at the question you put to me as to whether I have any near that can assist me in keeping my wardrobe in order. Formerly I had the kind missionaries' wives at Canton and Amoy, but now, where I have none such near, I happily am independent of such aid, wearing, as you seem to have forgot, the Chinese dress, which can be renewed or repaired everywhere. The only articles in which I still in part keep by the old attire are socks and flannel-shirts. The socks are hard to get repaired, but the native substitute answers very well. Indeed we need nothing here in addition to what we have but health of body – a mercy still continued to me – and our Lord's gracious presence and blessing in our souls and in our work.

When there are ships here with English crews, we have frequently public preaching on ship-board. Yesterday we had not this privilege, but I enjoyed much the season when in the forenoon Dr De la Porte and I joined in English worship. The Saviour's promise is even to two, and I trust we enjoyed his presence. We long, however, to see his work prospering, and his kingdom established around us. Of this we have not as yet much evidence, but we are not discouraged!

'The kingdom is the Lord's: he is the governor among the nations,' and he hath promised that all nations shall yet be blessed in the Messiah, and all nations call him blessed. Happy those who are made God's instruments in helping on this consummation – first by through grace giving ourselves to the Lord, and then by prayer in the Spirit, or by active efforts, aiding to spread abroad the savour of Christ's name. May such happiness be yours at home, and ours in this far land where our lot is at present cast! Pray for us, and seek for us the prayers of God's people. Remember me specially to Mrs Davidson (formerly Miss Mylne) and ask her prayers for me and this people.

Fraternal regards to Mr Stewart, and my prayers for your infant son.

Your affectionate brother,
Wm C. Burns

Swatow, June 9th, 1858

My Dear Mother,

Dr De la Porte is at last about to leave us. He was here seeing patients yesterday, as I suppose, for the last time, and tomorrow, if the Lord will, I go down to Double Island to see him away. He goes down to Hong-Kong in the expectation of finding a vessel in which to sail for England. It was affecting yesterday to join with him in prayer, probably for the last time, in a place where we have liked so many meetings at the mercy-seat, and when he was gone, the thought that we should see him not again here caused a tender pang which found relief only in looking to him who hath said, 'I will never leave thee nor forsake thee.' We have already parted here with two of God's servants, Mr Taylor two years ago, and now Dr De la Porte. It has been by the Lord's special favour to this poor place and people that they were sent for a time to labour with us here, and now that they are being removed we trust that the same Lord has still chosen instruments in store whom he will send here, and support in doing his work among the poor heathen, and among countrymen more privileged but in many cases equally polluted and far more guilty....

Perhaps you have wondered that I have not alluded to the new dignity conferred on my beloved father. I felt, when I heard of it, in a way that hindered me from at once noticing it, for while I was unwilling to seem to make light of it, I felt on the other hand how poor and insignificant it was compared with that dignity to which, I trust, my dear parents are daily expecting to be promoted – even the crown and the palm of the redeemed in glory – in the presence of God and of the Lamb. To this glory let us hasten, in that glorified company may we meet, to give praises to him that sitteth on the throne, and to the Lamb who bought us with his blood. The face of Christ in glory, as one says, is the glorified church's Bible, from which we shall learn in one day more of divinity than now by faith we attain by many years of study.

Come, Lord Jesus, come quickly! Make us like thee, and in thy time take us to be with thee, to behold thy glory which the Father hath given thee! Unto him that loved us and washed us from our sins in his own blood, and hath made us kings and priests unto

God and our Father: to him be glory! Continue to pray for me, dear parents, and seek an increase of prayer in behalf of this place and people, that the desert may be made to blossom, that the glory of Jehovah may be revealed, and all flesh see it together.

Praying that my parents may be filled with the fulness of God, through the knowledge of the love of Christ which passeth knowledge,

I am,
dear parents,
your affectionate son,
Wm C. Burns

November 21st, 1867 at Nieu-chwang

My Dear Mr Douglas,

Your letter of August 31st reached me this p.m. per steamer *Manchu*, and as she is the last vessel for this season, I hasten to send a few lines by her to Shanghai. Many thanks for the life-like photograph of yourself which you have sent me. You are more like the man that you were intended to be, with than without the 'beard'.

May it please God in his mercy long to preserve you in the health and vigour which you seemed to have enjoyed when the likeness was taken, and may your soul 'prosper and be in health', even as the body 'prospers'! For the last five months, I have allowed my 'beard' also to grow on the lower part of the face. This both saves a great deal of time and trouble, and, in this cold latitude, the hair is a protection to the throat. I fear I cannot write home pressing the claims of Singapore on our mission, when their energies are likely to be fully tasked in maintaining and extending the missions at Amoy, Swatow, and on Formosa. It seems to me that no place more suitable (or perhaps so suitable) could be recommended to the Irish Presbyterians than Nieu-chwang, and Manchuria beyond, a vast, open, and unoccupied field, with a fine climate, and a population comparatively well off in a worldly point of view. In writing home, I have already made this suggestion, and I hope that on consideration you will see your way to second my proposal. If the Irish were here, would this not be a fine place to come to from the south for a change of air?

And you yourself, when needing such a change, would enjoy the opportunity of using and increasing your Mandarin. Mr Cowie, too, would be only sent back to his Che-foo dialect, a great part of the people in this town being from that quarter. You can have no idea of the extent of the trade that is carried on here in grain and oil, as well as bean-cake, furs, etc., etc. I shall only mention what was told me by a gentleman connected with the imperial customs, viz. that two years ago it was estimated that during one winter 80,000 carts came to this place from the interior laden with grain and oil. It is common for from 500 to 1000 to come in on a single day during the winter months, and throughout all the region which furnishes this supply, including the provinces of the Amour and Kirin, as well as the province of Kwang-tung, pure Mandarin is universally spoken. Mr Meadows is now absent on a three months' journey to the north and east, passing through the centre of these three provinces. Romish priests are found here and there, but the only representative of the Protestant churches is my solitary self!

I lately heard from Mr Grant, and also from Si-boo. Mr G has now removed to Singapore from Penang, and so Singapore is not so destitute as it used to be. Mr G is married too, to a lady who lately came out, as perhaps you may have heard. As to the repairs at Pechuia, I shall be glad that you put me down, say, for the sum of 20 pounds sterling, but it will be the end of February before I can furnish you with an order on our treasurer for that amount, my accounts for the year being already made up.

I am rejoiced to hear that while man is repairing the chapel, God himself is again graciously putting forth his hand to repair the spiritual wells of that little church. May backsliders return to their first love, as well as additions be made to the church of 'such as shall be saved!' Who was that young man – an assistant of Dr Maxwell's – who was lost in the Formosa Channel? Not, I hope, the young man from Chioh-bey, who was afterwards chapel-keeper at Sinkoeya?

I must now conclude, as it is getting late. Pray for us, and commend us to the prayers of the churches. I should have mentioned that Mr Williamson of Che-foo, who was lately here, left a native assistant to sell books here during the winter. He and the man who came with me from Peking occupy themselves in this work in the principal street, preaching at the same time to the people. I join them generally during a part of the time, and the opportunity is a valuable one, especially as our house is too retired for collecting passers-by. A separate house we thought we had got for preaching was at last held back, and is now an opium-smoking den!

Christian love to all the brethren,

Yours affectionately,

Wm C. Burns

January 15, 1868. At Nieu-chwang

To my Mother,

At the end of the last year I got a severe chill which has not yet left the system, producing chilliness and fever every night, and for the last two nights this has been followed by perspiration, which rapidly diminishes the strength. Unless it should please God to rebuke the disease, it is evident what the end must soon be, and I write these lines beforehand to say that I am happy, and ready through the abounding grace of God either to live or to die. May the God of all consolation comfort you when the tidings of my decease shall reach you, and through the redeeming blood of Jesus may we meet with joy before the throne above!

Wm C. Burns

P.S. Dr Watson is very kind, and does everything in his power for my recovery.

[To this letter was attached a small fragment of Chinese paper, also in his own handwriting, which consisted of a list of the texts on which he had preached at Nieu-chwang. He probably included it for his mother to have the interest in such a list that only a loving parent might have. We see that on the first two Sundays there was no meeting, and this was due to his bad state of physical health when he arrived from Peking.]

325

Texts preached on at Nieu-chwang

Sept. 1st	No meeting
Sept. 8th	No meeting
Sept. 15th	John 3:16
Sept. 22nd	John 15:14
Sept. 29th	Gal. 5:16
Oct. 6th	Matt. 5:3-12
Oct. 13th	John 6:27
Oct. 20th	Luke 18:1-14
Oct. 27th	Luke 19:1-10
Nov. 3rd – Mr Williamson	John 4:14
Nov. 10th	Matt. 25:1-13
Nov. 17th	John 1:29
Nov. 24th	Isaiah 55:6-7
Dec. 1st	Luke 15 (a good day)
Dec. 8th	Luke 18:18-23
Dec. 15th	James 4:7-8
Dec. 22nd	Rom. 3:20-22
Dec. 29th	Rev. 20:11-15

Retrospective Notes
of
Discourses
Preached in 1842

Sermons Introduction

There are, sadly, not many written sermons from the hand of William Chalmers Burns that are extant. Much of his preaching was extempore and the sermons presented here were, like the letters published in this same volume, discovered as unpublished handwritten manuscripts during research in Edinburgh University's Manuscript Collections. Again, they are presented here as Burns wrote them. I accept any and all responsibility for any mistakes in transcription that may have occurred. No words have been added, even for the purpose of adding clarity. These sermons were composed in the midst of real revival in Scotland and, as such, give us a wonderful glimpse into the vitality and energy and blessing of what God was doing in those remarkable days. The prayer of this editor is that God might once again move as He did in these wonderful days.

Retrospective notes of Discourse delivered June 30th p.m.

v.1 'Out of the depths have I cried unto thee O God!'

This Psalm describes the experiences of a backsliding saint seeking restoration, but may be treated also with a view to a sinner when first awakened, since his case is in most respects very similar to that of a backsliding believer. I shall first view it as applicable to a sinner, then as applicable to a saint.

1st. While a sinner remains unawakened, he seems to himself to walk at liberty, in plain paths. But when the Holy Spirit is given to convince him of sin:

a. He attains discoveries of his guilt. Occasionally his views of sin were superficial, general and did not affect his heart. He included others with himself, and so never felt as if he were the man charged by God as a transgressor. How the Law comes home to him with Divine authority and power, and binds him with cords of conviction which he cannot break nor snap off.

b. This taught his spiritual bondage. This he has naturally no idea of, but thinks he is free to do good, as to do evil, but when awakened he finds it far otherwise. He cannot repent truly for his sin. He cannot come to Christ. He cannot deliver himself from Satan's dominion. He can perform no duty spiritually and with his whole heart to God.

c. He is convinced of the reality of the wrath of God abiding on him on account of unpardoned sin. Every sin becomes like an adder in his heart, wounding, poisoning and ruining the soul. He hears the thunderings of Sinai and is terrified with the lightnings of the Holy Law which he has broken. All these convictions together bring the soul into depths which are as waters going over the soul, and threatening to drown it, or as a deep, dark, lonesome and miry pit, from which there is no prospect of escape. The sinner is like Jonah.

329

2nd. But to pass to the case of the backsliding saint we remark,

a. That the Covenant of Grace does not make absolute provision for preventing the saints from falling into such sins as will bring them into depths of conscience. There is provision for the pardon of all sins of infirmity which cannot be avoided, while sanctification is incomplete. There is also absolute provision made against the sin of final apostasy (Jer. 30), but between these two extreme limits there is a wide region in which believers walk. In it there are many safe and heavenly paths, and many deep and polluting quagmires in which we may be in the utmost danger of perishing.

b. The other sins by which believers fall into depths are either of a gross and open character e.g. the sins of David, and of Peter, or they are sins of a more hidden kind, committed with aggravations, e.g. careless walking with God after special manifestations of his love and near communion with him and through neglect of eminent opportunities of doing good and advancing his glory. Sins committed after special training. All these and similar sins are aggravated in the case of believers by these circumstances:

i. That though the soul is furnished with a principle of grace tending to oppose and to preserve it against the dominion of these.

ii. That there is full provision made in Christ for the supply of all the believer's wants which he is to come and freely receive.

3rd. Such sins as have been mentioned when not speedily repented of and cleansed by the special application of the blood of Jesus may have one of two effects. They will either keep the soul in perpetual barrenness, dry, withered and seemingly almost dead, or if God intends to restore the soul to fruitfulness, he will judge it with heavy chastisement and bring it for this purpose into deeper agonies of affliction, either bodily or spiritual or both. In such depths the believer will lose the sweet and abiding sense of reconciliation to God. He will be perplexed with distressing thoughts about his unholy and ungrateful treatment of a gracious God and Father. Yea he may be brought under new discoveries of sin unaccompanied with present and convinced views of God's mercy in Christ, so low as to be on the brink of despair, and so mourning under darkness many days. Satan also may obtain liberty to harass the soul with sifting and grievous temptations insomuch that the soul may despair even of life. These are depths indeed which fill the soul with alarm and horror of darkness, even though being still in the bond of the sure Covenant of Sovereign Grace, its eternal salvation is infallibly secured.

I would improve this subject for the purpose of:

    1st. Examining those who are true Christians

    2nd. And those who are not.

1st. Many think themselves Christ's people who never have had any true work of the Lord upon their consciences and hearts; that this is impossible, though it is a common delusion in this superficial and secure generation, when all that is deep and spiritual and really passive in religion is little in repute and less in exercise. We must have received the sentence of death through the law before we can receive the sentence of acquittal and life through the gospel. It is by the law only, with its holy, spiritual and imperative demands, that any one is shut up to the faith of Jesus, and all of you whose faith has not grown out of alarming discoveries of damning guilt, are building not upon the rock but upon the sand, which will give way beneath you and bury you amid the ruins of the house which you have spent your strength in building to protect and defend you.

2nd. I would call on Christians to examine themselves. Many of you are not in depths at present only, we may fear, because God is leaving you to yourselves. It is because many sins of omission and commission are lying upon your conscience unconfessed, or confessed superficially and impenitently, or forgotten, that so many are like to them that go down to the pit. Oh! listen yourselves, and examine why it is that you are as withered branches on which there are not few blossoms, little fruit, yea but few shrivelled and worm-eaten leaves.

But to you both saints and sinners who may be in depths I cannot now proceed to give direction how to escape. This however must be in a great measure left to a future opportunity and at present I shall only notice from the following verses that it is by applying to God the prayer that follows, resting upon Jesus alone through whom there is forgiveness with God.

2nd. Psalm 130:2 July 7th (1 Thess. 5:17)

In considering the first verse of this remarkable Psalm we have been led to look into those depths in which unconverted sinners, and saints who have backslidden from God are all without exception lying, whether they are aware of it or not. These depths are indeed full of danger and terror. The unconverted when made alive to their condition find that they are laden with sins of the heinous nature, bound under the strong cords of natural corruption and the tyranny of Satan, and exposed to that infinite wrath of a holy God. When these things are in any degree discovered to the soul, it feels itself indeed like one who is cast amid the overwhelming waves of the ocean when he has no footing to stand on and none at hand to rescue him from the devouring flood.

The saints again, we have seen, though they have pardon provided for all those sins into which through the imperfection of this holiness on earth they are always falling, and though they are secured against the sin of total and final apostasy from God, yet are in danger, through the power of the old man within them, the world around and the god of this world, of falling into all or any of those innumerable sins which lie between importunity on the one hand, and the sin of apostasy on the other. Now it is by their being guilty of these that they are brought into deep waters. They may have committed some gross sin as David, or Peter, or they may have been guilty of sins which, though in their own nature seem little, are particularly offensive to God by various aggravating circumstances in which they are committed; and for these the Lord withdraws the sweet and abiding sense of their reconciliation to him, gives them a sharp and affecting sense of their ingratitude and wickedness in sinning against so holy and gracious a God and

Father and perhaps leaves them for a time almost to despair of again seeing his face in peace. These are the dreadful depths into which the saints have often fallen and may fall again, and it is out of these that we are here taught by the example of the Psalmist the way in which we may be delivered.

Upon this part of the subject I just stopped at the close of the last discourse, so far as might give direction to any who might at that time be in the circumstances described, and might be groaning for deliverance.

It is now my object to open up more fully this most interesting and precious subject that so the way may, through the teaching of the Holy Ghost, be made plain to all, by which they may escape from the horrible depths in which they are lying, and obtain a secure and eternal and glorious resting place upon Jesus, the Rock of our salvation.

And here we may notice from the words of the Psalmist:

First, that deliverance from the depths of sin and misery is to be looked for from God alone. If there was a true and practical conviction of this great truth in the minds of all who find themselves in these depths, many would be delivered who continue withering there and perish, and those who do escape would escape with greater speed.

But alas! It is not natural to man to look for help to God. The convinced sinner cannot believe that he can find pardon, full and free, from that holy and blessed Being whom he has so vilely offended. And even those backsliding saints, who have already enjoyed the consultations of God's free and unbounded grace, are tempted to think that all their past experience has been only a delusion, and that their guilt is so peculiarly aggravated in having sinned against so much light and love as they have enjoyed, that they can hardly suspect that it cannot be forgiven.

And so my friends, both in the case of the awakened sinner and the backsliding believer there is a great natural tendency to turn to other refuges than to God. The awakened sinner is often so terrified at his convictions of sin, and finds them so powerful to his soul, that he tries in various ways to get them removed. And alas! In his cruel attempt, he but too often succeeds, so far that the sleep of death which seemed about to be broken, returns upon him in all its power and continues undisturbed, until the poor, perishing sinner is awakened by the muttering thunders of the Judgment and the flashing lightnings of coming wrath. He will flee to business, to company, to sensual pleasures, all in order to dispel the gloom that is settling on his guilty soul. He will often succeed in this, in hardening his heart against the voice of the Lord God. Or if he cannot thus find peace, he will begin to reform many of the grosser sins into which he has fallen, and if circumstances favour, he will become a specious hypocrite, or a laborious and improving formalist, perhaps not only abstaining from gross outward sin, and becoming outwardly respectable, but joining the company of the people of God, and beginning to attend to secret and family duties of devotion.

All this and much more may well be done by the power of men's natural conscience, enlightened and aroused by the common grace of God. But, my dear friends, when God has a purpose of saving grace toward any soul, he drives it by the keen and painful wounds of the fiery law from all such shadowy and hollow refuges of self-righteousness, out into the open field, where the sinner is compelled to stand and answer for his debt to a righteous God, or die under his holy displeasure. He has nothing to pay and the more he tries to work out a righteousness that may satisfy its demands, he is the more fearfully convinced that he is poor and miserable and wretched and blind and naked. He is now brought to despair and under this despair wants to die – did not the Lord, the God of Love, pass by him at that time, and say to him when in his blood, 'Live!' Quickened by the word of a Redeeming God, he turns his eyes from the law and, beholding the Son of God bleeding upon the Cross as a sacrifice for the sins of men, hope breaks with its reviving beams upon his benighted soul, and he turns to seek a message in that holy, majestic, and gracious God, against whom he has so long and wickedly rebelled.

And in like manner my friends, the backsliding saint when cast into depths on account of sin, is often chargeable with the folly and the guilt of seeking other Saviours than Jesus the Lamb of

God to secure his restoration to God's holy and blessed fellowship. Sometimes he too will try to stifle the conviction that he is really a backslider and must return to God with renewed heart-humbling repentances by a simple and steadfast reliance on the holy, sin-purifying blood of Jesus.

He will go, for instance, to mingle with religious company, and join in religious conversation, when he ought to be found in his closet, laying open his treacherous heart in the presence of his God. Or again, he repairs on a Sabbath evening to the Church that he may open his heart-searching mercies in private retirement, and so in many other ways even more specious than these, he will try to remove the accusations of an awakened conscience. And when he cannot succeed by any such means in this foolish attempt, he will then begin to repent and confess, and even pray for the Holy Ghost to remove his corruption, all in order that he may avoid a simple application to the blood of Jesus as his only hope, and a direct return to God as the sovereign and gracious Pardoner of sin at last. However, the backsliding saint, whom God intends to purge that he may bring forth more fruit, is like the awakened sinner driven from all his refuges, and with mingled shame and joy, returns to seek his Father's face.

Thus my friend, you see that both the awakened sinner and the backsliding saint can find deliverance from the depths of their sin and misery, only from the Lord Jehovah! '(Unto thee have I cried) out of the depths have I cried unto thee, O Lord.'

But second, we are taught by the words before us, that it is in the exercise of prayer that deliverance from these 'depths' is obtained from the Lord. 'Lord, hear my voice, let thine ears be attentive to the voice of my supplications.'

Some of you are accustomed, perhaps, to think of faith in Jesus Christ as the grace in the exercise of which particularly it and he is obtained. And in this you are right, for it is by grace that a sinner is saved through faith (Eph. 2:8), and without this faith in Jesus it is impossible to come to God with acceptance. But then you must remember that faith does not exclude prayer, 'Whosoever calleth on the Name of the Lord shall be saved' (Rom. 10:13). Both are needful, and the one could not do without the other. Indeed, prayer may be said to be the breath of faith. In the very act of believing on Jesus, the sinner becomes a beggar at the door of God's free grace, and that faith which does not bring a sinner to his knees that he may come to God or to his face, is not only dumb but also dead, and leaves the soul as dead as before.

'Behold he prayeth,' was what God told Ananias regarding Paul, when the Lord sent Ananias to declare to the converted persecutor this gracious intention regarding him. And the same declaration is true of every one who secures a pardon from God, either when awakened from the sleep of death at first, or when rescued from the dangerous slumbers of carnal security, to return from backsliding unto God, from whom the soul may have revolted.

Observe most carefully the characters which distinguish those prayers of the awakened sinner and backsliding believer which prevail with God, through the merits of Jesus, to obtain a full and gracious pardon. These characteristics are very clearly set before us in the Psalm before us.

1. This prayer is that of a self-condemned and humbled sinner. 'If thou, Lord, shouldst mark iniquity, Oh Lord, who shall stand?' These words discover to us one of the springs out of which the prayer in context flows (as a stream).

The Psalmist justifies God and condemns himself in God's presence, as justly able to be brought into judgment and punished for his iniquities, and this character belongs to all those prayers which we can offer acceptably to God. To enter into his presence seeking pardon without confession of sin, is the very greatest insult to God's holy majesty, and to confess ourselves to be sinners with the lips, while our consciences are not keenly alive to our just dessert, and our hearts are deeply humbled for our iniquity, is such impious hypocrisy as the God of truth and uprightness abhors and condemns, and will certainly visit, if it is not repented of, with infinite and abiding wrath.

Everyone, however, who is truly seeking pardon from Jehovah, is truly aware of his sin, and sincerely humbled in sorrow of heart on account of it. You remember the case of the Publican in Luke

18:13. He was one who came to seek for pardon and actually found it, and observe the humility and penitence that marked his conduct. He stood afar off, hardly daring to lift up his eyes to heaven and smote upon his breast, saying, 'God be merciful to me a sinner.'

Behold also the humility of the woman of Cana in Matthew 15:27. The Lord Jesus calls her a dog, and yet she does not give over her entreaty but turns his very objection into an argument and claims the dog's portion, 'the crumbs that fall from their master's table.'

2. The prayer of the Psalmist is offered out in faith upon God as the pardoner of sin. 'There is forgiveness with thee, that thou mayst be feared.' Without a belief that God pardoneth iniquity there can be no acceptable approach to his presence, never will any awakened soul dare to approach him in any other character.

When an awakened sinner or a backsliding saint entreats for pardon, it approaches God, taking hold of his name as the Lord God, merciful and gracious, longsuffering and abundant in goodness and truth, keeping mercy for thousands, forgiving iniquity, transgression and sin, and who will by no means clear the guilty. Casting all its dependence on the glorious sacrifice of his own Son, as all-sufficient (to cleanse from guilt), to purge the conscience from guilt, and as freely offered by God to every sinner to whom the gospel comes. This is the plea which the returning sinner uses, to prevail with a holy and righteous God. This is the Rock of salvation on which it stands to plead with Jehovah.

If we lose hold of this argument, we may cease to plead. The case is hopeless, for we may sooner pluck the fixed stars from the sky than move the heart of God without Christ as our Mediator. But if we truly lay hold of this, and cast away from us all other grounds of confidence, then we shall assuredly prevail with God. We shall thus take hold of the Lord's strength and make peace with him (Isa. 27:5).

It is through a want of faith in God through Christ as the forgiver of sin, that many convinced sinners come short of salvation. They believe that they are sinners, and are thus filled with well-grounded alarm lest the wrath of God should overtake them, but they will not believe God's readiness to pardon them and love them freely through the death of his beloved Son, and therefore they remain afar off and restrain prayer before God. Or if they pray, yet it is with little hope of being heard. They deny the truth of God and thus are in the most imminent danger of perishing through unbelief.

If we then would be saved, we must cry to God, not only with humble and contrite confession of sin, but with confidence in his willingness to pardon us, as a God who delighteth in mercy if we do but cleave to the free promise of his grace in Jesus Christ the Saviour, and plead with him the merits of his finished atonement. Many instances to illustrate this might be brought from the Divine record. I may refer you again to the woman of Cana.

3. The third character which we may here mark in the prayer of the Psalmist, is earnestness and importunity. This appears from the petition, 'Lord, hear my voice, let thine ears be attentive to the voice of my supplications', and, from the emphatic nature of the words which he employs. He supplicates and that too with his voice, crying aloud with all earnestness after God, and having thus prayed, he prays again that God would hear the prayers he has offered. (This holy earnestness of soul is commended in many parts of Scripture, and we have many striking examples of it.)

Then the soul is made truly alive to its sin and misery, either at its first awakening from the sleep of death, or when it arouses from the slumbers of carnal security after conviction, and being convinced also that there is hope of its obtaining pardon from God and reconciliation to him. It is stirred up to seek him with all its powers. This great work takes precedence of all other business. He seeks first the Kingdom of God and his righteousness, and though many worldly concerns may demand attention, he will make every other call give way to the great work of obtaining peace with God.

The sinner will neither give sleep to his eyes, nor slumber to his eyelids, until he obtains some good hope that the Lord hath heard his prayer. He will like David in Psalm 119:147 greet the dawning of the morning with his cries to God. He will break through all obstacles and shake off all sloth and rid himself of unwillingness, stirring up himself to call upon God and give him no rest until he hear and answer his entreaties. Woman of Cana. Anxiety of men about worldly concerns, about natural life. If a man were to give over labour, if that were needful, and live for a month on alms, that he might attend to the concerns of the soul, it would be most reasonable.

Preached at Blairgowrie on Sacrament Monday, 8th July.

Psalm 130:3   July 14th   (N.B. Psalm 114:2)

In discoursing upon the two preceding verses, I have had occasion to allude pretty fully to the truth contained in this one. For in speaking of the depths out of which the sinner cries, I was naturally led to describe in some degree those convictions of sin which make him feel that he is lying in these. And again in setting before you the nature of that prayer which he presents to God for deliverance, I was led to speak of the conviction expressed in this verse as one of the springs from which that prayer takes its rise, and to describe its nature as far as was requisite, in order to give a first idea of that humility and penitence with which it taught him to pray.

I might therefore pass immediately to the consideration of that forgiveness which is set before us in the following verse, were it not that the nature and origin of true conviction of sin is set before us in this verse, in a light which has not yet been considered. And that is of the utmost importance, to set the truth of God regarding our guilt before the mind in every view, in order that it may be prepared for welcoming with joy the glorious offers of free grace and mercy, which are afterwards to be considered.

The language of this verse is formed with reference to the Judgment of God. David appears to have been realizing the transactions of that great and solemn day on which he was to appear before the Judge of all, and receive his final sentence. And having weighed his own character and conduct in the scales of Divine Justice, he finds his righteousness infinitely deficient, his guilt unspeakably heavy. And midst this affecting conviction, he appeals to God and confesses that if he should bring this iniquity to the light and charge it against him, he could not endure the trial, but crumble under just condemnation and lie exposed to the inflicting of Divine wrath and curse.

Now it may be useful for us, in endeavouring to confirm the conclusion to which he comes, first to follow him in some of the steps through which we may suppose he went in arriving at that conviction, and second to weigh what is contained in that conviction itself. We may then suppose that he considered, first, the character of the Judge by whom he was to be tried and may state,

1. That this Judge is omniscient. It greatly happens that when men are brought before human tribunals for their crimes, that the charges cannot be brought home to the offender for want of evidence, and that thus he escapes the punishment which he deserves. But it is far otherwise with God the Judge of all. He is present in every place, at all times, and there is not one event that occurs in all the vast universe of his dominion, which he does not witness, and record in the Book of His Remembrance.

He has been with every one among us from the very first moment of our being, and has noticed every thought and desire, and word, and action. Many things we have done in darkness, or in secret places where no human eye was upon us, but there the eye of Jehovah beheld us and marked our conduct. We have cherished many thoughts and formed many desires in the recesses of the heart, which no fellow creature discovers. But all these the 'Lord who searcheth the heart and trieth the reins' (Ps. 7:9) is more intimately acquainted with than we ourselves.

The Lord has searched us and known us, he knoweth our downsitting and our uprising, he understandeth our thoughts afar off. He compasses our path and our lying down and is acquainted with all our ways. Yea there is not a word on our tongue but lo! the Lord knoweth it altogether. If we should say, 'the darkness shall cover me', the night shall be light about us. Yea the darkness hideth not from him, but the night shineth as the day: the darkness and the light are both alike to him. If then we are chargeable with any iniquity, it cannot escape detection. He who is to be our Judge at last, is our witness now. He will bring to remembrance all that we have forgotten. He will bring to the light all the hidden things in the darkness, and make manifest the motives of the heart (1 Cor. 4:5).

2. The Judge is spotless in holiness. The holiness of God expresses his character as perfectly free from all moral infirmity and entirely contrary to it. He is not only separated from inward pollution, but is utterly opposed to it. He is the Being who scattereth evil with his eyes. He is glorious in holiness. The angels before him, cry continually, Holy! Holy! Holy! In consequence of this glorious character, Jehovah is the unchangeable enemy of all sin, and will not allow any sin to pass unpunished.

3. That not only is he holy, but also righteous. Righteousness is that disposition which victims cry one to give every being that which is his due. In a private individual, righteousness is consistent with passing by offences without punishment which it requires, that every one receive the good which he deserves. In a Judge however, righteousness demands as much that the guilty be condemned as that the innocent be acquitted. We would not blame but commend a righteous person, who when he is faced by another should meekly pass over the offence. But that Judge who should take upon him to grant release to an occasional man from pity or goodwill, would hardly be thought fit for his high and solemn charge, and thus it is with Jehovah as Judge. He proceeds according to the exact demands of the law, and the real character of the person tried, either to inflict punishment on the guilty, or to grant acquittal to the innocent. There is, therefore, no hope of a sinner escaping through any leniency which he may expect to find in the Judge.

4. The Judge is omnipotent and therefore he is capable of executing the sentence against all offenders against his majesty however numerous they may be, however powerful as individuals, and united in their rebellion. Though hand join in hand, the wicked shall not go unpunished. The Lord killeth and maketh alive. He woundeth and healeth, and there is none that can deliver out of his hand. He doeth according to his will among the armies of heaven and among the inhabitants of the world. None can stay his hand from working, or say unto him, 'What doest thou?'

These are the characteristics of the Judge. How full of security and joy to the holy! How pregnant with alarm and terror to all the guilty! Nothing can escape his omniscience, nothing can bribe his holiness and righteousness, to prevent the judgment of the guilty! Nothing can withstand his omnipotence! These glorious attributes of Godhead thus set in array against the sinner, may well arouse his most dreadful apprehensions of damnation and make him cry out, 'O Lord! Who can stand?'

But next we may consider the rule by which judgment is to be given by God upon the sons of men. This is clearly made known to us. It is the law of the Ten Commandments prescribing our duty to God and men. And must this law be perfectly obeyed? Is there no allowance for the fallen, depraved nature of man which cannot keep it perfectly? No! The law is holy and just and good, and though we have lost by the Fall the power to keep it, its objective remains unchanged and unchangeable. The rights of God and of our neighbour, which it defines and protects, continue uncompromised and cannot be attacked with violence, being true to the principles of eternal righteousness, which are a transcript of the matchless perfections of Jehovah.

Unless we have from the first moment of our being loved the Lord our God with all the heart and strength and mind, and our neighbour as ourselves, without the least intermission or defect, we are charged by the law as transgressors and must fall in judgment. Yea though we had kept every command perfectly during all our life with the single exception of having omitted one duty or committed one offence, we should for this become liable for condemnation, and be exposed to eternal wrath. For he that keepeth the whole law and yet offendeth in one point is guilty of all. The authority and terror of the Lawgiver are as much connected with each command, even the least as with the greatest, as with all, and therefore it is really the same to violate one as to violate all.

We have now come to the means by which we may suppose the Psalmist arrived at the conclusion contained in the verse before us, and we thus proceed to consider,

Secondly: What is implied in this conclusion to which he comes:

1. It implies a deep and self-condemning conviction of sin. This conviction appears both in the supposition he makes, and in the inference which he draws. If thou, Lord, shouldst mark iniquity, O Lord, who should stand?

This is as if he said to himself, I have considered the character of my Judge and the rule according to which I am to be tried, and am convinced that he is righteous and the law most holy, just and good, and therefore I conclude that all which the law finds and which the Judge condemns is really iniquity and deserving of punishment.

And again when I examine myself and other men by the holy standard of the law, I find that there is none righteous, no not one, that every imagination of the heart of man is only evil, and therefore I feel that not only I dare not stand a righteous trial, but that none of any of the sons of men can hope to do so. Every transgression of the law is sin, and not only I, but even the wisest of men come so far short of obedience that none can stand before God if he enter into a righteous judgment.

2. This conviction is a practical and operative one. It is not a notion in the head, but a feeling of the conscience and the heart, which stirs up the sinner to all the affections suitable to such a condition. This appears from the sinner being brought into depths by his views of sin and from his crying with importunate contriteness to Jehovah for deliverance. Many individuals hold sound views of the nature of sin in general: they are convinced that they are sinners and that they are guilty of this and that particular sin, but then they are not suitably affected by this belief. They are like David after he had sinned in the matter of Uriah the Hittite, and before the prophet Nathan came to him: not like David after Nathan came to declare his sin, and his heart was broken in godly sorrow and contrition.

3. There is in this verse, a confession of sin to God. The verse is itself simply a confession. It is not enough to feel the guilt of sin and condemn oneself by the Divine law. It must also come before

God and make an open acknowledgement of the evil of what we have done. And this confession must be genuine and not forced, penitent not proud and stubborn!

Left unfinished when going to Kilsyth before the beginning of God's glorious work, since which time till now, April 2nd 1842, I have written almost nothing for the pulpit.
Edinburgh April 2nd, 1842

Thoughts with a view to preaching on Tuesday to students.

Alas! My thoughts were barren and few are worthy of being put down.

Sermon for forenoon of Sabbath, April 10th

Hosea 13:9: 'O Israel, thou hast destroyed thyself, but in me is thine help.'

To whom is this addressed? It is addressed originally to 'Israel after the flesh', and thus to the visible Church of God in every age and throughout the whole world. It is evident that the name of Israel is not always to be taken literally, but that as the ancient people of Israel were typical of the Church of God, that names are also so. It is indeed a matter of the greatest difficulty in examining the prophecies which relate to times still future to ascertain in what cases such names as that of Israel, Jerusalem, etc, are to be viewed as describing his universal church.

It would seem that neither the one mode of explanation, nor the other, is to be used exclusively, but it is hard to define the respective boundaries of each, and to mark where the influence of the one principle is lost in that of the other. Closely connected with this difficulty is that of fixing the precise time and event to which particular prophecies relate. And this difficulty is not inferior at any rate to the other.

It seems clear that events the most distant in time are compared together, and are referred to in the same language, in such a way that while part of the language cannot be applied to what is farthest off, part of it can as little be explained by what is nearest, a central part as it were being applicable to both, though probably more strictly to that fulfilment, which is the more remote and general.

We are to view, then, the language of the text as addressed originally and most properly to the nation of Israel at the time when the prophet wrote, and as applicable generally to all who enjoy the outward privileges of the gospel, but still continue impenitent, or have gone back from a certain profession of godliness which they once made. 'O Israel, thou hast destroyed thyself; but in me is thine help.'

In these words, Jehovah speaks in faithfulness, condescension and love, first of security, and then to lead them to himself as the only source and author of salvation. From his words here set before us, we learn the following truths which we shall simply point out, and then consider in their order:

1. Unrenewed sinners are devoted to destruction
2. The destruction of sinners is owing to themselves
3. There is help for self-destroyed sinners to be found in God
4. They can find help in none else
5. God is so anxiously set on the salvation of sinners, that he condescends not only to provide help for them, but most faithfully to warn, and most tenderly to invite them to himself

On these great truths which are so evident in the words of the text, we shall briefly meditate, praying that Jehovah may lead our souls into the deep and hidden mysteries of his own words, and cause us to hear him speaking in them, as with an audible voice from heaven.

Unrenewed sinners are devoted to destruction

This is confirmed by manifold proofs. To allude to one among many, we are told in 2 Thessalonians 1:8 actually quoting vv. 7–9 that, 'the Lord Jesus shall be revealed from Heaven with his mighty angels in flaming fire taking vengeance on them that know not God, and that obey not the gospel of our Lord Jesus Christ, who shall be punished with everlasting destruction from the presence of the Lord and the glory of his power.'

Here we see who the unconverted are and what shall be their doom. They are those who know not God and who obey not the gospel. Their end shall be destruction, inflicted as vengeance, and that by Christ directly, even from the presence of the Lord and from the glory of his power. Destruction implies an utter ruin and annihilation of the sinner, so that both soul and body shall be rendered incapable either of dignity or blessedness, and shall be devoted to shame, contempt, torment and horror.

a. Destruction of the body
This does not consist in reducing it to nothing, but
1st. In its being stripped of all beauty and rendered loathsome, and
2nd. In its being the seat of the most terrible torments of which its nature admits. The worm shall never die, the fire shall never be quenched. What is more terrible than the gnawing of worms, or the consuming of fire?
Left unfinished.

Thursday May 5th, 1842

John 4:24: 'God is a Spirit, and they that worship him, must worship him in spirit and in truth.'

The occasion on which this wonderful declaration was made renders it doubly wonderful. It was spoken not to a council of the priests or to an assembly of the wise of this world, but to a poor Samaritan woman of abandoned character, coming to draw water at the well of Jacob. It consists of two parts:
1. An exhibition of the nature of the Godhead as immaterial and spiritual, and
2. An influence founded on this view of the Divine Nature, viz. That the worship which is offered to him by his creatures must be the worship of the heart and of sincerity. 'God is a spirit'.
God: this is the general name of the Supreme Being. It is not

used for the purpose of setting forth his nature like 'Jehovah', but simply as a name distinguishing the particular being intended in what is said. It is, therefore, of no consequence to enquire into the meaning of the word, though we notice that some derive *theos* from *theow* (to run), and they connect it with Zeus, meaning to shine.

'God is a Spirit.' A spirit means a being having no body or material parts which can be seen or felt. Our ideas of the nature of a spirit are chiefly negative. We may indeed know many of the attributes or properties of a spirit, as that it is intelligent, but of its essence we can only form an idea of a negative kind. That is by separating from an idea of it all those properties which belong to matter as having parts, being visible or tangible, being divisible and liable to corruption.

Properties of all spirits:
1. They cannot be discerned by the senses
2. They have no parts
3. They do not occupy space
4. They are not liable to corruption and therefore can only die by an act of power annihilating them
5. They have intelligence, will, memory, capacities of love, and hatred, of joy and sorrow. Indeed all the capacities of the human soul without those modifications of perception, thought, and feeling, which result from the union of the soul in man to a material body
6. They are immortal, i.e. free from those natural tendencies to decay which belong to a material frame, such as that which belongs to man.

God is a spirit, and is characterized by all the general attributes of created spirits which have been mentioned. In addition to these however, he possesses attitudes which raise him infinitely above all other spiritual beings.
1. He is a self-existent spirit
2. He is without beginning
3. He is omnipresent
4. He is omnipotent

5. He is infinitely powerful, wise, holy, just, true, benevolent

6. He is unchangeable and incomparable

'They that worship him must worship him in spirit and in truth.' Here we have the appointed manner of acceptable worship, 'in spirit and in truth'. What does this command and what does it forbid? It commands the worship of the heart, or the homage of the immortal spirit in all its powers to Jehovah. It forbids:

1. Formality or resting in an outward service from which the heart is wanting

2. It forbids our worshipping God by rites of man's invention, which may be added under the pretext of decorating or adorning diverse ordinances. These may please the carnal nature of man, but they offend the holy and spiritual nature of God. It is true that in the infant state of the Church under the dispensation of Moses, rites were appointed by God. But in this passage the Lord tells us that such carnal ordinances were now to come to an end, 'the time cometh and now is....' This does not mean that it was only now that true spiritual worship has to begin, but that now it was to be required exclusively, and that its former accompaniments, which were typical, were to be laid aside, the great antitype having appeared.

3. It also forbids, as we see from the context, the connecting of God's worship with particular places, as being more sacred than others. This had been done by Divine appointment in the case of Jerusalem, so that the Samaritans offended God by choosing only their mountain for his worship. But now we are taught that neither at Jerusalem nor in this mountain should men worship the Father. And it is evident that here the sacredness of any particular place whatever is denied, seeing the contrast is made not between these particular places and some others which were to be substituted for them, but between particular places as a carnal and temporary ordinance and the spiritual worship of all God's true people. It is a matter of convenience and order that

particular places should be selected for the solemn worship of God, and it would display impiety of mind and offend the Lord as well as the minds of all his people to use the same buildings for profane purposes as are used for his worship, but this is not owing to any sacredness in the spot, but only due to the ungodliness of feeling which it displays and the sacredness which it violates.

We have last of all to notice the connection between this latter and the former.

'God is a spirit and they that worship him....'

1. This dependence of the one truth on the other teaches us that the nature of God is the foundation of all obligation to worship him. It is his infinite perfection, not less than his relation to us as our Creator and Governor, which inevitably binds us to adore and serve him.

2. That nature of God as the rule of all acceptable worship, as well as the reason which obliges us to render worship to him. Nothing can be acceptable to him which is not agreeable to his nature.

3. Since God's nature is spiritual, a spiritual service and that only can meet with his approbation. 'They that worship him must worship him in spirit and in truth.' Were not God a pure spirit, he might be delighted by outward splendour in his ordinances, but as he is a spirit these things cannot please him. Nor are they to be allowed for their supposed influence in the minds of the worshippers. It is true that as man has a body as well as a spirit, he must serve God with both, and therefore ought to have a form of outward worship, but this is commanded under the New Testament to be the simplest possible, flowing entirely from the nature of the spiritual duties, such as praise and prayer, which are enjoined him, and having all its value from its being the expression of what is inward and spiritual.

We may learn from this subject:

1. The absolute necessity of regeneration in order that we may worship God truly and acceptably.

2. How little true worship of God there is in the world.

Thursday May 12th 1842: The Holiness of God

Isaiah 6:3: 'Holy, Holy, Holy is the Lord of Hosts.'

Colossians 1:21, 22: 'And you who were some time alienated and enemies in your mind by wicked works, yet now hath he reconciled in the body of his flesh through death.'

For the understanding of this passage, we would require to know the exact meaning of the principal words: 'alienated' and 'reconciled', and with this explanation we shall set out 'alienated'. The word thus translated literally means 'belonging to another', to another person, or to another land. The territory to which we belong by nature is the Kingdom of Satan, our prince is the god of this world. We are alienated from the Commonwealth of Israel with its Head, its privileges, its members. Alienated from the life of God, from its principle, its exercise, its object, yea from the knowledge of it. In regard to all these we are strangers.

1. In as much as we are not possessors of them
2. Because anything we know of them is only from the report of others
3. Because our hearts are utterly turned away from the love of these things and wholly engaged in the pursuit and enjoyment of other things.

'*Enemies* in your mind by wicked works.' It is possible to be a stranger and yet not an enemy. A person may belong to one commonwealth and yet be on friendly terms with the rulers and the members of another. In this case, however, it is different. We are not only alienated from God, from his Kingdom and from his life in the soul, but are enemies to him and to those in it. We hate them, and seek their ruin in ourselves and others.

'In your mind by wicked works.' It is by wicked works that we fight against God, his Kingdom, his life in the soul, and in doing these we are his enemies, not only because these are in their nature evil, contrary to his will, but because in doing them, we aim a blow at his sovereign authority, and show that we love not only what is evil in itself, but that we love it as a thing forbidden to us by God. This seems to be the force of the words, 'in our mind', as connected with those that follow, 'by wicked works'. It is this enmity to God in the 'mind' of the sinner which gives his sin the specific character of a rebellion, and renders it the waging of a direct offensive war against the Most High.

'Yet now hath he reconciled.' The idea contained in the word 'reconciled' seems to be agreement between those who have been enemies with a special reference to an offended party, viewed as him pardoning his adversary, and treating him with favour. It seems to point rather to God – as laying down his enmity to God – and yet this last is also implied or included in so far as to allow of the sinner cordially accepting the terms of pardon which are offered to him by his sovereign.

That this is the idea of 'reconciliation' is further evident from the persons who are reconciled being described as previously 'enemies', and still more seems to be evident from the nature of the means by which this reconciliation is said to be brought about. This is the death of Christ which, though indeed it opens up the way for the enmity of the sinner's heart being slain through the agency of the Holy Ghost and also proves a powerful means of slaying that enmity, yet leads directly and immediately as its effect to the proclaiming of peace and pardon from the Throne of God. The foundation of reconciliation is fully and exclusively laid in the merit of the death of Christ and the only thing subsequently necessary to its completion in the case of any soul, is that the beauty of Christ be welcomed as an all sufficient and exclusive ground of peace.

'In the body of his flesh through death.' Here 'reconciliation' is ascribed to Emmanuel as its author, 'you ... hath he reconciled'. In other passages it is ascribed to God, even the Father, as in 2 Corinthians 5:19, where it is said that, 'God was in Christ reconciling the world to himself.' It is thus with salvation in all its parts and in all its aspects. The Father, in the exercise of his own free and eternal love, formed the scheme of redemption, and purposed to accomplish it through the Mediation of the Son. The Son again voluntarily undertook the office of a Mediator and it is in fulfilling this office that he reconciles sinners to God. He does so 'by the blood of his Cross' (v.20), or again 'in the body of his flesh through death'. He shed his 'blood' and suffered 'death' on 'the cross', in order to make reconciliation for iniquity.

The sufferings are rendered necessary, because although God was wholly disposed to pardon guilty sinners and indeed formed the plan of reconciliation, he could pardon sin and be reconciled to sinners only in such a way as would fully declare his infinite abhorrence of all iniquity and fully satisfy the claims of eternal righteousness, as the Lawgiver, Ruler and Judge of the Universe. The guilt and heinousness of sin could be discovered in no other way than by its being followed by suffering. And so when Jesus undertook the office of a Mediator between God and his guilty people, he became bound to suffer what they deserved in his own holy body on the tree.

Death is the wages of sin and so he died, the just for the unjust, that he might bring us to God. And again, in as much as sin is infinitely evil, and deserves according to the righteous judgment of God an infinite punishment, had he been a mere man, or no higher in dignity and glory than the highest creature, it would have been impossible for him to have exhausted the curse of God even by his death. He was, however, God as well as man. It is in this character that he is exhibited in the chapter before us, and it is in consequence of this that his sufferings and death are of sufficient value to redeem a lost world from death eternal.

To this Saviour we must turn if we would be reconciled. God is in Christ reconciling the world to himself, not imputing to men their trespasses, but out of Christ he is a consuming fire to all the workers of iniquity.

Sabbath evening, St George's Church, Edinburgh, July 24th, 1842.